HOUSE OF
Scorpio

The Ascendant Series   Book IV

Whitney Estenson

Flint Hills Publishing

Flint Hills Publishing
www.flinthillspublishing.com
Topeka, Kansas U.S.A.

ISBN-978-1-7332035-3-1

To those who supported me from the beginning and believed, that those who **can**, teach.

"Those who live today will die tomorrow, those who die tomorrow will be born again; those who live Maat will not die."

~ Egyptian Proverbs

Chapter 1

Roman

The city was sleeping.

I leaned against the pillars of Council Chambers, staring upward, watching as a black cloud traveled across the night sky on an unseen wind, revealing behind it hidden stars.

I let the wind fill me and recharge my strength as I stared at the stars. There were four of them. Three clustered together, their lights bright and twinkling, the fourth off to the side. Near the others, and yet separate, not as bright. As quickly as they appeared, they disappeared again, covered by a different cloud. It was strange for the skies above Awen to be hazy. Apart from when we burned a funeral pyre, I couldn't remember a time where I hadn't been able to look up and see the clear sky. When the stars hadn't shone down brightly on the city, illuminating the buildings with their brilliant light. Now, the buildings cast an eerie orange glow, the torch light reflecting off the dense clouds that covered the island.

I scanned the city, my gaze jumping from one building to the next as I marked the areas that still showed signs of battle, that had not yet recovered from the attack late last year. We'd made progress, the various cleanup crews focusing on the most important buildings first. Like the arena, which had suffered the most damage—I'd personally seen to that. Now the walls were repaired, the destroyed dais removed as if it was never crumbled upon the sand. We didn't have enough soldiers to dedicate to the recovery effort, and several of the secondary buildings were still broken and unattended. Glaring reminders of the chaos Set and his hybrids had created.

Chaos *I'd* created.

I pushed away those dark thoughts, instead opening the notebook in my hands and shifting through the pages, trying to find an empty spot. The papers were covered in scribbled notes and roughly drawn sketches, their corners turned down from use and years of wear. I couldn't count how many times I'd opened this thing. How many times I'd wrung it between my hands, frustrated that all it did was raise questions rather than provide answers.

I managed to find an empty corner on one of the back pages. I grabbed the pencil from a hidden pocket in my tactical pants and scribbled down a few words, adding to the growing list.

No weapons.

Healthy.

Sage.

I underlined that last one several times, the tip of my pencil digging into the paper. I'd been recording everything I could remember all day, any chance I got, desperate not to forget anything, just in case it could be the key.

The key to finding her.

Last night, after six months of no leads, six months of silence, I'd seen her. It had only been for the briefest of moments, but she had been real. I had felt her presence as if she were standing next to me. I had no idea how it happened, no idea if I could do it again. All I knew was one moment I was lying in bed, thinking of her, and the next she was there, standing on my balcony.

"Kyndal?" I had said, not believing it was really her. I shook my head at my own stupidity. I'd imagined over and over what I would say to her when I finally held her again. How I would tell her I love her, declare it in front of everyone, shout it from the rooftops if they let me. How I'd promise her that *no one* would ever take her from me again. Ever. But last night, face to face with her, I hadn't remembered any of that. Instead, I bumbled around like a fool, unable to say anything but her name.

I closed my eyes, imagining her smile, remembering the mischief I'd seen dancing in her eyes at my obvious lack of speaking ability. Kyndal always enjoyed poking fun at me whenever given the chance. In fact, she was one of the few who wasn't too afraid to do so. She was fearless. Just one of the reasons I loved her.

One of the many.

I heard them coming from several hundred feet away. No one was walking the city at this time of night. The general population was confined to their housing under Amina's new citywide curfew, so I knew the only people walking the streets were those given special permission to do so. That was a short list that only included her personal sentries and the Guard. After our return from Cairo, Amina cleaned house, eliminating all Council guards and replacing them with soldiers from her own armies. Soldiers loyal only to her, as the Guard was now expected to be. I listened closely to the cadence of the steps. The Guard was on tenuous ground with Amina's sentries. Her soldiers thought they were better than us, and they took every opportunity to lord their assumed power over us, knowing we couldn't afford to step out of line. I was in no mood to deal with them tonight. Luckily, the steps didn't move with the casual arrogance of the sentries, but rather firmly and with purpose, moving directly north toward where I now stood on the top of the Council Chambers stairs. There were three distinct sets. I recognized two of them, the sound and pattern of their gaits familiar to me now. I knew that Grady Dunn was on the right, his heavily-booted foot echoing louder than the quieter steps of his partner, Brynn Hughes. He'd been injured in Cairo, and although he was healed long ago, he still carried a slight limp, favoring his right leg. Most people didn't notice small things like that, but I always did. I learned early in life that tiny details like this could be the difference between victory and defeat in battle.

Quickly, before they could round the corner that would bring me into view, I rolled up my notebook, concealing it in my boot. I straightened my back, standing up tall and shifting my face into a neutral mask. Moments later, they rounded the final turn, bringing them onto the main road that led to the bottom of the steps. They walked exactly as I knew they would, the soldier they were escorting walking a half step ahead of them. This time it was a woman. I didn't recognize her, but I could tell she was a warrior. She was dressed in traditional fighting gear, although her dagger wasn't strapped to her belt. Grady or Brynn would have confiscated that when they arrested her. Her hair was buzzed short on the edge, revealing faint scars along the side of her neck. The original wounds must have been deep to leave a permanent mark such as those. It was difficult to scar a Kindred, but not impossible.

As I studied her, I immediately knew it wasn't going to end well for this soldier. Her back was ramrod straight, her eyes steely and defiant as she looked up at the imposing building before her. Just as she understood why she had been summoned in front of the Council, she must have understood what her fate would be, and she didn't hesitate to approach that first step.

As the trio reached me, the soldier paid me no attention, instead keeping her eyes trained on the ornate front door. I nodded respectfully at Grady and Brynn, each of them returning the gesture. None of us allowed our masks to slip. A short time ago, I never would have believed I would ever show the two of them an ounce of respect, but a lot had changed. I now counted Grady and Brynn among my closest friends. Friendships that had been forged in battle and proven time and again.

This was the first I'd seen of either them since my dream, and I was dying to tell them everything, to tell them I'd seen her and see if they had any idea how I could do it again. But it wasn't safe to tell them. Not here. Not when others could be listening.

Almost as if he could read the tension on my face, Grady raised an eyebrow at me in silent question. I shook my head, blowing him off. Just as quickly as I'd done it, Grady turned back around, back to the task at hand, as if the exchange had never occurred. I pulled open the doors to Council Chambers, escorting the three of them into the marble foyer. The torches inside flickered with the breeze, but I turned from their heat, unable to watch the shadows dance on the walls without thinking of her. Of how my Rafiq made fire seem so alive, and how it held no such life since I'd lost her.

I led them down the silent hallway, our boots thundering across the hard floor the only sound. I didn't stop until I reached the next set of doors at the top of the main chamber. There were sentries stationed on either side, though they neither acknowledged us nor moved to open the doors between them. Nearby, Grady bristled, noticing the slight. I pulled the doors open myself, making sure to glare at the sentries as I revealed the waiting Nomarch Council in the chamber below. Letting them know the insult didn't go unnoticed.

Behind me, there was a sharp intake of breath. It was quick, a show of weakness that the unknown soldier swiftly stifled. *She is brave,* I thought. *Good.* She'd need that strength if she planned to survive the next ten minutes. It was easy to tell what made her nervous. It was rare for the Council to be waiting. Typically, they enjoyed making their subjects sit and squirm before making a grand entrance, but not tonight. Tonight, they wanted each person to feel the full effect of the power waiting for them as they descended into the pit. From our place at the top of the ascending gallery, we could see all the thrones, each carved from a single piece of stone, including the one that still sat empty. For there were no longer twelve Nomarchs.

Now there were only eleven.

The Council hadn't replaced Nero, even though it had been half a year since he'd defected to Set's side, taking his army of Coterie soldiers with him. They hadn't even bothered to pretend like they planned to promote the next in line to the Aries throne. Since Nero wasn't dead, technically his seat still belonged to him, but circumstances as they were, he could be replaced. They'd done it before when Ezekiel betrayed us, replacing him with a new Nomarch at the next full moon. That was when the Council still functioned properly. When each Nomarch had a voice.

It had been a long time since the Council worked the way it was supposed to. Now, the Council was nothing more than a trick, a thinly veiled illusion meant to pacify the masses. Those of us behind the scenes, the ones privy to what happened inside Council Chambers, knew the truth. The Council no longer existed. Instead, we only had one ruler.

Amina.

Former Nomarch of House Scorpio, Amina was now Governor of the Kindred, sole ruler of us all. She had declared herself as such after the battle of Cairo. She'd returned to Awen as the victor with the was-sceptre firmly in her possession, spinning a story to the Council about how *her* soldiers recovered the weapon, and only thanks to *her* leadership did we now have the one weapon that could put Set away for good. She made promises of retribution for the deaths of our warriors and ensured a swift victory for the Kindred, united under her rule. Whether through ignorance or fear, the weaker Nomarchs had been eager to agree with Amina, gifting her immediate executive power of the Kindred, making her Governor of us all.

It was a power she was supposed to relinquish when the war is over, but those of us that knew what she was really like, didn't trust she would. She had played the situation perfectly, capitalizing on the efforts of others to further her own agenda. We knew she would never return the power, and as soon as the war was over, she would eliminate the Council completely.

The entire power shift had taken place behind closed doors, without informing the people, and yet slowly, through those of us that resisted her rule, news of Amina's takeover had spread. The soldiers were outraged, demanding that she relinquish her power and return it to the Council. Others called for a complete overhaul of the Council, demanding instead a free election of our leaders. Their cries fell on deaf ears. Although Amina was widely disliked, she'd gained the favor of enough Nomarchs, controlled enough of the House armies, that the individual voices of the people no longer mattered. As a result, pockets of soldiers had grown restless, agitated. Fights broke out in the streets between the warriors who felt slighted by House Scorpio skipping their turn on the wheel and those who believed in her cause or had gained her favor. Infighting between the Houses increased, until it got so out of hand, not even the Nomarchs could keep the peace anymore. Amina, desperate to hold onto her power, began throwing soldiers in the Hollow just to stop the fighting or shut them up. Eventually, once the others realized that those who went into the Hollow weren't returning, it was enough to scare most of the others into silence.

Once her sentries controlled the city, Amina did her best to keep the focus away from herself, instead finding a new villain in the story—the Guard. She claimed it was our insubordination that almost cost us the battle in Cairo, that it was us the people should be blaming for the soldiers we lost fighting Set. She told the people Kyndal was working with Set and had been a traitor the entire time. A spy sent to rip the Kindred apart. Without Kyndal here to defend herself, many people—those that hadn't left Awen to see for themselves—believed her lies. Amina took it a step further, stripping the Guard of our property and reputation, doing everything she could to demean us, just stopping short of disbanding the Guard completely. Instead, she tightened the reins, forcing us to fulfill her every whim and grounding us to the island.

I knew if she could, she would debrand each of us and cast us out. The only reason she didn't was because of The Book of Breathings. Only the Guard could use it.

Despite Amina's campaign against us, the truth of what happened in Egypt had spread slowly. The soldiers, the ones who had been on the ground in Cairo, knew the truth. They saw through her deceit. They knew it was the Guard, not Amina, that found the sceptre. That it was *Kyndal* that retrieved the weapon. They knew she wasn't a spy. That she traded herself to the Chaos god to keep the rest of us safe.

They knew she had sacrificed herself to protect us.

It was dangerous to support the Guard. Amina was always searching for dissent, always looking for the smallest slight, the weakest excuse to find someone guilty and make an example of them. Another rebel to throw in the Hollow.

That exact reason was what brought me to Council Chambers this evening.

We descended into Council Chambers, Brynn, Grady, and I stopping short of entering the circle of thrones. The soldier continued, marching into the middle, her eyes jumping from one Nomarch to the next. I followed her gaze, my eyes lingering on one Nomarch in particular. A woman with stark white hair that hung over her equally pale shoulders and down to her waist—Astrid of House Cancer.

The closest thing the Guard had to an ally on the Council, Astrid had been quietly undermining Amina from the start. Astrid was ancient, over 1,000 years old if the rumors were to be believed, and as such had plenty of connections and warriors loyal specifically to her. She wielded that loyalty like a sword, using it to protect the Guard as much as possible. What would she think when she learned I'd seen Kyndal?

"State your name for the record," Amina commanded the soldier, bringing my attention to her. From where I stood, just behind her throne, I couldn't see Amina's face, but I could picture it. Her eyes would be stern, her face as tense as the rest of her body. As tightly strung as the hand resting on the edge of her throne. She wore a deep blue pantsuit, the only color I'd seen her wear since assuming her new position. A visual reminder of what House, what element controlled the Kindred.

"Briar," the soldier answered evenly. "From House Taurus."

My eyes cut to Grady, also a member of House Taurus. He stood not two feet away from me, but I saw no flicker of emotion on his face. Idly, I noticed Brynn glance toward Grady as well. Waiting for him to say something. To speak up. We both knew he wouldn't. There was no way he could.

"Although you hail from House Taurus, you serve in my army, do you not?" Amina questioned.

Briar nodded once. "That is correct, Governor. I have been a member of your army for twenty years. I have served you proudly."

"Have you now?" Amina asked, the lilt in her voice making it clear that she thought the exact opposite. "Then why is it that you disobeyed my orders?"

"With all due respect, Governor, I have not betrayed you. You are mistaken."

"But you have," Amina disagreed instantly. "You were overheard in the training ring spewing lies to my soldiers, claiming it was not my warriors that defeated Set, but rather giving credit to the Guard. Do you deny it?"

"Adamantly, Governor." The soldier's—Briar's—voice was like hard granite.

Amina lunged forward from her throne. "Are you calling me a liar?" she spit back at her.

"I didn't say that," Briar answered, her tone sharper than was wise. Completely unfazed by the raging Governor. "What I am adamantly denying is your statement that what I was saying was lies. What your source heard was accurate, but all I did was tell the truth. As you mentioned before, I have served in your army for many years. I was in Cairo, and I *saw* what happened that day." That caught my attention. I didn't recognize her from Cairo, but there had been so many soldiers, it was possible I missed her. Amina sat back slowly, her cold eyes never leaving Briar. To her credit, Briar didn't back down. "I will not allow the sacrifices of our own soldiers to be brushed under the rug, replaced by the unwarranted claim of a false leader."

The room went still, each of us waiting to see what Amina would do. No one had spoken to her so brazenly before. Slowly, with the stillness of the deadly warrior she was, Amina stood from her throne.

"You are a traitor. Your kind can not be allowed to remain among decent warriors, lest your poison spread amongst them like a disease."

Briar cut her off. "Then send me to the Hollow with the countless others you have falsely condemned. I am more free beneath its stone than I am under your rule." Next to me, through the bond that connected me to the Guardsmen,

I felt the smallest tendril of Grady's power stir before he clamped it down.

"I am inclined to oblige you," Amina sneered. Her head snapped to the side, her eyes cutting to us. To her Guard, oblivious to Grady's slip. "Take her to the Hollow," she ordered.

Obediently, the three of us stepped forward, Brynn and Grady grabbing Briar by her arms. She made no move to resist. We turned her toward the exit, even as she twisted to stare at Amina, "You can't throw us all in the Hollow," she shouted over my head. "There are more of us than you realize, and we will only support our true leader." I glanced once at Grady, then past him to Astrid, who was watching Briar with intense interest. "She is born of true blood, and when she returns, she will set us all free. You won't be able to hide from us then."

She. Such a small, simple word, but it rocked me to my core. There could only be one person she was talking about.

"You are a false ruler!" Briar continued as we ascended the gallery, pushing Briar through the same door we'd entered. "When the Descendant returns, we will be delivered!"

The door slammed behind us, cutting off Briar's rant and leaving her alone with the Guard. I took two sharp steps forward, pushing Briar out of Grady and Brynn's tight grips and into the marble wall. Two more steps and I was invading her personal space. Neither of my Guardsmen tried to stop me. "What do you know of Kyndal Davenport?" I hissed in the soldier's face. She couldn't know anything. It was impossible. I'd been searching for her for six months and still had no leads.

Briar smiled smugly. "I know that she lives. And I know that only through me will she return to Awen."

Chapter 2

Kyndal

The sound of drumbeats echoed off the stone walls.

The vibrations shook the dirty ceiling above me, raining dirt and sand down on my head, yet I hardly noticed. What did it matter? My hair was already greasy, dirty, and tangled, and I'd long since forfeited my vanity. I couldn't even remember the last time I'd been permitted a bath. Sunlight streamed in from the tiny barred window high up in the cell—my only source of light. I wasn't permitted a torch, no fire of any kind. They didn't seem to understand that it didn't matter. I didn't require a fire source in order to create my element. I could create fire in the dead of winter, in the middle of a blizzard, or even under water—although I'd admit I hadn't tried that one.

Yet.

I leaned over the side of the stone bench, a knife in one hand, a flattened stone in the other. Slowly, with a precision that came only from months of practice, I ran the knife over the stone, honing its edge to razor sharpness. I knew what waited for me outside the cell door. In my mind's eye, I could see the sand arena, the high stone walls, and makeshift seats that hovered above the pit. Lined with hunks of stone, broken boards—or less common—a trunk of a tree. I could picture the spectators staring down on the gladiators, throwing stones, food, weapons, whatever they can find at us. Smaller than the one in Awen, this arena was a pale comparison, but its beaten-down appearance only added to the savageness of the pit.

It'd been two days since my last fight. Typically, I was forced to fight every day, sometimes several times in a twenty-four hour period, but the last one had been difficult. I'd taken on two Fire User hybrids at once. Each of them was armed with daggers and I was weaponless. It'd been challenging to defeat them, and while I proved victorious, I was badly injured and had taken longer than normal to recover. The extra day was not a kindness, but rather, necessary. The pits were meant to be a show, entertainment for the hybrid troops who had grown restless during the last few months of inactivity. It simply would not do for me to die a quiet death.

I looked now at the gash in my upper thigh. The bleeding had stopped last night, but the tissue was still bright red and tender to the touch. Truth be told, I could use at least another day to heal it. Leaving it open as it was left me susceptible to infection. But without my element, my healing powers worked slower, and I was left with no choice. I knew Set would not let me rest any longer.

Carefully, I ran the sharpened knife over my forearm, pleased when a thin red line followed the blade. Just as the cut was sealing itself, a small magic, the metal door on the other edge of the cell groaned open. The drumbeats flooded the cell, no longer an echo, but now filling every inch of the tiny space. A large, burly soldier stepped into the doorway, shrouded in shadow. I expected him to be a hybrid, this place was crawling with them, but as he stepped into the faint light of the cell, I realized he wasn't. There were no pulsing dark veins, no serrated teeth. Technically, he was Kindred like me, except I recognized him as a member of the extremist group known as the Coterie. An exclusively male group that renounced Maat and solely worshipped her consort, Thoth. The Coterie soldiers had defected from the Kindred decades ago and now were foot soldiers for Set— following in the footsteps of their commander, Nero.

The soldier stared at me expectantly. I stood slowly, minding my injured leg and faced him. "Tell me something," I began, my voice dripping with disdain. I hated the Coterie soldiers and took any opportunity I could to piss them off. They were traitors, not to mention they had tortured Roman and I just a few short months ago. "The Coterie only worships Thoth, right? You renounce all other gods. . ." I let the sentence drop.

The soldier crossed his arms, his biceps bulging outward. "Yes," he answered. "What's your point?"

I shrugged, sheathing my knife in the belt of my pants. "I just wanted to know what it felt like to be serving the sworn enemy of your deity. I mean, I knew you were all a bunch of heartless bastards, but you must really hate yourself for switching sides. Taking Set's orders. Doing everything he tells you. If you thought serving Maat was bad, I can't even imagine how you look yourself in the mirror." I reached the doorway, but the soldier stepped in front of me, his large frame hovering above my obviously smaller stature. I glared up at him. "What? Did I hurt your feelings?"

He paused, glaring down at me, so close I could feel the power and bloodlust radiating off him. He wanted to hit me. Part of me wished he would. I would welcome the chance to beat on a Coterie soldier. We stared at each other for a moment longer, each of us waiting on the other to make a move, when suddenly the drumbeats stopped. I raised my eyebrows. "Looks like that's my cue."

I pushed past the man, marching out into the corridor. I wound through the makeshift hallway, studying it as I always did, as if it would suddenly divulge new information. Carved from the same stone as my cell, the walls were jagged and awkwardly cut. In some places, giant pieces of the wall were missing, like they'd been blown apart in a battle and never repaired. Every so often, sunlight streamed in from the same type of window as that in my cell, but they were situated at a greater distance, forcing the hallway into alternating blocks of light and dark. The floor was sturdy, clearly formed by rock as well, but the top layer was made of sand. Not the soft kind you would find at a beach, but the irritating type that seems to find its way into your clothes, forcing you to spend the next month pouring it out of your shoes.

The Coterie soldier followed me through the passageway, even though the walk was short and there weren't any turn offs or ways of escape. The corridor from my cell led to one place only.

The pit.

As I rounded the final turn, I felt the pounding of their feet. The audience was already there, the mix of hybrids, wraiths, and Coterie soldiers practically salivating as they waited for the fight to begin. As they waited for blood to spill. I reached the end of the corridor, pausing at the iron bars that blocked my entrance to the arena. There was no natural light in the pit, as such it was the only place that allowed torches. They were bolted to the walls, their strength filling me as I pulled their magic into me, replenishing my depleted power supply.

I unsheathed my knife, gripping it hard with my right hand. The fit wasn't exactly right, not like the cool metal of my Kindred dagger, but it was all I was given. I knew that being given a weapon at all was a sign of how difficult this fight would be. If I was forced to fight two hybrids without a weapon, what would today bring?

I received my answer moments later. Metal scraped against stone as the set of iron bars on the opposite end of the arena opened and my opponents entered the sand. Three wraiths marched out, each with dagger in hand, and I breathed a sigh of relief. Wraiths were easier to kill than hybrids. They burned easily and I didn't have to aim for the heart, but my relief was short lived. For the wraiths were not all that came out of the other gate. They were also followed by two hybrids; a Water User and an Air User.

Five against one.

Behind me, the Coterie soldier snickered. Now I understood why he hadn't taken my bait earlier, why he hadn't attacked me when I provoked him. He knew what I was going against. There was no need for him to hurt me. There was plenty of pain waiting for me in the pit.

Another soldier appeared on the opposite side of my gate, unlocking it and pulling it open. My opponents snarled in anticipation as they waited for me to take the final two steps into the arena. I paused a moment longer and their snarls turned to twisted smiles at my hesitation. They thought I was scared. A normal person would be, but I hadn't felt fear in months. Fear only came from having something to lose, and I'd had everything I cared about stripped away months ago.

There was nothing left that could hurt me.

I called to the power that slept deep inside me, using the torches as fuel to give strength to my limbs and dull the pain of the cut in my leg. My eyes changed from a vivid green to a sharp red, and suddenly everything was clearer. Sharper. I could hear the individual grains of sand grind underneath the boots of the wraiths, smell the metallic tang of old blood that stained the walls. I could feel the power course through my veins, a liquid inferno that sang with the promise of blood. I wanted to fight them, to tear them apart. There may be five of them, but I was a Descendant. The most powerful Kindred that walked the planet, and I would not, could not, be stopped.

I stepped onto the sand.

Immediately, the wraith to my left lunged for me. A stupid, reckless move. I dropped low, his arm sweeping wide over my head, even as I swiped with the blade. It cut across his stomach with razor sharpness. A wound like that made with a Kindred blade would have killed him. With a regular knife, all it did was piss him off. I heard him hiss with anger but I had no time to turn around. The first hybrid was running for me, gold eyes ablaze. He threw his arm out toward me, a burst of air following its path, blasting me into the rock wall. I bounced off the rough surface, swallowing a growl. It wasn't so much the pain that had me growling, but the annoyance of getting hit by an elemental attack. If the other Guard members had been here, I could've shielded myself from it. Alone as I was, I couldn't risk using the necessary strength to uphold the spell.

The hybrid followed his attack, his right hook swinging for my jaw. I raised my arm, blocking the blow, returning with a right of my own, directly in his stomach. He buckled forward, just close enough for me to headbutt him directly in his nose.

A satisfying crunch echoed in my ears, quickly drowned out by the jeers of the crowd. They hated it when I did something well. Over his head, I saw all three wraiths coming for me again. They would be on me in moments. I kicked the hybrid in the back of the knee, bringing him to the ground as I lunged for his Kindred dagger in the loop on his belt. I grabbed it, rolling through to the other side of him, putting more distance between me and the wraiths. Buying me precious seconds. I came up from the roll, blade poised, and threw it as hard as I could at the lead wraith. It buried itself in his abdomen and moments later he was gone. The other two wraiths continued their advance on me, not even blinking as they marched through the dust that had once been their ally. I may have eliminated an enemy, but I also had forfeited my best weapon. Forced to improvise, I reached up and grabbed the scalding handle of the torch, ripping it off the wall. I threw the torch at their feet, spreading the small flames with my power, creating a wall between them and me. They immediately quit moving, hissing at me over the growing flames. I pushed the fire closer to them, the growing flames adding to my power, making me even stronger. They were stupid enough to stand too close and the edges of their pants caught on fire. With one final shove of my power, the flames flew up their bodies, engulfing them in a fiery death.

The crowd roared as the wraiths burned. I knew it wasn't excitement for me, just the thrill of watching someone die. With all my focus on the wraiths, I never saw the other hybrid coming. The Water User barreled in from my right, knocking me onto the ground. My knife flew out of my hand, skittering across the sand and into the flames. The hybrid jumped on top of me, straddling my hips, his knee digging into the wound on my leg, that thanks to him was bleeding again. A sharp left ricocheted off my cheekbone, my face instantly swelling. The hybrid raised his dagger, bringing it down directly toward my face. I barely moved fast enough to get my head out of the way. The dagger embedded itself in the ground, so close it sliced my ear on the way down.

I bucked my hips, trying to get the hybrid off me, but he was too heavy. I lunged up, throwing a hard right. It snapped his head to the side, but he came back just as quickly, hissing in my face, his teeth sharp and serrated. I tried to hit him again, this time with my left, but he grabbed my arm, pinning it to the ground. It took him seconds to do it, but it was all the time I needed. While he'd been focused on controlling my arm, I snuck my right hand in between us. Faster than he could see, I built a fireball and blasted him at point blank range.

Directly through the heart.

He flew backward, his lifeless body smacking against the rock wall before landing in an awkward heap on the floor. The crowd roared with disapproval as I jumped to my feet and ran for the dead hybrid, ripping his dagger out of his belt.

I spun around to face my final opponent. Across the small pit, his dagger firmly in his grasp, was the Air User hybrid. Blood had quit gushing from his nose, but it stained his face, adding to his sinister appearance.

"I'm going to rip you apart," he snarled. I let him talk. Let him detail exactly all the creative ways he was going to kill me, the whole while building my power. I pulled from the sand under my feet, the rock in the walls, the flames in the torches, bringing it into myself until I couldn't hold it anymore. Then, with a scream, I released it all, aimed it directly at the hybrid. Just as I had once done on the streets of Cairo. The hybrid went up in flames, his screams cutting off as he fell to the ground, dead.

The audience went quiet, the wealth of my power stunning them silent. I threw my stolen dagger down on the ground, knowing I wouldn't be allowed to keep it, as I glared back at them.

Victorious.

Chapter 3

Kyndal

After the fight, I expected to be returned to my cell. Instead, the same Coterie soldier marched me through the opposite gate, into an area I hadn't seen in months, and next thing I knew I stood in front of the Chaos God Set.

My escort left quickly, slamming the door shut behind him. Idly, I noticed he didn't lock the door. I guessed there was no need to. It wasn't like I could run away. Even if I managed to escape, I had no idea where I was. Where I would go.

The room I was in was huge, but it didn't matter, Set's power filled every inch of it. There were more of the small, high windows in this room. They allowed in the sunlight but were too tall for me to see out of, to catch a glimpse of the outside world. I could hear the wind blowing outside but no rustle of leaves like the ones that dominated back home in the Allegheny. Wherever we were, there must not be very many trees.

The god stood on the opposite side of the room, his back to me, preoccupied by what appeared to be old papers scattered on a table. Five feet behind him was a monstrous bed made of a deep cherry wood. It struck me as odd. I had never thought about whether or not Set slept. I had always assumed he didn't. The sheets were rumpled, as if the god had a fitful sleep. I shuddered. I didn't want to think of Set lying in that bed.

Across from the bed, standing silently near one of the few torches in the room, was Set's new general—Nero.

Dressed in his traditional all black gear, the blood red pommel of his short sword peeked over his shoulder. I'd seen that blade in action, watched as the onyx blade swallowed the screams of those it had cut down. It was a dark, dangerous weapon.

Just like the man that wielded it.

I hated Nero for many reasons. He had tortured me. Tortured Roman. He'd betrayed us all, selling us out to Set. But mostly, I hated him for what he had planned to do with Roman. For what he would have done, had he been able to raise him like he planned. I hadn't spoken to Nero since Set took me away from The Hall of Two Truths. He'd learned the truth about his family that night, that the son he thought was dead was in fact alive and well. Roman had only revealed his heritage to keep Nero from killing me. Nero had denied it then, claiming that he had no son, but I could see it in the way I sometimes caught him watching me. When I would sometimes see him open his mouth to speak before closing it just as quickly. Nero believed that Roman was his son, and if what Astrid had told me was the truth, his legacy was the most important thing in the world to Nero.

Which made it his weakness.

I glared at the Coterie general as his cold eyes traveled slowly over me. I could almost see him cataloguing my injuries, his eyes pausing at each bruise, each cut, especially as he paused at the wound in my leg. I slowly shifted my weight to my good leg, taking the weight off the left side that was bleeding again, the wound hot and irritated. I was pulling whatever power I could from the torches in the room, but I was tired, drained, and my element responded slowly, only small embers making it to me.

"Kyndal, thank you for joining me," Set announced, his booming voice filling the room. I resisted the urge to roll my eyes. He welcomed me as though I had been invited as a guest, not escorted like the prisoner I was. It was something Ezekiel used to do, and I wasn't sure if the greeting was a leftover piece of him or purely coincidental.

"Don't you ever wear a shirt?" I answered, my tone sharp. It seemed every time I saw Set, he was always walking around half naked. A fact that didn't make me uncomfortable, just irritated. There was no sign of the red veins I'd seen running through him during the heat of battle, no dark smoke emanating from his skin. To the untrained eye, he would appear perfectly normal.

"You fought well today," he commended, ignoring my jab. "You didn't hesitate to kill. Much has changed for you."

I curled my lip in disgust, uncomfortable with the compliment. He was right, of course. A lot had changed. I'd been fighting in the pits for a while now, how long exactly, I wasn't sure. Long enough that I had become numb to the feel of the dagger in my hand, the sound of the blade slicing into flesh. I no longer felt remorse for the hybrid lives I took or for the Kindred soldiers they used to be. None of which I was willing to admit to him. "I wasn't aware you were there," I diverted.

"I wasn't," Set said casually, finally turning to look at me. His red eyes swirled, reminding me that he was not normal. Not by a long shot. "Nero told me of your prowess."

I refused to look over at the general. "I kill because it is required of me. I don't take any pride in it."

"All the same, you have become ruthless. It is a necessary thing if you are to survive."

I knew he didn't care about my survival. He was the one making me fight in the first place. "I doubt your men find it necessary. At the rate this is going, you aren't going to have much of an army left," I snipped at him.

He shrugged, his large, exposed muscles flexing with the movement. "If they cannot defeat one Kindred, they are no good to me. I can always make more." I suppressed a shudder, thinking of exactly how he would do that. For the first few weeks I'd been Set's prisoner, he brought me in regularly to drain me of my blood, a necessary ingredient in making Kindred/wraith hybrids. As far as I knew, he hadn't used it yet, but clearly, he had plans to.

"What do you want with me?" I asked, cutting through to the point. I leaned on my left leg, a move I quickly regretted as pain shot up my body. I smothered a wince before shifting back to my right side.

Set reached back to the table, grabbing a piece of weathered paper. "I find myself in need of your skills. You remember you made me many promises. Promises I expect you to uphold."

I didn't move. "I remember," I answered tersely, anticipating what he was going to say next.

"In two days' time, my army is moving." Here it comes, I thought. We were headed back to Cairo. Back to The Hall of Two Truths where he would force me to cross the river into the Inbetween. I opened my mouth to protest, to come up with any excuse to stall him. I was nowhere near strong enough to enter the river and come out alive. "The Kindred have been sending search parties throughout the continent, and according to my scouts, they are getting uncomfortably close to our location. Not to mention, my army has grown too large for this place. It is only a matter of time before we are noticed. My men need supplies; food, gear, weapons. Most of all, they need space. There is a Kindred compound a day's travel from here, one of the largest in this area of the world. My men are going to attack it and take it for themselves. And you are going to help them."

My mouth snapped shut. I tilted my head in confusion, momentarily stunned by his statement. "No." The word ripped out of me, almost on accident.

"Did you just say *no*?" Nero questioned. The first thing he'd said since I walked in the room.

I knew it wasn't smart to disagree with a god. Even less intelligent to deny him something he wanted, but I didn't regret it. "I won't help you raid compounds and kill Kindred. That wasn't part of our deal. I promised to take you to Maat."

"And you think you are up to that task?" Set questioned, his eyes traveling over my injured body.

I struggled not to show that I had just been worried about the exact same thing. Struggled and failed. "Maybe if you hadn't been forcing me to fight day after day, I would actually have enough strength to take you into the Inbetween."

31

"I don't want you to take me to the Inbetween," Set disagreed, his voice unnervingly soft.

"Why not?" I demanded. I was growing more frustrated by the moment.

Nero pushed off the wall. "My lord doesn't answer to you," he spit.

"Screw you," I threw back at him, "you *pathetic* excuse for a Kindred."

Nero lunged forward, his hand instinctively moving for his sword, but a single flick of Set's hand had Nero flying backward, his head smacking off the wall. He growled in pain, the muscles in his neck bulging as he strained against Set's power. My eyes widened in surprise. I'd never seen Set push his power out like that before. Either he'd been hiding the ability or he was growing stronger.

Slowly, Set turned his stormy gaze to Nero, who remained pinned against the wall. "You do not speak for me." Set turned back to me, moving slowly across the room, not stopping until he was in my personal space. I held strong, determined not to step back an inch. "You will do as you are told. You will help my army get into the Kindred compound undetected so that no alarms are raised."

He was working under the radar, which could only mean one thing. "You're scared the Kindred will find you. That the Guard will find *me*."

Set's eyes churned, and while he didn't move a muscle, a hot grip grabbed ahold of my neck, lifting me off my feet and cutting off my air at the same time. My toes only brushed the ground, as I now hung eye to eye with a very pissed off god. "I am scared of no one," he growled. The air around him crackled and thickened with power. Whispers of black smoke crept from his skin. "I am the ruler of the Redlands. Creator of wraiths and father of chaos. I tremble in front of no one. It is others that bow down at *my* feet. You would be wise to remember that. You will help my army raid the Kindred compound or I will abandon our deal and march directly into Awen, making sure that the first person I kill is that blue-eyed lover of yours."

The invisible hand released me, dropping me down to my knees. I grabbed at my throat, coughing and desperate for air. Set turned to Nero. "See that she is properly cleaned up, then see her well fed and rested. I want her prepared to move out in two days' time," he ordered.

From my spot on the ground, I didn't see Nero's response, if he had any reaction to Set's threat against his son, but soon his dark boots were in my vision and he grabbed my arm, ripping me to my feet. He pushed me toward the door. "Let's go," he commanded.

The moment the door shut behind us, I ripped my arm out of his grasp. "Don't touch me, pig." Nero grabbed my arm again, but I tore out of his grasp, taking a step ahead of him and out of arm's reach. I wheeled around to face him, my eyes a livid scarlet. "Keep your filthy hands off me, traitor," I spit.

Nero's dark eyes looked down at me but he made no move to touch me again. "Careful, Descendant. You may be Set's new pet, but you do not have the same favor with everyone here. That mouth of yours could get you in trouble." I glared up at him, ignoring his thinly veiled threat. I didn't care if he thought I was pushing my luck. We stared at each other a moment longer before I turned around and continued my march through the rocky corridor.

We didn't speak for several minutes, Nero only commenting when I needed to turn a specific direction. As we walked, the corridor walls smoothed out and became less rudimentary, more controlled, and clearly shaped by human hands. Through their thick walls I could hear the voices of the others—the hybrids and wraiths that filled the halls. "So much anger in such a small package," Nero continued after a while. "I can feel it coming off you in waves. I understand what Roman sees in you. You truly are made of fire."

"Don't talk about him like you know anything about who he is," I growled in response. I started to say something else snarky, to tell him to shut up about Roman, but I paused. If Nero brought up Roman, there had to be a reason why. Something he wanted to know. Something I could exploit and use to my advantage. I chose my next words carefully. "What do you care about Roman, anyway?" I asked. "You said so yourself, he's nothing to you."

"He isn't," Nero insisted quickly. Too quickly. "I am simply admiring his choice in women." I rolled my eyes, knowing fully well he couldn't see me. I came to a stop in front of the door at the end of the hallway. I could hear babbling water on the other side of the cherry wood.

I turned to face Nero. "Whatever your reasons for being interested in Roman may be, do yourself a favor. Stop. You may not claim him, but he *is* your son. Something that whether he admits it or not, means something to him. So, do him a favor and stay the hell away from him. He doesn't need you."

Nero's Adam's apple bobbed as he swallowed whatever words he was going to say next. I raised an eyebrow, giving him a satisfied smirk. I knew my words had cut him as deeply as I'd hoped. Nero reached past me, turning the knob on the door. "The bath is through there. I'll have fresh clothes delivered. There will be a guard at the door, so don't try anything stupid. You have thirty minutes." Then, he abruptly turned and left.

I lingered in the bath for at least twenty-five of the thirty minutes. It was the first real bath I'd had in months, and the water was deliciously warm, even though it did bite at my wounds in the first few moments. The bath was sunk into the ground, much like the springs of Awen, and large enough that even with all the dirt and grime that was stuck to my body, the water didn't turn a dingy color. A steady stream of water poured into the bath from a groove chiseled into the ground. The whole thing reminded me of an ancient hot tub. Dark tapestries were hung around its edges to give some semblance of privacy, even though I was the only one in the room. Soaps and shampoos were waiting for me and I almost cried with joy when I saw the razor that sat among them. I tested the blades with my thumb, not surprised to find them dull. I knew they wouldn't give me anything that could be used as a weapon, but they would work. It had been forever since I'd shaved my legs. I scrubbed at my skin until I could see something that resembled my skin tone again before starting on my hair. I finally pulled myself from the water and wrapped my body in the soft towels that had been provided. There were clothes waiting for me as promised. A set of tactical pants and a black tank top were neatly folded on top of a set of boots. Atop the shirt was a small jar with some sort of green lotion inside. I picked it up to inspect closer when a small slip of paper fluttered to the ground. I reached down to pick it up. *For your leg*, it read.

Scrunching my brows, I twisted the top off the jar, sniffing the lotion carefully. It smelled good, my time helping Cassie in the infirmary telling me there were hints of aloe and sage. Tentatively, I dipped my fingers in the mixture, dabbing it onto the wounded area of my leg. There was a quick sting, but almost immediately the ache eased, replaced instead by a light tingle. Uncomfortable, but not nearly as painful. I gasped at the relief it provided. I rubbed more into the wound, making sure not to use all of it in case

I needed more later. Careful not to disturb the wound, I pulled my fresh pair of pants on first, then lifted the shirt over my wet hair. Just as I was lacing up my boots, Nero returned, pushing the door open roughly.

"Did no one ever teach you to knock?" I demanded.

He snorted, giving me a singular glance, taking note of my improved condition. "I'll show you to your new accomodations."

The new room was a moderate improvement over my cell. They were about the same size, and this room, just like the other, was absent fire and torches. The high windows were the only source of light, also like before, but there was one large difference. This room had a bed. I made no attempt to act tough, instead I nearly sprinted for the small cot that was on the opposite end of the cell, lying down on the thin mattress. The blanket was scratchy, and the pillow was flat, but it was the softest thing I'd had the opportunity to sleep on in months. My muscles immediately responded, the tightness in my back loosening just a bit. "Fantastic," I muttered under my breath. I closed my eyes, not bothering to see if Nero had left yet. I didn't know what time of day it was, but I was suddenly, overwhelmingly tired.

It was only moments until exhaustion took over, and I fell into a deep sleep.

Chapter 4

Roman

"Begin!"

I attacked immediately, sprinting across the dirt, dagger raised. Isaac had only a moment to step backward and lift his own dagger above his head to block the blow. My weapon clanged off his, the sound echoing off the rough stone walls of our new training facility. *New* was a strong word. Realistically, our training facility was an old ruin on the edge of the island that Astrid had converted to a small sparring area with an even smaller weapons rack. She had tried to convince us it was traditional for the Guard to separate themselves from the other soldiers and train in private. Secretly, I knew that was just an excuse, and our new facility had less to do with tradition and more to do with Amina. She had eyes and ears everywhere on the island, soldiers who would rather spy for her than risk the Hollow. They would be all too willing to report back to her about what they saw or overheard during one of our training sessions. And after Grady got into two fights at the common training facility, both with people he thought were reporting back to Amina, Astrid had to make a change. She used the lingering pieces of her influence to move us here, then bribed one of her people to put up our own set of wards. No one would get within miles of the facility without us knowing about it.

I had to admit, while not as spacious as the other facility, this one was definitely easier on the eyes. As if it grew from the ground, the limestone walls scaled to twice my size, accented on both ends by large columns, wrapped in vines and natural growth. What was once the roof, now existed only in part, small pieces of the sand underfoot shadowed by its peaks. The rest left open to the elements, the wind came rushing through freely.

I struck at Isaac again.

Once.

Twice.

Three times.

The third blow knocked him down to one knee, and when I struck a fourth time, he rolled out of the way, putting a few feet of distance between us, giving him room to breathe. He jumped to his feet, attempting to covertly brace his hand across his torso. I noted the movement, the speed at which he got to his feet. Faster than a human, sure, but slower than he should have been. I took a step forward, prepared to lunge again. "Roman!" the sharp reprimand came from the side of the sparring ring, bringing me up short. I glared at Cassandra White, the source of the voice. Her bright red hair was pulled back in her signature braid, her typically smiling mouth set into a hard line. I'd known Cassie since I was twelve. She'd overseen a large part of my training when I'd been branded, and I considered her my sister. Not like Diana had been but as close as I would ever get to one again. She was also one of the few people I actually listened to. "Give him a moment," she hissed.

I narrowed my eyes. "Don't you have somewhere else to be? Isn't Mallory coming home soon?" Cassie's girlfriend had been sent on a mission almost a week ago but was due to return soon.

"She flies in in two days," Cassie answered, knowing I was trying to dismiss her. She crossed her arms, making it very clear she wasn't going anywhere, then looked knowingly at Isaac.

I rocked back on my heels, pointing at Isaac's abdomen with my dagger. "Are you bleeding?" I asked him.

"It's fine," he answered, brushing me off. I ignored the tense set of his jaw, the tinge of pain in his eyes.

"See," I said to Cassie, "he's fine."

She rolled her eyes at me. Something else I chose to ignore, instead eager to return to sparring. "Isaac, you should take a break," Cassie suggested. I shook my head, irritated at her interference. It wasn't that I was eager to hurt Isaac, but Cassie was coddling him, something that would do him no favors in the real world. Isaac had been gravely wounded during the battle of Cairo. A hybrid blade laced with poison had split him open from hip to collarbone. We didn't have the proper tools to treat it in Cairo, and when Amina and her forces had bombarded us at our safe house, they'd taken Isaac as leverage to keep us in line.

They refused to treat him, instead doing only enough to keep him alive. The delay in his treatment had cost him. The poison had reached his blood stream, pumping through his whole body. He had been too injured to heal himself and using magic would only seal the wound shut, trapping the poison inside him. When we'd returned to Awen, the healers had been forced to treat him with traditional methods, putting him through countless blood transfusions, desperate to cycle the tainted blood out and replace it with a fresh, clean substitute. When that hadn't worked, they were left with no option but to treat the symptoms of the poison and hope for the best. They stitched his abdomen closed, lowering his risk of infection, but with the poison still in his system, his body was under attack. It wasn't uncommon for him to spike a fever, a condition complicated by the fact that as a Sagittarius, he naturally ran at a higher temperature. At one point it had gotten so bad, he had been thrown into a fit of convulsions. The healers had been forced to put him in an induced hypothermic state to protect him from doing any permanent damage. From then on, no matter what the healers did, they couldn't bring him back to normal. It wasn't until Brynn had stepped in with a spell from The Book of Breathings that we found a solution.

"Do you need your tonic?" Cassie pushed, already stepping toward the door. "Brynn and Grady are working with the sceptre next door, I can get her to bring you some." Brynn had created a drink infused with a set of spelled herbs that temporarily erased the effects of the poison. Isaac's body temperature had almost immediately returned to normal, and he was up and around quickly. He remained that way, as long as he drank his tonic every day. As he improved, it became obvious that the antidote had one serious downside. Since the poison was magically based, Brynn's antidote had to be too. Which meant it blocked not only the magical properties in the poison, but all magic it found in Isaac's body. Which meant that as long as he drank the antidote, he no longer could feel his element.

Leaving him powerless.

Now Isaac was glaring at Cassie too. "I said *I'm fine*." She raised her eyebrow, obviously not believing him. Wisely, she let it drop. Isaac turned to me. "Let's fight."

I smiled, returning to fighting position. This time it was Isaac that lunged forward. Even with all his training, his lack of magic left his moves slow and sluggish, and I was easily able to read where he planned to strike. I parried the attack, letting him attempt three more before I knocked his dagger out of his hand, clattering to the ground. He growled with frustration, a sentiment I understood and didn't blame him for. Isaac was strong, there was no doubt about it, but without his magic, he never stood a chance at winning against a wraith, let alone a hybrid or Set. That made him a liability.

"You have to move faster than that, Isaac," I admonished him. "You're never going to get to go out in the field if you're that slow."

"I know!" he screamed at me, momentarily losing control of his temper. I knew I wasn't being fair to him. It wasn't his fault any of this happened. But better I was tough on him now than let him go on a hunt and get himself killed just because I wasn't willing to hurt his feelings.

I dropped into position again, signaling Isaac to attack, when an explosion rang out from just past the training ring walls, followed quickly by a shout. Training immediately forgotten, the three of us sprinted for the opening at the end of the sparring ring, rounding the corner of the ruin and running for the small building that lived in its shadow.

"Grady!" Cassie shouted as she pulled open the door. "Brynn!" We entered the small room, Cassie immediately coughing and waving her hand in front of her face to clear the smoke that was rolling through the space. "What the hell happened?" she asked.

When no answer came, I called on a small piece of power, willing the smoke toward me and out the door. The room was clear in seconds, revealing to us what was going on inside the room.

Grady leaned against the wall, his hair ruffled, with flakes of what appeared to be rock in-between the strands. Behind him was a large divot in the wall with scorch marks bursting from it like an angry sunburst. No doubt the source of the explosion we had heard. Across the room, Brynn stood with her eyes wide and mouth agape, staring at Grady. On the table in front of her was the was-sceptre, its metal inlay swirling with life. "Did you shoot Grady?" I asked Brynn incredulously. There seemed to be no other explanation.

"Not intentionally!" Brynn answered, her voice higher and faster than was normal for her.

From behind me, Isaac was chuckling. "That's awesome." Cassie had already moved toward Grady and was fussing around, trying to check him for wounds. He promptly shooed her away.

"How did this happen?" I demanded, my voice taking a slight edge. This was exactly the type of stupidity I didn't want to deal with right now.

"Chill out," Grady answered me. "We were trying to find a different spell in the book. One that would let us use the sceptre without draining us of all our power." We'd had the sceptre for months now, and one of the first things we realized was that none of us were strong enough to use it.

The sceptre was made to be wielded by a god. None of us came close to that kind of strength.

"Clearly, whatever you tried didn't work," I felt compelled to point out, eyeing the smoking hole in the wall.

"It's not as bad as it seems," Brynn defended herself. "It *did* work." She looked at Grady, shrugging her shoulders. "Briefly."

Grady continued. "We just have to figure out how to extend the spell. We need more power."

"Maybe you three should try combining power again," Cassie suggested.

I immediately shook my head. "Horrible idea," I muttered. We'd tried it before. It wasn't enough. Brynn and I had nearly sucked Grady dry. He'd passed out and was unconscious for almost a day.

"What's your problem?" Grady demanded, crossing his arms and staring at me.

Before I could answer, Cassie jumped in. "He's had a bug up his ass all day."

I ground my molars together. "I'm fine. Your idea was just awful. We're wasting our time with this damn thing. You know we don't have enough power to use it, and the one person who does isn't here. So, excuse me, but rather than keep playing with a weapon we can never use, I think our time is better used elsewhere."

"Like looking for Kyndal," Brynn finished for me. We'd had this argument before.

"Precisely. She's the strongest Kindred on the planet. If anyone can use the sceptre, you know it's her. Our Guard isn't complete without her."

"We want to find Kyndal as much as anyone, Roman, but what do you want us to do?" Grady questioned. "There's been no sign of her, no sign of Set or his army, for over half a year now. Astrid has sent out as many scouts as she can spare without drawing Amina's attention. They are scouring the world trying to find her. We don't even know if she's alive."

"She's alive," I responded immediately, cutting off whatever he was going to say next. "I know she's alive."

Grady ran his hand through his hair, miniature pieces of rock raining down to the floor. He took a deep, frustrated breath before turning to Cassie. "Talk to him."

"Look, I know you all think I'm clinging to some sort of denial that Kyndal is gone, but I'm not!" I said, before Cassie had to opportunity to say anything. "We are connected through the Rafiq bond. If she were dead, I would know. I wouldn't be standing here."

"Mallory said you told her the bond had gone silent. That you couldn't feel her anymore. Maybe you wouldn't know. Maybe the connection is gone." Cassie said the words kindly, and I could see the pain it caused her to give them voice.

"She's alive. I know it." I turned back to Grady. "What about Briar? She said she knew Kyndal would return to Awen. That she could help."

Grady shook his head. "Briar is crazy," he disagreed. "She always has been. Did you see that scar of hers? She was blown up during a battle decades ago and hasn't been right since. She started trying to convince people she could see things. Things that haven't happened yet."

"But maybe she knows something. If you had just let me question her last night. . ."

"You would have gotten nothing but the ramblings of a delusional woman," Grady finished. "Trust me."

I glared at Grady, even as Brynn walked around the table, stopping halfway between the two of us. Cassie and Isaac had wisely stayed where they were, realizing this was Guard business. Brynn's dark eyes were sharp, and she studied me now, as if she could see straight through me, right into my soul to see what I was hiding. She eyed me for a moment longer before rocking back on her heels and crossing her arms. "What are you not telling us?" she asked me. I looked to each of them in turn. Last night, I'd been dying to tell them about seeing Kyndal in my dream, but now I wasn't so sure. Would they even believe me? Brynn noted my hesitation. "Roman. . ." she prompted.

I closed my eyes briefly. "I saw Kyndal."

All four of them erupted, their words a mix of astonishment and anger. It was Cassie's voice that broke through the din. "How?" she asked.

"I dreamed of her, two nights ago. She was standing just as close to me then as you are now."

"You miss her," Isaac said simply. I could tell he didn't believe me. "It's normal to think about someone. . ."

"It was real," I interrupted. My shoulders slumped as they all looked at me with disbelieving eyes. I pinched the bridge of my nose. "When I was possessed, I dreamt of Kyndal. We were back at the lake in Marienville, and I was me again. I was normal. I wasn't sure at the time if it was real or not, but she remembered it, like she was actually there. Kyndal has always been able to dream walk. What if," I huffed a breath, "what if the Rafiq bond lets me do it too, and I can talk to her?"

Brynn took a step closer. "Tell us what you saw when you dreamt of her. Don't leave anything out."

So, I didn't. I told them everything. Where she had been, what she looked like, I even told them how I'd stumbled over myself, forgetting everything I wanted to say.

When I'd finished, Grady spoke quietly, "Let's pretend for just a moment, that you really did see her. Did you see anything that could lead us to where she is?"

I thought of the notebook still tucked neatly inside my boot. "Sage."

"Sage," Isaac repeated.

I nodded. "I could smell it. But it wasn't like it smells when someone burns it. It was cleaner than that, more natural. It reminded me of when Ezekiel used to plant it in his garden. When it would rain, the whole garden would smell like wet sage."

"That's not much to go on," Grady pointed out.

"No shit," I barked.

"The desert," Brynn threw in.

"What?" Grady asked.

"Sagebrush is one of the few things that can grow in the Sahara desert. You can find it along the bank of the Nile. When it rains, the air is filled with the smell of sage," she explained, unfazed by Grady's attitude. She turned to me.

"Do you think you can do it again?" she asked. "Do you think you can see Kyndal again?"

I heard it then. She believed me. And if what she was saying was true, we might be able to narrow down her location. "I'm not sure how I did it the first time," I admitted.

"We need to figure it out. Now. If Kyndal is alive, your dream might be the best opportunity we have to find her," Brynn responded.

"And if we find her," Grady added, "we find Set."

If I had it my way, we would've gone directly back to a secure location in order for me to attempt to dreamwalk. Unfortunately, we had responsibilities to attend to first. Amina had called for a special assembly of the Council, and the Guard had mandatory attendance. "No doubt she has more warriors for us to throw in the Hollow," Grady mumbled under his breath, even as he twirled the was-sceptre with his left hand. We were winding our way through the city, back toward Council Chambers. Not only did we have to attend this special meeting, we also had to return the sceptre to its rightful place, locked up in the basement of the Chambers.

"Quiet," Brynn admonished Grady quickly. Not because she disagreed with him, but because we had neared the Chambers by then and it was possible to be within hearing distance of the sentries. They stood guard all hours of the day, even when the Council was not in session. They wore the same black gear as the rest of us, but a silver pin adorned their collars, marking them as those who worked directly for the Nomarch Council. We couldn't risk them overhearing us.

We jogged up the large staircase into Council Chambers, past the sentries posted there. We kept our heads high, ignoring the jeers and angry stares we received from them. When we reached the center of the building, we veered in two directions. I stopped at the door to the throne room, Brynn and Grady continuing on toward the staircase at the back. It led down to the dungeon where the sceptre was kept. There was no sense in me going with them, or waiting here for them, so I turned to the sentry standing just five feet from me.

"Open the door," I instructed him. Just as before, he didn't budge. There was no flicker of recognition on his face to indicate he'd even heard me. I knew the sentries hated the Guard, but their disgust and mistreatment was growing real old, and frankly, it was pissing me off. "Open the door," I repeated, this time with more force. Still the sentry did not move. I stepped forward, into the sentry's personal space. He couldn't ignore me anymore. I was taller than him, and he pulled his head back to look me in the eye. "If I have to ask again, I'll open the door myself, and I'll use your head to do it," I growled.

"I would like to see you try," the sentry responded. His words sounded tough, but I noticed the shifting of his weight from the front of his foot to the back, the tightening of his hand around his spear. I made him nervous. He obviously knew who I was, what I was capable of. I glared at the man, pulling a small amount of power forward, just enough to change my eyes gold. The air behind me kicked up, my power reaching out to the element, and just as I was about to make good on my threat, a voice ripped through the stone hall.

"Roman!" Astrid yelled. "Stand down immediately."

For a split second I didn't move, didn't pull myself back. I wanted the sentry to worry for a moment longer that I might do it, I might actually throw him through the door. Slowly, I stepped back, quieting my power in the process. The wind, which had appeared out of nowhere, died just as quickly, until I'd moved far enough away to be standing next to the Cancer Nomarch. I could feel her ice-cold eyes boring into me, but I didn't meet her gaze. Instead, I kept mine trained on the sentry, knowing that one day, when I wasn't bound by duty and circumstance, I would have the opportunity to repay him for his disdain.

"Open the door, you fool," Astrid ordered the sentry. There was no hesitation this time. The sentry turned and pushed the large door open, standing to the side to allow us to enter. I didn't take my eyes off him for a moment, not until Astrid and I had entered the room. "I don't ever want to see anything like that again," Astrid hissed in my ear.

"That guy is an asshole," I answered her, unrepentant. "Someone needs to set him straight."

Astrid stepped in front of me, forcing me to quit walking. She was tiny, and I could see clearly over her head into the empty throne room. There was a large table in the center of the thrones, something I'd never seen before. It was covered in papers and maps. *Odd. Where was everyone? Why weren't the other Nomarchs here?*

"You don't have the luxury of picking a fight with every person that hates you, asshole or not. You have to be better than them. Stronger," she admonished.

I knew she was right, even if I was reluctant to hear it. "I'm sorry," I responded through gritted teeth.

"Good," Astrid said, nodding once, assuming that would be the end of it. "Where is the rest of your Guard?"

Still pissed, I was tempted to pop off and explain that *the rest* of my Guard wasn't here, one was still missing, just as she had been for months. "They are returning the sceptre," I answered instead. "Where is the rest of the *Council*?" My words held a bite. We both knew the Council was a joke anymore. "Amina summoned us for a special meeting."

Astrid glared at me, noting my tone. "The others will arrive shortly." Astrid's eyes flicked up to where Brynn and Grady had just entered. "But you should know, Amina wasn't the one who summoned you, nor will she be pleased at your presence. I was the one who summoned you."

"Why?" Brynn asked, her voice growing closer until they were both shoulder to shoulder with me.

"I am still a Nomarch of the High Council, no matter what Amina thinks about it. She cannot strip away my power completely, and I will use what little power I have left to whatever end I see fit," Astrid snapped.

I raised my eyebrows in surprise. It was odd for Astrid to lose her calm facade, even for a moment. Grady whistled quietly under his breath. "All right then," I eventually said. "What's with the table?" I asked in an attempt to steer the conversation somewhere useful.

Thankfully, Astrid took the que. For the moment we were the only ones in the room, but our privacy wouldn't last for long. "Amina's scouts returned this morning with their reports. It is anticipated Amina will announce our next move. I want to petition her to release the Guard into the field."

"Let us off the island?" Brynn restated, her voice raising with surprise. I couldn't blame her for her shock. We'd been grounded to Awen for so long now, it was almost unthinkable for Amina to let us out of her sight.

"Do you think she'll go for it?" Grady asked. It pained me to hear the hope in his voice as well.

I shook my head, refusing to believe it. "There's no way. She knows she can't control us once we leave Awen." *She knows I'll go searching for Kyndal,* I thought.

Astrid peered over her shoulder to the door that led to the private quarters of the Council, as if she could hear the Nomarchs beyond it heading this way. She was centuries older and stronger than me, perhaps she could. She leaned in closer, dropping her voice to a barely discernible whisper. "If enough of the Nomarchs side with me, we may be able to sway her. Either way, I need you three here to listen to what is happening next. At the very least, you will act as a witness to her plans."

Just then, the large ornate door at the back of the room cracked open. Astrid immediately turned to face the entering Nomarchs, striding forward into the center of the room. She stood proudly at the head of the wooden table, waiting. To the others, there would be no sign that the four of us had just been huddled together, discussing our secret plans. Unsure what to do, Brynn, Grady, and I hung back, behind the thrones. The first through the door was Maks, the Leo Nomarch. Kyndal had saved his life once, and he'd voted in our favor before. Maks was one of the few Nomarchs I counted as an ally. He gave us a simple nod, as if he weren't surprised to see the three of us standing there. I knew he and Astrid had worked together before. It was possible she'd warned him of our attendance. After him came Cyrus, the Gemini Nomarch, someone who was definitely *not* in our corner. He was a selfish, bitter man, one I knew hated me due to his history with my father. Cyrus had been the leader of the Coterie until Nero staged a coup and stole it from him. He glowered at us the whole way until reaching the newly placed table, standing uncomfortably next to Maks.

The next four were Zayna, Gabriel, Haru, and Elias; Taurus, Libra, Sagittarius, and Aquarius respectively. I'd never given much consideration to the four of them, but as I did now, I held little hope for their support. They were each relatively weak-minded, and could be easily swayed by the person in charge. It would be out of character for them to vote against Amina and try to get us released for field work. They paid the Guard no mind, probably assuming that our presence was at the demand of the Governor.

The next two Nomarchs were Riley of House Capricorn and Joran from House Pisces. Both were new to the Council. Riley had taken Ezekiel's place, and Joran stepped in after his predecessor was killed during the raising of Set. I knew little of Joran, but given how he came to power, I couldn't imagine he was a fan of mine. Riley had always struck me as a strong-minded woman. I knew she wouldn't allow Amina to push her around. The last one to enter the room before Amina was Madigan of House Virgo. One of the few people I'd seen whose hair was a brighter shade of red than Cassie's, Madigan was fierce. A warrior in her own right, she'd sat on the Council for decades and had always been an independent voice. Her decisions almost always worked in favor of the soldiers, the warriors that put themselves in harm's way on a daily basis.

I liked her.

Finally, almost a full minute after Madigan, Amina appeared. She walked through the room confidently, giving no care to the fact that the rest of the Council was standing and waiting for her. She moved slowly, forcing them to wait on their feet. A total powerplay. So caught up in her own hubris, it took her until midway through the room to realize Brynn, Grady, and I were there. She froze in her tracks, her eyes large, mouth tensed in her signature pout. Far away as we were, I could almost feel how pissed she was. We'd taken her by surprise. From the corner of my eye, Astrid smirked, pleased with herself.

It took a moment for Amina to say anything, as if she were struggling to get herself under control before she reacted. Finally, she found her voice. "What the hell are you doing here?"

Chapter 5

Roman

The room was still, the silence deafening.

None of the Nomarchs answered Amina, the three of us standing perfectly frozen, backs rigid, our faces set blank. The perfect soldiers.

"Answer me, Guardsmen!" Amina seethed.

Brynn stepped forward, facing the woman who had been her Nomarch for years, a woman she'd once respected. "We received an official summons, Governor, informing us of a special Council meeting. We were told our presence was mandatory."

"I sent no such summons," Amina argued.

"With respect, Governor, it carried your official seal." A careful correction. Brynn was telling the truth. Our summons had been marked with the wax seal of House

Scorpio. What Brynn failed to point out was that Astrid had most likely borrowed the seal and marked them herself. Brynn reached into her back pocket, producing a yellowed piece of paper. She'd been smart enough to bring the summons with her. She held it out to Amina. "See for yourself."

Amina stomped across the stone floor, the click of her heels echoing off the walls. She ripped the paper out of Brynn's hand, her face twisting with confusion at the proof of her words. "No matter, you aren't required. Get out."

"Governor," Astrid spoke up from the table, "perhaps we could benefit from their presence."

Amina spun around to Astrid, eyes afire. "Of course you would advocate for them to remain. No doubt you had a hand in them being here in the first place."

Astrid didn't even flinch at Amina's accusation. "Regardless of *how* they got here, it is imperative they stay. It was a Guard who entombed Set long ago, we cannot expect to defeat him without using this Guard." Several of the Nomarchs rumbled their agreement to the reminder of our necessity in this war. With one look from Amina, they were quickly silenced. Astrid was walking a fine line between challenging Amina and insulting her, she needed to ease into her request or this whole thing could blow up. "I demand you release them back into the field."

My eyebrows shot up. So much for subtlety.

The room erupted into a flurry of debate and arguing, Amina immediately moving away from us and toward the table to quiet the Council. A muffled huff escaped Grady, "I didn't expect her to just blurt it out like that," he whispered to Brynn and me. "She just ripped the Band-Aid right off, didn't she?"

I crossed my arms, carefully watching the Nomarchs. Who was arguing with whom, which ones were advocating for us, who appeared to be against us.

"It's genius," Brynn added in quietly. "Astrid forced the issue before Amina could flip the conversation in her favor." Typically, it would be dangerous to talk this way, but with the Nomarchs' attention elsewhere, we knew no one was listening to us.

Over the din of noise, one voice rose—Madigan. "Astrid is right. The Guard have sat idle for too long. They should be released into the field." I had no idea if she was working with Astrid or simply taking advantage of the situation. At the moment, I didn't care. Not if it got us what we wanted.

"That is not your decision to make," Amina snapped.

"Let's put it to a vote, then," Madigan countered. "Or do our votes no longer count at all? Why keep the illusion of the Council if you are going to ignore everything we say?"

Amina gave Madigan a look that told me she was wondering the same thing. Part of her no doubt wanted to dissolve the Council immediately, but even she was too smart for that. There was already too much unrest. Fracture the Council, and it would rip the Kindred apart, making us easy targets for Set.

"A vote!" someone echoed. Maks, I thought.

Astrid and Amina stood at opposite ends of the table, staring at each other. Amina may have the title of governor, but the women were equally powerful in their own right, both refusing to back down. "Fine," Amina eventually conceded, practically spitting the words. "A vote for allowing the Guard to return to the field. Those in favor, raise your right arm." Five arms rose. Astrid, Maks, and Madigan, unsurprisingly. With them was Riley and Joran. "All opposed?" Amina asked. Cyrus, Zayna, Gabriel, Haru, and Elias all raised their arms. The decision was split five-five. That was until Amina raised her own arm, tipping the scales in favor of the opposition.

She smiled, a move that reminded me of a feral cat after they'd caught their prey. "The noes have it."

I grimaced, even as a rumble went through the table, resonating with those who had voted on our side. Astrid glanced my direction from across the room, but her eyes did not hold the apology and disappointment I expected.

"Although the Guard will not be allowed back in the field," Amina continued, her voice taking on a sweet tone—I immediately distrusted anything she was about to say—"as proof of my good will, I will allow them to stay for this meeting. As Nomarch Astrid said, they are an important piece of our arsenal and they may yet have a part to play in this war."

"Thank you, Governor," Brynn, Grady, and I responded together, resuming our roles of perfect soldiers. I didn't miss the small rise of Astrid's eyebrow. She'd never expected to get us off the island, but she knew it would cause this rift. Force her to concede something.

"That is *if* you can prove yourself loyal," Amina continued.

There it is, I thought. She wanted something. "Of course, Governor," I answered quickly before Grady could say anything. He wasn't as good at keeping his emotions in check. "Whatever you require."

"There are rumors of a small group of soldiers that are organizing against me. Attempting to infiltrate various elements of the island, Hollow guards, instructors, even my inner circle, in order to conspire to kill me." I kept my face still, giving no hint that I knew to whom she was referring. "If it is true, these soldiers are traitors and deserve to be shown no mercy. I want you to find out if the rumors are true, and if they are, bring me the head of their leader. Then, and only then, will I allow you off Awen."

"This feels weird," Grady announced.

"Shut up and lay down," Cassie admonished him, pointing to the floor of her and Mallory's cottage.

He raised his hands defensively. "Sorry, but somebody had to say it," he answered before laying his tall frame out on the stone floor about five feet from where I already laid.

From the other side of the room, Brynn's stern voice explained, "This is the best way to find out if Roman is really dreamwalking, or if he's simply hallucinating Kyndal. Now do what Cassie said and shut up."

I snorted, as Grady laid his head back, properly admonished by our fellow Guardsmen. I leaned my head up, looking to Brynn. She was leaning over The Book of Breathings, surrounded by the various herbs and ingredients that populated Cassie's personal collection. Fire light flickered off her dark skin, the sun having set hours ago. There was a bowl in front of her, and I watched as she cut small pieces of a nearby herb and dropped them into the bowl. "If I ask a question, are you going to yell at me?" I asked her tentatively.

She didn't bother turning to acknowledge me. "It depends. Is it a stupid question?"

"I had a teacher once that said there's no such thing as a stupid question," Isaac interrupted from the chair on the other side of the room. I cracked a smile. Leave it to Isaac not to take the situation seriously. Brynn turned and glared at Isaac before silently signaling Cassie who stood nearby.

Wordlessly she reached out and smacked Isaac across the back of his head. He glared up at her. "Hey!" he protested before pouting as he took another drink of his tonic.

"Anyways," I added, redirecting the group, "theoretically, I understand the basics of how this works. The three of us combine powers and you guys boost me into a dreamspace where I can talk to Kyndal."

"I still don't hear a question," Brynn interrupted, turning with the bowl in hand.

"What happens if I can't fall asleep? Or worse, if I don't dream?"

She walked the short distance across the room, sitting down in between Grady and me, the whole time careful not to spill the contents of her bowl. Contents I could now see looked like some sort of herbal tea or soup. "That is what this is for," she answered.

"It smells awful," Grady commented. I felt inclined to agree.

"Regardless of its aroma, this tea is spelled from The Book of Breathings. Think of it like a magical sleeping pill. You'll be out in under a minute. As far as the dreaming goes, that's up to you."

"Fantastic," I muttered.

"Are we going to talk about the Council meeting?" Grady asked. "You know, before the mystical dreaming."

"There's nothing to talk about," I answered quickly. "We're not doing what Amina wants."

"Why not?" Grady asked. Cassie pinned him with a look. "What?" he asked defensively. "I'm just asking."

"The Council meeting was never about getting us off the island. It was about getting Amina to admit something she wanted so we could use it against her," I explained.

"Amina is looking for the leader of the rebels," Cassie continued. I'd filled her in on the details. "That means two things. One, she doesn't know who is leading her opposition, and two, she's scared. If she's scared, then she doesn't have as much control of the people as she wants us to think."

"Not to mention," I added, "the group she's referring to is led by Daniela, someone whose efforts have saved your ass more than once. You should be more grateful," I reminded him. "Or is loyalty still an issue for you?" I questioned. A dig at his former life. The one before he was in the Guard.

"Screw you, Roman," Grady responded. "I just thought if we had a way of getting off this damn island and into the fight, we should at least discuss it. I wasn't going to actually do it."

"We don't make a habit of selling out our friends, you jackass," Cassie answered harshly. I didn't move to defend Grady. Cassie was right. We don't turn on our friends.

Brynn ignored us all. "Everyone, shut up and focus!" The room immediately quieted. "Thank you. Remember, Grady and I won't actually be with you in the dream, you'll only be able to feel our magic. Don't use too much or you may not be able to bring yourself back." I was happy to hear they wouldn't be dreamwalking with me. If I did get to see Kyndal, the last thing I wanted was an audience.

"All right, let's do this," I said, reaching for the tea. The first drink was bitter, but I closed my eyes and drank it all down. The three of us laid back on the floor. I shut my eyes as the tea started to take effect. Next to me, I heard Grady and Brynn begin to chant and within moments I could feel their powers combining with mine. The earthy scent of soil filled my nose first, then was quickly washed away by the taste of the sea. I held onto their powers, wrapping my own around them, as I filled my thoughts with Kyndal.

I built her in my mind as I always did. Her hair first, then her eyes, the curve of her hip, the smoothness of her skin. I focused on the things about her only I knew. I imagined what it felt like when she was near, the heat that traveled along my spine and drew me to her. The sound of her voice when she first woke up, still raspy with sleep. The image of her brought with it several memories, the most potent of which was the last time I'd really seen her, disappearing with Set. I pushed that memory to the side, not wanting to remember her that way. Instead, I focused on her in a good memory. The last time we'd really been alone together, inside the Allegheny up in the treehouse. I remembered everything about that night, what she'd been wearing, the sound of Cherry Run babbling by. The more I thought about it, the stronger the memory grew, until finally, I opened my eyes and found myself standing at the foot of the tree.

The sky is dark, the stars above twinkling brightly. I'm surrounded by old growth trees I instantly recognize as the Allegheny. The sounds of wildlife envelope me, and I can only just hear Cherry Run flowing smoothly on the other side of the embankment. The familiar, giant sycamore looms above me, the wooden deck barely visible off the north side of the tree from this angle. It doesn't matter that I can't see through the trees, I can feel her. A heat centers at my spine, wrapping itself around me in a soft embrace. Using my own strength, but careful not to touch Grady or Brynn's magic. I can still feel pulsing inside me, I call to my power. My eyesight sharpens and the wind behind me instantly responds. I leap into the air, riding the air current up to the base of the treehouse. I land in a soft crouch, my eyes trained to the small open deck. She had been sitting with her legs dangling over the edge, but she twists her body at the sound of my landing, and I'm met with her fierce green stare.

"Roman?" she questions, and I almost fall to my knees at the sound of her voice. She jumps to her feet, taking an eager step toward me. I do the same, but just before I reach her, she pulls back. "You—you're not real," she stammers. I step forward again, but she matches the step, moving backward and staying out of reach. "Don't touch me. You can't be real," she repeats.

I hold my hands up, as if dealing with a wounded animal. "Kyndal, it's me, I promise."

She shakes her head. "No. You're just another one of Set's tricks," she mutters more to herself than me.

My heart aches at her words. What kind of torture is Set putting her through, that she doesn't even trust her own eyes? I chance a small step forward. She notes the movement but doesn't step back. "I'm not a trick," I say slowly, my arm outstretched. "It's me."

She stares at the hand. "Prove it," she challenges.

"The last thing you said to me in person was that you loved me. And you were sorry."

"Set was there when I said that. That proves nothing."

I grit my teeth. I don't know how long I can stay in this dream. I had to get her to believe me. I look around the small treehouse. "I brought you here once. You yelled at me and then I told you the story about how I built this place. You couldn't believe that Cassie had dumped me in the forest to fend for myself." She scrunches her face, and I can tell she isn't fully convinced. "If you don't believe what I'm saying, at least trust what you are feeling. *The bond has been silent for months now, but it's back, isn't it?* Can't you feel me?" *She pauses, and I feel her power stir, her eyes turning a sharp red. The bond strengthens, rushing to the forefront as if it is trying to help prove my point. "Good," I encourage her. "I know you feel it. Set can't fake that. It's really me, Kyndal."*

She looks again at my outstretched hand, tentatively lifting her fingers to brush my palm. Heat immediately fills my hand, and her body relaxes. She lifts her eyes to mine. "It's really you," she says. I release a breath I didn't realize I had been holding. She believes me. "How are you here?" she asks. "How long do we have?"

I smile, threading my fingers through hers. The feel of her skin instantly comforting me. "I don't know how long we have. The last time it was only moments. Brynn and Grady gave me a little power boost, but I'm not sure how much power they can spare. Kyndal, you need to tell me where you are so we can find you."

Her eyebrows knit together in obvious confusion. "Last time?" she questions, ignoring the most important part of what I said. "What do you mean, last time?"

"Two nights ago, I dreamt of you. You were standing on the balcony of my room. Don't you remember?"

"I thought it was a hallucination," she explains, her eyes welling with tears. "I thought Set was making me see things. I didn't believe it was you."

I reach up and wipe away a tear that escapes, stealing a moment for myself by holding her cheek in my hand. She leans into the touch. "You need to tell me where you are."

"I can't," she responds.

"It's okay if you don't know specifics," I encourage her, thinking of my list I'd made. I can compare what she knows to what I've already figured out. "Are you in the desert? Just tell me anything you can."

Kyndal takes a step back, out of my reach, and looks me square in the eye. "I can't," she repeats. "I can't tell you."

I snap backward as if she'd struck me. "Why not?"

"If I tell you, you'll try to find me."

"That's exactly the point, Kyndal. I. . ." I rough my hand through my hair. "I don't understand."

"You guys can't come here. Set's army is too big, his power is too strong. If you try to come for me, he'll kill you. It's best if you guys just forget about me."

My eyes bulge. "Forget? Kyndal, I'm not just going to forget you. . ." How could she ever ask me that?

She steps back again, and her image begins to fade. The dream is ending, one of us is beginning to wake up. The background, the trees and night sky, fade away, replaced instead by the faint image of sunshine and endless sand. Although I can't see it, I just faintly hear the rushing of water. I pull on my power, not caring that I'm using Grady and Brynn's too. "Kyndal, don't go yet!"

"I'm sorry, Roman," she says even as she fades more. The words put me right back in The Hall of Two Truths. "I love you."

I bolt upright off the floor, my breaths coming out in ragged gasps. I'm sweating, and my left hand is shaking, a sure sign I've spent too much of my power. Cassie was there almost immediately. "What happened?" she demanded. I ignored her, turning to Grady and Brynn who were both sluggishly opening their eyes and leaning up off the floor. Grady's face was ashen, his breathing as rough as mine. I had pulled hard on their magic, desperate to stay in the dream.

"Did it work?" he asked.

I nodded. "I saw her. I think Brynn was right. She's in the Sahara."

When I didn't provide any further explanation, Cassie pressed. "Did she say anything?"

I swallowed, my heart sinking. "She said she doesn't want to be found."

Chapter 6

Kyndal

I sat on the bow of an old barge, my head propped against the metal siding. My legs were curled into my body, my arms wrapped around my shins. My chin had been resting on my knees for the past six hours as I eyed the various hybrids that sat on the barge with me.

I'd spent almost the entire day in my room, behind my barred door. When I'd woken from the dream, I'd been a mess. The sun had been shining into the small room, but the colors were still the muted shades of sunrise. The memory of the dream was clear in my mind, but every time I tried to shake it loose, or tried to forget the look on Roman's face when I refused to tell him where I was, I broke. I'd never seen him look so betrayed before. I'd curled up on my tiny cot and cried for hours.

I'm doing the right thing, I tried telling myself. I had to do this in order to protect him. No matter what excuses I created, I couldn't stop the flood of emotions. There was a hollowness in my chest, an empty spot where I knew the bond should be. It had been months since I'd felt Roman's power. I'd learned to ignore the ache caused by his absence, but now, after seeing him, the pain had returned tenfold. My magic yearned to be reunited with its counterpart, and not just for a moment, but for good. While my heart ached for Roman, my mind replayed Set's threat—that he was willing to attack Awen just to find Roman and kill him—a threat I fully believed. If he was willing to go to those lengths, I couldn't imagine what he would do if Roman found him first. I had to do everything in my power to keep Set away from Roman. Even if it meant I'd never see him again.

It wasn't until long after the sun had set that my door opened. It was Nero, there to prepare me for the raid. "You look like hell," he said by way of greeting.

I didn't even have the strength to muster a comeback. I simply rose from my cot and followed him out of the cell. He escorted me through the building and into the outside air for the first time in months. The sky was dark, an unnatural fog hanging in the air and obscuring my view of the surroundings. Nero shoved me through the fog, and I stumbled over my feet, unable to see even just a few feet in front of me. I tried turning and looking at the building I'd been held in, but the details of it were obscured and I was only able to tell that it was huge and made of some sort of tan-colored rock.

Through the fog, I could hear the voices of the soldiers and oddly, the lapping of water. It wasn't until I pushed onto the sandy shore of a river that everything clicked into place. Set wouldn't be attacking the Kindred compound by land. He would use the river to travel, no doubt using his Water and Air Users to accelerate the pace.

The fog was thinner on the water, but I still couldn't see the shore on the other side, only what seemed like endless black water. I was escorted onto the metal barge, thrown into the corner and forgotten. I sat and watched as dozens of hybrids joined me, although interestingly, not a single Coterie soldier or wraith. Apparently, the different parts of Set's army were segregated, and I'd been lucky enough to be placed with the hybrids, the people that use to be my brethren but had been corrupted by my blood. I looked at their faces as they passed by me, unseen in the corner. I was partly responsible for each of their fates. When the last hybrid boarded the ship, Nero stepped aboard. He paid me no mind, simply turning to face the shore.

Out of the fog, Set appeared. His red eyes glowed in the darkness, a white linen vest draped open across his broad chest. The shadows had returned, swallowing the fog around him into oblivion. The chaos god smiled at me as he made his approach, a conqueror's joy on the eve of victory.

As soon as Set's foot stepped onto the deck of the barge, his red eyes blazing through the dark sky, we began to move. I could feel the power in the air change as one by one, blue and gold eyes illuminated the darkness. Just as I had thought, the Water and Air Users were using their power to push the boat down river.

Not boat. Boats.

Dozens of them.

The speed of the boats cleared the fog, opening up the view of the waterway. Ahead of us were dozens of vessels. From what I could tell in the darkness, they came in an assortment of shapes and sizes, from old school wooden boats with sails, to covered, motorized barges. Each held soldiers, the wraiths on some, Nero's Coterie men on others, at least thirty to forty for every vessel. My heart sunk. I recognized the river, its deep, black waters. The tiny grass-covered islands and lush greens that provided the only splash of life in a world of tan and beige. It was the Nile. And that meant there was only one compound we could be heading to, a place that last I knew was full of Amina's soldiers.

"It's beautiful, isn't it?"

I'd been sitting alone for hours, lost in my own thoughts, but the sound of Nero's brusque voice woke me from my daydream. The large man sat down next to me, his legs stretched out in front of him. My eyes cut to the Commander, moving away just as quickly. After my dream, all I could see in him were his son's features.

"Beautiful isn't exactly the word I would use for it," I answered dryly.

"Of course not," Nero answered. "That's because you still cling to the illusion that we're the bad guys in this scenario." I shook my head, refusing to be baited by him. "You understand the role you are to play?"

Begrudgingly, I nodded. "Protect the fleet. Any fireballs that get thrown our way, I'll push them into the water. If the compound catches fire, I'm to pull it back. Minimize the damage."

Nero nodded his approval. "You're smart to follow Set's commands and fight for our side."

"I'm not doing this for Set," I bit. "Do not for a moment mistake my actions with agreeing with your side. I'm doing this to protect my people. To protect *him*." I didn't have to say who he was. "There's nothing I wouldn't do to keep him safe." Nero paused a moment, absorbing my words. For a second, I thought he'd argue with me, but instead he simply stood up. "You are," I called after him. He turned around, a question in his dark eyes. "The bad guys. You fight for a god that doesn't care about human life. He corrupted the Kindred and twisted them into something evil. How can you fight for someone who doesn't give a damn about you?" I didn't care that every hybrid and Set himself could hear everything I was saying.

"Coming from the girl that fights for the Nomarch Council. How much do you think the Council cares about your life?"

I shook my head, huffing out an agitated breath. "I don't fight for the Nomarch Council. I fight for the people. For the soldiers that have to fight the battles that are waged by self-important rulers that refuse to risk their own lives." Nero laughed. I turned and looked at him incredulously, even as he threw his head back further. "What is so funny?"

"Your ignorance," he answered, once he quit laughing. "You think you can just declare yourself a fighter for the people and that makes it so. The truth is, as long as you fight against Set and his army, the Council will own your every move. Every victory, every defeat, they will claim for themselves. You are in their Guard and are attached to them whether you like it or not. Even if you were successful in defeating us, which you won't be, the Council will still exist, and you will still be one of their pawns. One person cannot overthrow a government as old and corrupt as that of the Nomarch Council."

"You came close," I felt compelled to point out.

"Close, yes," he responded, letting the thought drop. "But the Nomarch Council will not be able to withstand our forces. Not this time. You need to stop fighting us and realize we're on the same side."

"My side is with your son," I interrupted. "Always will be." Even if I couldn't be with Roman, I could at least fight for him from a distance.

At the mention of Roman, Nero's eyes cut sharply to me. There was a depth to them I'd never seen before. An earnestness I didn't associate with the Commander. He dropped to a crouch, now on my level. "I'm not as bad as you think I am," he whispered.

I raised my eyebrows, doing everything I could not to snicker. "Oh, really?" I challenged.

Nero's eyes traveled down slowly, landing on my left leg. He looked knowingly, right where I'd been wounded. As if he could see through the fabric to where the cut had healed from the serum that had been waiting in the bath. For a moment, he looked as if he was going to say something, but the sun peeked over the horizon, drawing our attention. "We've arrived," he announced.

I stood up, stretching my limbs as I looked to the horizon. Cutting into the Nile waters was a large outcropping, a tall, sand-colored building sitting proudly in the middle of it. It was several stories tall, dozens of windows dug into the hard building. There were high walls surrounding it, torches and braziers lit atop them, but no one patrolling that I could see. The compound was sleeping.

I took a deep breath. "Helwan."

The first wave of attack hit the walls of the Helwan compound just as the sun was fully visible over the horizon. From where I was, several boats back and locked into the water, I watched in horror as wraiths came pouring off the ships, climbing the limestone walls with their bare hands. It didn't surprise me that Set used them as his first line, especially as I heard a horn sound from the center of the compound, raising the alarm. It may not have looked like Helwan was guarded, but I knew every Kindred had twenty-four hour patrol and guards. One by one, wraiths came flying off the walls, dissolving into ash before they hit the ground. Hope swelled in my chest. The Helwan compound wasn't caught as unaware as Set expected. "Don't get too excited yet," Nero warned.

I turned, looking behind me to where Set stood calmly in the middle of the barge. His arms were crossed, his red, stormy eyes watching the raid with intent. There wasn't a single thing about him that made me believe he was worried that his wraiths were dying. Instead, it looked more like he expected it. A simple nod of his head had the soldiers I'd identified as the Water Users reaching over the edge of their ships, placing their hands along the river surface. At first nothing happened, and then one by one, soldiers started jumping off their boats and into the water. Except they weren't falling in like I expected. They were standing on the water's surface, now as solid as stone. I peered over the edge of the barge. I could see the fury of the Nile racing below even as a soldier ran across its surface toward the compound. I'd once seen a similar trick in Awen but nothing of this magnitude. Nero's hand came down hard on the back of my neck, pushing me over the edge of the boat. I landed on all fours before Nero jumped nimbly onto the river next to me. I stared up at him.

"Better move quickly. The Water Users won't hold this for long," he advised, even as he stepped toward the shore, unsheathing his sword. He was right. One by one, the Water Users were jumping from their vessels and onto the still water. As they marched forward, the water behind them began to surge again.

Ahead of them, I felt my element spark to life, a whole row of Fire Users building fireballs in their hands. They launched them over the tall walls and into the compound. I scrambled to my feet, running for the shore, even as I felt the river under my feet lose its stability. As my boots finally found ground in the lush riverbanks of the Nile, I got a complete picture of what was going on.

The sun had fully risen, its golden rays illuminating the Helwan compound and the smoke that rose from its center. An explosion sounded from the wall, and I ducked to avoid being hit by the debris. A large hole had been blown through the base of the wall. Two fireballs came flying out of it, but I raised my hands, quickly pushing them into the sand. The Coterie men surrounded me, their daggers raised as they breached the wall and entered the compound. The clash of metal rang through my ears. Nero was still next to

81

me although I hadn't noticed until he reached for the sleeve of my shirt and yanked me forward toward the wall. I stumbled over the rubble and inside the compound.

Once I passed the wall, Nero left me to join the fray, satisfied that I wouldn't try to run. There was no way I could. Inside was all out war. The entire compound was overrun with Set's men. The Helwan Kindred hadn't been ready for an attack of this magnitude. They'd fought back at first, but they held nowhere near the numbers Set did. Everywhere I looked, his men were capturing and killing the Kindred, and my enhanced hearing told me there was more of the same going on inside. There had been what looked like a small garden next to the opposite side of the wall, no doubt cultivated by the Earth Users, but now all the vegetation was ablaze. I called to my element and pulled its power into me, extinguishing the flames a little bit at a time. It was always harder to suffocate flames than it was to release them. Whatever made my magic work demanded my power be released into the world, and the idea of pulling my element away from the outside always felt wrong. My hand began to shake with the strength of the flames. It'd been six months since I'd had this much magic in me. I felt my eyes change to a sharp red as I surveyed the compound, looking for an outlet for the magic and power raging inside my body.

Across the courtyard, not far from the scorched garden, three hybrids were attacking a soldier. The soldier was crouched in the corner, having been knocked down by her enemy. Her face was bruised and bloody but her blue eyes were determined as she waved her dagger in front of her in adamant refusal to submit. I looked around quickly. Everyone was fighting. No one was paying attention to me. I focused my power on the three men surrounding her, even as I ran across the courtyard. I released my inner flames, two of the hybrids instantly dying a fiery death. The third remained untouched; a Fire User himself. It didn't matter though, I'd already reached them, and in one smooth motion, I scooped up a forgotten dagger and ran it through his heart. He dropped to the ground, the look of shock frozen on his face.

I held my hand out to the Helwan soldier. She looked up at me, her face just as shocked as the hybrid had been. Reluctantly, she grabbed my wrist and I pulled her to her feet. "You all right?" I asked her.

She nodded once, wiping the blood from her forehead. "I know you," she mumbled.

"What?" I asked, not sure I'd heard her.

"I know you," she said louder this time. "I've seen your picture. You're *her*."

I squinted my eyes. "Who?" I demanded. I'd never seen this woman before in my life.

"We've been looking for you for months. We've scoured every inch of Egypt trying to find you. I think she was beginning to give up."

She, I thought. I knew she was talking about Amina. This was her compound, her soldiers. If she had been looking for me, sending soldiers to scour the area, I was in even greater danger than I thought. Amina hated me. She'd no doubt already found some way to blame me for the mess that was Cairo. If she knew where I was, she'd kill me just to keep me from returning to Awen. I looked around again quickly. Our small exchange was still unnoticed. I debated knocking the soldier out and leaving her. No one would see. No one would care. "She will be so pleased you are alive. That you've survived. She needs your help."

My help? More like Amina wanted to use me for whatever nefarious scheme she was plotting now. I had to get rid of this soldier. Now. "You need to go." I grabbed her by her shoulders, spinning her toward the wall. She might be one of Amina's, but she hadn't done anything to me, and I refused to punish her for the resentment her commander held. I gritted my teeth. "Tell no one you saw me. But run, now."

She spun right back around, trying to push past me. Weakened as I was, she was nowhere near as strong as me. "I can't run," she argued. "I can't leave my people behind."

"Listen to me," I said sternly, gripping her arm. She winced, and I knew I was squeezing too tightly, but I needed my point to stick. "There is a god on that river. An actual god. If you stay, you will die. Your compound does not have the strength to beat him." Another explosion rang out behind us, punctuating my point. "There is no shame in running in order to fight another day. *Now go!*"

She reached for the wall, preparing to climb, but paused last second. "Come with me," she begged.

I paused, pursing my lips. I wanted to go with her more than anything. I could escape with her, then lose her later before she could report to Amina where I was, but I could feel Set moving closer. He would be looking for me. If he didn't find me here, helping with the attack, others would pay the price. "I can't," I told her. I could tell she was going to question me, but I didn't have time for it. Neither did she. "It's for the best, trust me." With no more explanation, I gave her one final shove toward the wall and ran back into the compound.

Chapter 7

Roman

"Where's Roman?! We have a serious problem!"

That was Cassie's greeting as she burst through the entrance to the Guard training facility, her girlfriend Mallory hot on her heels.

I set down the sharpening stone on the slab next to our weapons board, sheathing my dagger in my boot and met them halfway across the training ring. Grady, who had been working on the other side of the ring, joined us. "Where have you been?" he questioned Mallory, choosing to ignore Cassie's outburst for the moment. I didn't blame him. As much as I loved her, Cassie was a Pisces and had a flare for the dramatic. Mallory's caramel skin was dirty, her usually well kept hair a bit out of sorts. "You were supposed to be back three days ago," Grady continued.

"Wait until you hear why she was delayed," Cassie answered for her.

Mallory raised her eyebrows, pausing to indulge her girlfriend before turning to me. "As you know, Astrid sent me to Egypt to tie up loose ends. Check around with the locals, see if there was any remaining chatter about what happened in Cairo so many months ago. The good news there is they don't suspect anything odd. They've blamed it on local extremist groups. But, while I was in the city, I heard rumors of soldiers who were defecting from compounds in surrounding areas."

"Deserters?" Brynn asked, hanging her sai up on the weapons board.

Mallory pointed at her. "That's what I thought at first. It took some bribing and threats, but I managed to track them down and find where they were staying. They're just outside of Cairo in a small village. Turns out they're not deserters. At least not in the traditional sense. They're rebels. After they caught word of Amina's takeover, they refused to follow her rule and defected from their compounds."

"That's great," Brynn added.

"How many?" I asked. The more soldiers we had on our side, the better. Especially if they were off the island and out of Amina's reach.

"Fifty, roughly." Mallory answered. "Not enough to make a difference yet. But that's not the most important part. You'll never guess who their leader is." I crossed my arms, waiting. Thankfully, Mallory didn't leave me in suspense for long. "Sandra."

The name rang through me like a bell. I found myself wandering over to lean against the ancient stone wall, my legs suddenly unable to hold me upright. Sandra. She was alive. When Nero had turned on us last fall, Sandra had been stationed within the Coterie army's camp. I'd heard nothing from her since then. I wasn't even sure if she was alive, and yet I should have known she would be. She was one of the strongest warriors alive. She would always fight to survive. Vaguely, I was aware the others were still talking, although their voices were far away now, as if I were listening from the opposite side of a wall.

My mother was alive.

I wasn't alone.

"I still don't hear a problem," Grady pointed out. "Sandra leading rebels sounds like all good news."

"Maybe if you stopped interrupting and listened for a second, you would hear the problem," Mallory snapped. I snickered. Mallory and Grady weren't on the best of terms. Hadn't been since—well—since he killed me. "I was able to stay with the rebels for a day, feeding them as much information as I could about what was going on in Awen. Then after I heard from you, I cross-checked what you'd said about sagebrush and the Nile. I used Sandra's resources to find areas—compounds—big enough to hide Set's army. I found a lead."

"Wait," Brynn interrupted. "I didn't know you contacted Mallory."

I shrugged. "You didn't ask." She glared at me, unsatisfied with my blasé response. I knew this was a conversation we'd finish later. She'd see to it.

"Anyway," Mallory interjected. "Just before I was set to leave to investigate, I received a frantic call from a woman named Ume. She was stationed in Helwan as part of Amina's army."

"If she's one of Amina's, why did she call you?" Grady dared to interrupt. Mallory shot him a death glare but let it slide.

"She's one of Daniela's implants," Mallory explained. Cassie gave Grady a pointed look at the mention of Daniela, no doubt to punctuate her importance, why we could never turn her in. I knew Cassie hadn't told Mallory that Grady had considered doing just that. If she had, we wouldn't be talking. Mallory would be beating Grady's face in. "She said the Helwan compound was hit by Set and his army the night before. She barely escaped."

"Why did it take so long for us to hear about this?" I demanded, coming out of my fog. This was the first sign of Set in months and it had taken days for us to hear about it?

"Rome, stop. Let Mallory finish," Cassie demanded, cutting off my protest. I rolled my eyes. Now I was the one getting in trouble for interrupting.

Mallory paused, taking a deep breath. What more could there be to say? She'd already told me my mother was alive. That Set had finally been spotted. What could be so momentous that she paused now?

"Tell me," I demanded.

Mallory didn't blanch at my harsh tone, although Cassie shot me another disapproving look. "She said Kyndal was there. That Kyndal saved her life."

My breath escaped me, the air completly leaving my lungs. If I hadn't already been leaning against the wall, I would have fallen to the ground. Grady stepped forward, as if he knew I was incapable of speaking. "Kyndal's in Helwan?"

"At least she was a few days ago," Mallory confirmed.

"Where is Ume now?" he asked.

"I brought her back to Awen with me," Mallory answered. "I had to. Sandra and I both thought it was too dangerous to leave her with the rebels. Her presence could have drawn Set directly to them. Not to mention, if a compound was hit, I wasn't going to be able to hide that from the Nomarchs. They would have questioned why I didn't inform them about it since I was so close. Ume is debriefing the Council now."

That evening, I paced inside the foyer of Astrid's house. My boots echoed off her marble floor, my silhouette throwing shadows from the fire candelabra that hung high above me. I'd been waiting hours for the Council to dismiss and Astrid to return to her house. As desperate as I was to know what else Ume had to say, I wasn't stupid enough to go to Council Chambers and demand information. After the last meeting, I knew Amina didn't want the Guard there, and we couldn't risk showing up unannounced again.

Some time later, after I'd given up my pacing and instead stooped on the bottom of the stairs, the front door finally pulled open and Astrid entered. The Cancer Nomarch was not the most obviously intimidating Kindred I'd ever met. She was small by any standard, her muscles thin and lean. Her most striking feature was her straight white hair that hung to her waist. Paired with her crystal blue eyes, she looked like an ice queen. While she didn't appear threatening, I knew her to be one of the most dangerous Nomarchs on the Council. A fact that was proven as she still managed to challenge Amina's authority and survive.

Even after everything she'd done for us, Astrid always played her real intentions close to the vest and I was cautious around her, knowing that saying the wrong thing to her could come back and bite me later. After Kyndal disappeared with Set, I'd been staying in one of her many lavish guest rooms, a necessary evil after losing all my possessions. Astrid had offered up her house as a way of keeping me close, as a way of keeping connected to Kyndal. I'd agreed to the arrangement, needing her power and connections to further my own agenda. We both knew it was a temporary arrangement, and that when we succeeded in getting Kyndal back, we'd be at odds again.

While Astrid wanted Set gone as much as I did, we had very different opinions about how to make it happen. Astrid wanted to use the Guard and was-sceptre to kill Set and then sacrifice Kyndal and use her blood to seal his soul inside his prison. I was adamantly against the sacrifice and was willing to do whatever it took to make sure Kyndal survived, even if it meant dying in her place. A fact I'd no problem sharing with Astrid anytime she'd been brave enough to broach the subject. Any spare moment I'd been given, I'd been in the library researching alternatives to imprisoning Set's soul. Anything that was as strong as Descendant blood.

So far, I'd come up empty.

Astrid unwrapped the gray shawl from around her shoulders, setting it on a nearby table. "I have been looking for you."

"Mallory found me. She told me about the attack in Helwan and about what Ume said," I responded, jumping right into it.

"I know," she answered quickly, bringing me up short. "Did she tell you about the other thing?"

"You mean my mother being alive?" I drawled, choosing to ignore her flippant tone. Sandra and Astrid had a contentious relationship. It did me no good to argue with her about it.

She stared directly at me, her crystal eyes making me feel like a child. "Yes, that. As well as—" she flitted her hand through the air, "other things." I knew she was referencing Kyndal, but I didn't bring her up. Not yet. A part of me wanted to see if Astrid would tell me herself. "I sent Ms. Saenz to find you," she added, when I said nothing.

"Why would you do that?" I asked.

Astrid ignored me and instead walked through the house and into the kitchen. I followed closely behind. "Because you wouldn't have found out otherwise. Amina is paranoid, you saw that yourself. She sequestered Ume immediately, kicked the Nomarchs out of Chambers. I sent Ms. Saenz to find you, because I knew she would tell you the news."

"Why not just tell me yourself?" I pushed.

She turned on her heel. "Because I thought you might have wanted to hear about it from someone you actually trust."

I didn't acknowledge the dig, her obvious acknowledgement of the loose thread that held us together. "If Amina kicked the Nomarchs out of Chambers, why were you gone for hours?"

"I was meeting with the other Nomarchs on our side, quietly passing along the little information I knew, trying to find out what exactly happened. To see if their own people could fill in any gaps." She pressed up on her tiptoes to grab two glass tumblers from a nearby cabinet. "Kyndal Davenport is alive." I crossed my arms, silently watching as she pulled a bottle of scotch from a cabinet, a bottle I happened to know was several decades old and worth thousands of dollars. "From your silence, I take it that was not surprising news." She poured a large glass and shoved it across the marble island toward me. "How long have you known?" she asked, even as she grabbed the bottle by the neck and took a long swig.

I reached for the crystal tumbler in front of me, swishing the brown liquid. "I always knew she was alive. I never thought otherwise." A careful answer, truth and yet not completely.

She glared at me out of the corner of her eye. "Something tells me there's more to it than that." When I didn't answer, she shook her head, clearly frustrated. "I simply don't

94

understand. After all I've done for you, all I'm *still* trying to do for you, you don't trust me."

"Trusting Nomarchs has proven to be a dangerous pastime."

She shrugged, almost as if she understood my blunt response. "Fine. No matter the logistics of *how* you knew, my question is: are you ready to get her back?"

My mouth dropped and I openly gaped at her. Astrid smiled at my pure shock, leaving me in the kitchen and moving out to the open deck. I scrambled after her, hastily grabbing the drink she'd poured for me. Astrid lived on the coast of Awen. Her multilevel back balconies cut over the high cliffs of the island and overlooked the ocean. She leaned out over the balcony, taking another generous drink of her scotch. I stood next to her, looking down at the crashing waves below. Even from this height, the sound of the waves was deafening. I couldn't hear anything else, although there were several other houses along the coast. Astrid had chosen to come out here for a reason. No matter what she had to say, she knew no one would hear us. I turned to face the Cancer Nomarch. "What do you mean *get her back*?" I did everything I could to keep the desperation out of my voice, almost positive I failed.

"I don't know how much Mallory told you, but Set and his army wiped out the entire Helwan compound."

"I assumed," I responded simply. I probably should've been more upset, more sympathetic, but it was hard to muster a reaction. I'd been so focused on finding Kyndal, getting her back was all I focused on.

Astrid raised an eyebrow at my lackluster response but otherwise chose to ignore it. As old as she was, Astrid was long past emotional reactions to war. "The compound in Helwan was one of our strongest outposts, one of the few places we could use to safely access Cairo and keep an eye on the entrance to The Hall of Two Truths. With this defeat, Set not only took that position away from us, but by our best estimates, he captured, killed, or turned over four hundred Kindred." Another large drink from the bottle, the only sign this defeat affected her at all. This time I joined her, sipping the scotch she'd poured for me. The liquid was surprisingly smooth, and I could feel its heat in my chest as it went down. I waited for Astrid to continue. I had a million questions, but one thing I'd learned long ago was that it was better to stay quiet in moments like this. Saying the wrong thing could make her quit talking. Eventually she continued, "We've been behind on this war from the very start. Amina has been more focused on her political career than strategizing how to fight the enemy. Her lust for power is tearing the Council apart. Tearing our people apart. You saw for yourself how the Nomarchs reacted in Chambers."

"That's what you wanted us to see. Why you pushed for us to be let off the island. You wanted the Guard to see there are Nomarchs that oppose her."

She shrugged. "I figured it was best to get all allegiances out on the table. While Amina keeps the Guard—her greatest weapon—hidden on the island, she instead plans to send more troops to Egypt to investigate the Helwan defeat." She shook her head in frustration.

"But not rescue Kyndal," I finished for her. I wasn't surprised. Amina hated Kyndal and would never prioritize her safety. She'd already done everything she could to discredit her. The people were already doubting Amina's rule and looking to Kyndal for a last hope. I'd seen it myself when Briar had been pulled in front of the Council. Amina would never allow her to return if it meant she would lose her grip on power. She'd rather lose the war on her own than risk losing her seat to Kyndal.

"Kyndal is not her priority, no," Astrid agreed, no doubt thinking the same things I was. "In fact, the troops she's sending are under strict orders to observe but not engage. Even if they see Kyndal, they aren't to do anything about it." Just as I thought, Amina was happy to let her rot in Set's hands.

"Does Amina know about my mother? That she's alive? What's she's doing?"

Astrid shook her head. "No. I am the only Nomarch that knows Sandra lives."

I nodded, pleased with that at least. "So, I ask again, what do you mean am I ready to go get Kyndal? If Amina is sending her own soldiers, there's no way any of the Guard can get into Helwan unnoticed."

Astrid shook her head, taking another long drink. "You're right. You'd never make it into Helwan," she responded cryptically.

I pinched the bridge of my nose. "Then what are you talking about?"

"I need you to be one hundred percent honest with me," Astrid answered, her voice suddenly serious and her crystal blue eyes pinning me in place. "Because this plan is extremely dangerous with a high probability of failure. And even if we're successful, it will almost guarantee Amina calls for our execution. Not just you and me. But the Nomarchs who support you, Brynn, Grady, and Kyndal as well."

I turned fully to face her. "All right," I answered.

She smiled, pleased to see I didn't hesitate. "How did you know Kyndal was alive? And I'm not talking your gut feeling, I mean *proof* that she was all right."

I took a deep breath, contemplating what she was asking. Not just my information but trust. Astrid was asking me to trust her. Everything she'd said seemed sincere, but I was still hesitant to reveal this last bit of information. It was the last card I held. My last piece of leverage. "I knew she was alive because I spoke with her five days ago," I admitted.

"How." Not so much a question but a command.

"Kyndal has always been able to dreamwalk, ever since she was branded. Best I can tell, as her powers have grown, so have her abilities. As her Rafiq, we're able to reach out to each other through our dreams. But there are conditions. We have to both be sleeping and thinking of each other."

As I finished explaining, I could see Astrid's mind working, her 1,000 years of experience at play. "Can you control it?" she began. "We're going to need Kyndal's help if we're going to pull this off. Is it reliable enough for you to talk with her whenever you want?"

No, I thought, but I nodded anyway, "I think so." If Astrid had a plan to get Kyndal back, I didn't want to give her any reason to doubt me.

"When Amina's soldiers leave for Egypt, there will be a brief window of opportunity. Knowing our fearless Governor, she will make a large showing of the event, and the people will be distracted. I've spoken with a few of the others. We can use that time to create a window and sneak the Guard off the island."

"And go where?" I asked. "You already said we can't go to Helwan."

"We won't need to. Kyndal is going to come to us. We need to make a statement. Which is why I want us to take

Ozero Lobaz," she answered, before drinking the remainder of the bottle of scotch.

"The Coterie compound?" I questioned, "It's nothing but a pile of rocks. Set won't care about it."

"But Nero will. He loves nothing more than his Coterie legacy, the kingdom he built for himself and planned to one day pass on to you. That compound was his symbol of victory over the Nomarchs, of his prowess and greatness. No matter his loyalty to Set, I think if we claim it for the Kindred, he won't be able to resist coming to fight for it."

I smiled wickedly. "Splitting Set's forces in the process. I like it. Doesn't hurt that the man taking it will be the son that hates him."

She raised a single eyebrow. "No, it doesn't hurt."

"Where does Kyndal come into this?" I asked, trying to piece together her plan.

"She needs to know what we are doing, so when we take the Coterie and Nero comes for it, she makes sure he takes her with him."

"How is she supposed to manage that?" I questioned. Astrid shrugged, and I rolled my eyes, wondering for the first time if she was drunk. I scruffed my hair, considering her offer. "We'll do it, on two conditions."

"Name them," she responded.

"It can't be just the Guard. I want Cassie, Mallory, and Isaac too. Once the Guard leaves it won't be safe for anyone connected to us, you know that. They don't have the resources the Nomarchs do. Amina will throw them in the Hollow, or worse."

"Fine," she answered. "And the other condition?"

"I need you to get someone out of the Hollow."

Chapter 8

Kyndal

The Helwan compound burned for three days.

Not that the battle had raged for that long. The battle had been over in a matter of hours. Dozens of Amina's soldiers had been killed, the rest forced to surrender as they were overwhelmed by the sheer strength of Set's armies. He had marched through the wall, a dark conqueror, and just as I had suspected, almost immediately sought me out. I made myself easy to find, meeting him at the wall, even as I hoped the soldier, whose name I hadn't bothered to learn, had escaped. He forced me to create bonfires in the courtyard, forced me to watch the fires grow as one by one, my fallen Kindred brethren were thrown to the flames. No ceremony or rites that would allow their souls to rest. No ritual at all.

Just thrown to the fire like trash that needed to be burnt.

The soldiers that hadn't been killed had been taken prisoner. Set grouped them together, using his power to lock them inside some sort of invisible prison on the edges of the courtyard. They sat in the desert heat all day long, deprived of water and food, their powers stripped away by the dark magic of their cell, as they were forced to watch. Watch, just as I did, as Set's hybrids danced and drank around the fires at night, celebrating their victory. Each of them marked with a was-sceptre on their arm, a tattoo that couldn't help but make me think of Roman and how the ink would always mark his skin.

There was no real music for the hybrids to dance to, just the harsh beat of drums, although that seemed to be enough for them. But as the sun rose and the drum beats died, Set would descend from his makeshift throne and choose a Kindred soldier from the masses. The warrior would be tossed to the hybrids like a bone to a starving dog. A reward for their loyalty and efforts. The hybrids would feed from the warrior, slowly draining them of their life force until nothing remained but an empty shell. It was those moments that were the most agonizing. I was helpless to save my comrades, forced to endure their deaths and the stares of the other Kindred as they wondered why I didn't help. Why I didn't do something to stop the hybrids from killing our people.

By the second night, I realized that it was only the hybrids that were in the courtyard at night. Most of the wraiths had been wiped out in the assault, but dozens of Nero's Coterie soldiers had survived, and yet they were nowhere to be seen. Had they separated themselves intentionally, or were they relegated to another area under Set's orders? Too tired to think about it, I leaned my head against the rock of the compound wall, tuning out the sounds of another night of sadistic revelry and closing my eyes. Just a moment to rest, I told myself. Not sleep, just relax.

I hadn't been sleeping well. Truth be told, I'd barely slept at all in the last several days. Every night Set dragged me outside, making me sit and watch as his warriors celebrated, and while they slept during the day, I did not. The hybrids were replaced by Nero's soldiers who were ordered by their commander to work, a sentence I didn't escape. Nero forced me to help his men clear the courtyard and repair the wall. While I'd never been good at taking orders, I dug into the work willingly. I didn't want time to sit idly by and think about the horrors of what I'd seen at night, and I definitely didn't want time to sleep.

If I slept, I knew I'd see Roman, and I couldn't face him. Not after everything that had happened.

My short moment of rest was interrupted by the blasting of a horn. Different than the one the Kindred had sounded when Set attacked, this one was deep, filling me with a dark sense of dread. I peeled my eyes open, ignoring the fact that my vision was blurring at the edges. The horn sounded again and this time it was followed with the groaning of wooden doors. It took me longer than it should have to realize the sound was of the large gate opening at the far end of the wall. I had never seen it opened, had no idea who could possibly be arriving at the compound. I staggered to my feet, my muscles tired and achy from exhaustion, skin cracked from the relentless sun, in order to get a closer look. The drums had quit, the shouts of the hybrids immediately ceasing as the strangers entered. From what I could see in the dark, there seemed to be two lines of them, hundreds or more in each line. Beyond that, I couldn't see anything else that was of note. They marched straight into the compound, their backs rigid, their heads held high. I looked to Set, who was still perched on his throne on the opposite end of the courtyard. Even from this distance, I could see the churning storm in his eyes, the tiny satisfied smirk that played at his usually stern mouth as he watched the strangers enter. Whoever these people were, he'd been expecting them.

They marched past me, and although they looked normal, the hairs on the back of my neck stood up, the power in the pit of my stomach churning to life in reaction to their presence. I'd felt this way before. Felt it in Marienville, in Awen, in Cairo. It *always* meant the same thing.

Wraiths.

As if he heard me say the word, Set stood from his throne, his eyes focused completely on me. He stepped down the two stairs from the platform his throne sat upon, the movement a silent signal to those around him. The hybrids that had been dancing fell into rows reminiscent of the ones I'd seen when Roman had endured the gauntlet, watching in perfect silence as he passed through them.

Not sure whether from exhaustion or something else, I still didn't understand what was going on. From behind me, several Coterie soldiers filled the courtyard, closing in behind the wraiths. Whatever was happening, Nero had found it important enough to break Set's orders, allowing his own men into the courtyard at night. The Commander himself was at the back of the line and stopped next to me. I looked up at him. "What's happening?" I dared to ask.

He didn't answer, instead kept his eyes on Set, who was now joined by two hybrids on either side. I had no idea where they'd come from. One held a large bowl in her hands, the other a jagged knife. Set's eyes churned, the dark shadows returning. They wrapped themselves around his arms and over his broad shoulders as the ground beneath me shook. It rose up in front of Set, creating a raised table made of rock. The hybrids lowered the knife and bowl onto the makeshift table, giving me a clear view of its contents. The bowl was filled with blood, and immediately I knew whose it was, the power inside it calling to the power in me. Like calling to like.

The blood was mine.

Like the final piece of a puzzle, it all clicked into place. The wraiths, why Set captured the Kindred instead of killing them. He was going to use my blood to create more hybrids.

The power in the air shook again and Set dropped the invisible prison around the captured Kindred. Dehydrated and exhausted, barely any of them managed to put up a fight. Those that did were quickly beaten down, their limp bodies dragged the rest of the way until they were all dropped at the feet of the wraiths. Their hybrid captors each pulled their blades, individually slicing across the brands of the Kindred. No matter their physical state, every one of them cried out, not from pain but loss of their last form of protection. For many of us, possession was a fate worse than death.

From the back of the wraith lines, my name echoed, a broken rasp from a Kindred warrior that knelt in the sand. "Kyndal," the man begged. I didn't recognize him. How he knew who I was, my name, I had no idea. His eyes were the same shade of red as mine. Was he an Aries too? Or a Sagittarius or Leo? "Save us, Descendant. Save us or see us avenged."

My heart broke at his words. At the hope in his eyes. Stop the possession, he begged. And if I couldn't stop it, finish them. For a Kindred possessed, there was freedom in death.

I couldn't watch this happen. Not again.

I don't think I actually decided to start moving, but next thing I knew, I was running across the courtyard. I made it past the Coterie soldiers, moving too quickly for them to even realize what I was doing. When I reached the first hybrid, an Earth User, he reached out to stop me, but my power was already coursing through my body. I ducked below his fist, coming up quickly, my hand wrapping around his throat. I twisted, snapping his neck. It wouldn't kill him, but it got him out of the way.

Three more hybrids broke toward me, and I dispatched them just as easily. A fireball to the chest for one, a broken arm and cracked nose for the other two. I'd watched them torture and kill my people, helpless to do anything about it. Now all that pent-up rage was pouring out of me like liquid fire. "Set, stop this!" I roared as I grew closer, my eyes a livid red, bright enough to rival that of the god himself. I could feel the hybrids behind me, but I threw my arms wide, calling to the nearby fires. They raced to do my bidding, a wall of flames rising up behind me, separating me from the angry hybrids. I could still hear them behind me, hissing in anger, but not even the Fire Users dared to test my power. They'd seen me fight in the pits. They knew none of them came close to my strength.

Only the two hybrids that flanked Set stood in my way. They attacked me as one, their daggers drawn. I blocked the first attack, but the second was fast and managed to swipe their dagger across my bicep. I cried out, a mixture of pain and anger, as I answered the blow with a backhand of my own. From behind me, the first hybrid kicked at the back of my leg, dropping me to one knee. I jumped to my feet, prepared to finish the fight, when suddenly Set took a step forward. Power erupted from his center, a lightning bolt shooting out of him, hitting me directly in the chest. The last thing I remembered was flying backward, my head cracking off the rock tabletop.

When I wake up, I know I'm dreaming. I'm not in the treehouse like before, but a clearing in the middle of the Allegheny Forest. The sun is shining, the leaves on the trees rustling in a light breeze. By all accounts, a perfectly beautiful day. I look closer, quickly realizing it's the same place I saw Roman and the others use their powers for the first time, just a short run from where we use to party at the Ridge. Why would my dreams bring me back here? A branch snaps behind me and I wheel around, even though I know who will be waiting. Sure enough, Roman stands there. He's dressed in the same black gear I am, his standard dagger tucked in the belt of his pants, the second one hidden in his boot, exactly where I knew it would be. He looks stressed, the light that usually lives in his eyes a little dimmer than before. His hair is mussed, and he hasn't shaved in several days. Through the bond, I can feel the distress and worry coursing through him. Uncontrollably, my heart aches for him.

"Finally!" he greets me. There is a sharp edge to his voice, one I grew accustomed to hearing when we first met. A sure sign he's agitated. "I've been trying to reach you for days."

Images of what was happening in Helwan play through my mind. Like scissors cutting through twine, I snap out of my emotions. "I don't have time for this," I tell him, turning to move away from him. I've woken myself up from dreams before, maybe I can do it again. I open my mouth to scream at myself to wake up, but a sharp pain splits through the back of my neck, and I bring my hand up to cover it out of instinct, cutting off the sound.

"You're hurt," Roman says, the concern in his voice obvious. He runs over to me, but I put my hand up to stop him.

"I'm fine," I tell him.

He ignores me, grabbing my hand. "I can feel your pain, Kyndal. And look, you're bleeding." He turns my palm to face me, and sure enough it's covered in blood.

"It's nothing," I assure him, pulling my hand away. I must have hit my head on that table harder than I realized. I look up at the blinding sun, "Wake up!" I yell.

"What are you doing?" Roman asks. I ignore him.

"Wake up!" I scream again, ignoring the throbbing in the back of my head. Why isn't it working? I yell again.

Roman grabs me by the shoulders shaking me, "Kyndal, stop it!" he roars at me. "What is wrong with you?"

I smack his arms away, a weak move that I knew he could block if he wanted to but wouldn't. Roman would never force me to do something I didn't want to do. "Nothing is wrong with me," I answer, my voice tight. I move to the other side of the clearing, well out of Roman's reach. I scream again. Again.

Nothing changes.

My head is throbbing, and I'm forced to brace my hands on my knees and close my eyes to wait for the pain to subside.

"I'm so disappointed in you." His voice is quiet, but it cuts through the clearing, worse because I can hear the pain in his voice, feel it in my heart. "You're a coward."

My eyes snap open. "What did you just call me?"

"You heard me," he says challengingly. "You're a coward. You've given up."

I stand tall. "No I haven't," I argue.

"Of course you have." He throws his arm out, gesturing at me. "Look at you, running away. Again. You've stopped fighting. You're going to just lay down and let Set win."

"I'm not letting him win," I counter. My temper flares, and I can feel my power rising. My vision sharpens, my senses heighten. How dare he say that to me? He has no idea what I'm going through. No idea because you won't tell him, *I think bitingly.*

"Sandra is alive," he blurts. Immediately, I stop in my tracks. Sandra?

"How?" I ask. She'd been with the Coterie. There's no way she could have gotten out of their camp alive. "If she was alive, I would know. I would have heard them talking about her." I'd been looking for her in the compounds, expecting to see her in the eyes of every hybrid I meet.

"Mallory saw her with her own eyes. She's alive and she's still fighting. She's in Egypt, gathering a force of Kindred loyal to the Guard, but she needs our help. Your help."

"I can't help anyone."

Roman takes a step forward, his eyes a bright gold. Whether an example of his own temper or a reaction to the rise in mine, I'm not sure. "Have you forgotten who you are? You are the strongest Kindred on the planet. Possibly the strongest to ever be born. You don't have the luxury of giving up because we can't win this war without you. If you quit, we die. Me, Grady, Brynn, Isaac, Cassie, Mallory. We all die. It doesn't matter how many soldiers we have, how many weapons. Without you, we will lose." Another step forward. "I know you don't care about yourself, you've made that perfectly clear. But don't you at least care what happens to them?"

I think of everything that's happened. All the horrible things I've seen, all the pain and death that became inevitable the moment I was branded Kindred. "I can't stop anything. Trust me." Angry tears well up in my eyes.

Roman pauses, understanding exactly what I was thinking about. "I heard about Helwan. That's not your fault."

He doesn't know, *I think. He doesn't know about the new hybrids. I think about telling him but that would just give him another reason to come for me. Another reason to put himself in danger. I shake my head, trying to erase the images of the rows of wraiths marching into Helwan. When I refocus, Roman has moved closer. So close I could reach out and touch him if I wanted. His eyes have softened, only flecks of yellow remaining. "You weren't supposed to know about any of that. I'm sorry you found out," I tell him sincerely. The side of me that was still logical wondered how he had found out. Even if that soldier I helped escape survived, she would have reported to Amina, and Amina definitely wouldn't have told Roman where I was.*

Slowly, he reaches out, gripping either side of my face with his hands. "You can't give up," he whispers. "I won't allow it." He presses his forehead against mine, our lips inches apart. Selfishly stealing a moment for myself, I close my eyes, letting the strength of his power wash over me. From the first moment I knew him, he had the ability to calm me down, to extinguish the flames that lived inside. He takes a deep breath in through his nose, and for a moment, I think he's going to kiss me. I want him to, even though I don't deserve it. Even though I know it's possible he doesn't even think of me that way anymore. It's been months since we actually saw each other. I wouldn't blame him if he'd moved on. He doesn't kiss me, but instead pulls away, raising my face to his, forcing me to reach his eyes. "I don't believe you," he says quietly.

My eyes well with tears and it takes every bit of my strength to keep them from falling. "I don't understand."

He can sense I'm on the edge and continues. "If you didn't want me to know what happened, if you didn't want me to know where you were, you wouldn't have saved Ume. You had to have known that she would find me." He says it very matter of fact, no judgment, just logic.

I wanted to question him, to ask how Ume ended up reporting to him, but I didn't bother. It didn't matter anymore, it was done. He knew where I was.

"She's alive?" I ask, needing him to say it again.

"She's alive," he reassures me. I almost collapse, the relief is so intense. I didn't know why I cared so much. She was just one soldier. One soldier against the countless others that hadn't been as lucky.

"Kyndal, I need you to listen to me. We have a plan. Astrid, the Guard, we have a plan to get you out."

I shake my head. "No," I protest. "You can't come here." Not now, *I think again. By now Set must have turned all the Kindred. His hybrid army is bigger than ever.*

Roman can see the panic rising up in me. "We won't. . ."
he says quickly. "We don't have to go to Helwan. Astrid
found a way for you to come to us."

"You trust Astrid now?" I question. "You realize why she
wants me back, don't you?" It was my blood that could seal
Set's cage. Astrid knew that and was more than willing to
use my death to defeat Set. It was a sacrifice we'd both
been willing to make, but Roman never had.

"You let me worry about Astrid's motives," Roman says,
expertly avoiding my question. "We're getting you back
one way or the other. Either you listen to my plan and come
to us, or I will march the Guard straight into Helwan."

"You'll be signing their death sentences," I retort.

"I have a way to keep them safe. To keep everyone safe.
You force me to bring them to you—their deaths will be on
your conscience. Not mine." His words are harsh, but I
couldn't deny the truth in them.

I pause, wiping an errant tear from my cheek before
looking straight at him. Through the bond I can feel his
determination, his absolute resolve in what he's saying. If I
don't come to him, he will put all our friends in danger
trying to get to me. There was nothing he wouldn't do to
protect me. "How?" I ask.

"Do you think it's possible to separate Nero from Set?" he
replies.

Instantly, my tears stop, and a feeling I haven't experienced in months takes hold in my chest, spreading through me as I replay his words, combining them with the things I'd seen, the information I held. It took me a moment to give the emotion a name, as if I was too scared to recognize it.

Hope.

For the first time since leaving with Set, I feel hopeful. I'm quiet for so long, Roman repeats his question. "Kyndal, will you fight?"

Hope.

Desperation.

Love.

I don't know if they're coming from me or him. I take a deep breath, knowing that after I answer, there will be no going back. "What do you need me to do?"

Chapter 9

Kyndal

When I woke up, I was on the floor of a strange room. I groaned from the knot in my back, put there from sleeping on the hard floor. At first glance, the room looked nice enough, there was even a bed tucked away in the corner. It was a luxury that apparently whoever carried me here thought I didn't deserve. I honestly couldn't remember the last time I'd slept in an actual bed. Had it been at home in Marienville? The cottage in Awen? *No,* I thought. *Cairo.* The last bed I'd laid in had been at the safe house in Cairo, the night before the gala. That house had been extravagant, the beds filled with down comforters and plush pillows. Who knew if I'd ever have the opportunity to sleep in anything like that again? That house had also been the last time I'd enjoyed modern conveniences. Electricity, running water. I'd kill just to be able to turn on a light switch or a faucet.

I sat up slowly. The back of my head still throbbed from where I'd hit it against the stone table. I reached my fingers around, checking to see if it was still bleeding when a voice cut me off.

"Don't touch that."

I turned slowly, careful of the pain, to see Nero sitting on a short stool in the opposite corner of the room. His sword was laid across his lap, a polishing stone in his hand. The obsidian-colored blade glinted in the small flicker of torchlight that sat next to him. I lowered my hand from where it hovered behind my head. "What are you doing here?" I asked him.

"I cleaned the wound the best I could," he answered, ignoring my question. "But I couldn't find more of the salve, so I'm afraid you're going to have to heal it on your own this time."

A snarky response rested on the tip of my tongue, but I thought of Roman and what he'd asked of me. If I was going to separate Nero from Set, I had to start by being nicer to him. "Thank you," I said carefully. "You didn't need to do that." Nero didn't respond, just returned to polishing his sword. "How long was I out?" I asked.

"Not long," Nero replied, continuing his task. "It's just the next morning."

I glanced around the room again, staring longingly at the bed. "I'm surprised I'm not in a cell."

"I saw no need for locked doors or bars."

"Was it too much to ask to sleep on the bed?" I asked, pushing my luck.

Nero snorted a laugh. "My apologies, girl."

"Don't call me that," I snapped, forgetting I was supposed to be nice. I'd always hated when he called me girl. But before I had been forced to endure it, back when Nero was my superior. There were no such lines anymore. "The Kindred?" I ventured to ask, forcing my voice to quiet, although I kept the tone. "Did Set turn them all?" Without a word, Nero nodded. I sat in silence for a moment, watching the mesmerizing movement of the stone against the blade. Again, I wondered at its story. "Does your sword have a name?" I'd never dared to ask before.

Nero's movements paused. "Yes."

"Do you care to share it?"

He flipped the blade, wiping the metal with the bottom of his shirt. "No."

I rolled my eyes, unsurprised by his attitude. "What about your Coterie men?" I was jumping topics. I needed to focus my thoughts to pull this off.

"What about them?" he asked.

"Did Set turn them as well?"

"No," he answered simply.

"Why not?" I pushed, not letting him off with a onecword answer this time. "Why turn Amina's soldiers, but leave yours alone?"

"We have a deal," he responded. "My allegiance, in exchange for my men staying pure."

I pondered his words. It had never occurred to me that Nero had made demands before joining Set's side. I had always assumed he had switched sides because he was an evil bastard.

Maybe I was wrong. Maybe he'd done it to protect his soldiers, as horrible as they were.

I stood up slowly, careful not to move too quickly, in case my wound made me light-headed and I lost my footing. As nice as the room was, a definite improvement from my last set of accommodations, there was still no window. The small torches along the walls worked as the only source of light. Although I was exhausted, I pushed my power out toward the flames, seeking their strength and comfort. The flames crackled in response, and Nero's eyes jumped to the closest torch and then me, almost as if he could see the power flowing from the fire into me. He was an Aries like I was, so maybe he could.

My room walls were thick, but even through the rock, I could hear the hybrids milling around outside, working toward some unknown goal. "Why aren't you outside with the others?" I asked Nero.

His polishing stone worked down the blade. "I am not currently required," he answered, his tone biting.

I spun around to look at him, turning my head to the side. "Do I sense a tone?"

His hand paused and he glared up at me from under lowered brows. "I don't know what you're talking about."

I huffed a laugh, one I used to reserve for my brother when I could tell he was lying. "I don't buy that for a second," I mumbled. I knew he could hear me, but he didn't say anything. Silence stretched out between us, and I wandered closer to the bed, the sounds of stone on metal filling the room. My fingers brushed the top comforter of the bed, sinking into the soft cotton. I considered sitting down but held off. I worried if I did, I'd never get up. I turned my head to eye the Commander. "You know, you could just ask."

He raised his eyebrows, but his hand didn't stop moving. In fact, he carefully flipped the sword and began polishing the other side again. I knew he didn't need to work on it any longer, that he was stalling, looking for a reason to stay with me. "Ask what?" he finally said.

"There's only one reason you would be here," I said cautiously, knowing I was on dangerous ground. If I was going to get Nero to trust me, I knew Roman was the way to do it. "It's obvious you have questions. My guess is Set wouldn't tell you anything about him, even though he has all of Ezekiel's memories and knows more about him than I do."

"I don't want to know about Roman," Nero replied evenly.

"You're here, aren't you?" I pointed out. "You helped heal me. Twice. You must want something."

"And why would you be willing to share information now?"

I shrugged, feigning indifference. "I don't like owing people. You helped me out, so I figure if I answer a couple of questions, we're square."

I crossed my arms, waiting. For the longest time, he said nothing. Usually, the silence would make me uncomfortable and I'd work to fill it, but I held back, taking a play out of Roman's playbook. He was the master at using silence to his advantage. During my wait, I lost my resolve and laid back on the top of the bed, sinking into it. I closed my eyes, holding back a groan as every aching muscle relaxed.

I forced myself to focus on the torchlight and pulling my element into me, the heat slowly filling my veins as the throbbing in my head lessened. The wound wasn't nearly as bad as it had been in my dream. Had being near Roman, even in my dreamscape, helped heal me? "How did he come to be raised by Ezekiel?" The question came quietly, almost as if he was as surprised as anyone that he had actually asked it.

It took every ounce of my restraint not to smile. *I got him.* I opened my eyes, but stared at the ceiling, rather than the Commander. Part of me considered lying, spinning some wild tale about Roman's childhood, in order to protect his privacy, but I couldn't risk it. What if Ezekiel had told him some things and my story didn't match? "Roman and his sister Diana were raised in foster care. When he and Diana were branded, they were young and scared so they ran away. They took care of themselves for a while, but eventually the wraiths found them. Ezekiel and his soldiers intervened, although they were too late to save Diana." At that, I looked to Nero, but his face was a stone wall. No emotional reaction for the dead daughter he never cared to know. I shouldn't have expected otherwise. Diana was of no interest to him—she could never have been a part of the Coterie. He only cared about Roman. "Afterward, Ezekiel brought Roman to the compound and began his training."

Nero remained still, only the movement of his eyes showing he was processing everything I was telling him, matching it to what he had believed to be true for so many years. "And the possession?" he asked after a while. Roman had told him his story while we'd been in Siberia.

"It happened last year. Ezekiel had tricked us into thinking he needed The Book of Breathings for a spell that would help the Kindred, but as you know, he betrayed us. There was a battle and Roman was turned into a hybrid. For a while, he was the only one." I did my best to stick to the facts, avoiding anything that would take me back to that night. One of the worst nights of my life.

"Why did Ezekiel target him? Why turn someone he considered a son?" he asked, faster this time. The question surprised me. It wasn't one of a strategist trying to understand the motives of an ally. But of a father, trying to discern how another father could do such a thing to his son.

"He's strong," I said, knowing that would play to Nero's ego. He would take credit for Roman's strength, even though he had no right to it. "He's faster than warriors decades older than him, one of the best fighters I've ever seen, and a brilliant strategist." I paused, hesitating on the next part. I didn't want to admit it, but I knew I had to give part of myself to gain his trust. "And Ezekiel knew it would hurt me. That if he turned Roman, he could control me because I'd do anything to get him back."

"Because you love him," he finished for me. I didn't deny it. There was no point in it now. I expected him to mock me, to say something about me being weak for loving his son, but he remained silent.

"You must know who she is," I said, and Nero's eyes jumped to me. "Roman's mother. He doesn't remember her. But you would know."

"What would it matter if I told you?" he responded. "You'll never see him again, never have the opportunity to tell him."

I opened my mouth to respond, when suddenly the large metal door was ripped open. I had been so distracted talking to Nero, I hadn't even heard them coming. *Had Nero?* In the doorway stood two hybrids, their eyes glowing green and blue. The once beautiful jewel tones were surrounded by blood shot eyes and black veins, marking their new state. I recognized them as two of the Kindred that had been stationed here. Two of Amina's soldiers that had recently been turned. They looked to me then to Nero. "Set wants to see you. Both of you."

Wordlessly, Nero and I followed the hybrids out of the cell and through the compound. I expected to be brought to whatever room Set had claimed for himself, but as we wound through the hallways and past the hundreds of hybrids and Coterie soldiers, I quickly realized that wasn't where we were headed. Set had been right. The Helwan compound was much larger than wherever we'd been before. The hallways were open and bright, their windows providing glimpses of the Nile through the broken exterior wall. Banners decorated in the colors and sigils of the Houses littered the floor, no doubt ripped from the walls by the compound's newest occupants. Eventually, we reached a stairwell on the far side of the compound, a winding set of stairs that descended into what I assumed was the basement or dungeon of some sort. Even a year ago, I never would have guessed how much of my time I would spend underground.

The torches bolted into the wall crackled and popped as Nero and I descended the steps, and I wondered if he was syphoning their strength, same as I was. The smell of the dungeon hit me long before my foot ever touched the floor. A stagnant air, heavy with the copper smell of blood and death. It permeated the dry air, sticking to my skin like a thin layer of wraith ash. I risked a glance at Nero. There was no way he didn't notice the same smell I had, although he gave no outward indication. His sword was sheathed across his back again, the red pommel sticking out over his now stoic face. Looking at him, I never would have guessed that just moments before we'd been having an open conversation. That Nero was gone. Left in his place was the hard shell of the Coterie Commander.

The hybrids walked us past several cells, ones similar to those I'd seen in Awen and the safehouse in Marienville. I knew the bars were made of the same metal as our daggers, capable of draining a wraith or hybrid of their strength. We often used them for interrogations, including when Grady had thrown Roman into one in the basement below Council Chambers. The smell grew more pungent as we walked farther down the hall. It was too fresh to be residual, but as I scanned the area, I couldn't find where it was coming from. The cells were empty. Finally, the hybrids stopped at the end of the hall in front of a heavy wooden door, inlaid with metal braces for reinforcement. The Water User reached up, pounding his heavy fist against the door twice.

I didn't hear any sound from the other side, no permission to enter, but the hybrids pushed it open anyway, stepping to the side, allowing us room to walk past. Nero stepped through first, and I followed a step behind. As soon as I entered the room, I almost fell to my knees gagging. It was painfully obvious that this room was where the reek was coming from. The walls were covered in blood, the floor dirty, the grit dark even when highlighted with the oranges and yellows from the torches on the wall. Metal rings were screwed underneath the torches, chains hanging loose from them toward the ground. At first, I was so distracted by the room I didn't even see Set, though I could *feel* him. I followed his power to the far corner of the room. There, shrouded in the shadows, I could just make out the curve of his bare back. He was hunched over, his head bent, arms curved as if he was holding something in a gentle caress.

A sick feeling built in my gut and I used the smallest bit of power in order to see better. The room came into sharp focus, the smell so much worse with my senses enhanced. I realized he wasn't just standing in shadows, but rather, he *was* the shadows. They leaked from his body, through his veins that protruded out of his skin. I remembered the first time I'd seen him like this in Siberia. I remember thinking then that it was the real him, the god leaking out of its human form.

Suddenly, and with the rigidity of something not quite human, Set stood up straight, dropping whatever was in his arms to the hard floor. It landed with a thud, but I still could not see what it was through the shadows. Then slowly, the darkness dissipated, sucking back into the god's body, filling him with a dark, unnatural magic. His veins morphed from a stark black to a livid red, before finally disappearing under the skin's surface. He turned, his eyes glowing brighter than I had ever seen. Methodically, he lifted his hand to his mouth, wiping the edge of his lips. It wasn't until he took a step forward that I finally saw what, or rather who, he had dropped to the floor.

It was a woman. From what I could tell, she appeared to be not much older than me. Her skin was dark, her bright blue shirt ripped down the front. Her skin was stretched over her cheekbones, her clavicle and elbows protruding from beneath the tightened surface, sure signs she'd been fed on. Repeatedly. Her eyes were wide and bulging, her mouth open in a silent scream. At first I thought she was dead, but as I looked closer, I noticed the smallest movement; her chest rising and falling in short, shallow breaths. Behind her lay a pile of other victims, at least four more as I could see, the source of the foul smell that hung in the air.

They were all dead, and if I didn't do something, this woman would be too.

Rage gripped me, running through my veins and filling me with ire. The torches flared in response, both Nero and Set taking notice. *I am going to kill him,* I thought. He had to pay for everything he'd done. The flames jumped from the torches to my waiting hands, but before I could even pull my arm back to throw, Nero's hand gripped my wrist extinguishing the flames. I glared at him, at his matching red eyes, but he shook his head slightly. Not a command, but a request.

Not here. Not now, he was telling me.

I ripped my arm from his grasp, but quieted my power anyway, crossing my arms defiantly as I turned to Set. He'd been watching the whole thing with amused interest. "I admire your spirit," he said.

"What do you want?" I demanded. "Did you bring me down here just to gloat about how horrible and evil you are? To show me more of the innocent lives you've destroyed?" I was near hysterical, but he didn't react.

Instead, he walked over to the opposite wall, grabbing a piece of paper off a small table that was housed there. He read it over with great interest, forcing me to stand and wait. "Did you know," he began, "that Amina was a fastidious record keeper?"

I scrunched my eyebrows, not understanding. "You brought me to your red room of pain to talk about paperwork?" I said snarkily. I may not be able to physically attack him, but throwing attitude was the least I could do.

Set didn't react, but I could have sworn I heard Nero swallow a laugh. "Amina kept a ledger with the names of every soldier in her compound," Set continued. "What House they were from, their various skills, known associates, etc. It seems she is a very untrusting individual." *Don't have to tell me that,* I thought. I'd been on the business end of her paranoia more than once. "So untrusting that she hid this ledger in a place only her second in command knew of. Since that soldier is now loyal to me, he was kind enough to share it with me." I didn't like where this was going. "You might be interested to know that your beloved Scorpio Nomarch also required her soldiers to stand in the courtyard every morning for roll call, so she could note who was accounted for, and who wasn't. A tradition her second in command continued in her absence." Set took several steps forward so that he now stood directly in front of me, although Nero was now to his side. "On the morning of our invasion, there were four hundred and seventeen soldiers in this compound. I've taken stock of those who became hybrid, and those we killed during the battle, and they all come up accounted for," his eyes lingered, the red storm clouds boring into me. "Except one."

I went perfectly still, forcing myself not to look away from the Chaos god's eyes. To not give away any movement that would confirm his suspicion. I counted to ten before I spoke, waiting for my nerves to steady. "Why are you telling me this?" I asked, proud of how even my voice was.

"You are the only person stupid enough to defy me. So, I will ask you this question *once*. Did you help one of the soldiers escape?"

My heart was racing, as Set's power churned in his eyes. The hair on my arms stood up as electricity crackled off his skin. I'd seen him use that power before. I'd seen the damage it could do. As much as I didn't want to be on the wrong end of it, I couldn't tell him anything. It would mean selling out my Guard. Selling out Roman. "No," I answered.

Set's eyes narrowed, his head turned slightly as if he were listening to something too far away or too small for me to hear. "You're lying," he accused, and before I could even defend myself, a shock of electricity jumped from Set and wrapped itself around my arms. Thousands of volts of electricity pulsed through my body, my muscles locking up as I dropped to the floor, screaming. It only lasted for seconds, but I remained on the disgusting floor, writhing in pain as my muscles regained use. "What did you tell her?" Set roared, his voice filling the room, pushing its way past the ringing in my ears. "Where did she escape to?"

"I don't know what you're talking about," I protested, yelling back at the god. Another jolt ripped through me, my back bowing off the ground before I curled in on myself instinctually, my arms locked around my midsection. That jolt was followed by another shock. Then another. When I still didn't say anything, Set changed tactics, rearing his heavily-booted foot back and kicking me square in the face.

The force of the blow threw me into the air, and I landed on my back, arms spread wide, a moan falling from my lips. Set lifted his foot again, but surprisingly, Nero stepped in.

"That won't work," he said, and thankfully Set paused before lowering his foot to the ground. "She doesn't care what happens to her, and if you kill her, you'd only be doing her a favor."

"Then what is your suggestion, Commander?" Set sneered, using Nero's position as an insult.

Nero stomped over to the woman curled in the corner and ripped her to her feet before throwing her in the middle of the room, directly in front of me. A raspy moan broke between her cracked lips. "She's trained to protect the innocent at all costs," I heard Nero say to Set, although I couldn't see him from where I was still curled on the ground. I heard the sound of Nero's sword loosing from its sheath. He kneeled in front of me, his hand gripped firmly in the woman's hair, exposing her throat. The tip of the obsidian blade pressed into the sensitive part of her neck, nicking the skin and drawing blood.

"She's dead either way," I rasped, before Nero had the chance to say anything. It pained me to say it, but it was true. There was no way Set would let her live.

"Then tell him what he wants to know and I'll make it quick."

A cough racked my body, my mouth filling with blood and saliva. I spit it harshly on the floor, pushing myself up to face the god. It was a horrible choice to make, but it seemed those were the only decisions I had left in life. This woman had already suffered more than enough. If I could give her a quick death, it was the least I owed her. "Her name is Ume. I saved her from one of your hybrids and helped her escape."

"Where did she go?" Nero pushed. "Did she report back to Awen?"

"I don't know," I lied. "But I doubt it."

"Why?" Set growled.

A plan formed in my head. "I recognized her. She wasn't loyal to Amina like the others but a spy that worked for one of the other Nomarchs. Before she climbed the wall, she asked me to come with her. To run away. She said she knew of somewhere safe I could go, and since Amina isn't particularly fond of me," I spit, "she couldn't have been talking about Awen." Partial truth, partial lie.

"Did she say where?" Set asked. Each word was precise, filled with restraint, as if any moment he could lose control of the leash on his power and kill us all.

I pursed my lips, pretending I wouldn't answer. Nero slid the edge of his sword over the woman's neck, and a thin red line formed behind it. Not enough to kill her, just wound. She didn't even protest, she was so out of it. It killed me to watch it, but I had to let it happen if I was going to sell this story. *I'm sorry*, I thought to the woman. *I'm sorry this is happening to you.*

"Fine, fine. I'll tell you." I huffed a large breath. "She said there's a safe house, one that a few of the other spies like her had been sent to prepare. She said it's empty now, but if we got there quickly, that there were others coming soon. People who would help me. People that cared."

"The Guard," Nero said, not to me, but to Set. "She's talking about the Guard. If we can get the rest of them, the Kindred wouldn't even think about opposing us. The Guard is their greatest weapon."

"No!" I cried out, feigning my outrage, letting Nero believe he had figured out the one piece of intel I hadn't wanted him to know. "She never mentioned the Guard. I swear it!" I turned fully to Set, "I swear it!" I yelled again.

Nero ignored my outburst. "They'll have The Book of Breathings with them," he added. "Possibly your was-sceptre too." I could practically feel the sense of victory and accomplishment radiating off his skin, as he believed he'd beaten me.

Electricity crackled around Set as he stared down at me, helpless and defenseless on the ground. "The location," he hissed.

I closed my eyes, a small tear escaping. Defeated. Let them think they had defeated me. "Ozero Lobaz," I whispered. "They're headed for Ozero Lobaz."

Nero yelled in anger. I opened my eyes just in time to see him ram his sword through the throat of the woman and rip it back out. Her blood splattered my face, hot and sticky before he dropped her dead body roughly to the floor.

Nero had kept his word. The woman was dead. There would be no more pain for her. In death came freedom.

Nero stomped to the other side of the room, ramming his fist into the rock wall. Once, twice, as he roared at the top of his lungs. I pulled the edge of my shirt up, wiping at the blood on my face, trying to ignore the shaking of my hand. I looked up to Set who stood above me. He no longer looked murderous. The storm clouds in his eyes had settled, replaced by a calculated sharpness. A look I recognized when Roman was planning. "What are you going to do?" I asked him.

His red eyes lowered to mine. "The Kindred have made a grave error in moving toward Ozero Lobaz. They allowed their hubris to guide their actions, believing they could sneak their Guard around behind my back and use their old tricks to try and put me back in my cage. I plan to show them how wrong they are." He looked up to Nero, who had quit pounding his fist at this point and was staring at the god. Idly, I noticed his knuckles were cut and bleeding.

"News of your conquests will have reached Awen by now," Nero answered him, surprisingly calm again, his voice giving no hint to the great show of anger I had just witnessed. "We have to assume they will send soldiers to retaliate. You cannot afford to leave Helwan. We may lose this compound if you do." No matter his faults, Nero was a brilliant strategist.

Seemingly forgotten for the moment, I looked back and forth between the Commander and the god. "Then *you* will go to Ozero Lobaz and reclaim what was once yours, and when her Guardsmen arrive, you will be waiting for them," Set ordered.

Nero pulled his shoulders back, his pleasure at his new assignment obvious. "Yes, sir. I will bring you back their heads."

"No," Set responded. "I want them alive."

Nero's jaw clenched tightly, but he gave a curt nod. He kneeled down, glaring at me. "When will the Guard arrive?" he demanded.

"I don't know exactly. Five days, maybe seven. It will be difficult for them to get off the island with Amina watching," I snipped. A lie. One I hoped bought Roman time to get to Ozero Lobaz first. If Nero arrived before he did, we were screwed.

"How many with them?"

"I don't know," I answered. The truth this time.

Nero straightened. "With such limited intel, I'll need assurances. If there are more Kindred than we're aware of, I'll need collateral to bargain with if things so south."

The storm returned to Set's eyes. He didn't like that Nero was adding to the plan, that he was thinking on his own. "What did you have in mind?" he sneered. I raised my eyebrows, shocked he was even entertaining the idea. I watched, waiting for Nero to answer, but when he didn't say anything, I spoke.

"Me. He needs to take me."

Chapter 10

Roman

Three sharp raps sounded on the wooden door.

I crossed the small room in four large strides, pulling the lock aside and opening the door just enough to look outside. Grady and Brynn stood still, their faces silhouetted by moonlight. I glanced over their heads, using my enhanced senses to check the small strip of beach behind them. I saw nothing but white sand, heard nothing but the crashing of waves. "You're late," I admonished them.

Grady placed his hand on the door, pushing his way inside. Brynn followed closely behind, The Book of Breathings tucked tightly into her side. "Sorry, but it's not exactly like this place was easy to find, and you were pretty secretive with your instructions." I'd been watching the street guards and sentries for weeks, timing their rotations as they moved through the various dirt and cobblestone roads, so when I left instructions for the others to meet me at this abandoned shack at the bottom of the cliffs, I'd told them specifically which roads to take and at what time, in order to avoid being seen. If they were discovered by a sentry, there would be no explanation for where they were going. The Guard was allowed to be out after curfew only if the Governor allowed it. If they were caught and lied about being on a task for Amina, I knew they would check and learn the truth.

I shut the door behind my Guardsmen, sliding the lock home. Closed doors and locks were typically useless in Awen—everyone was strong enough to break them—but for this meeting it was imperative. "Why is it so dark in here?" Brynn asked, referring to the single candle that flickered on the table in the middle of the room. Enough for someone like us to see but also keep the corners in shadow. I ignored her question.

I pulled a small dagger from my belt, slicing it over my finger and quickly scribbling the silence sigil on the back of the door. The power in the room changed, the soundproof shield locking around the small building. Brynn and Grady wheeled around, sensing the power shift, even before they spotted the sigil. "Did you bring everything I requested?" I asked them.

Grady swung a large bag from his shoulder. "It's all here. Weapons from our personal collections, three sets of tactical gear, and as many medical supplies as we could find."

Brynn stepped forward, so much shorter than Grady or me, and yet in many ways, stronger. I knew so little about her. How she was branded, which family member she'd lost. If we survived all this, I'd make a point to hear her story. "Tell us what is going on. Why are you being so shady?"

"Follow me," I said simply, grabbing the candle and leading them across the dusty floor and to the back of the room. There, only visible if you knew to look for it, was a small door latch. I pushed the hidden doorway open, ushering Brynn and Grady inside. They eyed me warily as they passed, each peppering me with questions the whole way. I ignored all of them, knowing it was pointless to answer any of them now. They would know the plan soon enough, and it was too risky to repeat it unnecessarily. I shut this door behind them, just as I had the other, repeating the silence sigil here as well. The power drain it created was small, like the drip of a faucet. I was aware of it yet it wasn't enough to affect me. The second sigil was probably unnecessary, but I had to be sure. If someone stumbled across our meeting place and inside the first room, this would keep us protected.

Grady and Brynn's questions came to an abrupt halt, and I knew they had finally taken in the room. I turned around, my back against the door as I looked at them. All of them.

Not just Grady and Brynn, but Mallory, Cassie, and Isaac, each standing against the western wall in a show of solidarity. And finally, Astrid. The Cancer Nomarch was seated in a high back chair, the only chair in the room. She was dressed in tactical gear, but instead of the standard black, hers was a stark white—a fur sash clipped from her left shoulder to the opposite hip.

"What the hell is going on?" Brynn demanded. "What is she doing here?"

"Watch your tone, Scorpio," Astrid admonished, her voice ice cold. "You are speaking to a Nomarch of the High Council."

"Get off your damn high horse, Astrid. This isn't Council Chambers," Cassie barked from the side, her sharp eyes cutting to the Nomarch, completely unafraid. "You're not in charge here." Surprisingly, Cassie looked to me. They all did.

I took a deep breath, choosing to cut to the chase. "The six of us are leaving Awen in two days. We're going to Ozero Lobaz, and we're going to get Kyndal back."

Brynn shook her head, "But Amina. . ."

"Amina will not be a problem," Astrid interrupted, attempting to take control of the meeting. I let her. For now. "Three days from now is the Summer Solstice. As you know, the Houses shift from Gemini to Cancer, and Awen will move from the middle of the Pacific to just off the southeastern coast of North America to what the humans call The Bermuda Triangle. Once that shift occurs, Amina is sending a fleet of her troops into Helwan to attack

Set. But because it is the Solstice, Amina is forced to hold to tradition. Celebration begins that morning at dawn, continuing well into the night. Amina has already announced there are to be various competitions inside the great arena, as well as public trials for those awaiting sentencing. The entire Kindred population is expected to attend."

"If everyone is expected to be there, doesn't that include the Guard?" Mallory asked. "Amina may not notice if we aren't there," she continued, gesturing to herself, Cassie, and Isaac, "but she will definitely notice if they aren't."

Astrid nodded. "It's true. Absence of The Guard will not go unnoticed, which is why you must all leave the night before. Amina's greatest weakness is that she is still attempting to appear as the selfless leader to the warriors. She has to work to keep up that facade, and under no circumstances can she afford to lose that mask. By the time Amina realizes you are not at the Solstice celebration, she won't be able to do anything about it with all the eyes of the warriors watching. When she finally can take action, it will be too late."

"Then she'll send warriors after us," Cassie finished for her. "She'll hunt us down and kill us."

"She won't be able to find us," I answered her, ignoring the fact the question had been aimed at Astrid. "She won't even know where to begin."

"How does going to Ozero Lobaz get Kyndal back?" Mallory asked Astrid. "She's in Egypt."

"Specifics are not your concern," she answered coldly. "Just be ready when you are given the signal."

Mallory raised her eyebrows in astonishment—looking directly at me—as if to ask if I was going to let that answer slide. I didn't want to, but I needed Astrid for this plan to work and couldn't risk upsetting her. I turned away from Mallory, ignoring her silent question. I didn't miss her huff of disapproval. I would be hearing from her later.

"How are we getting off the island?" Grady asked, steering the conversation away.

"That information is protected," Astrid answered cryptically.

When she gave no further explanation, Brynn leaned forward, looking at Astrid expectantly. "You're not giving us a lot to go on here." She turned to me. "Tell us *something*, Roman. How is Kyndal getting out of Egypt? Did you talk to her again?"

Mallory pushed off the wall at that. The others had been there when I'd talked to Kyndal in my dreams, but Mallory hadn't. I assumed Cassie had filled her in. Looking at her expression now, maybe she hadn't. "Yes, I spoke to her again."

"Roman," Astrid hissed. A sharp reprimand.

I turned to the Nomarch, stoic and unyielding. "You cannot expect them to risk everything with no information. If they don't know what's going on, they won't be prepared and mistakes will be made. We both know we can't afford any errors."

"What's wrong, Nomarch?" Isaac drawled from the sidelines, speaking for the first time. His words stung with their usual sarcasm. "If your plan is so airtight, why not share it with the group?"

"In case you fail," Astrid answered harshly. "This plan relies on several Nomarchs, including myself, sticking our necks out for you. If any of you are caught, Amina will not hesitate to torture the information out of you, that I can guarantee." Her eyes roamed over Isaac, her disapproval obvious. "I doubt someone as weak as you would do well when faced with the knife. If you don't know anything, at least when you crack, I can guarantee she won't learn anything useful."

Isaac crossed his arms, his reply found only in his silence. "Look," I said, refocusing the group. "We all know the risks. What I'm asking you to do goes in direct violation of our orders. If we're caught, we *will* be killed. But I can guarantee you, if we do nothing, we're dead anyway. Since Amina took control, we've all watched as she tightened her grip on the warriors, finding the smallest slight as an excuse to throw her opponents in the Hollow. She hasn't been able to touch us, at least not yet. Astrid and some of the other Nomarchs have been working to make sure that doesn't happen. How much longer can we expect them to be able to do so? As long as we're in Awen, Amina has us trapped. This is our one opportunity to get out and for our Guard to finally, *finally* be complete again. So, if you're not up for this, tell me now."

"I'm in," Grady announced immediately, shrugging his shoulders nonchalantly. "Damn the consequences. Let's go get Kyndal. It's no fun around here without her, anyway." I nodded my thanks, choosing to ignore his comment. I was always uncertain about Grady's intentions toward Kyndal. That uncertainty made me uncomfortable.

"Me too," Brynn agreed. "I'm in."

After Brynn came Isaac, agreeing to the danger despite the greater risk to him. He claimed he owed it to her. I knew after he was injured in Cairo, it had always bothered him that he hadn't been with us at the museum. That he hadn't been there to fight Set. He'd been trying to make up for it ever since. Cassie answered with a simple *yes*, then finally my eyes landed on Mallory. "Of course I'm in. It's the least I can do after what she did in The Hall of Two Truths. Kyndal has saved all of our lives more than once. Tell us what to do."

So, I did.

Over the next hour, I detailed the plans for our escape. Astrid and I had gone over them tirelessly the night before. How to collect supplies, the best routes to take through the city, how to avoid the street guards. They all listened intently, only stopping to ask questions when something needed clarification. The time for sarcasm and joking had ended, each one of them was intent on the mission at hand. The whole time, I kept part of my attention on the silence shield, making sure it held strong, that there was no possible way anyone could hear what we were planning. When I finally finished, Astrid, who had stayed surprisingly quiet, stood from her chair.

"In the next two days, it is imperative that you all act as if nothing has changed. Amina cannot suspect that we are planning anything. If she gets suspicious, she could tighten her grip even more and we lose our window of opportunity."

I agreed. "Grady, leave your duffel bag here. Astrid will see that it makes it to the plane. The rest of you gather whatever supplies you can, quietly. When Nero comes for Ozero Lobaz, we have to be ready for anything."

Slowly, I lifted the silence shield, all of us remaining perfectly still, our individual powers reaching out to the surrounding area, searching for an unfamiliar presence. I found nothing in my search, but even as we worked our way back toward the front door, we let Grady leave first. He jogged out to where the soft sand met the beginning of the forest, disappearing among the trees. He returned moments later, shaking his head. Confirmation that there was no sign of recent power signatures. One by one, the small group left, taking different routes back to the heart of the city, just as they were instructed. I watched the last of them vanish and prepared myself to leave, but before I could step into the night air, Astrid placed a strong hand on my arm.

"There is one final thing to discuss," she said.

Quickly, I thought through the plan. "I didn't miss anything."

"The Guard has The Book of Breathings in your possession, and as you know, Amina took Set's cage from the safehouse in Cairo, but there is one other artifact at play. Something you must procure for me before you leave Awen. Set's was-sceptre."

My eyes narrowed. "We discussed this. It's too risky." We had talked about it already, the night before. Astrid wanted the sceptre, which was locked beneath Council Chambers every night. The Guard was allowed to test the sceptre during the day, but we were also required to return it. It was locked in the dungeon under Chambers, not far from my old cell, actually.

"I've changed my mind," Astrid said simply. "I want you to get it for me."

I ground my back molars to keep a lock on my temper. My power stirred deep in my abdomen, but I pushed it down, refusing to release it. I'd been practicing stifling my temper for years. I knew that reacting too quickly would give Astrid an edge. I couldn't let her know what I was thinking. No matter how pissed off I was.

"Why not just get it yourself?" I asked her. "You're a Nomarch, it should be easier for you than me."

Astrid reached out, tugging lightly at the edge of my black T-shirt, her icy blue eyes traveling up my arm and leaving a chill in their wake. "I noticed you didn't mention to your friends that you asked me to break Briar out of the Hollow. Why is that?"

My power flared again, and this time I didn't try to contain it. I felt my eyes change, the details of the room becoming sharper. I clenched my fist, refusing to answer the question. There was no need. She knew why I hadn't told them. I had been stupid enough to explain to her they didn't believe in Briar's abilities. She smiled. "There is no mission without the sceptre. Bring it to me," she ordered and then sauntered out into the night, the moonlight reflecting off her silver hair.

Chapter 11

Roman

The next two days were brutal.

Preparations for the Solstice began the morning after my clandestine meeting on the beach. Every Kindred had been ordered to help with the preparations, and the Guard was no different. We'd been ordered to attend to the arena and build a stage in the sands, one that faced the dais. Although Amina hadn't told us what it would be used for, the specifications she gave us made it pretty obvious. It would be a holding area for those on trial. The "criminals" that would be sentenced during the celebration. We'd done as we were told, keeping our heads down as we followed her orders. Awful as it was, there was nothing we could do to help those soldiers. Not now. The best we could do for them was to get off the island and regain our power. Then, we could return and liberate those left.

When the night of our escape arrived, I'd woken early from a restless sleep. We were not to leave until after midnight, so I'd returned to Astrid's home after curfew to get a few hours of sleep. I wasn't tired, yet I wanted to try and speak with Kyndal again. I had tried to reach her the night before but had been unsuccessful. This night had produced the same results. For reasons I didn't understand, I couldn't reach her. Maybe she wasn't asleep, maybe I was doing something wrong, or maybe there was another reason I couldn't get through to her. A nagging voice in the back of my head told me that something could have happened to her. Something that kept her from using her powers. I didn't delve too far into that train of thought, I couldn't. If I started thinking about all the horrible things that could be happening to her, I would drive myself crazy.

Frustrated and too agitated to sleep, I finally gave up. I stood and began final preparations to leave. I took my time, securing my leather vest over the short black T-shirt I always wore. I strapped a leather arm sheath to my forearm, a new acquisition that concealed the was-sceptre tattoo inked into my arm. I picked up two daggers from my bedside table, tucking the first into my belt, hiding the second in my boot. I paused briefly, staring at the third blade that laid there. Smaller than the others, the blade was just as sharp, with a loop at the top made for fingers smaller than mine, more delicate. It'd been sitting there for months now, a physical reminder of her. I couldn't count how many times I'd stood staring at it, and yet it never moved. It never felt right to take it.

Until now.

I grabbed the small ring dagger and tucked it into the arm sheath.

I left the room without a final glance, even knowing I would most likely never return. The room meant nothing to me, held no sentimental value. Everything I cared about lay ahead of me.

Nothing else mattered.

When I left the house, the moon was high, the stars twinkling brightly, and yet the air was still warm, a true sign that summer was almost here. I wound through the streets of Awen, away from the large mansions where Astrid resided, and along the river. Many of the street torches were still lit, but I used my power to snuff them out, one by one. The release of power took the edge off my agitation. As I neared the heart of the city, I was met with the sounds of activity. The bakers were up, working overtime to prepare food for the upcoming festivities, while others prepared gear and weapons for the warriors that would be departing soon. While they were working like normal, the city lacked its usual chatter, its almost musical quality that always accompanied the marketplace. Instead, there was no conversation, each Kindred carrying out their duties with stoic obedience. I stuck to the shadows, moving silently from one to the next, taking care that no one saw me. It was easy to be silent, I had no bag with me, no other effects. I'd packed them the day before and gave them to Astrid, who assured me they would end up on the plane.

The sound of boots on the cobblestones had me pressing back into a shop wall. It was a street patrol, at least three sentries. Amina's people had finished their decorations, the royal blue banner of House Cancer hanging out of the shop window above me. I squeezed myself behind it, using it for cover. My right hand moved slowly to my belt as I kept one eye on the street. The boots had stopped, the hushed, tense voices of the soldiers mixing with those of the shop owner. The guards were stealing her bread and refusing to pay or trade for it. She was arguing with them but it was no use. I grit my teeth, desperate to intervene, even as I knew I couldn't. It was too risky. I held my breath as they laughed at her and walked away. When they came into my view, they were pulling the bread apart and sharing it among themselves. I marked each of their faces, burning them into my memory. One day, I would pay them back for the way they had treated the baker.

When I reached the other side of the marketplace, I turned and crossed the river to a different part of the island. Not far from where I used to live, the houses here were smaller, each built almost exactly the same. I stopped at the fifth one, jogging alongside it and around to the back where I knew the house would be open to the elements. This wasn't her house, of course. That had been taken from her months ago. She told me once it belonged to a friend of hers who was stationed off the island. She allowed her to use it while she was gone. I crouched down at the gossamer curtains that hung off the back of the house, the only barrier between me and the hot spring I could hear bubbling on the other side. There was no firelight coming from inside that I could see, but I knew she was here. I could hear her moving around at the front of the house. I could have easily walked in, but I didn't dare.

"Brynn," I hissed into the darkness.

There was only the briefest of pauses before a door opened and a small flicker of candlelight appeared in the house. Brynn walked through, dressed in full gear, dagger in hand, staring at me incredulously.

"Roman?" she whispered back, not bothering to hide her shock. "What are you doing here?"

I stood from my crouch, pulling the curtains back as I entered her house. "I need to talk to you."

She waved me in further, although I knew she was unsure. Brynn and I didn't spend a lot of alone time together, so my behavior would be considered strange on a normal day. And tonight was definitely not a normal day.

"It's not safe for you to be here, we leave in two hours."

"We have a problem," I said, ignoring her concern. "I'm going to need the book." She stared at me, the candlelight flickering off her dark irises. I glanced around her living room. The whole area was dark. I looked again at her gear. "What were you doing?"

"Sharpening my blades."

"In the dark?" I questioned.

Brynn glared at me. "Roman, what's the problem?"

I took a deep breath, scruffing my hair out of habit. Here goes nothing. "Astrid wants us to get the sceptre for her before we leave Awen."

Brynn's eyes bulged out, and for a moment she forgot to whisper. "Are you kidding me?! That's the most ridiculous…"

"Keep your voice down," I interrupted her. She swiftly changed her volume but not her tone.

"How the hell are we supposed to do that? It's locked under Council Chambers. Behind guards. Only Amina can give the order to open. . ." this time she cut herself off. "Oh," she said, understanding dawning on her. She knew *exactly* how I planned to get the sceptre. What I needed to do and why it brought me here. "You want the Changeling Spell."

"Yes," I said simply.

Brynn pinched the bridge of her nose, a small sign of stress that I wasn't used to seeing on her. Brynn rarely showed when something upset her. "Let's ignore for a moment that Sandra directly told us not to try that spell, that it presented its own dangers."

"Sandra isn't here," I interrupted harshly, ignoring the shot of pain that went through my heart at the sound of my adoptive mother's name. *She's alive*, I reminded myself. She was alive and fighting. I'd see her again one day.

Brynn didn't falter. "You can't masquerade as Amina inside Council Chambers, in front of her own soldiers. It's too risky. What happens if you run into someone who knows where she really is? What if you run into Amina?"

"There is no other choice," I urged Brynn. "If we don't bring Astrid the sceptre, the plan is off and we're all dead."

Brynn shook her head, her mouth forming a tense line. "What does she want with it, anyway? She knows she can't use it. Only we can."

"I think that's exactly the point," I told her. "Astrid knows we need the sceptre to defeat Set. Having it in her possession ensures we don't double-cross her. It keeps us tethered to her." Brynn crossed her arms, angry. "At least if Astrid has the sceptre, that means Amina won't. It takes the weapon out of her hands. Brynn, I don't need you to like this plan, but it is our *only option*."

"Why didn't she bring this up at our meeting the other night? Why only tell you?"

I gritted my teeth. *Dammit, I wish she hadn't asked that.* I thought about lying to her, but for whatever reason, I just couldn't bring myself to do it. "I asked Astrid to get Briar out of the Hollow for me. She used that to blackmail me into doing this for her."

"Briar?" Brynn demanded. "Seriously? I thought Grady told you she was crazy."

I reached out toward Brynn's arm, but at the last minute pulled back. Brynn wasn't much for physical contact. "Which is why I'm here, talking to you, and not Grady. Will you give me the damn book or not?"

Brynn set her candle down, pacing over to the other side of the room. "I'll do one better," she said. I waited patiently. "I'll go with you."

"No," I said immediately.

"You don't know Amina well enough to pull off pretending to be her. I'm House Scorpio like she is. For years I idolized her, studied her battle tactics and moves. I know how she talks, how she responds, everything. Not to mention, that spell is going to take some serious magic skills, and we both know I have you beat there." I sucked in a deep breath, counting to ten while my temper simmered under the surface. I didn't want her with me. Didn't want to put her at any more risk. Apparently I waited too long to respond as Brynn said, "If I go with you, I won't tell Grady how Briar ended up on the plane."

"Fine," I eventually relented. "Let's get it done."

"We can't start the spell until we get to right outside Council Chambers," Brynn began, immediately taking control of the situation. She walked across the living room and into her bedroom, reemerging with The Book of Breathings. She laid the ancient tome out in front of us on a nearby table, next to the one source of light. She flipped through the pages quickly, with the knowledge of someone who had spent hours poring over its contents. She found the page easily. "The longer I stay under as Amina, the more difficult it will be for me to pull out of the spell. Also, walking down the streets as her is asking for someone to discover us. We'll have to wait until just before we go in."

"There's an alcove underneath the chamber stairs, hidden from view. We can do it there."

She nodded, her finger moving over the ancient words on the yellowed page. Her eyes flew along with them, committing the spell to memory. I promptly shut up, allowing her to focus. "I'm assuming the street guards won't be an issue," she said.

"I have their patterns timed, we can avoid them," I assured her.

She slammed the book shut, "Good. Let's go."

We wound through the streets in the same manner I'd made it to Brynn's house. I took the lead, pushing Brynn back into the shadows and around alcoves when necessary to avoid detection. Our pace was slower, the change in plan forcing Brynn to bring her remaining supplies and the book with her inside a small backpack. Council Chambers was a decent hike from where she lived, but luckily we could stick to side streets and alleyways, making it easier for us to hide. The closer we got to Chambers however, the more heavily patrolled the streets were, which slowed our pace. Finally, the stairs came into view. I turned back from where we hid around a corner, making sure to keep my voice low. "There's no cover between here and the stairs. The courtyard is too exposed. I can hear three sets of boots, three sentries. We're going to have to time it perfectly and make a run for it." She nodded. "On my count," I told her. "One." I held up two fingers, then three.

The two of us lept from our hiding spot, sprinting behind the turned backs of the guards that were walking the opposite direction now. Brynn's hand held down her backpack, preventing the weapons inside from clanging together and giving us away.

We were fast and silent, just as we'd been trained. We reached the side of the massive steps, tucking ourselves underneath the small ledge that hung over our heads, losing ourselves in shadow. The fit was tight, Brynn's shoulder pressed against mine. Brynn wasted no time, dropping her bag and beginning to chant under her breath. I called to my power, splitting its strength in two. Half to listen for guards approaching, the other half open for Brynn to pull from. We couldn't risk this spell failing. The mask had to hold.

I took a small step out into the light, risking a glance over the stairs' edge. "It's clear, we should go," I said, turning back to Brynn. "Woah." For Brynn had stood up, but it was no longer Brynn in front of me. Her height had changed, and she was now at least three inches taller. Her buzzed hair had grown long and jet black. It fell straight down her back. Her face morphed in front of me, Brynn's sharp cheekbones softening slightly, her round eyes taking on an almond shape. Brynn's usually full lips now sat in a thin line, the perfect imitation of Amina's pursed annoyance. Her clothes had stayed the same, but it would not be strange for Amina to be seen in tactical gear. Not on the eve of soldiers leaving the island.

"Did it work?" Brynn asked, Amina's voice breaking across her lips.

I blinked stupidly for a moment. "I'd say so." The glint of something silver caught my eye. Brynn's sais tucked in her belt. I pointed to her weapons. "You're going to have to leave those here. Amina doesn't carry sais. We can come back for them after."

Begrudgingly, Brynn pulled them from her belt loop, placing them quietly on the ground next to her bag in the shadows. She stood tall, straightening an invisible wrinkle in her shirt, just as Amina would. "Stay behind me," she ordered. "Whatever you do, whoever we run into, don't speak. Let me handle it." Then she stepped out into the courtyard.

Brynn—*Amina*—stepped onto the steps, her head held high, the perfect image of regality. I walked two steps behind her, an appropriate distance for someone inferior. I no longer had to worry about being seen. Although it was after curfew, no one would dare question me as long as I was with the Governor. We reached the top step, and I moved around Brynn to pull the door open for her. She walked through proudly. No recognition for me. No thank you. Just as Amina would.

As soon as we made it through the atrium of the building, we were met with a series of sentries that stood outside the official chamber. I had anticipated them, as I knew Brynn had as well. I checked my power, ensuring it was still open to Brynn. It responded quickly, strong and stable. As we passed the guards, they lowered their heads in deference, but Brynn didn't so much as spare them a glance. I had to force myself not to turn around and check after we passed them to ensure they weren't calling for backup. To make sure we hadn't been discovered.

We made it to the end of the hallway, to the large oak door that led down to the dungeon. Brynn paused for a moment, cutting a glance to me. We couldn't risk talking to each other, not with so many ears on us, but I knew what she was saying anyways. These steps were the only way down and our only way out. Once we were down there, Amina's most elite sentries would be waiting, the ones that knew her best. Our biggest test. I pushed my power out toward her, giving her more of my magic. As much as I could spare. A small show of silent support. Then she pulled open the door.

The cold air of the dungeon was sickeningly familiar. There was a single long corridor with a series of doors similar to the ones we just came through on both sides. I'd seen the inside of one before, back when I had been possessed. Grady had brought me here and thrown me in a cell, torturing me for hours to try and learn Ezekiel's plan. I'd avoided coming back here, always making the others return the sceptre. Being back was more difficult than I anticipated. I cleared my throat, ignoring the rising emotion.

At the end of the hallway were four sentries, standing in front of the last door. I recognized each of them. They had been with Amina when she'd followed us to Cairo. They had held their daggers to our throats in the safehouse as Isaac laid dying on the cold floor. One of them had been the man who'd refused to open the chamber doors for me. I would never forget their faces. As we approached, one of them stepped forward. He was a large man, almost as tall as I was. I didn't remember his name, just that he was from House Leo. A Fire User. And he was the one that had struck Brynn with the hilt of his dagger. "Surprised to see you here, ma'am," he greeted, his voice deep and thickly accented. *Italian,* I thought. "You said you were headed to the arena for the night, to check that the preparations had been done correctly." I tucked that piece of information away. If Amina was in the arena, that meant she wasn't far from where we were now.

"Last I checked," Brynn answered, her voice haughty and irritated, the perfect Amina, "I didn't have to check with you whenever I changed my mind. Open the door and step aside."

"Absolutely, ma'am," he replied. "After you provide the password."

I quit breathing. My hand inched slowly closer to my dagger.

Brynn didn't skip a beat. "It is late and I am tired after a long day. I do not wish to play games," she admonished. "Open the door."

"My apologies, Governor," said the guard. "But it was your order that requires the password. I'm not to let you through without it."

Brynn scoffed. The outside guards moved slowly to our sides. Their daggers were sheathed in their belts, but two more steps and they would outflank us. My hand moved the final inch, now gripping the cool handle of my dagger. I stared straight ahead, watching the sentries from the corner of my eye. In front of me, Brynn continued to try and talk her way into the room. Silver flashed out of the corner of my eye as one of the sentries pulled his dagger from its sheath.

I didn't hesitate, didn't think.

I called my power forward, and it flew to the surface eagerly. For too long it had been stifled, too long I'd had been forced to keep my magic inside me. The room immediately sharpened.

I grabbed Brynn, pushing her to the ground as a burst of air blasted outward from my center, rocking the sentries into the stone walls. The air overcame the torches, and the dungeon plunged into darkness.

Chapter 12

Roman

"Get the key!" I shouted at Brynn.

She sprung up from her crouched position, her form barely visible in the looming darkness. She lunged for the closest sentry. It was the leader, the one that demanded the password. He was sprawled out on the ground, momentarily disoriented. My air burst had caught them all off guard, but it was an advantage that wouldn't last for long. Brynn, still in the visage of Amina, dug through the sentry's pocket, throwing a lighter, pieces of paper, and other random junk to the floor.

"It isn't here!" she yelled back at me.

From my right I heard the sound of another sentry coming to, rolling onto his front, no doubt trying to push to his feet. I reared back, kicking him harshly in the face, and back to the ground. I hoped it was the man from Chambers, he deserved a swift kick in the face, but I couldn't be sure. I

rummaged through his pockets blindly. No key. I reached
for his neck, feeling for a necklace, a leather chord,
anything that could hold what we were looking for.
Nothing. "Check the others," I ordered Brynn. I spun
around at the sound of a lighter flicking to life behind me.
Brynn had taken it from the fallen sentry, using it to help us
see.

"Got it!" she shouted, holding out a long, old-styled key.

I jumped over a third sentry, taking the key from her hands.
I fit it to the lock on the wooden door, pushing our way
inside. I was immediately met by the sharp edges of two
daggers, both pointed directly at my throat. More sentries.
Judging by their bright red eyes, two more Fire Users.
Silently, I cursed myself for not anticipating this. I should
have known Amina would have more than one line of
defense.

The torches were still lit in this room and over their
shoulders, I could clearly see the center of the room where
the was-sceptre was kept. It was laid out on a table, a sheet
of velvet beneath it, the swirling mercury of the staff
writhing like a living creature. Half a step behind me,
Brynn entered the room. When the sentries saw her—saw
Amina—their surprise was obvious. Not only were they
surprised to see their Governor standing in front of them,
but alongside a Guardsman, no less. For the shortest of
moments, they dropped their guard. It was all I needed.

I leapt forward, lunging for the sentry on the right. I tackled him through the center, his dagger slicing wide over the top of my head. We fell to the floor, and I landed a hard right to his cheekbone, followed by another straight in his nose. From my left, I heard the clash of metal on metal as Brynn battled the other sentry using a dagger she'd stolen from the remaining guards. The sentry landed a strong kick in her midsection, pushing her back against the wall, and she lost her grip on her weapon. I pulled my own dagger from my belt, sliding it across the floor to her. *We don't have time for this,* I thought angrily. Our plane left in less than an hour and we still needed to get the others.

Below me, the Fire User reached back for the torches, the hair on my arms standing on end as the oxygen in the air sped toward the torch to feed the flames. Quickly, I murmured the ancient words under my breath, snapping an elemental shield around both me and Brynn. It wasn't a large spell, but I was still connected to Brynn, and along with the burst of magic I'd just used, my power supply was running low. The shield had no more than closed around us when the fireball blasted against me. I could feel the heat of the flames as they blasted into my shoulder, spinning me around. I grunted in pain at the impact, but otherwise, the shield held and I was unharmed.

I caught a glance of the corridor. The first four sentries were back on their feet, three pulling their weapons and heading our direction as one ran toward the stairs. Toward back up. I slammed the door shut in their faces. With the key inside with us, it bought us precious moments.

Brynn's elbow flew backward, crunching into the sentry's nose. "Roman, we need to go!" she shouted at me. "We have to run!"

"I'm not leaving!" I yelled back at her. "Not until we get what we came for!"

She only nodded once, not bothering to argue.

The room was small, the fighting quarters cramped, but still Brynn and I pushed forward, each attacking our sentries again. Amina had chosen her personal guard well. The sentries were skilled fighters, and for every cut, every hit Brynn or I managed to land, they returned it in kind. With our shields, the sentries' element was useless, but so were ours. The fire was sucking the oxygen out of the room, thinning the air around us and making it difficult to manipulate, and there wasn't a drop of water in sight to help Brynn. The fight raged on, the sound of the other sentries barreling into the door behind us like the pounding of war drums.

I had just managed to work myself to the side of the sentry, to put myself in a position where I could finally get the finishing blow I'd been working for, when Brynn's cry of pain sounded from the other side of the room. She'd been thrown by the sentry, her back slamming into the table holding the was-sceptre. Her opponent was stalking closer, his movements slow and calculated. He knew he'd won. Two more moves and Brynn would be dead.

With a roar, I summoned what remained of my element. I jumped as high as I could, spinning and kicking my opponent squarely in the face. He went down, face first into the floor, unconscious. I had no more than landed on the floor when I lunged for the sceptre, ripping the weapon off the table. I ignored the thrum of dark magic that leaked from its staff, the almost-painful burn from its metal. I spun a second time, using the sceptre as an extension of my arm, smacking the end off the face of the sentry that stood above Brynn, knocking him out cold.

My chest heaving from exertion and the rising temperature of the room, I reached down with one hand, grasping Brynn's arm and yanking her to her feet. She shouted in pain. I looked to her shoulder, dark red blood was seeping from a large cut. Judging by the angle of it, the cut would make it difficult for her to raise her arm. I thrust the sceptre into her other hand. The pounding from the other side of the door continued, louder and more insistent. "When that door comes down, I want you to run. Get the sceptre to Astrid then you get the others and get on that plane."

"What about you?" she asked.

I raised my arm, wiping the blood and sweat from my forehead. "I'll meet you there. But if I'm late, you do *not* delay. Not even for a moment. Do you understand me?" Brynn's eyes pinched shut and her mouth pursed. I knew she didn't like the idea of leaving me behind. It went against everything she was trained to do. I gripped her good arm, forcing her to look at me. "You leave me if you have to. Say you'll do it."

She nodded quickly, her face softer, more vulnerable than I'd ever seen it, even though she was still under the mask of Amina. Behind her, the wooden door split, the head of an axe breaking through. The sentries would be on us in moments. "Try not to kill them," she answered instead. "They're only doing as they were ordered. You don't want their deaths on your conscience."

I rushed to the center of the room, kicking the table over on its side then dragging it to the near side wall. It wasn't much for cover, but it would have to work. Brynn pushed her back against the wall next to the door, the sceptre flat against her stomach. Her eyes glowed a bright blue against the reds and oranges of the firelight. When the sentries came through the door, they wouldn't be able to see her.

The axe split through again. Then again. Two more and they would be able to reach the handle on the inside. I nodded to Brynn across the room before I ducked below the upturned table. I readjusted my grip on my dagger, digging as deep as I could into my power, into the smallest reserve I could find. Still connected to Brynn, I could feel her do the same, pushing some of it toward me. The boost of her power filled me, as refreshing as a summer rain. The axe hit again.

Again.

I cast my power outward like a net, searching for the two torches that lit the room and snuffed them out, descending the room into darkness.

The roar of the sentries was louder now, the large door swinging open on its hinges. Fresh air blew into the room from the corridor, the sentries moving quietly now in the darkness. I closed my eyes, listening to the sound of their heavily- booted steps as they came into the dark room. Three steps forward, they would have just cleared the edge of the door. A shortened step as one of them stubbed their toe on their fallen comrade. Two more steps and Brynn would have enough room to get around them unseen. The heat of a flame as one of them ignited their element. I peered around the edge, still in shadow. They were dragging the unconscious sentry from the center of the room, out of their walkway as they took the last two steps. I leapt from my position, staying low as I slid across the floor, slicing my dagger across two of their calves. The dagger went deep into the muscle, slicing them open and dropping them both to their knees. They screamed in agony, the torches behind them roaring to life as their power burst out of their hands. I pushed my hands forward, using the wind to shove the other two sentries against the far wall and hold them there. "Now!" I shouted at Brynn.

She pushed the broken door away, sprinting out into the corridor, the sceptre heavy in her grip. I held fast to my power, not letting the sentries budge an inch until Brynn had disappeared from view and up the stairs. I'd been so focused on her, I never saw the fireball coming. One of the fallen sentries had managed to create one again, the fireball smacking off my back shoulder. I grunted in pain, faltering a step and losing control of my element, forcing me to drop the sentries. My shield held just enough to keep the flames from burning my skin. I knew I couldn't take another blow like that. My shield wouldn't hold. I felt the air change, sizzle with heat. I turned in time to see four of the sentries, four Fire Users, their hands full of living flames. I dove toward the overturned table, the only chance for cover, just as the flames ricocheted off the wood, setting it ablaze.

Out of nowhere, a rush of power filled my lungs, a pocket of cool air in an overheated room. The connection between Brynn and I had snapped. She had broken the Changeling Spell. That part of myself that I'd given to her surged through me, filled every inch of my bones, my blood, my muscles. Another fireball hit the table, rocking it back into me. *I have to get out of here, have to make a run for it.* I knew if I stayed here, tried to battle it out, I would die.

With a roar, I ran out from behind the table, darting for the open door. Fireballs flew all around me, hitting the wall, the back of the door, until finally one landed, breaking through my shield and hitting me in the back of the leg. I screamed, the flames burning through my tactical gear, scorching my flesh. I didn't stop running. I was in the corridor now, the steps on the other end just a short distance away. With one last effort, I threw my power backward, creating a different kind of shield. A solid wall of air. I felt it as all four of them pounded against it, first with their flames, then with their fists. The wall held true.

I ran down the hallway, dragging my leg and slipping on my blood. I reached the steps, crawling on my hands and knees toward the top. I hadn't seen any other sentries yet, any other guards, but I knew what waited for me at the top. There was no way I'd make it past them, not like this. I sat down on the top step, daring to pause a moment. I dug through my non-existent power, whispering the same words I'd heard Brynn speak just an hour before. While I said them, I focused on his image, on the small details of his face, his hair. I stifled a scream as I felt my body change, my muscles constrict and contort, as if they were being ripped from my body. *How had Brynn endured this in silence?* When it finished, I looked down, but no longer saw myself. The spell had worked and I was now the exact image of my least favorite sentry.

I pushed myself to my feet and rounded the corner to the main floor. I didn't try to ignore the burning in my leg, the pain I felt with every step. Instead, I leaned into it, used it to my advantage. I dragged my hand along the curved wall of Council Chambers, until I practically fell at the feet of the Council guards I could sense standing there. There were two lines of them—at least fifteen warriors—daggers already drawn. Why they had waited up here instead of going down to the dungeon, or how Brynn managed to get past them, I had no idea. "Down there," I said hoarsely, pointing to the steps. My voice matched the sentry perfectly. "We managed to contain the traitor, but the others are hurt, and they need your help. He's a Guard member. He's using his magic against us. I fear if you don't help, we'll lose the sceptre." At first no one moved.

"Now!" I screamed. That spurred them on and the entire unit ran for the steps. When the last one disappeared, I crawled to my feet, immediately dropping the spell. It wasn't difficult for me to lose it. I'd barely had enough strength to create it in the first place.

I sprinted through Chancel Hall and down the open steps. At this time of night, I didn't have to worry about running into anyone but the street guards, and I was long past worrying about them. I had only minutes until the plane would leave. I had no doubt Brynn would do as I told her. They would leave without me.

Out in the open air, surrounded by my element, I pulled it to me, letting it fill my lungs and deaden the pain in my leg. It wouldn't stop the bleeding, but it would keep me from collapsing. The airstrip wasn't far from Council Chambers, just a few short roads, and I ran through them like a wild man. Finally, the airstrip came into view, the tiny plane barely visible in the shadows of the night. Next to it was a small figure, obviously female, but it wasn't until she moved and her red hair glinted in the moonlight, that I knew who it was.

"Cassie!" I shouted, not bothering to be discreet anymore. By this point Amina knew she had been betrayed, and no doubt she knew who was responsible. "Cassie!" I yelled again, stumbling on the uneven ground. Her head snapped my direction, a split second later she took off toward me. I tried to push to my feet, but my leg gave out. Cassie slid to the dirt next to me, cradling my head in her lap.

"Roman! Roman, what happened to you?"

"Plane," I managed between coughs. "Get me on the plane."

Isaac had joined Cassie by then, both of them hauling me to my feet. I cried out, the burnt flesh pulling at the muscle of my calf. They each supported an arm as they limped me to the plane. As soon as my feet touched the metal of the plane floor, I fell again and this time I knew I wouldn't get up for a very long time.

Chapter 13

Kyndal

The flight to Siberia was long.

It had taken Nero two days to prepare to leave. Going with us would be Dirk, his second in command, and twenty others Set had allowed. All hybrids, all soldiers that had proven themselves loyal to his cause. It took another day to secure the necessary payments and bribes to earn us a direct flight out of Egypt to Siberia. Travel in and out of the country was strictly limited by the local government, something I had witnessed when I'd entered Egypt so many months earlier. Apparently, Nero didn't have the same connections as Sandra, so he was forced to resort to a rich local with his own airstrip. He paid him handsomely for the use of his plane, making no promises to return it.

This plane was different than the ones the Kindred typically employed, with no room for cargo, just simple seats. I sat in the front row, tucked into my cushioned chair, my head against the window. Sleep had evaded me and I watched the skyline. Although the sun had just set roughly six hours before, it was already reappearing on the eastern horizon. Best I could figure, we were heading almost straight north at this point, where the days were longer, the sun barely resting.

My fingers worried at the edge of the simple tan T-shirt Nero had thrown to me before we'd left Helwan. Along with denim jeans and boots that he had stolen from who-only-knew-where, it wasn't much. Although I was happy to be rid of the clothes I'd been wearing that reeked of the blood and death of the dungeon, I hadn't been permitted a bath before I left, so the ends of my hair were thick and tangled with blood. I'd managed to tie it back in a loose braid to get it out of my face for now, but first chance I had, I planned to cut it off. I'd never appreciated the simplicity of short hair until I was forced to live without shampoo and conditioner.

"What are you thinking about?" Nero's deep voice cut through my thoughts, drawing my attention across the small aisle to where he was laid out across three seats, his long legs pointed toward me. His ever-present sword leaned against the plane wall next to him.

I glared at him, not about to admit to him that I'd been fantasizing about shampoo. "I was thinking about your sword. I want to know its name."

"Batil," he answered surprisingly. "The sword is named Batil."

"What language is that?"

"Arabic. It doesn't translate exactly, but roughly it means, extinct, or to the void." His sharp eyes cut to me. "Which is where my enemies end up after they face me." He didn't even attempt to keep the swaggering bravado out of his voice.

I snorted. "I think I'll use that sword when I kill you."

He raised his eyebrows, surprised by my outburst. "Will you now?" he asked.

"Did I stutter?" I snipped at him.

He chuckled darkly. "Still so angry. I would have thought you'd be thanking me by now."

Now it was my turn to laugh. "Thank you? Why the hell would I do that?"

Lazily, he crossed one foot over the other. "For getting you out of Egypt and away from Set. Delivering you from that cell, for however brief of a time. I thought you would appreciate the change in scenery."

I crossed my arms. "The bars may be gone, but the cell isn't. I'm still a prisoner." He shrugged, blowing me off. I peeked over my chair to the rest of the plane. "Why is this plane so full of hybrids? It seems strange to me that Set only allowed you to bring one of your men. Your men who would know the Coterie the best. But. . ."

"But what?" Nero interrupted.

I shrugged, showing the same indifference he had shown me. "It seems to me he wanted to separate you from them. So you couldn't stop him from turning them."

Nero pushed off the wall and leaned forward, his dark eyes boring into me. It was a struggle to not smile. I'd hit a nerve. "You think you know everything, don't you, *girl?*" he sneered, slipping back into his old habit. "I think you will find that I am not the fool you believe me to be."

"I don't think you're a fool," I disagreed. "I think you're a fraud."

"How is that?"

"When I first met you, you boasted that you weren't scared of anything, and yet you were so scared to challenge Set, you switched your allegiance at the first opportunity."

"It is not cowardice to survive," he interrupted.

"It is when it comes at the cost of your morals. You claim to worship Thoth, say he is the only true deity, and yet you threw away your entire belief system to work for his enemy, even though it is clear that you hate the hybrids. The Coterie was built on a system that reveres strength,

178

purity, and legacy, a system you intended to pass on to your son. And yet here you are, traveling to kill him. So, tell me, what kind of man does that make you, *Commander?*"

"Set won't kill Roman," he contested. "He wants to keep the Guard alive."

I shook my head. "And you believe him." I turned my back on Nero, curling up in my seat and returning to window watching. My body was suddenly overcome with exhaustion and before I knew it, my eyes closed, and I felt the beginnings of a dream.

I am standing at the base of the tree house, the familiar sounds of the Allegheny surrounding me. The sun is out, shining brightly through the thick canopy. Cherry Run is moving swiftly next to me, the waters glinting beautifully in the midday sun. The Rafiq bond courses through me proudly, announcing my arrival, and before I can move toward him, I hear his steps rush through the undergrowth. They're off somehow, his right foot not stepping as strongly as the left.

He's limping.

Four quick steps and I'm up the ridge, meeting him at the top. He's standing there, his breaths coming in the same short rasps as mine. I look him over quickly, and just as I thought, he's putting all the weight on his left leg. Self-consciously, my hand goes to my hair. Luckily, I don't look like I do in real life, whatever magic that runs the dream, changing me into different clothes. The blood is gone from my hair, the tresses long and combed. "Hi," he says simply. I can't help but smile. It has been days since I've seen him, and I'm overwhelmed by the relief that comes with the sight of him. Before I realize what I'm doing, I close the distance between us, throwing my arms around him, nearly knocking him back. I squeeze his neck tightly, burying my head in the crook of his neck. He returns the gesture, locking his long arms around my waist, pressing me to him. I close my eyes, breathing in his familiar scent of burnt leaves and open wind. Finally, after several long minutes, I step back out of his embrace.

"I'm sorry," I say, my eyes on the ground. "I shouldn't have done that."

His fingers gently grab my chin, raising my eyes to meet his again. "Don't apologize. Ever," he says softly. His emotions course through me. Love. Relief. Concern. They mix together in a heady combination that makes it difficult to tell the difference between them.

"I'm sorry," I say again, but before he can stop me, I hold up my hand. "Not for the hug, this time." I take a deep breath. Apologies have never been my strong suit and this one had been weighing on me for a while. "I'm sorry for the way I acted last time I saw you. I shouldn't have argued with you like that, but I was just trying to protect you."

His hand moves from my chin, his full palm cupping my cheek. I wait for him to kiss me, but he doesn't move closer. "Like I said, no apologies necessary. It's good to see you, I've been worried."

I step out of his reach, clearing my head. "Worried? Why?"

"I've tried to reach you for the last few nights and I never could. I thought something might be wrong."

Flashes of the dungeon floor, Set's power ripping through my muscles from shock after shock tear through my memory. They had kept me down for days, long after I'd been dragged from the dungeon. Whatever it was about Set's magic, it prevented me from accessing my power, rendering me practically useless. I couldn't summon a single flame, let alone dreamwalk. I shake my head, pretending to be less concerned than I am. "Nothing to worry about," I tell Roman, clearing my voice when it falters. "I did it," I say, moving the focus away from me.

Roman pauses for the briefest of moments, no doubt reading my emotions, which I promptly lock down. The last thing I want is him worrying about me even more. "Did— did what?" he stammers and I cringe. Roman never stammers.

"I separated Nero and Set. I'm on a plane to Ozero Lobaz with Nero as we speak. We'll be there in a matter of hours. Please tell me you're off the island and already waiting in

Siberia." Roman's eyes bulge out, his excitement bursting forth. His face would be comical under any other circumstances, but I didn't laugh now, I was too worried.

"Kyndal, that's fantastic!" he yells, he arms flying wide. He grabs the sides of my face, his gaze slipping to my lips and again I think he's going to kiss me. Again, he doesn't. It's hard to not feel the sting of rejection. It takes a moment for his excitement to slow down, for him to realize that I'm not celebrating like he is. "What's wrong?"

"Why do you do that?" I ask him.

"What?" he responds, clearly confused.

This so wasn't important right now, but I couldn't help but ask it. I may never have another chance. "You look at me like you want to kiss me, your emotions tell me you want to kiss me, but you don't. Why not? Do you not—do you not want me anymore?"

"Of course I want you," he says immediately. I check the emotions behind his words, pleased to find they match. Resolve. Honesty. "I just didn't want to assume. After everything you've been through, everything that happened..."

I cut him off with a kiss.

It was no light or innocent kiss either. I press my mouth to his, clasping my hands on either side of his face. It takes him half a second to respond, then his arm snakes around my waist yanking me forward and molding my body to his. I move my hands through his hair, pulling playfully on his long ends. He pulls back just enough to speak, pressing his forehead to mine. "Are you trying to say I need a haircut?" he whispers.

"I'm not one to judge," I answer, tugging on his light ends again. "Anyway, I think I like it." He smiles, closing the distance between us and kissing me again. I melt into it, allowing myself a few more moments of happiness before I finally pull away, although I don't leave his arms. "I'm scared," I admit. "Set sent twenty of his strongest hybrids with Nero. Them, plus Nero and Dirk, that's twenty-two warriors. They're expecting a large force to be at the compound. How many are with you?"

"We arrived at Ozero Lobaz two days ago. There are seven of us. Isaac, Cassie, Mallory, Grady, Brynn, and a warrior named Briar. You make eight."

"Who's Briar?" I ask immediately, the name unfamiliar. "She better not have anything to do with that limp you're trying to hide from me, because if she does, we're going to have some words." I don't bother to temper my tone, allowing its sharpness to show I'm not happy that he hasn't mentioned it yet. As if he could hide it from me.

"You're cute when you're jealous," he responds, calling me out on my attitude, softening it with a sweet kiss. I simply cross my arms, waiting on an answer. "Briar had

183

nothing to do with my leg. I had a small run in with a Fire User while escaping the island," he explains, his nonchalant tone not matching what I could feel behind them.

"Someone burnt you?!" I respond, immediately livid, but before I can say anything else, he interrupts.

"Like I said, it was nothing. I'm healing it. And as for Briar, she is from House Taurus but served Amina in her army. Amina threw her in Maat's Hollow for treason, but Astrid got her out for me."

"Why?" I push. I had never heard of Briar before, didn't understand why he would risk breaking her out of the Hollow at such a dangerous time.

"Honestly, I'm not sure," he answers. "It was something she said during her trial about helping you return to Awen. I think she can see things we can't." He chuckles quietly at some silent memory. I hadn't heard that sound in months. It almost breaks my heart. "Grady thinks I'm crazy—that Briar is crazy."

I smirk. That sounds like him. "I agree with Grady," I admit. "Even with Crazy Pants, eight versus twenty-two. I don't like those odds."

"We've faced worse," Roman responds. "And we have the advantage of location. This compound is a fortress. When we arrived, it was a wreck. No one had been here since

Set's attack months ago. It was snow-covered and broken down, but we've been working nonstop for the last two days. We've rebuilt the wall and are currently working on interior repairs. We all left so quickly after Set's attack, several of the Coterie men that died then were still here, frozen underneath the ice and snow. We burnt their bodies." Better than they deserved, *I think bitterly, although I'm smart enough not to say it aloud. "Once we cleared them out, we raided the weapons cache and distributed them around the compound. No matter how Nero attacks, we'll be ready."*

"Set ordered Nero to bring the Guard back alive."

"A fact we can use to our advantage," Roman responds. "If he isn't authorized to kill us, then he'll hesitate."

"He's going to use me as a shield," I say. "It's the whole reason he brought me. He thinks you won't attack if it means risking my life."

"He's right. We didn't come all this way just to lose you. You have to find a way to get away from him, and once you do, we'll unleash hell."

I woke from the dream to the plane loud with activity. The hybrids were growing restless, many of them now out of their seats. With no humans around them, the hybrids did little to hide their true selves. Their eyes were bright, surrounded by bloodshot veins, their teeth sharp and serrated as they prepared themselves for the coming battle. We would be landing soon, I could already feel the plane descending slightly. I cut a glance over to Nero, who still sat facing me, his eyes intent, completely immune to the flurry of men and women around him. I trained my face to a still mask, making sure I gave no emotion away, nothing that could indicate that I had just been with Roman. My dreamwalking was no secret, but my ability to communicate with Roman was. My last secret.

"What's the plan?" I asked him. I needed him to tell me *something*, so I could figure out how to escape it and reach my friends. My Guard.

"We'll land shortly," Nero answered. An answer and yet not.

"And then what?" I pushed. "You obviously can't land right by the compound. Where will we hike from? If you expect me to march with you as your shield, I want to know what you are planning."

"I never said you would be my shield," Nero corrected quietly.

I was taken aback. "But you told Set. . ." I interrupted.

"I told Set that I required collateral. I said nothing of a shield."

"You aren't taking me to the compound?" I demanded, not caring that my voice was rising. The plane was small. They could all hear me anyway.

"No," Nero answered simply and I clenched my fist in anger. "You are not going to the compound."

Chapter 14

Roman

I stood atop the Coterie rampart, overlooking the frozen lake and the tundra beyond. The wind was biting at this height, whipping across my cheeks. There was no heat to fight the cold, the braziers that were staked into the stone sat unlit. We couldn't risk the fire, couldn't risk giving the hybrid Fire Users access to their element. If I wanted to, I could use my power to push the cold away, to keep it from cutting at my already sensitive skin, but I didn't. I couldn't afford to use the strength. Battle would be coming soon enough.

It had been hours since I spoke with Kyndal, and still there was no sign of Nero and his men. I'd told the others everything Kyndal said about Nero's band of warriors. Hybrids meant we had to go for the heart to kill them. Unlike a normal wraith, our Kindred blades wouldn't expel the demon through a flesh wound. Boots sounded on the stairs behind me. I didn't have to turn to know it was Cassie.

"For the record," she said, coming to stand next to me, "I hate this place. It's freezing and there's no color here. Everything is white." She was right, of course, but I didn't respond. I knew her well enough to know it wasn't necessary. She looked out over the landscape, scanning the horizon. She wore gear similar to mine. It was a mixture of the whites and grays that annoyed her so much, but it would help us camouflage into the environment. Cassie had added a stocking cap to hide her bright red hair. Two daggers were strapped to her belt. A spear in her hand. "Everyone is in position," she said after a moment.

I nodded, "Good." I'd taken our small band of warriors and split us into groups of two, making sure to separate the Guard members and mix up the elements. With such small numbers, we had to stretch ourselves as much as possible. Cassie and I, Water and Air, were positioned atop the wall above the front gate, charged with protecting not only the main entrance, but also the newly-constructed wall. Our repair job had been quick and with minimal available materials. We knew it was a weak spot, one Nero might try to exploit. Grady and Mallory, Earth and Air, monitored the opposite end, watching the mountain side, making sure Nero didn't try to sneak in that way. Brynn and Briar, Water and Earth, were positioned inside the wall for the moment. They were tasked with monitoring their elements, searching for any changes in the lake below us or the trees and hills that spotted the horizon. Brynn also held The Book of Breathings. She'd modified the amplification spell we'd used in Cairo. When Nero's men attacked, Grady, Brynn, and I would combine powers and put up our elemental shields. Then Brynn would use the newly modified spell to expand our shields to cover the others. If we could take away the enemies' elemental weapons while maintaining ours, it would even the playing field. It would take a large amount of power to sustain the spell over so many people. Yet another reason Brynn was inside the wall, on the lake surface. She was our power source. We'd lose her as a fighter, but the closer she was to her element, the easier it would be for her to have the necessary strength to withstand the spell.

Finally, Isaac was posted inside the compound. We'd argued for an hour about it, Isaac insisting he could still fight. "You need my element. I'm your only Fire User," he'd pointed out.

I'd ground my molars, knowing that on the surface, he was right. His element was highly offensive, something we desperately needed, but I couldn't do it, I couldn't risk his life. "You quit drinking your tonic to access your powers and your wounds come back. You won't be strong enough to use your element anyway. You stay in the compound. If Nero gets past us, you're our last hope."

"You're hiding me inside like a helpless child," he'd accused, his voice rising.

"I won't allow it," I'd shouted back. "You take one step outside the compound during the fight, and I'll knock your ass out myself."

He'd stormed off after that, pissed but following orders. I'd take it. He could be mad at me all he wanted, as long as it kept him alive.

"Do you feel anything yet?" Cassie asked, pulling me from my internal review.

I pressed my power forward again, same as I had a dozen times. I used the biting wind to cast it out across the land, simultaneously shooting the Rafiq bond like a spear into the air, searching for Kyndal. Both came up empty. "Nothing," I responded. Something was wrong. They should have landed in Siberia by now. Why wait to attack? What was I missing?

"Roman." My name hissed through the wind, whipping me around to the center of the compound. Brynn was crouched next to the meat shack, sitting cross legged, The Book of Breathings open on her lap. Her eyes were closed as she chanted quietly. She looked perfectly comfortable, as if she didn't sit atop a frozen lake in the freezing cold. The voice I heard hadn't been hers, but rather Briar's. I looked to the woman next to Brynn. Her chest was rising and falling heavily, her sharp green eyes glowing wildly as if they were seeing things far off, things only she could see. "The earth is trembling," she warned. "It burns."

Just as the words left her lips, a surge of power flew through me, as cool and refreshing as the rivers of the Allegheny. Brynn's power reaching out to me. I grabbed ahold of it, pulling it into me, wrapping my own power around it, before sending it to Grady like a rain-soaked wind. Moments later, the smell of fresh earth filled my nose. Grady had added his power to the triad, completing our circuit. I could feel both of them, pull on their power and strength if I wanted to, and they could do the same. Brynn's chanting changed, and I recognized the sound of the shield spell, could feel the drain on my strength as she formed the shield, as she expanded it to fit all six of us. The pull on me was small, nothing compared to what it should have been. I knew Brynn was taking the brunt of it, using her own power first in order to allow Grady and me to conserve our magic.

With the added power, I called to my element, my eyes changing immediately, my senses heightening. I'd always been able to use the wind to enhance my hearing, even more so than other Kindred. The wind brought the sound to me. Strong as I was now, I tapped into that strength and that was when I heard it. The stretching of cords being pulled tight, followed by the whistling of something moving quickly through the crisp air.

Arrows.

"Cover!" I yelled. My warning came not a moment too soon. Cassie and I dropped below the wall as a dozen fire-tipped arrows sailed over the rampart and into the courtyard of the compound.

I looked to Cassie crouched next to me. "They missed," she assured me. I didn't know if she was talking about herself or Brynn and Briar. I knew Brynn hadn't been hit, I would have felt it through the spell.

I leapt to my feet, not bothering to try and hide behind the stone wall. "No," I said, my stomach dropping. "They didn't." They weren't aiming for us. They meant to hit the courtyard. The compound was made of several different buildings. Most of the arrows had landed innocently in the snow, but a handful of them had landed in the roof of one of the training buildings, catching its roof ablaze. The fire started small, the wooden roof damp from the snow, but steadily, unnaturally, they grew until the entire roof roared with flames. There had to be Fire Users close enough to control them. They knew we wouldn't have any of the braziers and torches lit. They knew they would have to get fire into the compound somehow.

From outside the wall, on Mallory and Grady's end, a roar of battle cries emerged, drawing my attention. "They're coming," Grady shouted, his weapons drawn. Mallory raised her metal bow from her lap, knocking an arrow before letting it fly over the wall.

"How many?" I shouted to them. Another arrow flew. Then another.

"Ten!" Grady shouted back. "Maybe twelve!" Only half Nero's force. Where were the rest of them?

"Roman, look!" Cassie was pointing out onto the frozen lake, where five hybrids were now advancing, less than fifty yards away.

"Drown them," I told her. Not having to be told twice, Cassie summoned her power, calling to the icy depths below us, cracking the lake apart underneath the hybrids' feet. They had been advancing slowly, but as the ice began to crack under their feet, they picked up their pace, running for the front gate. One dropped into the icy water and Cassie quickly closed the ice over her head, locking her in her watery grave. The others, however, didn't quit. Didn't even pause to look after their fallen comrade. Cassie broke the ice at their feet, but when the ice turned to water, they simply ran on top of it.

"They're Water Users," she pointed out needlessly. They were moving faster now, twenty yards from the front gate. I couldn't allow them to reach the gate. If they breached our defenses we were finished. I summoned the air, the wind kicking up around me, blowing the too-long-strands of hair into my face. I threw my arms out toward the enemy, blasting them backward, skidding on the ice. It would buy us precious moments.

The fire still roared behind us, consuming the training building. "Get that fire out," I ordered Cassie, when suddenly a sharp pain erupted in my stomach. I screamed in pain, doubling over. Another hit, this time across my cheek, cutting the skin open.

The burning building forgotten, Cassie grabbed my shoulders, her eyes searching me frantically, desperately trying to find the source of my pain. "Roman! Roman, what's happening?!"

I growled, straightening myself, although I kept pressure on the pain in my stomach, at the burn that lived there. "It's not me," I grit through my teeth, a different kind of pain taking hold. "The wounds aren't mine. They're Kyndal's. Someone is hurting her."

"Kyndal?" Cassie echoed. "She's not even here."

"She's close," I growled. She had to be. If she wasn't, I wouldn't be able to feel the echoes of her pain. "I have to find her. I have to get to her."

I staggered for the steps, but Cassie moved in front of me, blocking my way. "You can't leave us."

"This is Kyndal we're talking about," I argued. "I'm not going to leave her to be tortured." I tried to step around her, but again she stood in my way. "Move Cassandra."

She didn't even blink at my use of her full name. "They won't kill her. They'd lose all their leverage. Nero is baiting you, trying to draw you away from the compound because he knows he can't penetrate the walls. It's a trap."

"I don't care," I growled. A slow, searing pain ripped across my bicep, one that I knew came from a blade. "I'm sorry." I leapt over the outer rampart, using my element to ease my landing on the frozen lake.

Above me, Cassie screamed at me, cursing my name and ordering me to return to the rampart. I ignored her. I disconnected myself from Brynn and Grady, knowing that the further away I got, the harder it would be for them to hold on to me. Ahead of me, the four remaining Water User hybrids were advancing again, having regained the ground they'd lost. I didn't think. I zoned out everything except my singular goal.

Find Kyndal.

The hybrids broke for me at the same time I took off sprinting across the lake. I unsheathed my daggers, tucking the sharp blades under my forearms. Two steps from the first hybrid, I jumped, riding the air over his head and landing behind him. Before he could turn to attack, I flipped the dagger in my left hand, ramming it through his back, between the two ribs that I knew led directly to the heart. I held my dagger there for only a moment before ripping it back out and shoving the dead hybrid to the icy ground.

Three remain.

I could feel the next two hybrids approaching. They weren't even attempting to conceal their footsteps. I spun, dropping to one knee. Their weapons swung high and I took my twin daggers, ripping them through the thick meat of their thighs, making sure to cut their femoral arteries. Blood splattered across my arms and neck, thick and hot, as they each dropped to one knee. Their screams tore through the crisp air, but were soon silenced when a pulse of air flew from my center, forcing them onto their backs. I switched the grip on my daggers, slamming them both down simultaneously through the hybrids' hearts, until I heard the metal embed in the ice below.

Only one left.

I stood to my full height, wiping the hot blood from my face. The last hybrid was several paces away, smarter, more cautious than the others. He waited with his dagger in his hand, a snarl across his face. I could feel the blood lust coming off him, his desire to kill me. It would do him no good. He was all that stood between me and Kyndal. He might not know it yet, but he was already dead.

I took one step forward when a sharp pain tore across my shoulder blade. The cut was deeper, sharper than the others. No doubt because I was closer to Kyndal. I roared as I felt the skin open up underneath my heavy gear, the hot blood trickle down my back. The unexpected wound pulled my focus, and for the shortest of moments, I hesitated. The hybrid took advantage. He lunged forward, tackling me to the icy ground below. My daggers flew from my hands, skittering across the ice as the hybrid pushed his knee into my abdomen, into that first echo. His fist ricocheted off my cheek, further opening the cut there. I worked my hands between my body and his, and with all the might of my element, pushed him off me and flying into the air. As he flew backward, I got to my feet, reaching for the dagger that had landed not too far away. The hybrid was strong and well trained, and had managed to land on his feet, but the moment his feet touched the ground, I threw my dagger, the blade embedding deep in his chest. He fell back, dead before he hit the ground.

I heard the sounds of battle echoing off the mountain side and stone walls of the Coterie as I gathered up the weapons within reach. The hybrids were still trying to breach the wall. I didn't look back. I felt Kyndal's presence, her strength and magic coursing through my veins as the power of the Rafiq bond drew me to her. I took off, leaving behind Ozero Lobaz and moving over the small ridge that separated the lake from the rest of the land. There was a small nest of evergreens just over a hundred yards away. The only cover even remotely close to my location. I ran for it, ignoring the growing ache of my muscles, the burning of my wounds. *I could feel her. She was there.*

I slowed my approach as I neared the trees, smart enough to know I couldn't go barreling in to save her. She wouldn't be alone. I pulled on my power, using the air to cushion my footsteps, dampen the sound they made on the snow. There was a large evergreen on the outside of the treeline, and I crept up to it, using its large trunk for cover. I peered around the side, my heart breaking at what I found.

She was there, kneeling on the ground. Dressed in a ragged T-shirt and simple jeans that were soaked through from the snow, her hands were bound behind her, tied with vines to the trunk of a large tree. Her head was sagging forward, her long brown hair obscuring her face. The snow was stained red at her feet. She wasn't alone. There were four of them. Two hybrids I didn't know, but judging by their eyes, were Earth and Water Users. And Dirk and Nero.

Nero stood next to her, his obsidian blade hanging from his side, the tip of it dripping blood. Her blood.

Rage ignited inside me and I burst through the trees and into the small clearing.

Chapter 15

Kyndal

I'd felt him coming.

Nero had picked this location to hide me for many reasons. The tactical advantage, for one. With the trees around us, it obscured us from view but also kept the harsh elements of the tundra off our faces. It was also close enough to the compound that Nero knew that if he tortured me, Roman would feel it and wouldn't be able to resist coming after me. I was the bait in his trap and it had worked perfectly.

The one thing Nero hadn't considered was how pissed Roman would be when he did find me.

Roman tore through the trees of our hideout, wielding his double blades, his eyes glowing bright and golden, his tan skin splattered with the blood of his fallen enemies. Not a dream. Not a hallucination.

He was real.

The closest hybrid never stood a chance. Roman ripped one dagger across his throat, the other thrust through his chest before the Water User could even raise his hand in defense.

I pulled at my restraints, trying to muscle my way out of them, but they were tied by an Earth User. There would be no way to break them on my own. The Earth User and Dirk broke toward Roman, the battle officially on. Nero, although he'd moved a few steps away from me, his back turned my direction now, still hung back, watching the fight instead of jumping into it. For the life of me, I didn't understand why he didn't join the fight.

Forgotten for a moment, I began to chant quietly under my breath. The words were sluggish, difficult on my unpracticed tongue, some of them almost forgotten, as it had been so long since I'd used them. But as I finished, my power rushed out toward Roman, filling him with the strength and familiarity of me. I felt his power wrap around mine, welcome it as the missing piece of his strength. I was instantly in tune with his strength, the power of his magic and element. So much stronger when we connected to each other, even more than our other Guardsmen, fore there was no one like us in the world.

A Descendant and her Rafiq.

I pulled on our bond, taking the necessary power from him to heal my injuries, knowing that it would fix him too. I called to my internal fire, to the rage that had been boiling beneath the surface for so long, waiting to be set loose upon the world. My hands ignited, a scalding heat that burnt through the vines holding my wrists captive. I ripped my arms outward, snapping the vines and releasing me. I leapt to my feet, knowing I had a split second before Nero realized what had happened. I lunged for him, knocking the large man onto the ground. I scrambled to my feet, launching a fireball toward Dirk. He saw it coming and dove out of the way at the last moment, but the result had been the same. That small distance he'd created gave Roman the opportunity he needed to gain the upper hand on the Earth User hybrid. He spun, kicking the hybrid in the face, then drove his dagger straight through his heart.

Nero had climbed to his feet by now, his movements unhurried, calculated. He dragged the tip of Batil through the snow as he stalked closer to me. That same stupid blade he'd used to carve through my skin. The Void, it meant. "I should have killed you the moment you showed up at my gate," he growled. I matched each of his steps with one of my own, moving backward for every one of his forward. My element could not help me, for fire could not harm another Aries, and I was unarmed.

"I made you a promise about that sword," I answered, nodding to his weapon. "I plan to keep it."

Nero struck. His left arm lashed out, swinging for my face, forcing me to dodge to my left, toward his sword hand. The blade sliced forward but I jumped back at the last moment. The tip of the blade nicked my shirt but missed my skin. I ducked low, kicking out at the side of Nero's leg, buckling it underneath him. He growled roughly as his knee hit the snow. I kicked again, this time at his shoulder, hoping to loosen his sword from his hand, but his other arm came across, knocking my leg away. From that same arm, his hand built a fireball, hitting me with it at point blank range.

The fire couldn't hurt me, but the strength of the blast threw me into the air and across the clearing. My back smacked into a nearby tree before I dropped to the ground, next to the dead Water User hybrid. I groaned in pain, a cough breaking loose. The snow beneath me splattered with red, but I ignored it. Beyond the dead hybrid, Roman and Dirk were still locked in battle, each beaten and bloodied. Just as Nero and I had been matched for element, so were Roman and Dirk. I still didn't know Dirk's House, but his eyes shone with the same golden intensity as Roman's.

I pushed to my feet when something silver glinted in the sun, drawing my attention. In the hybrid's belt, forgotten by everyone, was his dagger. I ripped it from its sheath, twisting the familiar hilt in my hand. It had been months since I'd held a true Kindred blade. Months since I'd felt the comforting weight of its metal.

"That blade will make no difference," Nero jeered. "You cannot beat me. I am decades older and stronger than you."

I rolled my neck, loosening the knot that had formed there. His condescending tone was really starting to get on my nerves. With a shriek, I lunged at him, dagger drawn high. He raised his sword to block the blow, sparks flying off the clashing metal. I landed at his feet, his left cross swinging toward my face, dropping me low. I retaliated with an uppercut, one that connected with his jaw. I felt the small bones in my hand crunch under the impact. Broken. Again. I hissed at the sharp pain that was zinging up my left arm. I was unable to ignore the growl I could hear from Roman behind me, absorbing the echo. Nero and I parried back and forth for a while, each taking our fair share of hits. He was physically stronger than me, and his sword gave him an extended reach, but I was faster, able to weave in and out of his reach. No matter what either of us did, neither of us could seem to gain the upper hand. Behind me, Roman and Dirk were stuck in the same battle, neither able to overtake the other.

We don't have time for this, I thought. Something had to change if we were going to be victorious. The others were still fighting in the compound and needed our help. My hand was throbbing, the small bones already trying to reconnect and heal themselves. With no other idea of what to do, I built a fireball in my hand. Before I could throw it, before I could even pull my arm back to release, a fireball shot out from behind me, zinging so closely to my face, I could feel its heat on my cheek. It went past me, past Nero, right in between Roman and Dirk—breaking them apart. I wheeled around to find the source, prepared to fight another enemy. But it wasn't a hybrid.

It was Isaac.

Dressed in the same white and gray gear that Roman wore, his eyes a bright red, Isaac held a torch in his left hand. Excitement leapt through me. I hadn't seen Isaac in months. The last time I'd seen him, he was bleeding-out on the floor. I knew he was alive, Roman had told me as much, but there was a difference between being told something and seeing it yourself. Without a word, Isaac reached over and grabbed a piece of flame from the torch, rolling it in the palm of his hand. He launched it at Dirk again. Then another. Another. Dirk turned and ran from the attack but he wasn't fast enough. I called to my element, lifting a wall of flames in front of him, cutting off his retreat. Dirk skidded to a halt, but the edge of his tactical pants caught the fire, lighting him ablaze. He was so focused on putting the flames out, he had no hope as Roman took two simple steps forward, turned his dagger and hit him across the face, hilt first. Dirk hit the ground, unconscious. The flames crept up his leg, and with a small burst of power, I pushed them to burn faster. Burn hotter. Within moments, Dirk's entire body was on fire. He didn't even have time to scream.

I watched him burn to death and yet felt no guilt, no remorse. It was a justified end for a man who had done so much evil in his life.

Roman stalked away from the burning body, standing near me, his strength and magic filling every corner of my being. I was acutely aware of him, every nerve in my body screaming at me to turn toward him, but I couldn't allow myself to look his direction. I knew I'd forget all about the battle if I did. *The others still need our help*, I reminded myself. There would be time for reunions later. Instead, as one, Roman, Isaac, and I turned to Nero, who'd stepped back, doing nothing to intervene as his second-in-command burned to death. He looked to each of us in turn, his dark, calculating eyes searching for a gap in our defenses. He found none. He was surrounded. Outnumbered.

He threw Batil into the snow at our feet.

Defeated.

We bound his hands with vines, the same kind he had used to tie me to the tree. They wouldn't hold him forever, but it was enough to get him back to the compound. Once there, Grady could reinforce them. Holding my dagger loosely in my broken hand, I picked up Nero's sword, eyeing him as I felt the weight of the blade in my hand. It was lighter than I anticipated, perfectly balanced. My blood stained the tip. "What's happening at the compound?" I asked Isaac, keeping my eyes trained on the Coterie Commander. Isaac and Roman were gathering the weapons, pulling them out of the snow, off of Dirk. At least what was left of him. I didn't bother smothering the remaining flames, they would die out on their own.

"The hybrids breached the wall. The stone held, but there were so few of us, a handful of them managed to get inside.

Brynn and Briar were forced to fight. When I left, they were still dealing with them."

"And *why exactly* did you leave?" Roman demanded. His tone was biting. I'd never heard him talk to Isaac that way. I risked a glance at the two men.

"That's a strange way of saying thank you, Rome," Isaac snipped back.

Roman took a challenging step forward. He appeared angry, but I could feel his emotions. He wasn't angry at Isaac, but at himself. For Isaac, he was *worried*. "I ordered you to. . ."

"Your orders were bullshit," Isaac interrupted, not backing down from his best friend. His commanding officer. "You were on your own. Stop giving me hell. . ." his words were cut off with a hacking cough that forced Isaac to lean forward and grab his abdomen. Their argument forgotten, Roman rushed forward, grabbing his friend by the shoulders, helping him to straighten. I flinched when I saw the blood on Isaac's lip.

Roman's eyes cut to mine. *Not a dream*, I told myself again. *Real*. "He's fine," he said, but I knew he didn't mean it. I was missing something.

"We need to get to the compound," I said, then looked to Nero again, who still knelt in the snow before me. "On your feet," I ordered him.

He glared at me but complied. Using the sword as a prod, I pushed him toward the compound. As we passed his fallen soldier, his second-in-command, Nero paused. "Don't even think about it," Roman said gruffly, a few steps behind. "I already put a shield around us. Your element won't help you."

"Pick up the pace," I said, pushing Nero again, back toward the compound. It was several hundred yards away still, and we needed to get there quick. The others could still need our help. We crossed the icy tundra but saw no sign of any remaining hybrids. When we finally reached the compound gates, we found them broken open, the large white doors cut in two. The air was still, no sounds of battle coming from within. I cut a quick glance to Roman, to gauge his thoughts. He shook his head slightly. He was worried. Just because the compound was quiet didn't mean the threat was gone. I knew Nero had sent thirteen hybrids to the compound. Some of them could be inside, waiting to ambush us.

Roman went first, moving soundlessly between the broken doors, around the main building and into the courtyard. Isaac followed him, Nero and I a step behind. The courtyard was quiet, and I saw no sign of my friends. There were three dead hybrids in the snow, another leaning half-off the stone wall on the opposite end, a metal arrow sticking out of his chest. One of the smaller buildings, the training one, was smoldering, its roof laying in cinders as if it had been lit on fire. Not far from it was a blood trail that led directly into the back door of the main building.

I whistled softly to catch Roman's attention. He turned and I pointed with my dagger at the blood trail. He nodded. He'd already seen it. We turned as a group toward the back door and into the compound. The walls here were made completely of stone, so any amount of sound traveled and echoed through the hallway. It wasn't difficult to find them. They were in the great dining hall, the same room we'd once sat in and eaten with the Coterie soldiers. The very place I'd watched Nero sink a dagger into Dirk's shoulder for disrespecting him. The table was still there, but the chairs were broken and overturned, the large chandeliers swinging wildly with fire, throwing shadows onto the walls in the shape of dancing demons.

All five of my allies were there, each showing signs of battle wear. Grady and Brynn fought fiercely against two hybrids, Mallory and Cassie finishing off a hybrid of their own. Another woman, one that could only have been Briar, fought bravely against a Fire User hybrid. The room was chaotic and no one noticed our arrival. I kicked Nero's knee out from under him, pushing the large man to the floor roughly, then handed my dagger to an ashen-faced Isaac. It would be no good in my broken hand anyway. "If he even thinks about moving, kill him."

I stepped fully into the room, calling out to the chandeliers that hung above. I was still connected to Roman, and my power filled me easily. With a single thought, three of the hybrids, all but the Fire User, went up in flame. Unlike Dirk, they screamed, their shrieks echoing off the walls, their arms flailing wildly as they tried to outrun the pain.

My friends jumped out of the way, watching with confused fascination as their enemies suddenly combusted. From the corner of my eye, I saw Roman take advantage of the situation. He joined Briar, and together, they killed the final hybrid. One by one, the three hybrids dropped to the floor. Once I knew they were dead, I pulled back on the fire, squelching the flames and returning my power to quiet.

Almost simultaneously, they all turned to stare. Their faces were covered in sweat and blood, their chests heaving with the exertion of the battle. I met each of their eyes individually until finally I landed on Mallory, whose caramel eyes shone with tears. Roman's presence neared as he took his place by my side. As if he couldn't bear to be away from me, even for a second. "Not a dream," I whispered.

They were all here. They were all alive.

I was alive.

I was free.

For a moment, no one said anything.

I felt increasingly awkward. Silence had always made me uncomfortable, and everyone was staring at me. I knew I looked like a wreck, but it was as if they were staring at a ghost. "Someone please say something," I begged them.

Cassie broke first, shoving a broken chair out of her way and rounding the large dining table. Her pace was quick as she came toward me, throwing her arms around me in a monstrous hug. I returned the gesture the best I could, careful of both my broken hand and the sword I still held on to. "Is it really you?" she whispered.

"It's me," I assured her.

She stepped back, keeping one hand on my shoulder, looking me over. It took everything I had not to flinch from her gaze. I looked like hell. "We've really missed you," she said. Next to me, I felt Roman's heart swell and yet still I didn't look over to him. Not yet. Not with everyone around.

Behind me, Nero groaned. "If you're going to do the heartfelt reunion thing, just kill me now. Put me out of my misery," he whined.

I turned, having forgotten about the captive Commander for a moment. "What are we going to do with him?" Cassie asked.

"I'll take care of him," Grady offered. He marched over to Nero, placing a soft hand on my shoulder when he passed. A simple gesture, but one I understood. I'd missed him, too. Grady pulled Nero to his feet, pushing him out another doorway and back into the hall. With a quick glance my direction, Roman followed him out. Isaac excused himself as well, although he didn't follow the other two. His coughs had returned, and I eyed him warily as he left the room.

With Nero gone, I took my turn greeting the women that remained in the room. A brief hug for Brynn, as she'd never been one for touch. Her hair was even shorter than the last time I'd seen her. She looked stronger, but there were worry lines under her eyes, a weariness that hadn't been there before.

Just past her, Mallory still stood where I'd first seen her. "Hello, friend," I greeted her, placing my injured hand on her shoulder, squeezing lightly. Her eyes still shone with tears, but if I knew Mallory, she was working hard to hold in her emotions. I didn't want to make it worse for her. "It's good to see you."

Surprisingly, she was the one to pull me forward and squeeze me tightly. "I looked for you for months," she said quietly in my ear, her voice breaking. "I'm so sorry I never found you."

My throat burned with emotion, my own eyes brimming over. "You have nothing to apologize for. Thank you. For trying."

I pulled away from her, looking to the last person in the room. "You must be Briar."

She nodded, a stiff gesture. "I am, Descendant."

"You don't need to call me that," I told her. "Thank you, for helping my friends. My—Roman."

"Your gratitude is unnecessary. It was my honor and my destiny to come here. To help deliver the Descendant back to her people, so you may restore faith to the Kindred."

I raised an eyebrow in astonishment, looking to Mallory. *Crazy*, she mouthed to me. I nodded in understanding. "Well, all the same. I'm glad you're here," I said to her.

"There's a lot to catch you up on," Brynn said, pulling my attention. "A lot to be done."

"Yes," I said wearily. "I know."

"Before any of that happens," Cassie interjected. "I think Kyndal would like to get cleaned up, get some rest. We could all use the break." A kindness. To let me clean myself up.

"Is that safe?" Briar asked.

I nodded. "For now. All the hybrids are dead. It will take some time for Set to realize Nero was defeated and for him to come for us. We can rest for the night."

"Then it is decided," Cassie said. "Kyndal, let me show you to your room. You can borrow some of Mallory's clothes."

I smiled at my friend, always the caretaker, always looking out for me. "Thank you, Cassie."

I trailed my fingers along the stone wall of the bath house. Different than the rest of the compound, these walls were smooth, painted with scenes of a god I assumed was Thoth. Part human, part animal, just as I had seen Set portrayed, Thoth stood between the sun and the moon, a book clutched against his chest.

After Cassie had shown me to my room, she gave me the clothes she had promised, along with an array of shampoos, conditioners, and soaps they had packed. The sight of them about made me cry. Then, she'd led me down a side hallway on the lowest level. "Best we can figure," she'd explained, "this was Nero's private living quarters. It's bigger than the rest of the rooms and far more extravagant. And—" she opened a small pocket door, "it has its own private bath house." Larger than my bedroom back in Awen, the room had a walk-in bath, way more than was necessary for just one person.

All around me, the candles glowed a soft orange, the flames dancing as I moved. I didn't know who had come in ahead of me to light them. It wasn't a lot of light, but it was enough for me to see. "Thank you," I said.

She placed her hand softly on my shoulder. "I can take a look at your hand if you want me to," she offered.

I shook my head. "It will be fine. I've healed worse." It was true. In the months of fighting in the pit, I'd gotten quite good at patching myself up. Cassie nodded. If she heard the unspoken pain behind my words, she didn't ask about it. She simply slipped quietly from the room.

I set the small pile of clothes and towels down on the floor, then lined the bottles of shampoos and soaps up by the water's edge. I shucked my dirty boots and socks off, throwing them into the corner of the room, then dipped my toe into the clear water. Quickly, I pulled it back, sucking in a breath. *Just as I thought, freezing.* But then, an idea formed, and I placed my hand on the water's surface, calling to my element. Not enough for a flame, but just enough to heat. I sent the power out into the water, willing it to swirl inside it, to reach the depths of the pool. Soon enough, steam billowed throughout the room.

Slowly, careful of my various injuries, I removed the filthy clothes I'd been wearing, tossed them away, and sunk down into the water. I groaned at the feel of it, the light sting of my cuts. I allowed the water to pull me under, soaking my hair. Using the supplies Cassie had given me, I washed my hair thoroughly, repeating the process until finally it rinsed clean. I cleaned my skin next, scrubbed at it until the dirt and blood disappeared. Suddenly thankful for how large the bath was, I waded to the other side, to where the water was clear and sat on a small stone seat. I let my head fall back against the ledge and closed my eyes. A tug pulled at my center, at the Rafiq bond. Roman was looking for me. I opened myself up to him, allowing him to follow the bond like a trail, until finally, I could feel him right outside the door. I waited for the door to open, could hear him breathing on the other side of it, but he didn't move. I sent a small emotion to him—curiosity. Both a question and an invitation.

Slowly, hesitatingly, the door pushed open. I didn't open my eyes to look at him. Not yet. Not as he shut the door behind him, or as I heard his clothes join mine on the floor. It wasn't until the water lapped gently against me as he lowered himself into the bath that I finally opened my eyes. The steam was thick in the room now, but it swirled on the water's surface, obscuring his body but giving me full view of his face. He was standing on the opposite side of the large bath, the water at his waist. He looked tired, worried. I wondered if seeing Nero had upset him, but I held off from asking just yet.

His eyes scanned over me slowly. I didn't shy away from his gaze, although there was little to protect my bare skin from view. I wasn't scared of him. I never had been. His gaze lit me on fire, making me desperate for more, a spark of life after months of keeping my emotions hidden. The memory of his kisses inside the dream were still fresh in my mind—and I couldn't help but wonder—would it be the same in the real world? His stomach was riddled with bruises from the battle, wounds too small for an echo and yet I felt them, nonetheless. The light scarring of his brand along his ribs shone in the flicker of the candlelight. "Where are the others?" I asked him as he stepped deeper into the bath.

"Grady, Briar, and Brynn are guarding Nero. Cassie and Mallory are out cleaning up the courtyard and monitoring the wall just in case. Isaac is pouting," he answered. Another step closer. "I think they are trying to give you some space. They didn't want to crowd."

"What's wrong with Isaac?" I asked. He took another step, but didn't answer. Instead, he reached past me, his body coming dangerously close to mine as he grabbed the washcloth and soap I'd sat there.

"I don't want to talk about the others," he whispered. I watched as he poured a generous amount of soap onto the washcloth, lathering it between his hands. He grabbed my right hand, running the washcloth along my skin; up my arm and around my shoulder, his hand dipping dangerously low. I didn't bother telling him I'd already washed myself, instead my head lolled backward, my eyes shutting involuntarily as he moved across my neck and to the other side.

"That feels amazing," I admitted.

I could feel his satisfaction. Could imagine the sideways smirk that would play at his lips. "I told you I was good with a loofah." I giggled. It seemed so long ago he had said that. We were different people then, back when the world seemed simpler. When ancient gods weren't roaming the Earth, hell bent on killing us all. He reached my left hand, lifting it gently from the water. With heartbreaking tenderness, he straightened my fingers, cleaning each one thoroughly. "This seems better."

"Mmhh," I answered incoherently. "I heal faster than I used to. Can you still feel it?" I asked, finally looking at him. He was closer than I'd realized and I was immediately met with the brilliance of his blue eyes. He paused, his eyes dropping to my lips. Love, desire, and longing filled me. I couldn't tell if they were my emotions or his. I didn't care. I closed the distance between us, my lips pressing against his. He responded immediately, deepening the kiss. The washcloth forgotten, his hands gripped at the stone edge of the bath on either side of my head, and I knew he was using every ounce of self-control to keep his hands there. I sat up taller, breaking his hold on the wall but not my lips. I dove my hands into his wet hair, then turned him, sitting him down on the bench I had just been on, straddling his hips. His long arms wrapped around me, pressing my body to his, the bath water sloshing around us wildly. He stood from the bench, and I wrapped my legs around his waist as he stepped out of the bath, refusing to be parted for even a second. I kissed his lips, his neck, his strong shoulders as he walked us out of the bath house, using his power to open the door to the bedroom, to close the one that led to the hallway. I called my own power forward, lighting the candles and torches in the room, bringing the dormant fireplace to life. He laid me down on the soft furs of the four-poster bed, neither of us caring that we were dripping water everywhere. His hand trailed down my sternum, over my hip, leaving an icy fire in its wake. He paused, pulling back, even as his grip tightened, kneading at the skin, pulling at the old scar that marked my hip. "What's wrong?" I asked him, my voice breathy.

"I never thought I'd have this again," he admitted, marveling at me. "Part of me worries this is all a dream. That I'll wake up at any moment and you won't be here anymore. I don't think I could take it. I wouldn't survive if I lost you again."

My heart broke at the pain in his voice, the pain I knew I had put there when I left with Set. I caressed his cheek and he leaned into the touch, kissing my palm, my brand. "I'm not a dream," I assured him. "I'm real. I'm sorry for the pain I've caused you. Please forgive me. I love you." The words were simple, and yet I'd never meant anything more in my life. I wanted to promise him I'd never leave him again, but part of me knew I couldn't do that. War was coming, and neither of us knew what would happen.

As if the words broke him, he leaned down, capturing my lips again. I pulled him close, fitting his body to mine and for some time, there was no more talking.

Chapter 16

Roman

I woke before dawn.

Kyndal and I never made it out of the extravagant room, instead we had fallen asleep beneath the warm furs adorning the bed. When I woke, Kyndal's limbs were wrapped tightly around me, her wild hair covering her face. I leaned over, placing a soft kiss on her forehead and pulling the covers over her shoulder before sneaking out of bed and dressing in the gear I had been smart enough to bring with me the night before. I stood staring out the window over the landscape. It had started to snow, but without the brutal wind of the day before. The thick snowflakes covered the courtyard, removing the carnage of yesterday, making it almost appear peaceful.

There was a quiet knock at the door, followed moments later by Grady poking his head inside the room. "Roman..." he began, but I held my hand up, putting a finger to my lips to silence him. He looked at me in confusion until finally he noticed Kyndal. His gaze lingered for a moment longer than I prefered, so I grabbed him by his shoulder, pushing him out into the hallway and pulling the door shut behind me.

"What do you want?" I asked Grady, scruffing my hair.

"How is she?" he asked, nodding toward the door.

"She's been through a lot," I answered him, looking past him, deep into the hallway. The memories of what she'd admitted to me in the dark hours of the night were still fresh in my mind. "She'll recover. She's strong."

"And you're together again?" he asked.

My eyes cut to him. "Is that a problem for you?" I demanded roughly. Maybe rougher than I should have, but I didn't care.

"I just think that with everything going on, you're handing Amina a reason to lock you two up."

"And I think you should mind your damn business," I retorted. A spark of heat lit in my chest. Kyndal was awake.

"The Guard laws still stand," Grady pointed out, not backing down.

I shook my head. "Why are you talking about Council law? We broke Council law when we fled Awen to get away from Amina and her tyranny. We're already fugitives in the eyes of our beloved Governor. By now, there's probably a kill order out on us. At this point, whether Kyndal and I are together doesn't even matter. If you want to come up with an excuse to keep us apart, you're going to have to do better than that." I turned back to the door, then wheeled back around on Grady. "On second thought—from now on—you can keep your opinions on our lives to yourself."

"Whatever," Grady mumbled. "While you two were *occupied* last night, Cassie and Mallory went into the closest town to try and get word to Daniela and find out what's happening in Awen. They'll be back within the hour. We're all meeting in the dining hall to decide what to do next."

"Fine," I grumbled as I went back into the bedroom, slamming the door behind me.

Kyndal was walking out of the bathhouse, pulling her gear over her head. It was too big for her. She'd lost weight, lost muscle since she'd been away. Even with the fights Set put her through, she wasn't as toned as before. She raised her eyebrows at me. "You were kind of tough on him." Of course she had heard everything.

"Grady thinks just because he has an opinion, he has to share it with the class," I grumbled. "Taurus."

"You sure that's all it is?" she asked. "You haven't exactly always seen clearly when it came to him."

I sat on the edge of the bed, reaching for her. I pulled her forward until she stood in-between my knees. I toyed with the edge of her shirt, keeping my eyes trained there. "Why?" I asked quietly. "Because he killed me once, or because of his feelings for you?"

She ran her fingers through my hair, and I closed my eyes, reveling in her touch, at the warmth it brought. "Either," she answered softly, not denying that he cared for her. "Both."

I shrugged, finally meeting her eyes. "He irritates me."

She smiled down at me. "Understatement of the century." She leaned down kissing me once, softly. "You have nothing to worry about with Grady. I'm not going anywhere." She stepped out of my arms, grabbing her boots and pulling them on. "I want you to catch me up on everything before the meeting. I've missed too much." *To business, then.*

"What do you want to know?" I asked. So much had happened, where would I even begin?

"Start with Isaac," she responded. "Something is wrong with him. You yelled at him when he came to help us, then he was coughing up blood and Kindred don't get sick."

I sat back, choosing to cut to the chase. Kyndal didn't appreciate it when someone danced around bad news. "Isaac isn't supposed to use his element anymore. The blade he was injured with in Cairo was laced with a magical poison. When Amina delayed his treatment, the poison got into his bloodstream. In order to save him, Brynn made a tonic that he has to drink regularly. It stifles all magic in his body. It saved his life. . ."

"Yet he lost his connection to fire," she finished for me. "But yesterday. . ."

"I had ordered Isaac to remain in the compound, to only engage with the hybrids as an absolute last resort. He lied to me and didn't take his tonic like he was supposed to. His magic came back, but so did the poison."

"He risked his life to save us, and you yelled at him for it."

She didn't understand. "And right now he's upstairs paying the price for it. His fever came back, and he was puking his guts up last I saw. I don't want him taking risks like that."

She smiled. "It's not your choice what he does. Isaac loves you like a brother. You would have done the same for him. I think you should cut him some slack."

"I'll consider it," I conceded.

"Good," she responded, doing a horrible job hiding her growing smile. She knew she had won that argument. "What about Sandra? Have you heard from her?"

"No," I answered quietly. "I don't know if I will. It's too dangerous for her to reach out now."

She crossed the room again, dropping to a crouch before me. "I heard no mention of her within Set's camp," she said. The bond tugged with regret and guilt at her words. "If I had known she was there. . ."

"You would have done what?" I interrupted, leaning forward. Meeting her eye to eye. What did she have to feel guilty for? "You had no way to get to her."

"I could have told you that she was alive. I would have told you where she was if I knew. I swear it."

I nodded, grabbing the tips of her hair and twirling it through my fingers. "I know that."

She nodded, the bond settling again. Whatever need drove her to declare those words was satiated. "What happened on Awen?" she asked, changing the subject, even as she rose to her feet, putting distance between us again. "Why were you forced to flee the island?" She'd asked this question last night, but I'd refused to answer at the time. I didn't want to upset her so soon after getting her back.

I huffed a breath. "Simply put? Amina." She leaned back against the wall, crossing her arms, well aware that the explanation would be longer than that. I dove into the entire tale, starting from the moment Kyndal left with Set. I explained to her the change in Kindred politics, how Amina had declared herself Governor, claiming credit for our victory in Cairo. The warriors she was locking in Maat's Hollow on an almost daily basis, how she tried to get us to out Daniela, and the risks Astrid and the others had taken in getting us off the island and out of Amina's reach.

"You realize that the Guard escaping is going to piss her off," Kyndal said when I was finished.

"What else would you have had us do?" I answered, frustrated. I was tired of this same argument. "You still wish we hadn't left? You wouldn't be sitting here if we hadn't." How could she *still* think it wasn't worth it?

She leaned forward, intent. "That's not what I'm saying. But it sounds like a big part of her credibility with the Kindred was the pretense that the Guard was under her control. When they find out you fled, she's going to lose that facade. It could make her desperate."

"The others are expecting us in the dining hall," I responded, standing up and cutting her off.

"We need to talk about this," she pushed.

I scratched absently at the back of my neck. "I know, but not now. Later?"

She paused a moment. "Fine," she eventually conceded. I strapped my dagger to my belt, Kyndal doing the same. No sign of the blade she'd taken from Nero. "What'd you do with Nero's sword?" I asked her as nonchalantly as possible.

She paused, her dagger mid-sheath. "Batil?" she questioned. I'd never heard the name of the blade before. *Arabic for void,* I thought, remembering my lessons from years ago. Seemed appropriate. "I left it in my room. Why?"

I shrugged. "Curious," I mumbled.

Clearly not buying it, Kyndal sheathed her dagger and came to stand in front of me. "I don't want the sword. You can have it if you'd like, it makes more sense for you to carry it anyway."

I shook my head. "I don't want it. I think you should wear it."

She blanched. "Me? Why?"

"It's a good weapon, it would be a waste to not use it. Plus, I think it would really piss Nero off if a girl carried it." She laughed, and I remembered something I'd heard her say. "Back during the battle, you told Nero you'd made him a promise about the sword. What was it?"

Her smile disappeared, her face growing deathly serious. "That I would kill him with it."

I absorbed the words, waited for them to hurt, for me to feel *something*. Nero was my father, after all. I should be upset at the idea of his death. And yet I felt nothing. I'd mourned the loss of my father years ago. Nero was nothing to me. "Good, it's settled. You carry the sword."

Someone had put the dining hall back together. The table was centered in the room again, the chairs, at least the ones that hadn't been broken, tucked underneath it. The fireplace was lit, along with the torches on the wall, but the chandeliers hung cold and dark. With a flick of Kyndal's wrist, they burst forward with flames, properly lighting the room.

Although the change in lighting no doubt alerted the others to our arrival, no one turned to greet us. Grady, Brynn, and Briar sat at the far edge of the table, picking over a variety of food. Some of it was from the little bit of provisions we had brought with us, the rest they must have scrounged up from around the compound. Isaac was noticeably missing, probably still upstairs puking. I made a mental note to go check on him after the meeting. "What's with Briar?" Kyndal whispered in my ear. Confused, I looked up at the group again. Sure enough, Briar kept glancing at Kyndal, her mouth moving quickly, as if she was muttering something.

I shrugged. The behavior was odd, but my gut still told me Briar could be useful somehow, that there had been a reason I'd gotten her out of the Hollow.

Kyndal and I rounded the table, each taking our places. Kyndal sat down next to Brynn, and I took the seat next to her. With a smile, Brynn handed over her food, offering it to Kyndal. She accepted it gladly. *Good, she needed to put on some weight.* Grady was seated at the head of the table, doing his best to avoid looking at us. At me. "How'd you sleep?" Brynn asked Kyndal.

"Good," Kyndal responded plainly around the food in her mouth, although I could feel her deeper emotion. The cheekiness hidden behind her answer. Last night had been amazing. We'd been completely wrapped up in each other, as if after months apart we were both trying to make up for lost time. I smothered a smile at the memory. "That bed definitely beat the floor of a cell," Kyndal was explaining, no doubt trying to ignore the emotions I was giving off. Grady's eyes finally snapped up at that, staring directly at Kyndal, the pain at her admission obvious. She had explained to me already, during the wee hours of the morning where we laid in bed talking, how Set had treated her. The harsh conditions under which she'd survived. How he'd tortured her for information, forced her to compete in the pits—his sick version of gladiator fights. It twisted my stomach to hear what she'd been through, but it also explained a lot. Watching her fight out on the snow yesterday, she'd been different. Kyndal had never hesitated during battle before, never shown fear, but yesterday she was more aggressive, tenacious, bloodthirsty. She went for the kill when before she would have moved to disable. She'd burned four people alive, including Dirk, someone she knew personally. The scorch marks on the cement behind Grady were a permanent reminder of her actions. As I replayed those images in my head, there was only one word to describe it.

Ruthless.

"Cassie and Mallory are late," Brynn pointed out. She was right. It'd been over an hour. "They should be back by now."

"Travel isn't exactly easy up here," Grady answered, finally looking at me. "They'll be here soon, but we should begin without them. We need to decide what our next move is."

"We can't stay here," Kyndal pointed out. "Set knows this is where we are. He'll expect Nero to come back soon, or at the very least send word of his victory. When he doesn't, Set will send more soldiers, or worse. . ."

"He'll come here himself," I finished for her.

Kyndal nodded.

"We need to figure out what Set's next move will be," Grady said. "If we can figure out what he wants, maybe we can get there first, and finally get in front of this war."

"He wants Maat," Kyndal answered him. "When we were in Cairo, *before* he blew up the Egyptian Museum, he told me a story about how he and Maat used to rule Egypt together. According to him, she cheated on him with Thoth and kicked him out of the Blacklands."

"So, this entire thing is a revenge scheme to get back at an old girlfriend?" Grady asked, drolly. He was clearly skeptical.

"Revenge is rarely that simple," Kyndal snipped back, not taking kindly to his tone. I hid a smile. "She took his kingdom from him. Before he was banished to the Redlands, Set was worshipped. When Maat replaced him with Thoth, he was demonized, vilified. She stole his power from him. To a god, power is everything. He created the wraiths to try to get that power back."

Brynn leaned forward on the table. "Thoth, or Hermes Trismegistus as he is known, created the Kindred with Maat. An entire race of warriors built to defeat Set's creation."

"Exactly," Kyndal agreed with her. "He was defeated *again*. And now he wants to kill Maat."

Grady popped a piece of bread in his mouth, his eyebrows furrowed. "But Maat lives in the Inbetween, right? How does he plan to get there to fight her?"

"Kyndal," I said, looking to Grady. "Kyndal is the key. Her Descendant blood was the reason she could cross the river inside The Hall of Two Truths. He plans to use her to get to the Inbetween."

"This doesn't make sense," Brynn interjected. "If Kyndal is the one thing Set needs to get to the Inbetween, why hasn't he done it already? Why didn't he do it months ago?"

"Because he's a chaos god," Kyndal answered. "You guys haven't seen him work like I have. You don't know him like I do. Set rarely takes the most immediately course of action. He goes for the move that creates discord, that sews distrust. I've watched him do it with the Coterie soldiers. He's been pitting them against the hybrids for months. He set the hybrids up as superior, rewarding them for their efforts and then punishing the Coterie soldiers for the same actions. He doesn't just want to defeat the Kindred. He wants to humiliate us."

The wheels in my head turned as I began to put the pieces together. "He let Kyndal go. Why would he let her go if she was the only key he needed? Maybe she isn't the only thing that gets him to the Inbetween, he just wants us to think she is."

"Roman. . ." Kyndal interjected softly. I understood why. She thought I was being idealistic. That I was trying to find any excuse not to put her in danger, in the center of this all.

"I'm serious," I stopped her. "Why would he let you go, unless it gained him something he needed?"

Grady piped up. "He had too much faith in Nero, he didn't think we would beat him."

I shook my head. Something didn't feel right. Set was smarter than that. We were missing something, I just couldn't put my finger on it.

Just then, I felt the door to the outside burst open, the freezing cold air rushing through the hallway and into the dining hall, almost extinguishing the flames. Mallory and Cassie rushed into the room, both nearly frozen and wind whipped. Their eyes were large, panic written across their faces. I was immediately on edge, looking behind them for any imminent danger.

"We have a problem." The words came from Mallory this time, not Cassie. Mallory didn't exaggerate.

Kyndal stood, I followed her a moment later. "What's wrong?" she asked. I could feel the panic rising inside her as well.

"I spoke with Daniela. Amina went into a rage after you all escaped. She questioned any soldier she could get her hands on, demanding to know where you were. When no one would give you up, she started arresting soldiers, holding public trials in the arena. She whipped those who didn't give her the answers she wanted, executed others who flat out refused her. Then two days ago, Amina and a large battalion of soldiers disappeared. Left Awen."

"Where did they go?" I asked, ice water running through my veins. "She doesn't know where we are." There was no way she could be coming here.

"We weren't sure at first," Mallory answered. "Daniela didn't have any insiders in the battalion, she's pulled several of her people back after we tipped her off that Amina was on to her organization." She looked to Cassie for support, an odd showing of insecurity. "Then Cassie got a call from Darius."

"No." The word ripped out of Kyndal. A lance to my heart.

"Amina and her soldiers arrived yesterday." Mallory turned to Kyndal. "Amina is in Marienville."

Chapter 17

Kyndal

"I'll kill her!" I shouted. The torches, the fireplace, the chandelier all popped and crackled as my temper flared.

"Kyndal," Roman's voice whispered softly, his hand brushing my arm. I ripped mine away.

"No," I growled. "I mean it, Rome. If she touches Lydia or *Allie*," my voice broke at my aunt's name, but for only a split second. "I. Will. Kill. Her."

"What did Darius say, exactly?" Brynn asked, and I was grateful for it. She was much more capable of being logical than I was at the moment.

Cassie looked to Brynn, the relief on her face was obvious, happy to be given an excuse to look away from me and my anger. "His details were limited. He just said that Amina and a large force of her soldiers flew into the private airport yesterday morning and upon her arrival she took immediate command of the compound."

"And my aunt? Lydia?" I demanded of Cassie, not caring that Brynn was talking to her.

Mallory piped up, never one to shy away from me. "He didn't mention them."

"It's a trap," Grady said from behind me, forcing me to turn. For Roman to turn as well.

"What was that?" I demanded.

Grady's arms were crossed, his face hard. "She didn't pick Marienville at random. She couldn't find us and she knew that going to Marienville would push your buttons. It's a trap. One that we cannot afford to fall into."

Roman took a step forward, shoulder to shoulder with me. "Amina doesn't know that we have Kyndal back, why would she target her family?" My heart swelled at his immediate defense of me.

"Because they're an easy target," Grady responded immediately. "None of the rest of us have any family to speak of. Amina may not know for a fact that we have Kyndal back, but she isn't stupid. She had to wonder why we waited to escape the island, what would make us finally risk leaving. It wouldn't take her long to connect the dots. Not to mention we don't know what information she's learned since we left. Since she can't find us, she's trying to draw us to her. We can't let her do it."

"You really think Amina would hurt humans?" Cassie asked Grady. "Innocent people?"

Briar, who up until now had been silent, scoffed. "Of course she would. Look at what she's done to her own people. She's locking us up. Whipping us. Executing us for no reason. If she's willing to do that to the people she claims to care about the most, there isn't much she wouldn't do."

I stood up tall. "If she's in Marienville, she could decide at any moment to hurt my family. I can't let that happen, I won't. I'm going to Pennsylvania."

"That's exactly what Amina wants you to do!" Grady shouted. "You're playing right into her hands!"

"Shut up, Grady!" Roman demanded. "You were fine with the risks when it involved coming to Siberia, and now all of a sudden, you're unwilling to help?"

"Coming here was the *tactical* move. It gained us Kyndal, it eliminated Nero. There is no advantage to going to Marienville." His words cut at my skin. The man I thought I could trust, so idly throwing away the lives of those I loved.

"I don't buy it," Roman disagreed. "We both know there were other reasons for you to come here." There it was. An accusation, even though I'd told him there was no reason for concern. The others looked back and forth between the men, confused. *This is not the time or place for this to happen.*

"Careful what you say to me," Grady growled back.

Roman went silent, the muscles in his jaw pulsing with agitation. I popped my knuckles, annoyed with both of them.

Cassie shook her head. "Amina was supposed to attack Set. The Guard isn't enough of a reason for her to call off the attack. She wasn't planning on taking the Guard to Egypt anyway. What are we missing?" The healer was trying desperately to keep the group focused, from descending into arguing and chaos.

Roman's eyes cut to Brynn who had been quiet and stoic this whole time. The movement was quick, but Grady caught it. "What?" he demanded of both of them. "What are you hiding?"

I looked between my Guardsmen. Waiting for Brynn or Roman to say something. To fill everyone else in on the missing piece of the puzzle. "We stole the was-sceptre," Brynn admitted.

The room broke, erupting into yelling. Each person shouted at the other, with Brynn and Roman just standing there, like the eye in the center of a tempest. I joined them in their stillness. Roman had told me the night before about what he and Brynn had to do. Although we did not agree on everything, at least there were no more secrets between us. As everyone yelled and screamed, I sent my feelings down the bond to Roman. Reassurance. Love. I may be angry with him, but he didn't deserve to shoulder this burden alone. I knew he hated that everyone was angry, but he would do it again if he had to. He would always take the blame if he thought what he had done was right. He would always sacrifice his own feelings for those he loved.

"Why didn't you tell me?" Grady shouted at Brynn and Roman. Although not connected to him, I could almost feel his emotions. Knew exactly what he'd be wondering. *Why did you keep this a secret? From me of all people?*

"We didn't have a choice," Roman began. "Astrid forced my hand."

"You had a choice whether or not to tell us," Grady threw back at him. He raised his voice, drawing the attention of the others, silencing their protests. Even as Grady yelled, Roman just stood there, letting him get it all out. When Grady noticed I wasn't as upset as him, he whipped around, looking to me. "Did you know about this?"

There was no more time for lies. No time for games. "Yes," I answered simply.

"And you don't have a problem with it? Their choices are the reason Amina went to Pennsylvania. The reason your family is in danger."

I crossed my arms. "*Amina* is the reason my family is in danger. No one else." I wouldn't let him pin this on Roman and Brynn.

Grady scoffed, now glaring at Brynn. The Guardsmen he'd always been closest to. "When we left Awen, you both made the plane late, beaten and bloody. You claimed you'd been discovered by Amina's men during your escape, but there was no mention of the sceptre. You looked me right in my face and *lied*."

"We were trying to protect you," Roman cut in. It was strange, I thought. Just moments ago, Roman was accusing Grady of loving me. The two men were nearly at each other's throats. Now, Roman was trying to protect him.

"Where is it?" Grady asked. "Or do I not get to know that, either?" His tone was biting, but no one blamed him.

"We don't have it," Brynn answered, unfazed by how pissed off everyone else seemed to be. "Astrid does. She wasn't going to help us off the island unless we got the sceptre for her. So Roman and I used a Changeling Spell to get into Council Chambers and we stole it. End of story." I knew that wasn't the end of the story, but Grady let it be, for now.

"Well, Amina sure seems to think you still have it," Mallory pointed out. "Her control of the people hinged on that weapon. The Guard defecting simply plays into the narrative she's created. You guys are rogue, unruly, insubordinate. She can spin your disappearance to her advantage. But losing the sceptre," she tilted her head, "you stole it from Council Chambers, from supposedly one of the most secure locations in Awen, and you defeated her personal sentries to do it. It makes her look weak. No wonder she's looking for you. She's been looking for an excuse to kill you, and you two handed it to her."

"This could be an opportunity," Briar threw in. "If her public image is weakened, we could take advantage, push her out of power."

"You're wrong," Grady said through his teeth. "Amina is not the focus. We need to get to Set. Find out what his real plan is, like I said before."

"How do you suggest we do that?" Cassie snapped at him.

Grady's arm flew out, pointing down the back hallway. "There is a Coterie Commander locked in the basement! We interrogate him. Find out what Set is doing next."

I smacked my hand on the wooden table, the sparse tableware rattling. "He won't tell you anything." This debate was getting old, and we were getting nowhere. When I spoke again, my voice was tight. "Even if we knew *exactly* what Set was going to do next, there isn't much the seven of us can do about it by ourselves and without the sceptre. In case you forgot, he is a god, and his army of hybrids is thousands strong by now. We have to rally the Kindred to even stand a chance. We have to deal with Amina first. That means going to Marienville."

Grady threw his hands up. "Do what you want, Kyndal. You always have." He took two steps backward. "I'm going to interrogate Nero." Then, he turned and left the room. With an apologetic glance, Brynn followed him out.

I spun, facing Roman, a million questions passing between us, even without a single word spoken. "I need to check on Isaac," he said. I knew it was an excuse, that he needed to cool off after all the arguing, all the accusations toward him, but I nodded anyway. I let him go.

"I'll go with you," Cassie added, following him down the opposite hallway. I watched them go, my emotions a tangled mess. Part of me wanting to follow him, the other part rooting my feet to the floor. Mallory's feet shuffled across the stone as she joined me, watching her girlfriend go. "Leave him be for the moment," she advised. "Cassie will take care of him. Trust me." I could hear the smile in her voice. It was always there when she talked about her longtime partner. Mallory leaned over, nudging my shoulder. "Nobody is going anywhere today. Choose a weapon and meet me in the training building. We need to knock some rust off your skills."

I wasn't rusty. Not by a long shot, but Mallory didn't know I'd been fighting for months. Either way, training sounded good. I needed to blow off some steam. "The training building doesn't have a roof," I pointed out.

"And?" Mallory asked. "Suck it up. I'll meet you there in four minutes." I smirked. Mallory—always so precise.

Briar took a tentative step forward. "Might I accompany you?" she asked. "I could use the practice."

Mallory glanced at me quickly, then looked to Briar. "Fine. Just don't expect us to slow down for you."

The building was not exactly as I remembered. It had never been a particularly cozy place, made fully of stone and cement, but now after months of neglect, it was not only cold, but broken down. As far as I knew, Roman and I had been the last people inside the building. It's where we were when Set attacked the Coterie. The weapons were still bolted to the wall, the multiple punching bags still hung from the ceiling. The chalk outlines of the sparring rings were faintly visible in some places, completely gone in others. But now, after the entire back half of the roof had burnt, there were charred, wooden beams catapulting into the stone floor, crisscrossing over each other. Sunlight filtered over the snow-covered beams, the blackened sides peeking through the crisp, clean snow. Below them, among the wreckage, I could just make out the edge of the heavy leather bag Roman had ripped from the ceiling, still laying right where he'd left it.

I walked the room, placing my hand on each torch bolted to the wall, bringing them to life one by one. It was unnecessary for me to light them individually, but I wanted to do it that way. My heart was still pounding from the news of Amina's arrival in Marienville, the possible danger it put my loved ones in. I worked hard to control the rising panic I could feel. Being forced to focus my power on a small task helped to clear my mind and take the edge off that part of me that wanted to travel to Pennsylvania immediately, grab Amina by the throat, and demand retribution. The flames worked their magic, blanketing the room in a soft orange glow, just strong enough to keep the bite of the cold off our skin.

Mallory wasted no time with talking and pleasantries. She knew I was angry, set to explode, and that I needed to get my aggression out. She entered the training ring, Briar following suit, both armed with their choice of weapons. Within moments, the clash of metal rang through the training facility.

The first time I'd fought Mallory, my powers had just manifested. I was completely inexperienced, and she'd handed me my ass easily. She was lightning quick, her movements so fluid she oftentimes reminded me of a dancer. She'd cut me several times within the first two minutes of our sparring session, and by the end of it, my blade was still dry of her blood.

Things were different now.

I lunged forward with two large overhand hacks of my sword. *Nero's sword,* I corrected internally. I was carrying it, as Roman had encouraged me to, and yet I couldn't think of it as mine. Mallory raised her own sword to block my attack, pushing out with a strong front kick. I spun to the right to avoid it, moving right into Briar. Her dagger lunged forward, but I knocked it away with my blade. My hit was strong, loosening her dagger from her grip. It clanged loudly as it flew across the cement floor. Now weaponless, she was an easy target. I leapt at her, landing a hard left cross to her cheekbone, dropping her to a knee. Once down, a final front kick to her chest put her on her back, outside the training circle. I twirled the pommel in my hand, taking a moment to revel in the victory. The sword was magnificent; both perfectly balanced and surprisingly light. I understood Nero's attachment to it.

My body buzzed with adrenaline as I turned to face Mallory. I wiped the sweat from my forehead, pushing a few errant strands of hair off my face. I'd lit all the torches when I'd entered the building and Mallory's eyes glowed a brilliant yellow against the orange hue of the flames. She cracked her neck as she sized me up. I knew her, knew what she was going to do next. I murmured the words under my breath, snapping a shield around me just before a blast of air flew in from the ripped open ceiling. I could feel the wind, its biting chill pushing against my shield, looking for gaps, and yet I did not budge. I smiled at my friend, taunting her from behind the shield. She grimaced, a small growl ripping from her lips. Mallory did not lose well. I was stronger than ever, my abilities as a Descendant and Guardsmen unmatched, but I knew she would never concede. She pushed her element harder. The wind whipped around me, the hair I'd just adjusted now flying out of my ponytail, and yet still my feet remained rooted to the ground.

I ran at her, Batil poised to strike. She parried my attack, her footwork matching mine perfectly. I may be faster than her, elementally stronger, but she had years of fighting experience on me. We moved through the training ring, locked in a deadly dance. She pressed her element, but my shield held strong. I swiped at her midsection, and yet she jumped backward, the blade nicking her shirt, cutting a slash. She swung around, a wicked backfist jarring my head to the side. I staggered, but before I could recover, she kicked out at my sword hand, knocking it away.

I was unaffected by the loss of my weapon. I'd been in situations worse than this before. I answered her attack with a strong three punch combination. She blocked the first one, but the other two connected, pushing her back a step. I pressed my advantage and called to fire, pushing a small flame toward the short sword in her hand. The flames began at the tip of her raised sword, traveling down the blade and over the pommel, until finally they reached flesh. Her palm sizzled and Mallory roared at the pain, throwing the flaming sword to the ground. I took advantage, dropping to the ground, and swiping my leg behind her ankles. She dropped to the hard floor on her back, even as I reached for the still-searing blade. Before she could sit up, I raised to one knee, and brought the red-hot blade down, the tip of it suspended directly over her heart.

"Kill shot," I declared.

She scowled, even as she dropped her head back to the floor, accepting defeat. I jumped to my feet, dropping the sword, then offered her a hand up. She clasped it, and I pulled her to her feet, before going to collect Batil. "You've improved," she said to my back. I could hear the question in her words, but I let it be. Briar was standing outside the training ring, where she'd been since I beat her. Roman might trust her, but I didn't. Not enough to go into detail about what had happened to me the last several months. "Don't quite have the hang of that sword though, you shouldn't have let me kick it out of your hand like that. It's heavier than a dagger. Requires a stronger grip."

I smiled ruefully as I sheathed the sword across my back. It didn't surprise me that even in defeat, Mallory still found something to critique, some way to try and push me to be better. "I'll remember that," I answered, turning around. "You should consider gloves. It will keep a Fire User from burning your palm so easily."

Mallory raised her eyebrows at my brazen retort, "I'll remember that," she threw back.

I smiled, enjoying pissing her off a little. "Good," I replied, purposefully chipper. Mallory was used to people being scared of her. Most people couldn't handle her tough exterior. The foundation of our friendship was based on our ability to put up with each other when others would typically cower.

She glowered at me, grabbing a nearby towel and throwing it at my face. I caught it easily, wiping the sweat off my face, laughing.

I wrapped the towel around my neck. "I need to ask you something," I said, the moment of levity forgotten. "And you have to promise to be honest."

Mallory grabbed her own sword carefully, returning it to its place on the wall. "Okay," she prompted.

"What would you do if you were me?" I didn't say more. She knew what I was referring to.

She huffed a breath, her hands on her hips. "Why are you asking me?"

"Because I trust you," I answered immediately. "Almost more than anyone. And because I'm struggling between what my heart is telling me to do and what my brain is saying. You've never been scared to set me straight when I needed it before."

"And you think you need it now?" she asked.

I threw my arms out, slapping them against the sides of my legs. "I don't know. Maybe."

"What aren't you sure about?" she asked. *Again*.

"Are you just going to keep asking questions?" I snipped. "Because I asked for your advice, not a damn therapy session."

Briar, who had been organizing the weapons on the wall by size, stopped midmotion, turned, and abruptly left the building. The door made a loud, resounding thud behind her. Mallory didn't even flinch at her departure. She crossed her arms, stepping toward me. "I'm just trying to figure out why you, a woman who for at least as long as I've known her, has never once second-guessed her decisions, is all of a sudden unsure of what she's doing." Her words were hard, cutting.

"I'm scared," I admitted.

"Of what?" she asked, and this time the question did not annoy me.

"Of making the wrong choice!" I bellowed. "I've been here before. Ezekiel used my family against me to free The Book of Breathings. I made the choice that time. I chose Allie, and because I did, so many bad things have happened. I just don't want to be responsible for that kind of horribleness again."

"You don't have the luxury of second-guessing yourself Kyndal, or of checking out. We are in the middle of a war. Like it or not, the people need you, the Kindred need you. Everyone looks to you as a leader."

"But what if I'm wrong?" I asked. "Grady thinks I am. What if he's right?"

Mallory stared at me a moment, her brown eyes searching mine, looking for some sort of answer. Eventually, she found what she was looking for and spoke. "Grady *is* right." I suppressed the urge to interrupt. I asked for her opinion, I had to let her give it. I pressed my weight back to my heels, taking a deep breath in. "Grady is right when he said that Amina is baiting you. There is no doubt that she figured out the Guard escaped to meet up with you. She has no chance of finding you on her own, so she created the perfect trap in order to get you in a specific place at a specific time. Amina has been ruling the Kindred with an iron fist since you went away, and she knows that you are the only person that can really challenge her for leadership of the Kindred. The rest of the Guard can't. The other Nomarchs can't. She already proved that when she discredited the Guard and overthrew the Council in order to announce herself Governor. If you go back to Marienville, and Amina sees you, there is a good chance she is going to lobby the safety of your aunt against you. Force you to lay down your weapons. Once you do that, *she will execute you on the spot*. There is no chance she takes you back to Awen for a trial or public execution. Most of the people don't even know that you're alive, let alone free. She can't risk letting them see you."

"If I don't go. . ." I said, unable to get the thought out of my head. Of what would happen to Allie.

Mallory cut me off. "I didn't say you shouldn't go. I said Grady was right."

I blanched. "What?"

"Grady is right about Amina's motives, but not that there is no tactical advantage to going to Marienville."

"You lost me," I admitted.

"Amina has a large force of warriors that fight for her. They outnumber those that openly oppose her, but not by much. With the amount of warriors she's thrown in the Hollow, our numbers are even smaller on the island, and the scale is not tipping in our favor." I was yet to hear something encouraging, but I let her continue. "Not all of her soldiers fight for her out of loyalty. Mostly it is out of fear of joining those in the Hollow. Now, Amina would have been forced to split those warriors in order to go to Pennsylvania. She wouldn't travel without a large garrison, yet she would also be forced to keep the majority of her soldiers, her most loyal, back in Awen to keep the others from rising up against her. I think if you go to Marienville, if those soldiers see that you're alive, it'll shake their faith in Amina."

"You think they'll choose to fight for me, not her?"

She nodded once. "Maybe not all of them, but enough that if it came down to a fight, we could win."

"What about the rest of her soldiers back in Awen?"

"When I spoke to Daniela, I was surprised when she didn't mention Astrid being arrested for helping us escape. But after what Roman and Brynn admitted about the was-sceptre, it makes sense. As long as Amina thinks the Guard has the sceptre, she won't be focused on Astrid. She can use that advantage to help us take control of the island."

"I don't want a civil war. My issue is with Amina, not the soldiers. Set's numbers have grown into the thousands. We need every warrior we can get at the end of this if we're going to stand a chance against him."

"If a fully reunited Guard returns to Awen with Amina's soldiers at their back and two Nomarchs in custody, I promise you it will be all the inspiration the people need to fight back against the remaining loyalists. And those that don't concede, once they see the sceptre's power, they will have no choice but to submit."

Chapter 18

Roman

The stone hallways of the Coterie were dark and dreary.

I stepped out of Isaac's room, pulling the heavy door shut behind me. Cassie leaned up against the wall on the opposite side of the hallway, her red hair the only color in the otherwise gray corridor. It was cold here. The fireplace was roaring in Isaac's room, the heat reminding me of Kyndal, but none of that reached past the door. I yearned for the comfort of the flames. The warmth they contained. I held up my hand. "I don't want to hear it."

"Hear what?" she asked, feigning innocence.

I rolled my eyes, walking away from her, down the dark hallway that led to the staircase. Cassie had talked my ear off all the way to Isaac's room, trying to force me to open up. I'd blown her off. I didn't want therapy, I wanted action.

Part of me thought about going to the dungeon, in order to check on Grady and Brynn. I had firsthand experience with Grady's interrogation techniques. There was no telling what he was doing to Nero right now. Not that I cared for Nero's safety. Cassie's light footsteps sounded behind me, but I ignored them. Instead, I checked the bond, just to make sure Kyndal was alright. I'd heard Mallory invite her to train, but I still needed the reassurance that she was safe.

I can go there, check in on her, I thought.

It wasn't that I thought Kyndal was in any real danger, or that she couldn't take care of herself even if she was. I just knew what it felt like to lose her, and I never wanted to feel that again. The bond was reassurance that she was with me. That she was near. And yet it was nothing like seeing her in real life.

I could feel her presence now and her emotions seemed scattered. Agitated, yet intensely focused. Angry and yet scared. I felt an overwhelming urge to go to her, but I only made it two steps her direction before Cassie's voice stopped me.

"How is he?" she called after me.

"Why don't you check for yourself?" I answered, not pausing to turn. If she was going to push me, I'd push right back. Just as I had for the last fifteen years.

"You know why," she answered bluntly.

The pain in her voice hit me like a punch to the gut. I huffed a breath, pausing. I did know the answer. Cassie had been a Kindred healer for decades. Between her skills and years of experience, there was rarely an injury she couldn't fix. It was torture for her to look at a patient she couldn't save, and there was no cure for Isaac's condition. I turned finally. "He's better," I answered honestly. "He seems to be over the worst of it. The sweats have stopped, and he's asking for food. His wound is still bleeding a little, but it's slowing down. I would imagine it'll be closed within the next day. Brynn put extra doses of tonic in his bag, so he has plenty of that to help."

She nodded. "That's good." She looked me up and down, scrutinizing me.

I raised my eyebrows, aggravated. "He can't keep going on like this. That tonic is just a Band-aid. One that will keep getting ripped off if he stays around this war. We need to find him a more permanent solution."

"Like what?" she asked. I only shrugged, unable to produce any answers. "How are you doing?" she wondered.

I turned back around, grumbling, intent on getting to the training building and avoiding this conversation. A spark of recognition zapped through the bond. Kyndal was aware of me now, she knew I was looking for her. She was on the move, headed toward me. A deep urge to see her filled me, overwhelming and more powerful than anything else.

"Roman Sands, don't you dare walk away from me again!" Cassie yelled sternly. The angry voice of an older sister. Of someone who had whipped me into shape more than once. The voice of the woman who left me in the forest to sort out my attitude when I was just an insolent teenager. Begrudgingly, I stopped. She stepped up to me, putting herself between me and the staircase. So much smaller than I was, and yet not an ounce of fear in her. "I have known you for over half your life. Don't you dare play dumb with me, and quit avoiding my questions. I know you have a lot going on. You just got Kyndal back, your father is chained up in a dungeon, your best friend is wounded, and Grady was pretty harsh on you for the whole was-sceptre thing. You can't pretend like that doesn't affect you. Talk to me."

"I don't have time to pour out my feelings, Cass," I answered, with every ounce of patience I had left. Kyndal was in the main building of the compound now.

"Then you can listen," Cassie tossed back. I crossed my arms, awaiting the lecture. If Cassie was anything, it was determined. She wouldn't leave me alone until she'd said her piece. Sometimes it was easier to let her get it over with. I'd let her talk and then I could find Kyndal. "I know the others were harsh on you earlier, but I want you to know I think you did the right thing. Stealing the sceptre. You know my history with Amina, so you know what it means when I say she's different than who I first met. She's not the person she used to be, the one I used to love. I also know what it means to be in love with someone as much as you love Kyndal. To be willing to do anything for that person. Sacrifice everything for them. I would've done the same thing you did, if given the choice." I scruffed my hair, instantly feeling guilty for avoiding her. "I know you think you have to be in charge of everything. That you have something to prove because of your heritage. But remember, you have three Guardsmen to lean on. And you have me, too. We care about you, and we trust you. You should try trusting us."

Footsteps sounded on the steps, light and clearly female. I knew it wasn't Kyndal, she had stopped on the main level of the compound, which I had now figured out was near the dining hall. She'd been waiting for me there ever since. Out of the darkness, Brynn appeared. Her eyes were tight, small lines appearing underneath them.

"What's wrong?" I asked her brusquely. "Problems with Nero?" I tried to keep the sarcasm out of my voice, but I didn't succeed. I knew Nero wouldn't say a word, they were wasting their effort.

"You could say that," she deadpanned.

"What's wrong?" I pushed. I may have disagreed with their plan to interrogate the Coterie Commander, but I knew if Brynn was coming to me, there must be a problem.

"Nero won't talk to us," Brynn answered.

"Not surprising." I couldn't help the small dig. Cassie's hand flew out, smacking me across the shoulder. I glared at her from the corner of my eye.

"He says he'll only talk to you," she continued. That brought me up short. Me? Nero had never wanted to talk to me before. From the corner of my eye, Cassie flinched.

"Fine," I said sharply, rubbing the back of my neck. "I'll be there in a moment." Both an answer and a dismissal. Brynn nodded but made no move to leave. Apparently, we would be going together to the dungeon, leaving me no opportunity to speak to Kyndal. I turned to Cassie. "I'm sorry for being an ass." I leaned down, placing a soft kiss on her cheek. "Thank you, for looking out for me. *Really*."

She nodded. "You're welcome. I'll get some food and bring it to Isaac."

Nero's cell was eerily quiet. I stood at the outside of the door, hesitating. Brynn had escorted me down to the dungeon in tense silence. She was obviously still upset after the argument in the dining hall. I tried to think of what to say to her, what would help smooth things over, but nothing came to mind. Instead, I did what I'd always done. Kept my mouth shut. Better to say nothing than say something stupid.

Cassie's words ricocheted in my head, a reminder that I
didn't have to do everything on my own. That it was okay
to rely on my fellow Guardsmen. The four of us had been
shoved together out of circumstance and necessity, and
from day one, there had been a divide. As Rafiq, Kyndal
and I naturally defended each other, sided together, and
Brynn and Grady had banded together to do the same. Even
with our complicated, oftentimes violent history with one
another, the gap had lessened over time. And yet with
recent events, there was a danger of breaking apart again. I
knew Grady and I were at the center of that rift, my own
temper and ego as much to blame as his. One of us had to
put our differences aside and lay the rivalry to rest for
good. And it appeared like that person was me.

I pulled the door open, the metal hinges creaking loudly. It
was warmer down here than the rest of the building, the
dungeon naturally insulated by the surrounding
environment. It amazed me this compound even had a
basement, considering it sat atop a lake. The amount of
magic it took to keep a compound this size from sinking
into the freezing water below was staggering. Even more
impressive was that it was sustainable without active Water
Users on site.

Grady was posted on the opposite side of the cell, crouched
low, his weight on the balls of his feet. He was spinning a
dagger on its tip in front of his knees, but he went still as I
entered. Past him, impossible to miss, was Nero. He was
chained to the wall by his waist. There were manacles on
his wrists, each attached to heavy chains bolted into the

ceiling. The chains were pulled just tight enough to force Nero to stand on the edge of his toes to remain upright. Surprisingly, there wasn't a single mark on him. I had expected him to be beaten and bleeding, Grady's standard. Instead he hung there, steely eyed and determined.

And staring right at me.

I held his hard gaze for a moment, the man who was partly responsible for bringing me into the world. Who would I have become if he'd been able to raise me in his image? Would I be as sinister and cold as him? When I was younger, I used to allow myself to think about my parents. Who they were, what they looked like. Why they hadn't kept us. I never expected answers to any of those questions, and now I was face to face with the one person who could give them to me. I turned to Grady. "I'll need the room." Not a question, not a request.

He stood and walked out of the cell without a word or even a glance in my direction. I ground my molars. I was going to have to deal with him. Soon.

I shut the heavy door behind him. I didn't bother sliding the metal bar across the door to lock it. The center of my abdomen, where the Rafiq bond lived, was growing warmer. A sure sign that Kyndal was on her way.

I spun on my heel, going to stand against the wall opposite Nero. I put one foot up, crossed my arms, and stared at my father. "Thank you for coming," he said, almost immediately. "I didn't think you would."

"Don't thank me," I said quickly, roughly. "I'm not here to help you. You have exactly one minute to start talking, or I'll open that door and let Grady have you. He will be more than happy to cut the answers out of you."

"Is that any way to speak to your father?" Nero asked.

"Father?!" the word ripped out of me. It enraged me to hear him use the term. As if he'd earned it. As if he hadn't denied the position from the moment he learned who I was. "You lost your opportunity to call yourself that a long time ago. First, when you allowed your children to grow up not knowing who their parents were. For the second time when you betrayed us, selling us out to our enemy. And the final time, when you took from me one of the few people I have left."

"Still your family," he cut back, unaffected by my words. "And I'd remind you that I also delivered that same person back to your arms."

I pushed off the wall, seeing red. "*Diana* was my family. *Sandra* is my family. Kyndal, Cassie, Isaac. They understand that family is not just the people that share your DNA, but the people who stick their necks out for each other, who sacrifice for each other." I pointed a finger at his face, my hand shaking with rage. "You've never cared about anyone but yourself and your ridiculous legacy. As if

I could ever be proud of the things you've done. You may be my father by blood," I growled, "but do not think for a moment that I owe you a damn thing. You are a killer, a traitor, and a coward. Nothing more."

The door pushed open, Kyndal stepping inside. Her gear was sweat-stained, her hair slicked back from training. Nero pulled at his restraints as she entered, at the sight of his blade strapped across her back. Her eyes were on fire, cutting between Nero and me. I knew she was reading the room both visually and through the bond.

"Everything alright here?" she asked, although she already knew the answer. Her small attempt to stop the conversation, push me back to the point. I'd lost control, let Nero drag me into personal issues. I loved her for the correction. The reminder of why I was here. Brynn and Grady sulked in the doorway, using Kyndal's interruption as an excuse to get in the room. I didn't care. They could hear everything anyway.

"Fine," I told her, reeling myself back in. "Nero was just about to tell us everything he knows."

He laughed, but the sound of it was off. It was dark, full of secrets. "There is no need to act so strong, so *tough*, Roman. I will gladly tell you everything I know. It is after all, why I asked you here."

"And your price for this knowledge?" Kyndal asked before I could, seeing right through his bullshit.

"Simple," he responded. "That you remove Batil from your back, for one. You have not earned the right to carry that blade." I raised an eyebrow smugly. "And that you allow me to join you and fight by your side."

"Excuse me?" I drolled. I could not have heard what I thought I heard. There was no way he was really asking for *us* to trust *him*. "You want to help us?"

"Why would we allow that? You betrayed us," Kyndal added. "*Your betrayal* was the reason I was captured by Set in the first place." I felt the anger rise up in Kyndal, her temper slipping out of her control. I was torn, part of me wanting to calm her down, the other wanting to turn her loose, let her rip Nero apart.

My father's gaze slid to my Rafiq. "Where you see betrayal, I see strategy. *Survival.* You see me delivering you to Set, and yet I remember staying my hand and saving your life. Set was the tactical moment at the time, but I am not loyal to him. I never have been."

Grady snorted. "Of course not, you're not loyal to anyone but yourself." It took every ounce of control I had to keep from pointing out the irony of that comment.

"If we free you, you'll just slither back to Set like the snake you are." Brynn this time.

"Except I wouldn't," Nero snapped, his eyes crawling from Kyndal to me. "Much has changed since I joined Set's side. There are new reasons to fight."

"Like what?" Kyndal demanded, not giving the Commander an inch. "Name them."

Nero didn't respond immediately, but his eyes slid back across the cell, slowly.

To me.

He let them linger a moment, allowing the silence between us to serve as his answer. My heart rate increased, my blood pumping so fast, I thought my heart would burst. *No, it wasn't about me.* I wanted to say it, to shout it, but the words died at my lips. Nero hadn't known I was his son when he joined Set's side. He'd only learned that information at the last moment, when it was too late.

"You're lying," I managed to say, even though he'd never actually said anything. My voice shook slightly at the end.

"I'm not," he snapped, a hint of the cold killer I'd come to know sneaking to the surface. "Ask her," he said, tempering his tone. "Ask her if it's true." Kyndal said nothing, but her eyebrows were wrinkled, and she was popping her knuckles. Sure signs that she was thinking. *She couldn't possibly be entertaining this idea, could she?* "She knows I have no desire to work for that self-absorbed, maniac of a false idol. I never have. I want him dead. I only pretended to serve him to buy me time, to buy *you all* time, to form a plan and grow stronger. If you give me my freedom, I will help you kill him."

"What about your men?" Kyndel asked. "Your soldiers? You would just leave them in Set's grasp."

Nero shrugged, as much as he was capable in his chains. "By this point, Set has most assuredly turned them into hybrids. They are already lost."

"You said he'd promised you they would remain pure," Kyndal retorted. I looked back and forth between them, only understanding part of their debate. So much had gone on between them in the last six months.

Nero gave Kyndal a sly smile. "You are naive if you think I ever trusted Set and his word. I knew from the very beginning what he intended to do with my soldiers. What he would have tried to force upon me. But I would never allow myself to be tainted in such a way." I tightened my fist at his judgement, his blatant disapproval of what had happened to me. "If you were smarter, you would see that I've been helping you since the beginning. Set never once suspected my true intentions. He always thought I served him, but I knew he was simply waiting for an excuse to get rid of me so he wouldn't have any resistance when he changed my soldiers into his hybrid scum. I gave him the perfect reason when I begged to come here, to protect the Coterie that he believes I love so much. And I made sure he let *you* go with me."

Kyndal scoffed. "You're trying to tell me you orchestrated coming here? That everything since Egypt has been a ploy? Your allegiance to Set, the battle outside the walls, the soldiers you lost, everything?"

"Convincing, wasn't I?" he jeered. We both just stared at him. Grady and Brynn looked to each other. "Why do you think I brought so few men? It wasn't like I could exactly walk into the compound, waving a white flag. I knew there would be a fight. I just made sure I brought a defeatable amount of soldiers. Allow you to think you won. I even brought you Dirk so you could get your revenge."

"Revenge for a beating you orchestrated," Brynn pointed out.

"You're lying," I said again, this time with more force. "Same old Nero. Willing to say anything, do anything to keep yourself alive. Now you're lying again, taking credit for things you had no control over, in the hopes we spare your life. I think you don't have anything useful to tell us and you're grasping at straws."

Nero ignored me, instead speaking directly to Kyndal. "I told you once that we were on the same side. That still remains true. You want to destroy the Council, and I'm the only person who has even come *close* to doing just that. Free me from these shackles, take me with you to Marienville. I'll tell you everything you want to know."

"How do you know about Marienville?" Grady asked, speaking for the first time in a while.

"You may have me locked in a basement, but I can still hear everything that goes on within these walls." I sincerely hoped that wasn't true.

Kyndal turned to me, a question in her eyes. I nodded toward the door, following her, Grady, and Brynn to the corridor. I pulled the door shut behind us. It wouldn't keep him from hearing us, obviously, but I couldn't stand to see him anymore.

"What do you think?" I asked Kyndal.

She shrugged. "Part of it checks out. He was in Set's strictest confidence. There's a good chance he has the information we need."

"What did he mean about helping you?" Grady asked Kyndal.

She shook her head, her eyebrows pinched together. "There were a few times," she blew out a breath, like she couldn't believe what she was about to say, "a few times that he helped me. Worked against Set in small ways."

I wanted to ask her about the other part, about him pretending to be back for me, but I held back. Those were questions better left for private moments. "Do you trust him?" Grady asked her, but before she could answer, Brynn interrupted.

"I think we should kill him." All three of us turned to her. "What? He's shown us repeatedly that he can't be trusted. That'll he'll turn on anyone to save his own skin. We shouldn't trust him."

"We don't trust him," Kyndal cut back at her. "But we're running out of options. We need his intel. *Now*." She turned to Grady. "This is the only way we're going to get the info we need. Are you with us?" she asked. "We can't do this without you."

He let out an annoyed, exasperated breath. We were losing him, and I knew it. I took Cassie's advice and stepped forward. It was time to close the divide within the Guard. "Grady, anything we do at this point has risks. We are out of good options. The longer we stay here, the longer we give Set the opportunity to find us. If we take Nero to Marienville, we get his intel, just like you wanted. This is the only way."

"And Amina?" he asked.

"Mallory thinks once Amina's soldiers see me, some of them will defect to our side."

Yes, I thought. *They will*. I don't know why I hadn't thought of it before. One of Amina's biggest lies was letting the people believe Kyndal wasn't an option. If they saw her, it would break what faith remained in Amina. They would rise against her. "When we have Amina's soldiers, Astrid will give us the sceptre. Then, with Nero's intel, we can go after Set. We can't fight this war on two fronts."

Grady stared at the wall ahead of him, his head shaking back and forth. "How would you get us into Marienville? You know Amina will have scouts and spies all over town, watching the airstrip, Kyndal's house, the school. Forget about going to the compound."

Kyndal crossed her arms. "Actually, I think I may have an idea."

Chapter 19

Kyndal

I tiptoed through the soft vegetation of the Allegheny Forest. The edge of the treeline was in sight, the open yard behind it. It felt strange to be back here. Part of me had never believed I'd be able to return, not after everything I'd been through. Being back among the trees of the forest, the green grass under my feet, I felt alive again.

Roman walked up next to me, his shoulder pressed against mine. "I can't believe *this* was your idea."

I turned, smiling at the man I loved so much. The moon was high. It wasn't full anymore, but was still large enough to provide plenty of light as it streamed through the canopy of the trees, highlighting his face in the silver of the moonlight. I leaned over kissing him quickly on the lips. "Do you have an objection to breaking and entering?" I teased.

He smirked. "Not usually, but this particular house is a gutsy move, don't you think?"

I shrugged. "The patrol car isn't in the driveway. It should be fine."

"Should be," Grady hissed from behind us. "Excuse me if I don't find that comforting."

I rolled my eyes, looking at where he and Brynn were hidden among the trees. The others, Mallory, Cassie, Briar, and Isaac were deeper in the forest, keeping watch over Nero, but also watching for Kindred soldiers. We'd made it into Marienville unseen, but we couldn't chance one of Amina's soldiers happening across us on patrol.

"You ready?" I asked Roman. His eyes wandered down to my lips, then along my body to my hips, where my dagger was tucked into my waistband.

"Do you really think the dagger is necessary?" he questioned.

I smiled. "You never know. She could get feisty."

He chuckled quietly.

We snuck into the open yard, making sure to keep to the shadows. There was a shed not far from where we were hidden, and we backed up against it, next to a pile of firewood. I crouched down and grabbed a large log, throwing it into the yard. It landed with a thud, triggering one of the motion sensor lights. It flashed on, illuminating the backyard. Roman jogged around the side of the shed, edging the safety light just enough for us to make it to the back of the house unseen. The kitchen window was open, the summer wind blowing into the house. It was a small opening, but big enough for me to get through. I pushed lightly, popping the screen out of the window and dropping it to the ground. I hoisted myself up, slithering inside the dark house and walking around to the door to let Roman in.

"Which room is hers?" I whispered.

He raised his eyebrow. "How would I know?" he hissed back. I pinned him with a look. "I have no clue," he defended himself. "Honest."

"Fine, let's go." The house wasn't extravagant, just a simple one-story ranch. We moved down the hallway, careful of any creaking boards. We came to the first door and peeked inside. Empty. The next was the bathroom. There were only two doors left. One on the right side of the hallway, the other at the end of the hall. "This has to be it," I whispered to Roman. I reached for the doorknob, twisting it quietly. I held up one finger toward him, counting silently to three, then pushed the door open. It was dark inside, but the window was open, just as it had been in the kitchen. It gave off just enough light from outside to make out details. This was definitely her room. There was a dresser just inside the door, covered in various boxes of colored pencils, paints, and art supplies. *Huh,* I thought. *I had no idea she was an artist.* On the far side of the room, tucked against the corner of the wall, barely visible in the minimal moonlight, was a small shape curled up in bed. Her caramel colored hair, much longer than the last time I'd seen it, was spread out on her pillow.

I moved forward, Roman staying back at the door. We only had one shot at this. I didn't think her dad was home, but I couldn't be sure. If she screamed, we could be in big trouble. I reached the edge of the bed, striking quickly, slapping my hand over her mouth. She immediately bucked off the bed, a muffled scream ripping out of her. Her arms flailed, trying to fight me, even as I pushed her back onto the bed. Her fists smacked off my shoulders, barely registering. "Paige!" I hissed. "Paige, it's Kyndal. Calm down." She spun toward me, her eyes wild and unseeing. "I'm not going to hurt you," I whispered, desperately trying to calm her down. "It's Kyndal," I repeated. "I need you to calm down. I can't move my hand until you calm down." Slowly, her thrashing subsided, her eyes focused in on me, taking so much longer without the enhanced senses Roman and I possessed. I watched as she registered who I was, what was happening. The panic left her eyes, replaced with confused recognition. Finally, her body relaxed. "I'm going to remove my hand now, Paige. I need you to promise you'll stay quiet." She nodded. Carefully, I pulled my hand back.

"What the hell are you doing here?" she immediately demanded, her large voice filling the small room. I growled, lunging for her again to cover her mouth. She shuffled backward into the corner, out of immediate reach. "Get away from me!" The room went dark as Roman clicked the door shut, trying to prevent any noise from leaking into the hallway. "Who did that?" Paige questioned. I could hear the panic returning to her voice. I needed to get a handle on this quickly.

"Paige, shut up!" I snarled. Surprisingly, she listened. "I'm not here to hurt you. I need your help, but you have to listen to me." Silence. I let out a breath I hadn't realized I'd been holding. "Good," I encouraged her. "Now, is your dad home?"

"No, he's at the station." *A small victory.*

"That's good. We're going to turn the light on now," I warned her.

"We. . ." she began, but before she could finish her question, the light clicked on, and she saw who was with me. "Roman. I should've known."

"Hi, Paige," he said simply. I looked between them, part of me tempted to laugh at the absurdity of the situation. A year ago, I would've wanted to rip Paige's throat out for even being this close to Roman. She had hated me from the moment I showed up at East Forest High School, her ire only growing when she discovered Roman and I were involved.

Now that Paige knew she wasn't in danger, and who exactly had broken into her room, she was full of questions. "Where have you two been? You disappeared like a year ago. No one has seen you since. Half the school was convinced you got knocked up and ran away together. Everyone else thinks you died."

I stepped back into the middle of the room, halfway between Paige and Roman, doing my best to stifle a smile. A small part of me enjoyed watching Paige so thrown off her game. The *It Girl* that was always composed, always in control, left bewildered by the *New Girl*. "Clearly, we're not dead," Roman responded, completely unaffected by her panic.

"I'm not pregnant either," I felt compelled to clarify. Roman rolled his eyes. I shrugged. "What? It was an important detail," I whispered.

"Although we could be dead soon if you don't help us," Roman added.

"I'm listening," Paige responded.

"I need you to get a message to my aunt," I told her.

"Why can't you do it?" she asked. I held back a grimace. This was going to be difficult.

"It's not safe for us to be seen in Marienville right now," I began. "There are certain *people* that we can't risk seeing us. They could be watching Allie."

"Okay," she answered, drawing the word out. She was skeptical, and I couldn't really blame her. At least she wasn't saying no. "What's the message?"

"Tell her I need her to meet me at noon in the greatest amount of secrecy, in the place that is safe from all evils of the world."

"I don't understand what that means," Paige said.

"I don't need you to understand it," I responded immediately. "She'll get it. That's all that matters."

Paige crossed her arms over her chest, a familiar look settling in on her face. "What exactly are you guys into?"

"We can't tell you that," Roman answered from behind me.

"What if I said I wouldn't help you unless you explained?" Paige countered.

A sharp stab of annoyance, Roman's annoyance, shot down the bond. "Explaining things to you is not an option. The more you know, the more possibility we are putting you in danger. We are already risking too much by coming here. I hope you understand the gravity of the situation that we came to you in the first place," he answered.

Paige looked between the two of us, her eyes cutting back and forth. "Fine," she relented. "I'll get Allie your message."

I squeezed my hand into a fist, a small piece of relief cracking through. "Thank you, Paige. Really."

She waved her hand, blowing us off. "Whatever. How do I let you know she got the message? Where are you staying?" she asked.

I grimaced, casting an uncertain glance toward Roman. He stepped up, next to me. "We actually need one more favor."

"This is an old hunting cabin that belongs to my father," Paige explained as our small group trekked through an old trail deep inside the forest. "He hasn't used it in years, not since my mom left. You won't have to worry about him popping by or anything, but it isn't exactly in the best of shape. He only comes by to do routine maintenance, flush the water lines, things like that. So, the good news is you have running water, but there's no electricity and I'm not sure if the propane tank out back is filled or not."

"I'm sure it'll be fine," I assured her. Little did she know just having running water would be an upgrade from my most recent accommodations.

Paige turned, glaring at me, before staring down my friends. The bags they carried on their backs, the similar clothes we all wore. A few of us were even still sporting light bruises from the battle in Siberia. It had to be confusing for her. Over half of our group, Isaac, Roman, Grady, Cassie, and myself, were familiar to her. People she knew from school or had seen at parties. No doubt she had drawn her own conclusions about us long ago, all of which were being challenged with the evidence in front of her now. I noticed her gaze land on the back of our crew, where Mallory and Briar were walking, daggers in hand, behind a bound Nero.

"Don't ask," I reminded her. She turned back around, right as the trail opened up into a small clearing. In the middle of it sat a modest house. It was wooden, painted an evergreen color than matched the forest during the middle of summer. There was a small covered porch on the front, a single chair posted there, next to a large log that had been set up like a table. A deer hoist hung from a pulley system that had been rigged on the side of the porch. Paige stuck the key in the lock and shouldered the door open, dust falling from the door jamb down on her head. She waved her hand in front of her, airing out the dust then held it out in welcome. "Here ya go. Home sweet home." The others filtered inside, Roman giving me a knowing look as I hung back on the porch with Paige. Once everyone had gone inside, I closed the door and stepped back in the clearing, Paige sauntering after me.

"Thank you," I said with full sincerity. "You've done a lot for us. We won't forget it."

"I've always known something was weird about you, Kyndal. From the moment I met you, it was obvious to me. But I have to admit, this is a whole new level of strange."

"I'm not a bad person," I interrupted.

She smiled, a rare sincere smile. "I know." She glanced back, no doubt to see if anyone was watching us, listening in. I didn't have the heart to tell her they could all hear everything we were saying anyway. "Answer one question for me." I scrunched my eyebrows, intrigued. "That night at the dance, what happened to my hair?"

I chuckled. We'd danced around this conversation before, but she'd never flat out asked me. "I may have had something to do with that," I admitted.

Her face dropped in astonishment. "I knew it!" she shouted, pointing her finger at me. She didn't seem angry, just happy to have her theory confirmed.

I jumped to defend myself anyway. "You had it coming," I reminded her. "You kissed Roman!" I didn't feel bad for a moment of it.

She smiled now, recognizing that I wasn't repentant, and that she obviously wasn't either. "Maybe I was kind of rude," she conceded. I shook my head, finding myself smiling back at her. "Clearly, I lost that battle," she added.

I raised my eyebrows, shrugging with a satisfied smirk. I could feel Roman paying attention to us, his own satisfaction and humor at the conversation happening out in the forest. "Be careful when you deliver the message," I told her.

She nodded, taking a few steps toward the trail that would lead her back to where we left her car. "I will."

"And remember, you never saw us."

She raised her arms into the air. "Saw who?"

Chapter 20

Roman

We wasted no time getting the cabin prepared. The lodging was small, the main area filled with a kitchenette and what I supposed passed for a living room. There was only a couch and a recliner inside it, both pointed at an old TV in the corner of the room, covered in dust. With a flick of my wrist, the couch and recliner pushed to the walls, opening up space in the middle of the room. I sat a wooden chair from the kitchen in the center of the now exposed rug. "Sit," I ordered Nero, who still stood awkwardly near Mallory. Surprisingly, he did so without complaint, his bound hands sitting in his lap. His guards took up residence behind him, weapons at the ready. Brynn and Briar had already taken their spots in the opposite corners of the room, Brynn standing with The Book of Breathings open in front of her, as if she was prepared to whisper its words at the slightest excuse.

The front door opened and closed, the small space filling with the warmth of Kyndal. Her strong steps sounded on the wooden floor until she stood directly next to me, her shoulder just touching mine. It was always a heady thing being around her. She was the strongest Kindred in the world. Power radiated off her, so much that everyone couldn't help but feel a piece of it. This close to her, our skin touching, I had a direct line to her nearly endless well of power and magic. Sometimes I couldn't believe that I was her Rafiq, her counterpart. That out of everyone, I was the one chosen to walk the Earth by her side. At one point I had thought my feelings would taper off, that there was no way they could remain so strong, but if anything, the opposite was true. The more time I spent with her, the more I was around her, the stronger my feelings grew.

She bumped my shoulder, drawing my attention. My mind had wandered, and no doubt my emotions were spilling out of me, right down the bond. It was the effect she had on me. She made me forget about everything else, everyone else in the world. Embarrassed, I regained control of myself, sending her a silent apology through our connection. She responded, answering with what I could only describe as a laugh. She found amusement in my embarrassment, as she always had. Another emotion quickly took its place, and although I couldn't read her mind, whatever she was thinking about definitely wasn't appropriate to be thinking about in a room full of people. It was my turn to push against her shoulder. "Quit it," I whispered, although the words lacked any real force.

She laughed for real this time, her lips forming a wicked smile that now had *me* thinking inappropriate thoughts.

"You know, just because you aren't saying the words out loud, don't think we can't tell when you're talking to each other," Isaac whined from behind us. "And whatever you two are talking about right now is gross. I can practically smell your hormones from here."

Kyndal turned, putting her hand on my shoulder, a move that did nothing to slow my errant thoughts. Then she stuck her tongue out at my best friend.

Isaac laughed from where he was sitting at the kitchen table, next to Cassie. Thankfully, before the conversation could descend any further into childishness, Grady came out of the single bedroom, saving me. "Is it done?" I asked him.

He nodded. "Every window is shut and locked. I wrote Silence sigils on each window-pane. No one will hear anything that goes on in here."

"Good," I answered. It was overkill covering each window with the sigil spell, but I wasn't taking any chances. Although the Kindred compound was on the opposite side of the Allegheny, I wouldn't put it past Amina to send her warriors this far west on a patrol. From the exterior the cabin looked deserted, we needed to make sure we didn't give any indications otherwise.

All jokes forgotten, I turned to my father. "We held up our end of the deal," I began. "We brought you to Marienville, and now we expect you to honor your side of the bargain and tell us what you know about Set's plans."

"Your end of the deal was to give me my freedom, and yet..." He let the sentence drop and simply held up his bound hands.

"Don't give me more of an excuse to kill you," Brynn answered. "Intel first."

Nero let out an exasperated breath. "Fine. I assume you are all familiar with the story of Set and Maat."

"I am," Kyndal answered. "Set told me it in Cairo. He and Maat were lovers and they ruled over Egypt together for generations. The way he tells it, they were madly in love until one day he left to conquer the Redlands. He was going to present them to Maat as a gift, but when he returned, he discovered Maat had been unfaithful. She cheated on him with Thoth. She kicked Set out of the Blacklands and replaced him with Thoth. Thoth smeared his name, vilifying him in the process. Set lost worshippers, lost his faithful servants, so he created new ones—the wraiths—in order to gain his lands back."

"Then the Original Twelve prayed to Hermes Trismegistus for help, and he created the Kindred to fight back the wraiths," I added. This part of the story was familiar to me.

"And the war has continued ever since," Nero finished. "Neither side ever wins. Even when Marius and the ancient Guard managed to put Set back in his cage, he found a way back out. You all kill wraiths and then more return. No matter how many Kindred Set kills, more are branded every day. Set means to end the war. Forever."

"How?" That question came from Grady.

"By tipping the scales in his favor."

"That's not an answer," Kyndal pointed out.

"In ancient times, the gods lived among the humans, but when Set was defeated last time, Maat left this plane. She hated what the war did to humans, so she retreated to the Inbetween, the entrance to the afterlife and Duat."

"That's where I went to get the sceptre," Kyndal added.

"Set can't enter the Inbetween, it is forbidden by the spell Maat placed on it thousands of years ago. The spell created a wall, keeping him on this plane. He's tried to force Maat into leaving the Inbetween and fighting him on this side of the wall, but she won't take the bait. So now he plans to tear down the wall."

"I've been to the Inbetween," Kyndal argued. "There's no wall."

Nero rolled his eyes. "You need to quit thinking so literally. The wall doesn't have to *look* like a wall. It's simply a barrier, something made out of pure magic that divides the worlds."

"The river," she answered, figuring it out. Nero nodded.

"How does releasing his greatest enemy tip the scales in his favor?" I asked. This wasn't making sense. There had to be something we were missing.

"There's a reason Maat returned to the Inbetween. Some thought it was out of fear of Set's return, or indifference to those of us that fought in the war, but in fact it was because she had a job to fulfill. Maat is the keeper of balance, the guardian of the entrance to the afterlife. From the Inbetween, she is able to influence this world, while also keeping those in Duat at bay. Once a soul enters the afterlife, it cannot re-enter our plane without passing through the Inbetween and Maat." My eyes cut to Kyndal, the same confusion rolling through her as I felt. "Do none of you understand?" Nero demanded.

"Spell it out," I urged him.

He leaned forward, his cold eyes boring into me. "Have you never wondered where the wraiths go when you kill them?"

Brynn pushed off the wall, stepping forward. "You're saying Maat is the reason wraiths don't return after we kill them. That she is the only thing keeping them in Duat?"

Nero threw himself back in his chair. "Finally, someone intelligent." I didn't even have time to pause and recognize the fact that he complimented a woman.

Kyndal crossed her arms. "So, if Set breaks down the wall to the Inbetween, destroying the barrier between us and Duat, not only would he finally be able to get to Maat, but all those wraiths the Kindred have killed will come rushing back to our world?" Nero nodded, and my heart dropped. "That's thousands of wraiths."

"Millions," Grady corrected.

"Holy. . ." Kyndal began.

"Shit," I finished.

"So now you know," Nero responded. "Release me."

"That's not everything," I answered, ignoring his plea for release. "You told us *what* he wants to do, but you haven't said anything about *how* he plans to do it."

"There are only two things that can withstand the spell separating us and Inbetween. In small doses, they suspend the magic of the barrier and are allowed to pass through the river. In larger doses, they can break it apart," Nero explained.

"A Descendant is one," Brynn provided. "Kyndal could pass through the river."

"Yes," Nero responded. "Sacrificing Kyndal in the river would break the barrier, but Set would never do that. He needs her blood to make more hybrids. The only other thing is the was-sceptre."

"He doesn't know where the sceptre is," I said.

"No," Nero agreed. "But he knows who could tell him."

"Amina," Grady filled in. "Amina could tell him. She's the Governor. He'd assume she'd know."

"And who is the one person that could push Amina out of Awen?" Nero asked. "The only person that she would risk putting herself out in the open to capture?"

"Me," Kyndal answered.

"Which means Set could already be on his way to Marienville," I finished.

I needed space to think.

Nero had dropped so much information on us in the cabin, I couldn't stand to stay in such a small space, surrounded by everyone who was looking to me to do something. To know what to do next.

I retreated into the forest, going just far enough that I knew I could return quickly if I had to. Being back in the Allegheny after so long away, it was tempting to go to my old spots. The compound was on the other side of the forest, but there were several other places familiar to me. The Ridge was within walking distance, the treehouse just a few miles north of here, not to mention Sandra's bar on the edge of this side of the forest. I was craving something familiar, something comforting, and it took every ounce of strength I had not to run to one of those places.

I'd heard her coming. She'd made no attempt to hide her steps, giving me plenty of opportunity to tell her to leave me alone, if I wanted to. And I knew if I said the words, if I asked her to leave me be, she would turn and walk away without complaint. Her arms snaked around my waist from behind, her slender hands clasped at my abdomen. She squeezed me tightly, not saying anything out loud, but rather allowing me to feel everything she wanted to say. Her warmth filled me, the Rafiq bond purring with contentment. Without anyone else around, it was easy to surrender myself to her strength and lose myself in her magic. I reached up almost unconsciously and grabbed her right hand, my thumb sliding over the brand on her palm. I knew exactly where it was without looking, just like I'd memorized every inch of her skin.

"Are you alright?" I asked her.

She snorted, the blunt sound rumbling through my chest. "Why would you ask a stupid question like that?"

I turned around, and yet she didn't break her hold on me. I pushed her long hair back off her shoulders, lifting her head up to force her to look at me. Her eyes were beautiful. Green wasn't a strong enough word to describe them. They were emeralds that sparkled with life, mischief, and her internal fire. "Nero just explained that the only reason Set hasn't killed you yet is because he plans to use you as a human blood bag to make more hybrids."

She shrugged, the casual movement at odds with the torrent I could feel building inside her. "It's not like that's new information. I'm more concerned about him using the sceptre to break the barrier between us and the other side."

"Kyndal. . ." I began, but she lifted up on her toes and kissed me. I immediately forgot what I was going to say and pulled her to me, fitting her body against mine. I dug my fingers into her hair, the other hand firm against her back. She yanked at the bottom of my shirt, the edge of her fingers teasing at my beltline. I pushed into her, fully intent on taking it further, not giving a damn that we were in the middle of the forest. But as quickly as she had kissed me, she pulled away, breaking all contact. I staggered a moment at the suddenly empty space. "Why'd you do that?"

"Because I felt like it," she said. "And it seemed like a good way to shut you up."

I raised an eyebrow, fake pouting. "That's my move."

"I know what you were going to say, and it's a wasted conversation. I'm not going to let anything happen to you just because you're connected to me."

"You think I'm worried about myself?" I asked. She couldn't possibly believe that.

"Amina knows it is my blood that creates hybrids. If I'm out of the equation, Set's army can't continue to grow. She could decide to come after me."

"She also knows she needs you for the war," I argued, but even before I finished speaking, she was shaking her head.

"She doesn't care about that. We both know the longer this war goes on, the more Amina benefits. She has no interest in bringing it to an end." She took a deep breath. "If she comes after me, we don't know for sure it would kill you. When you died, I felt it, but the echo was slower. I was able to heal myself in time. Not to mention Marius didn't die when Davina did. Maybe with The Book of Breathings. . ."

She was rambling, her words pouring out of her without thought. It was my turn to interrupt. "Kyndal, Kyndal stop." I grabbed her hand, a rush of heat flying up my arm.

"I'm not worried about myself. I don't care what happens to me."

She closed her eyes for a moment, whether to absorb my power or collect her thoughts, I couldn't be sure. Either way, she waited before saying anything. She leaned forward, placing her head against my chest. I rubbed my hands along her shoulders. "You know even if Amina doesn't kill me, and we beat Set, there's only one thing that can put him back in his cage. This story only ends one way."

My hands froze. "This is a conversation I won't have. I've already told you, I won't let you sacrifice yourself to put Set away. We will find another way. I've been searching the books in the library back on the island." She looked up to me, and it was my turn to kiss her. She had tried to talk to me about this before, tried to convince me it was alright to sacrifice herself, but I always refused to listen to her. "We will find another way," I promised her. I wrapped my arms around her. "You do not have permission to leave me." I waited for her to argue with me, but she didn't. Not for a moment did I think it was because she agreed with me.

I held her a moment longer, then finally worked up the courage to ask what I was too scared to know inside. "Do you think he means it?"

Kyndal stepped back, out of reach. "Who?"

"Nero. Do you think knowing about me changed his mind? His allegiance?"

Sympathy poured down the bond, Kyndal knew better than anyone what it was like to not have parents. To not understand where you came from. "There were a couple times we were alone and he would ask about you. How you were branded, why Ezekiel raised you, things like that. I told him the basics."

"Did he. . ." I paused, stumbling on the question. "Did it seemed like he cared?" I hated that I even asked the question. That part of me sought his approval.

"It's tough to say with Nero, like always. He was interested, but whether that's because he cared about you or just about his legacy. . ."

I nodded, not needing her to say more. "I get it. I just wish it wasn't all so difficult. I don't remember the last time I got to make a decision that wasn't life or death." A truth I'd admit only to her.

"Do you ever wish we were just normal people?" she asked, her voice sounding wistful. "That I was just a normal high school girl with a bad attitude, and you were just a normal high school boy with a chip on his shoulder."

I huffed a laugh. "You realize if we were normal, we probably never would have met. We definitely wouldn't be in school at the same time. I'm ten years older than you."

"Nine and a half," she corrected. "I turned a year older while I was away. And you're ruining my fantasy," she pouted.

I tightened my grip around her waist. "Alright, then. Play a game with me."

"A game?" she asked. "Now?"

"Why not? You asked for fantasy," I responded. I wanted to talk about anything else. Anything but sacrifices and despot fathers.

She smiled. "Fine, what's your game?"

"Close your eyes." She did so. "We may not have gotten to be those normal people before, but that doesn't mean our lives can't be normal one day. Pretend it's a year from now. Set is dead, for good. We aren't fugitives anymore. Where do you see yourself? What are you doing?"

It took her a minute to say anything, and for a while I thought she wouldn't respond at all, until finally, "I'm packing."

"Packing?" I asked. "That wasn't the answer I expected."

"I just graduated high school, and I have my diploma in hand. Allie is there with Darius, a large diamond ring glittering on her wedding finger. They'll be leaving for their honeymoon soon, somewhere wild and exotic, obviously. I finish packing and a horn honks outside." She smiled. "It's you of course, there to pick me up for our cross-country road trip."

I smiled. "A road trip, huh?"

She tightened her grip around my waist. "Yes, a road trip. Just the two of us. You're going to take me to Philadelphia, to show me where you grew up, and I'll take you to Dayton to see where my family is buried."

"Sounds like a sad road trip," I couldn't help but notice.

She opened her eyes, glaring at me playfully. "This is my fantasy, quit judging."

I chuckled, "Alright, fine."

She continued, "After Texas, we'll go to California to see the Pacific Ocean. I've never seen it before. We'll swim in the water during the day, camp on the beach at night next to a small bonfire. Then we can travel up to the Redwood Forest. We can measure ourselves against the trees." She bumped her hip against me. "Even *you* look short compared to those. And then we'll travel from there. We can go anywhere we want. We'll be in charge. We'll be. . ."

"Free," I finished for her.

She opened her eyes. "Exactly."

"It sounds perfect."

"You can add stops of your own to our road trip if you like," she offered. "I'm not a complete tyrant."

I shook my head. "No. I want it exactly the way you said it. Everything you said was perfect."

She smiled, wiggling her eyebrows. "I know, right?"

I leaned down, bringing her in for another searing kiss. When we pulled away, she lifted her head, staring at the summer sky. "It's almost noon. We should leave soon, get there before my aunt so we can scout the area."

"We?" I asked.

"You're coming with me, right?" she asked, as if she couldn't imagine anything otherwise.

"Absolutely," I answered. "Where you go, I go."

Chapter 21

Kyndal

The sun had almost reached its apex in the sky, soaring above the canopy of the forest, shining down on the charred earth in front of me. I walked the exterior of the ring, where the new fresh grass met the burnt ground that used to live under the lake. It'd been long enough that the ground should have recovered by now. There should be fresh grass growing in the lake basin, fertilized by years of silt, and yet there were no signs of new growth. I wondered if anything would ever live here again, or if the magic had burned away all chances for the ground to recover.

There were so many memories for me here. This is where everything had gone wrong. Where Ezekiel betrayed us. Where Roman was turned. Dozens of Kindred had died here. Roman knelt down in the center of the charred circle, running his fingers along the burnt grass in the exact spot he'd once laid when a wraith crawled over his body and down his throat. No doubt feeling me watching him, he glanced up at me briefly before standing up straight to cover any unwanted emotions leaking through.

It didn't take our bond to know if he had his way, he'd never return to this place again, and I couldn't blame him. Unfortunately, it offered one of the few safe places to meet my aunt. It was highly secluded, well off any tourist trails, and only accessible by those who knew where to look. People like me and my aunt. Not to mention, according to Grady, there was no magical signature left in the earth here. Amina's soldiers on patrol would never find us, and those with similar abilities to Grady's wouldn't be drawn here either.

A branch snapped behind me, and I whipped around, eyes lit red. My natural instinct to protect myself kicking in. I knew Kindred would never make a sound like that. We knew how to stay silent in the forest. On the opposite end of the dead clearing, my aunt stood under the shade of an old maple tree. She wasn't in her work clothes like I had expected, but rather jean shorts and a tank top. It was the middle of the week, she should've been at Allegheny Explorers. Her hair was tied back, the dark tresses longer than the last time I'd seen her. Behind her was another shadow, a larger one I recognized as Darius, a Kindred Air User, a dear friend, and my aunt's boyfriend.

I don't know which one of us broke across the clearing first, but next thing I knew I was in the middle of the dried-up lake, holding on fiercely to Allie. "I never thought I'd see you again," she whispered. I wrapped her up even tighter, never wanting to let her go. We stood there for a moment, each holding on to our last living relative. "Kyndal," she eventually rasped. "Kyndal, I can't breathe."

"Oh, sorry!" I responded, instantly pulling back. "You alright? Sorry."

A small chuckle broke out of my aunt, even as I noticed her wipe a tear or two from under her eyes. "I'm fine. It's so good to see you."

"You weren't followed, were you?" I asked both her and Darius, who now stood alongside us.

"No one saw where we went," Darius responded, shaking Roman's hand, then mine. "I made sure of it. Are you alone?"

Roman shook his head. "There are six others. They're safe, in a cabin not far away."

Darius nodded, satisfied we had taken precautions. "The whole Guard?" he affirmed.

"Yes," Roman answered.

"I was worried you wouldn't come," I confessed to my aunt.

"I will admit, when Paige Christensen knocked on my door claiming to have a message from you, you could imagine my surprise. Last I knew, you two hated each other. But once she delivered the message, I knew it was real. She's oddly convincing, that girl," Allie answered.

I smiled. I knew Paige was the right girl for the job. "I would have come myself, but it wasn't safe."

"I know," Allie answered. "Amina."

I raised my eyebrows. "So, you've seen her?" Roman asked. *Dammit, I knew she would come for my family.*

She shrugged. "She paid a visit to my work a day or two ago, asking if I had seen you or heard from you. Things like that. I didn't tell her a thing, but she managed to create enough of a problem that when I yelled at her to leave, I was suspended. Darius filled me in on the rest, about what's going on. Where you've been."

I wasn't sure which to address first. That my 30-year-old aunt yelled at a several-hundred-year-old Nomarch, or that she lost her job because of it. "Did she touch you?" I demanded instead. "Because if she did, I swear I will. . ."

"She didn't lay a hand on me," Allie interrupted. "She was just trying to scare me, I think."

I turned to Darius. "Where do you land in all of this?"

"I'm Kindred," he replied. "As such it isn't wise to ignore a summons from my Governor. When she arrived, I answered her call."

"You've been inside the compound since they arrived?" I asked him.

He nodded. "I'm bound to uphold the law of our people, protect those that cannot protect themselves, although I will admit I'm not so sure that is why our brethren have come to our town. They are in a frenzy, looking for the Guard, although when she mentioned your name, her soldiers seemed surprised. They are under the impression that you are an agent of Set's and that you were working with him. It is wise that you have stayed hidden."

"Thank you for looking after my aunt," I said to him.

A sweet, soft look from Allie to Darius. "I swore to protect her, a vow I do not intend to break." I smiled. They were totally in love. I knew we could trust him.

"I need you to tell me everything you know," Roman said. "Who Amina brought with her, how many soldiers, what Houses they are from. Anything you know about her operation."

"What do you plan to do?" he asked.

"Confront Amina," I answered quickly.

Darius noticeably flinched. "We have reason to believe that Set is on his way here now," Roman filled in for him. "What Kyndal means is that we need to warn Amina, convince her to prepare her soldiers and work *with* us before Set shows up and demolishes us all." I rolled my eyes. Roman just said the same thing I had, only with fancier words.

Darius didn't panic at the news of Set's impending arrival, didn't even hesitate. A warrior to his core. "What if Amina won't listen to you?" Darius asked.

"If she's not going to listen, then we will take the compound by force," I answered harshly, not bothering to sugarcoat it. "Once we have control of the compound, the soldiers will have to listen to us, and then they can make their choice."

"What choice?" Allie asked.

Roman's voice was hard. "Either defect from Amina and join the Guard in the fight against Set, or be arrested alongside their Governor and await trial in Awen."

"Let's hope it doesn't come to that," Darius responded. "She came with a garrison of soldiers. Fifty, by my count. Most I recognized as warriors that came with her last time she was in Marienville. People that are relatively familiar with the area. She has an equal amount of Air, Earth, and Water Users."

"What about Fire?" I interrupted.

"Not any that I knew by reputation, but that doesn't mean they aren't there. I haven't seen all of them use their powers. It is possible there are more Fire Users than I realize."

"Her Fire Users were her most visible force back on the island," Roman added. "She may not have been able to bring many of them with her."

I turned to Roman. "If she's short on Fire Users, we can use that to our advantage."

"Fifty soldiers are too many to take on," Roman disagreed. "Even for us."

"If we do this right, we shouldn't have to fight at all," I argued. "We just need them to listen."

"Shouldn't that be pretty easy?" Allie asked. "I mean, I know Amina isn't exactly your fan, but this is Set you're talking about. She has to believe you. If she doesn't, her warriors could die."

I gave my aunt a sad smile. "It's not that simple."

Roman explained. "Amina hates Kyndal because she knows she's gained the favor and respect of the warriors. They are frustrated with the Nomarch Council and she thinks if the soldiers see that Kyndal is back, they will overthrow her and put Kyndal and the Guard in power. She'll be desperate to keep her seat of power, desperate enough to let her warriors die to make it happen."

"What about a diversion?" Darius asked. "Something that pulls the majority of the soldiers away, allowing you a chance to get to Amina directly?"

Roman shook his head. "No. It's imperative the soldiers are there to act as witnesses. Amina's hold on power is centered around her ability to control the information and lie to the people. We have to make sure everyone sees us. If we meet with her privately, she'll just lock us away or kill us, then deny it ever happened."

"When will you attack?" Darius asked.

"Tonight," Roman answered.

"You need to get out of town," I told my aunt. "I can't have you here, at risk, with all of this going down. I don't trust Amina or Set to not use you against me. If you can, warn Lydia, and then get out. We'll find you when it's safe."

"If you leave, do so discreetly," Roman advised. "If Amina's soldiers see you rush out of town unexpectedly, it might tip our hand." He turned to Darius, shaking his hand. "Kyndal and I will return with the rest of the Guard at midnight. Be ready."

The cabin was eerily quiet. It was nearly midnight and the four of us; Roman, Brynn, Grady, and me had secluded ourselves in the small bedroom to prepare for the upcoming attack. Isaac and Cassie were in the living room watching over Nero, while Mallory and Briar had gone to run patrol nearly an hour ago. Once they returned, we would have the all-clear to attack. None of us were particularly excited about the possibility of taking on our own people. Most of them were just soldiers doing as ordered. We had no quarrel with them and would take no pleasure in harming them if it did come down to a fight.

The small bedroom was lit by two kerosene lamps, the bed covered in a plethora of weapons. Everything from daggers and swords, to staffs and sais. Whatever we'd been able to bring with us from Siberia. Brynn and I stood on one side, the men on the other, as she reached for the sais, her weapon of choice, and tucked each of them into the backside of her belt. Then, almost as an afterthought, she grabbed a dagger, sliding it into her boot. Grady, always one to keep his weapons simple, grabbed a short sword and dagger, inserting them both into his belt scabbards. Roman was outfitted with his traditional dual daggers, although I noticed his fingers worrying over the small leather scrap that covered his forearm. I'd seen him wear it before, but never asked about it. I didn't think I needed to. He always wore it around the others, and yet never in private. I knew its placement was no accident, and that he used it to conceal his was-sceptre tattoo. He caught me staring at the small piece of leather, and I was surprised when he reached up, producing a tiny ring dagger from beneath it. My eyes lit up with excitement. Ring daggers had always been my favorite weapon. They were small, easy to conceal, and wickedly sharp. Most people overlooked them, instead going for something large and obviously intimidating, but I always used to carry one on me. Their small blades had saved my ass more than once.

Without a word, Roman held it out to me across the bed. I eagerly accepted it, immediately slipping my finger through the loop at the top, flipping the blade into the palm of my hand. The cold steel was familiar, comforting even. *Thank you*, I mouthed to him, hoping he understood exactly how much it meant to me that he had kept one of these for me all this time. He gave a simple nod in return, although the bond revealed more beneath the small gesture. I made a note that later, if we survived what we were about to attempt, I would thank him properly. I tucked the dagger away inside my belt then reached for the sword laid out in front of me. My hand wrapped around the ruby red pommel of Batil and I pulled it from its sheath for a moment to check the darkened blade.

"That is *my* sword!" Nero yelled from the other room, breaking the silence. "I was promised it back when I gave you the information, *which I've already done*. Return it to me and then set me free!"

I rolled my eyes. "We promised to release you!" Grady yelled back. "We didn't specify when! Now shut up!"

I glanced across the bed at Grady. "I told you we should have gagged him," I mumbled. He didn't disagree.

"You all know the plan?" Roman asked. Brynn and Grady nodded first, then I added my agreeance with greater reluctance. I wasn't a particularly large fan of his plan, considering it mainly hinged on me staying out of the fray and out of sight, at least until the right moment, while the rest of the Guard went into the center of the fight.

"Remember, we fight to disable, not harm. We need as many soldiers alert at the end of this as we can manage. But if someone forces your hand—" He paused. "Do what you have to do. We take the compound by any means necessary."

A stab of pain hit my abdomen, an echo of Roman's feelings. It wasn't easy to give this command. To approve the killing of our own people in order to save ourselves. I knew he would take every death personally, feel responsible for their lives as the one who ordered their death. Yet it was a burden he would gladly bear if it meant saving those closest to him.

A large thud sounded in the living room, as if a chair had been knocked over. As the one closest to the doorway, Brynn ripped it open, stepping into the living room, the rest of us following closely behind. "What was that?" she demanded. Everything was exactly as we'd left it. Nero was seated in his wooden chair, the restraints firmly in place, Cassie and Isaac standing behind him, weapons drawn.

"It didn't come from inside," Cassie answered. Everyone in the room froze, our senses on high alert. The hairs on the back of my neck stood at attention. Something wasn't right. I pulled on my power, heightening my sight, my hearing. I glanced quickly at Roman, noting he had done the same thing. His eyes were shining gold as he tried to detect anything out of place. For several moments, nothing happened. Then, another thud rang off the front door, this time louder than the first. As one, we broke toward the old piece of wood, yanking it open only to find an empty porch.

"No one is here," Grady pointed out, stating the obvious.

I pushed my way toward the front to stand next to him. I stared out into the darkness, the minimal night light making it hard to see anything. Behind me, Brynn leaned down to pick up something. "What is that?" Roman asked. She held it out for us to see. It was a rock, large enough to fill the palm of her hand.

Had that been there before?

Before I could voice my question, Grady yelled, "Look out!" only moments before pushing me out of the way. I faltered, nearly falling down, but managed to catch myself at the last moment. I turned to yell at him for shoving me, but before I could, another rock of the same size came whizzing past my head and into the cabin. It crashed loudly into some cups and dishes we'd had sitting on the table, knocking them over.

"Someone is throwing them," Brynn said.

"There's no one close enough to be throwing them," I pointed out. The surrounding area was empty.

"An Earth User could." Grady pushed his russet hair out of his face, his keen eyes glowing green, searching the land for any power signatures. "There!" he declared, pointing into the darkness at some power source only he could see. He leapt from the porch, taking off into the night.

The three of us followed, but a few steps onto the grass, I turned back to the cabin. "Stay here!" I ordered Cassie and Isaac. We couldn't risk this being a distraction, something to help Nero escape. By the time I caught up with the others, they were out of sight of the cabin and already huddled around a large mass curled up on the soft grass, a form I quickly recognized. "Briar." Barely recognizable, she was slumped on her side, one arm tucked into her torso, the other outstretched toward the direction of the cabin. Her pants were ripped in several places, her tibia broken and protruding through one of the tears. Her breathing was shallow and wet as if one of her lungs was punctured.

"What happened?" Roman demanded.

"Where is Mallory?" I added immediately.

"They took her," Briar managed to rasp. Her breathing was short and labored. "We were outnumbered and she took the brunt of the attack so I could run back."

They? Who were they? Amina's soldiers? Was Set already here? Too many unanswered questions.

"No more talking. Grady, Kyndal, support her leg while I turn her," Brynn ordered. She was right, so I quickly shut up and did as instructed. Carefully, Brynn turned Briar to her back. I flinched as she moaned in pain at the movement. Briar pulled away her arm, the one protecting her torso, exposing a large gash that was gushing blood. Brynn covered the wound with her hand, pressing down harshly to stop the bleeding. Briar screamed at the contact. Brynn looked to Roman. "I can't fix this. We need to get her to Cassie."

"We have to move fast," Roman answered, his eyes scanning the trees. "It isn't safe out here."

"Roman," I said, getting his attention. "They have Mallory."

The look he gave me, the fear I felt churning through the bond made my stomach drop. "One thing at a time," Grady cut in. "Let's get Briar to Cassie, then we'll go find Mallory." Roman knelt down, placing his hands under Briar's shoulders. Grady and I each had a leg, Brynn's hands holding firm to Briar's wound. "On three," Grady counted.

We moved through the forest as quickly as we could. It was not a long distance to the cabin, but we had to be careful of our steps and try our best not to jostle Briar, which slowed us down. When the cabin came into view, the door was still wide open and I could see the others inside, just where we left them. *We're going to make it in time. Everything will be fine. We'll patch up Briar and then save Mallory.* I repeated the words like a mantra, like the only acceptable outcome. We hit the steps and Roman called out, "Cassie! Briar is hurt!" We laid her down on the open floor, all of us focused on our injured comrade.

I expected to hear the thundering of Cassie's steps as she ran to help, but they never came, instead I heard her strong voice from across the room. "Kyndal."

I ignored her, instead stayed focused on Briar, on keeping her leg steady. "Her leg is broken," I answered without looking up. "You need to set it before she begins healing."

"Kyndal," my name sounded again, this time from Roman. Unable to ignore him, my head snapped up. He wasn't kneeling like I expected, but standing at Briar's side, frozen in place. His eyes trained ahead of him. Slowly, I turned to follow his line of sight. He was staring at Nero—where Cassie and Isaac stood behind him—just as they had before. Except now they weren't alone. Not anymore. There were five others. They had to have been hiding in the bedroom, waiting for us to return. Their eyes glowed brightly, their veins darkened, protruding through their necks and faces, weapons drawn and pointed toward my friends.

Hybrids.

We were too late.

Set had found us.

Chapter 22

Roman

For what felt like forever, no one moved.

I stared at the hybrids, their weapons poised at Cassie's back, at Isaac's throat. One move and they would run them through. In the middle of it all, Nero sat, his eyes surprisingly murderous, intent on the hybrids although they did not directly threaten him. Not the face of a man whose rescuers had come to his aid, but the face of a warrior prepared to fight for his life. Grady had turned toward the threat, abandoning Briar who was writhing on the floor in pain, the only source of movement in the room. Brynn held true, keeping her hands pressed down on Briar's wound, twisting as much as she could in order to keep an eye on the enemy. If she moved her hands, Briar would bleed to death.

The room was thick with power, each of the hybrids pulling their fill. Their eyes glowed brightly, skittering across the space rapidly like wild animals. Waiting for one of us to move, one of us to strike. I took stock of their elements. Two Air Users, one Water, one Earth, one Fire. There were only five of them for the moment, but I knew there had to be more. Set wanted to know where the sceptre was, he wouldn't only send a few scouts. He would have sent an army. Maybe even come to Marienville himself. He could be on his way to the cabin at this exact moment. If we were going to do something, if we were going to escape, we had to do it now, before any reinforcements arrived.

"We've come for the Guard," the Water User declared, his eyes landing on me. "You have been summoned by our master. Come with us now and there will be no violence."

Like hell there wouldn't be, I thought bitterly.

Kyndal rose from her crouched position slowly, her muscles taut, her eyes solely focused on the enemies in the room. Each hybrid turned their attention to her. Power radiated off her. She was clearly the largest threat in the room. I prepared myself for blind rage to barrel down the bond. These were the creatures that held her captive, that pushed her around, that forced her to bear witness to countless atrocities, but the rage never came. Instead there was a stillness to her anger, which was somehow more frightening. It was controlled, focused, like the edge of a perfectly-sharpened blade. Her fingers twitched toward her belt, to the hidden ring dagger. She didn't spare a single glance toward me, but I knew what she would do. We couldn't talk our way out of this one. We had to fight. "We aren't going anywhere with you. Your *master* can go to hell," she growled. Faster than I'd ever seen her move, faster than the hybrids could follow, she pulled her ring dagger from her belt, flinging it across the room. The tiny dagger struck the Water User hybrid next to Isaac directly through the heart.

Before the hybrid's body hit the floor, the room erupted. Isaac tackled the nearest hybrid, knocking him away from Cassie, buying her the precious seconds she needed to get out of the hybrid's reach. As one, Grady, Kyndal, and I rushed toward the hybrids, at the same moment Cassie broke toward Briar. The room was small, but we spread out as much as we could, Kyndal taking on the two Air Users, Grady squaring off with the Earth User, leaving me the Fire User, the one Isaac had knocked down.

I summoned my power, and wind tore through the open door, filling the cabin. I pushed it toward the Fire User, lifting him off the floor and throwing him into the opposite wall. He bounced hard off the wood, dust falling around him as he landed in a heap. I spun toward Isaac. "Help Cassie," I ordered him as I pulled my dagger from my belt. For once he didn't argue.

"Roman!" I heard the deep voice call my name, forcing me to turn back to the fight. I thought the Fire User was still prone on the ground, but instead I found him standing not five feet from me, a fireball ready in hand. Before I could react, he threw it at point blank range directly at my chest. It barreled toward me, too fast for me to evade. The shot should have killed me, and yet mere inches from my chest, it froze in mid-air. The flames still roiled, their heat burning my cheeks it was so close, and yet it came no closer.

It wasn't a shield that had stopped it. None of us had had time to raise one. Kyndal couldn't be the one who stopped it either. She was busy fighting her own battle. But it made no sense, she was the only other Fire User except—I turned—except Nero.

Still tied to the chair, Nero's eyes were a lively red, staring at the suspended fireball. As hard as it was for me to believe, he had just saved my life.

Refusing to look too closely at *that issue,* I stepped around the fireball. The hybrid was as surprised as I was and I took advantage, driving my dagger through his heart, up to the hilt. With his death, the fireball disintegrated.

"You're welcome," Nero growled.

I ignored him, instead running around him to help finish off the other hybrids. Grady and Kyndal were holding their own just fine, but we had no time to spare before other hybrids arrived. Kyndal was down to one hybrid and I felt her power building, knew she would be ending the fight soon. I jumped in next to Grady. He was matched for element with the hybrid, making his powers useless. I pushed a strong surge of air at the hybrid, sliding him into the wall and holding him there. Behind me, a burst of flames erupted from the floor. Kyndal finishing off her opponent.

"Finish him!" I shouted at Grady. He didn't hesitate. He leapt forward, burying his dagger in the hybrid's heart.

With no other enemies to fight, the bond demanded my attention, almost forcing me to turn and make sure Kyndal was alright. She stood not ten feet from me, her chest heaving from the adrenaline. Her eyes locked onto mine, a brilliant red to what I knew was my own bright gold. Grady stepped in line next to her, his own eyes shining green. None of us were prepared to lower our guard or release our powers. "We need to get to the compound," I told them both. "Now."

"Brynn, you're with us," Grady added, looking to our final Guard member. I didn't have to be connected to him to feel his bloodlust. It was written all over his face, obvious in the way he clenched his hand around the hilt of his short sword.

"Brynn is currently holding Briar's small intestine in place," Cassie interrupted, her voice rough. "She's not going anywhere." She made no mention of the blood covering her own hands as she furiously tried to patch Briar back together.

Grady took a small, threatening step forward. "Set could be at that compound. We need every fighter we can get. That includes the *entire* Guard."

"If she moves, Briar will die!" Cassie shouted back.

"If we don't go soon, we will all die!" Grady yelled in return, not backing down an inch.

"I'll stay with Cassie and help Briar," Isaac declared, stepping forward. He gave no room for anyone to argue, just simply dropped to his knees at Briar's side, sliding his hands underneath Brynn's. She pulled her hands away slowly, almost as if she didn't trust Isaac enough to let go.

"Roman," Cassie said, pulling my attention. I looked to my adopted sister, surprised to find fear in her eyes. "Find her."

I didn't have to ask who she was talking about. To Cassie there was no one else that mattered. "I promise," I answered. I spun around, running my dagger through the restraints that held Nero in place.

"What are you doing?" Kyndal demanded.

With a triumphant smile, my father stood from the chair, dramatically stretching his tall frame. I flipped the dagger in my palm, holding its hilt out to Nero. "Like Grady said, we need every fighter we can get. He'll either help us or betray us." I turned to my father. "And if he betrays us, I'll kill him myself."

The five of us sprinted through the forest at top speed. It was the middle of the night, so we didn't have to worry about hikers and tourists out in the forest who could see us. Anyone out at this time of night was dangerous.

Anyone out at this time was the enemy.

Thunder rumbled and lightning cracked across the sky, where only an hour before, the moon had shone clear. The same thing we'd seen in Siberia when Set arrived. We combined powers immediately after leaving the cabin, using each other's reserves to strengthen ourselves. Out in the forest, our power was a never-ending well. We could pull as much as we needed from our surroundings. We pushed faster through the undergrowth of the forest. There was no way to extend our power to Nero, but he managed to keep up on his own.

During the summer, the Allegheny was at its wildest. The grasses were overgrown, the trees thick and lush, their branches reaching across worn paths, creating obstacles where there used to be none. I took the lead, knowing the forest better than the others.

The cabin was on the opposite side of the forest from the compound, we'd chosen it for that very reason. It would be several miles until we reached it. As we ran through the forest, the sky grew darker, the claps of thunder getting louder and closer together until we felt them rumble in our bones. We ran around the town, past a trail that I knew would lead us to the school, beyond the dark and deserted *Sandra's* until finally we broke through to the clearing where the funeral pyres had once stood.

"No guards on patrol," Brynn called out to us, even as we kept moving. She was right. The compound was less than a mile away, Amina should have had guards watching the perimeter. Their absence did not bode well for what we were heading into. There was only one more treeline between us and the compound. Any other time of the year and the trees would be thin enough we would be able to see the compound from here, but now they were thick enough to obscure it from view, a blessing that meant no one would see us coming. Using that advantage and the rumble of thunder overhead to mask the pounding of our footsteps, we sprinted through the open field.

Just before we reached the opposite end of the field, another clap of thunder sounded directly overhead, followed immediately by lightning that struck the top of a giant maple tree. The ancient tree crackled and sparked, the branches catching fire, the flames jumping to nearby trees, consuming the smaller parts of the trees and working their way down the trunks at a speed that was too fast to be natural. "We have to move faster or those flames are going to block us from the compound!" I yelled to the others. This was the best way in. If we were forced to run around it, it would waste precious time.

We all pushed harder, but even as we grew closer, I knew we weren't going to make it in time. The flames spread to create an impenetrable wall, and I slowed, planning to turn and find another way in. "Don't stop!" Kyndal shouted, even as she and Nero sprinted past us. I didn't understand, not until I felt the shield snap around me. With our powers combined, the shield spread from me to Grady and Brynn. Kyndal leapt through the flames first, unsheathing Batil from her back mid jump; Nero following quickly behind. The shield didn't extend to him, but he didn't need it. Fire could not burn an Aries.

"Aw, hell," Grady hissed as we grew closer to the flames. I understood exactly. I'd seen the shield at work several times but stopping a fireball was one thing. Allowing us to jump through a giant wall of fire was something completely different.

"Don't think about it," Brynn yelled. "Just jump." Her final words before she disappeared into the flames.

Trusting in the shield, trusting in Kyndal, Grady and I leapt into the fire, throwing our arms up to shield our faces as we made our way through it to the other side. The flames were suffocatingly hot, but while I could feel their heat, there was no pain. I landed in a crouch on the other side, dagger in hand, Grady at my side. Both of us without a single burn. Thunder rolled overhead. Lightning struck, illuminating the compound and the battle being waged all around us.

Everywhere I looked, there were Kindred fighting to the death. They were in the training rings, on the back porch of the main house, even more up against the logs stacked for a bonfire long forgotten. Amina herself was in the middle of the fray, her long, dark ponytail swinging around wildly as she spun to slice her dagger across the face of an Air User hybrid. He roared in pain and Amina pressed her advantage, burying her weapon in his chest, throwing his body roughly to the ground before moving on to the next. For as many soldiers as she'd brought, they were still outnumbered at least two to one.

I searched the area for Set, but no matter where I looked, I didn't see him. *He has to be here. There's no way he isn't.* Thunder cracked overhead again, this time breaking apart the clouds, and rain poured down on our heads. The bond tugged at me, pulling my attention to the part of the property just behind my old house. Kyndal was there, already in the thick of it. Ten feet from her, Nero fought, too. Fire shot from the blazing trees behind him, blasting a hybrid across the yard. "Go help Brynn," I ordered Grady, drawn to help my Rafiq.

I sprinted into the fray, to where Kyndal was fighting three hybrids simultaneously. I called to my element, the raindrops stinging my skin as the wind whipped around me. I felt Kyndal's power build, as she no doubt felt mine. The obsidian blade in her hand burst into a flaming sword just as I released the wind to help her. She spun quickly, using the wind to extend the flames from the sword forward as she cut across the chests of all three hybrids. The fire caught their gear, moving with too much speed and power for the rain to put it out in time. Just as I reached Kyndal, the hybrids dropped to their knees, screaming.

We didn't wait for them to die, instead we turned to where the fighting was the most fierce. Back-to-back we fought the hybrids. Fully in tune to each other's powers, and infinitely stronger together, Kyndal and I were unstoppable. We cut through the enemies, downing every hybrid in our sight, giving no thought to their House or who they used to be. As the rain continued to pour, the blades became slick in our hands, the ground unsteady underfoot. But when one of us faltered, the other was there to cover.

The battlefield was chaos, hybrids and Kindred alike using their various elements as means to attack. Fire flew across the field, the roaring trees giving the Fire Users plenty to pull from. Gusts of wind ripped through the property, Air Users forcing the wind to do their bidding, even as the Water Users fought for the rain to heed their calling. The ground at our feet rumbled, as Earth Users tore apart the wet earth, ripping trees from their roots and sending them across the clearing. Kyndal and I worked our way to the center of the yard, to the area used for bonfires. We used the large logs as cover, setting our backs to them as we fought off one hybrid after the other. On the other side of the battlefield, near the steps of the main house, I could still sense Grady and Brynn, fighting just as fiercely as we were. Combined as we were, out in the open and surrounded by nature, our shield held strong, giving us the advantage against the hybrids. Their numbers were dwindling, and although I knew several of the bodies that littered the wet ground were Kindred, more of them were hybrids.

Just as Kyndal felled another enemy, the hairs on the back of my neck stood at attention. I spun to the right, instinct telling me to raise my dagger. The weapon clashed with mine a split second before I realized who was on the other end of the attack. Not a hybrid at all.

Amina.

I roared, pushing back with all my force, the ancient Nomarch only faltering two steps. Next to me, Kyndal turned, her sword, somehow darker from the blood of hybrids, pointed directly at Amina's throat. "What are you doing, Amina?" I yelled over the wind and thunder. "We're on the same side, we came here to help you!"

She eyed the blade pointed at her throat, the one she knew belonged to my father. "You came to kill me!" she shouted back, the rain pouring off her, sticking her hair to her back. Behind her, Grady and Brynn closed ranks. She spun, dagger raised, but when she found no gap in our defenses she turned back to Kyndal and me. "You're working with Set!" Around us, the battle raged, the remaining Kindred slowly wearing down the hybrids.

"You're insane!" Kyndal yelled. "We want to stop Set! That's all we've ever wanted! Tell us where he is!"

"I knew the moment I met you that you would be the downfall of us all," Amina spit at her. The facade was completely gone now, she wasn't performing for the people. This was the real Amina. "You are a disgrace to everything that is good and noble about the Kindred. We were a strong, proud people until you broke us apart. Your mother was a traitor and you have followed directly in her footsteps. You should have died in the arena during The Blinding or in Cairo along with your wraith of a lover. We would all be better off. Now look around us. You will be the death of us all."

"You brought this upon our people!" I yelled at Amina, unable to stand idly by and listen to her spew her venom. "You lied to the Kindred, you told them Kyndal was a traitor. That you were our people's only hope in defeating Set, and then every chance you've had, you've weakened us. You refused to let the Guard into the war when you knew we could save lives. You imprisoned those who dared to speak the truth and killed your own soldiers when they wouldn't fall to command. While you've been working to break us apart, Set has been building his forces against us. Now you put this entire town at risk just to protect your political position."

"No longer," Kyndal added simply, her voice rock hard. "You don't lead the Kindred anymore."

"Lay down your weapon, Amina," Brynn added. "We'll take you back to Awen and see that you get a fair trial."

Before she could say anything, there was a snarl behind us, an Earth User hybrid had slipped through the Kindred and was running our way, dagger raised high. I turned, preparing my weapon, when a dagger flew from around the bonfire, striking him dead. Moments later, a flash of red appeared in the darkness.

Cassie.

She ripped the dagger from the dead hybrid, a limping, and yet very alive Briar only a step behind her. I had no time to question how she had survived, why she was here. My adopted sister stood by my side, staring down her former lover. "Where is Mallory?" she demanded.

Amina laughed, the sound dark and twisted. "When will you realize just how bad that *Gemini bitch* is for you?"

Cassie's eyes turned in an instant, her dagger flying from her hand again, embedding itself in Amina's thigh. She screamed, dropping to one knee. "I will not ask again," Cassie sneered.

Amina ripped the dagger from her leg, dropping the bloodied weapon to the ground. "I don't have her, which must mean Set does." She staggered to her feet. "For what it's worth, I hope he kills her. I hope he kills all of you."

Thunder boomed overhead again, a bolt of lightning striking the bonfire logs not two feet from us. The electricity of the bolt blasted outward, sending all of us spinning through the air. Kyndal and I were thrown across the yard, too quickly for me to use my element to cushion our fall. We landed in a heap on the other side of the yard, our bodies smacking into the muddy ground. Shrapnel from the logs rained down on us, the wooden chunks ricocheting off our skin. My muscles spasmed as electricity pulsed through them, paralyzing me. I willed my arms to move, to push me up, and yet they didn't budge. "Kyndal," I coughed, my chest burning through the word. My pain or hers, I couldn't tell. She had landed in front of me, but her back faced my direction. I couldn't see if she was conscious or not. "Kyndal, are you okay?"

Finally, she groaned, the painful sound resonating through me. "Roman?" she asked.

"I'm here." Another burning pain.

"I can't move, Roman."

"I know," I replied, desperately wishing I could reach out to her, help her up. "It's the electricity from the lightning strike. Just focus on healing yourself. It's only temporary." I might not have been able to touch her physically, but I reached out with the bond, using it to soothe her, to comfort her, and let her know she wasn't alone.

Across the yard, the others were scattered. Amina, as close to the blast as Kyndal and I had been, was laying limply in the mud, unconscious. Brynn and Grady had been further away from the strike and were sprawled out a few feet from each other, near the main house. The shield had completely disintegrated, and I couldn't feel them anymore, but they both were moving, slowly pushing themselves up, pushing broken pieces of logs off themselves. Cassie and Briar had been the furthest away, and although they hadn't avoided it completely, they were already back on their feet. I expected them to rush to our aid, but they both stood, as if rooted to the ground, staring at where the gravel driveway met the open yard. I followed their gaze, still unable to move, my eyes bulging when I saw what had them so scared.

"Kyndal, it's Set," I rasped. "Set is here." And he wasn't alone.

Chapter 23

Kyndal

I'd been on the receiving end of Set's power more times than I could remember, but I'd never experienced the strength of his power like this before. I'd never felt the sort of pain like I did the moment that lightning strike ripped through my body. Not when I'd been stabbed or beaten, or when the bones in my hand had been ground to dust. Not even when Roman had been killed. It was like every nerve in my body was being ripped apart piece by piece and I had no control to stop it.

He sauntered into the backyard of the compound, his red eyes glowing, the storm clouds reflected in his irises. His veins ran a bright red, almost glowing in the darkness as they weaved over the tight skin of his arms, neck, and face. For once, the shadows I'd seen swirl around him were nowhere to be found, but I knew at the slightest provocation, they could return. While the thunder still boomed, the lightning and rain had stopped almost immediately, as if he'd flipped some sort of off switch. His large hand was twisted in the long, caramel-colored hair of a Kindred soldier as he dragged her behind him. Her feet slipped through the mud, and she tripped and fell several times as he continued to yank her forward. The woman's hair was tangled and falling into her face, and what part of her face wasn't covered with hair was bloodied and beaten. Even with all of that, I knew exactly who it was. I would recognize her anywhere.

"Mallory!" the name tore out of Cassie, as if she couldn't stop herself from calling out to her longtime partner. It broke my heart to hear the panic and fear in my friend's voice. To know the pain she felt as she watched the person she loved the most be dragged behind the Chaos god. "Let her go, Set!"

Obliging her, Set threw Mallory into the wet mud at his feet. She fell limply, barely able to catch herself from landing face first. Kneeling, she slowly sat back on her legs, raising her bloodied face to see Cassie. Her eyes glowed a soft honey instead of a brilliant gold, strong and defiant even in her weakened state.

"I will make this very simple," Set began, his voice echoing through the compound. Remaining hybrids and Kindred froze mid-battle to listen. "I want the was-sceptre. Bring it to me, and I'll spare her life. Refuse and she dies."

I dug deep into my power, trying to force my body to get up, to move, to do *something*. No matter how much I pulled forward, I could only manage to get my right hand to twitch.

"We don't have it," Cassie answered, her voice wavering slightly. A carefully worded truth. "It's not here."

Set's head turned, the movement slow and calculated, not quite human. "Then where is it?" he demanded of her.

"Don't tell him shit," Mallory growled. Set reached down, staring at Cassie as he violently pulled Mallory back by her hair, his other hand landing over her heart. Outwardly, nothing changed, but Mallory bucked backward, a scream escaping her lips as Set fed from her. He smiled at Cassie as he did it, before dropping Mallory to all fours. Her breath came in sharp, painful gasps. Rage filled my veins at the sight of my friend writhing in the mud. She wouldn't survive another feeding like that. She was too weak.

Cassie lunged forward, but Set cut her off, stepping over Mallory. "You can end her pain," he said. "She doesn't have to suffer for a moment longer, just tell me where the sceptre is."

"Do not speak a word, Cassandra White. That is an order," a newly-awakened Amina yelled. She staggered to her feet, attempting and failing to straighten her gear. "If he gets his hands on that sceptre, he will kill *thousands*."

"Millions," Set corrected, unrepentant. "But if you don't, I'll kill the one you love most. Now."

"One life is not worth millions," Amina finished for him. "Kill her, it makes no difference. We will not give up the sceptre."

We. As if Amina was on the same side as the rest of us. As if she even knew where the sceptre was hidden.

Cassie never took her eyes off Mallory, even as I knew her next words weren't for her. "You're right. A single life is less important than the lives of the many. But she is not *any* life. She is my love, my partner, my everything." Tears shone in Mallory's eyes, as her lover confessed the choice she would make. As if she knew she would have made the same one. "You don't speak for the people anymore Amina. You do not decide *for* me. The sceptre was stolen by Astrid, the Nomarch of House Cancer."

"You *stupid, ignorant. . .*" Amina sneered, reaching down and grabbing a dagger from the body of a nearby dead hybrid. She raised the dagger, intent on attacking Cassie. She only made it a couple of steps before another blade, one pointed at her throat, brought her up short.

"You raise another hand against a Kindred and I will see that it is the last choice you make as a free woman," Brynn growled. Amina twisted her head, her eyes boring into my fellow Guardsman, and yet she heeded the warning. She lowered her arm, although she did not drop the weapon.

Thunder clapped overhead, a maniacal cackle bursting forth from Set. "So much chaos!" he shouted excitedly. "It's almost a shame I plan to kill you all myself. It would be so much more entertaining to watch you rip each other apart from the inside." He shrugged, a strangely human gesture. "However, plans being what they are. . ." He turned to Cassie. "You were saying?"

"I already told you where the sceptre is!" she shouted frantically. "Let her go."

"Astrid is hardly an answer, child. She could have hidden it anywhere in the world by now. Where is it?"

"We know why you want it!" I yelled, pulling Set's attention. I dug to the very bottom of my power, surprised to find what could only be described as wet earth waiting for me. Brynn and Grady's power. I used it, pulled it into me as I healed my muscles enough to push myself to my feet. I was wobbly at best, but I managed to stay upright. Behind me, Roman was recovering as well, albeit slower. "Nero told us what you plan to use the sceptre for," I added, not caring that I was selling out the Commander, who was surprisingly still around, poised with a dagger in hand, intent on our conversation. "He also explained what you planned to do with me."

Set smirked. "And you think this makes a difference?" he taunted. "You knowing my plan. As if simply possessing the knowledge would be enough for you to stop me."

"You never wanted me to take you to the Inbetween," I continued, trying my damnedest to stall him. I had enough power to get to my feet, but not nearly enough to fight. Not yet. "You were just using me to build your army, to create more of your hybrids. You never planned on killing Maat."

The thunder clouds in Set's eyes rolled with excitement. "Oh, but I do! You see Maat hid behind her responsibilities, claiming it was her duty to keep the wraiths in Duat and that was why she had to return to the Inbetween, when really she was a coward. She was too frightened to face me on this plane, so instead she left her precious Kindred to do her dirty work. But if she will not come to me willingly, then I will tear down the barrier and bring the entire Inbetween here. After my wraiths have wiped out her children, and after I have rammed the sceptre through her heart, I will regain my rightful status as the ultimate supreme being. No one will be able to refute that. Then your blood will help me raise an army so vast, no one would ever dare challenge me again." He returned to Cassie. "For the last time, where did Astrid hide the sceptre?"

"I have no idea," Cassie responded immediately. "I swear it! I don't know!"

Set tilted his head, looking back at Mallory, then to Cassie, a fake pout resting on his lips. "That's really too bad. I suppose you were no help after all." He took a single step toward Mallory.

"It's in Awen!" I screamed, bringing him up short. I staggered forward, finally feeling the first spark of my power returning, brought to me on a cool breeze. Roman's power joining mine. "The sceptre is in Awen, but that's all we know, I swear it. She would never take it off the island, out from behind the wards."

"See, was that so hard?" he asked.

"It's protected by thousands of soldiers, you'll never get to it," I threatened. "If you go after it, we *will* stop you and bury you back under the Hollow where you belong."

"We shall see." Thunder cracked overhead, a lightning strike landing directly where Set was standing, blinding us all. I raised my arm to shield myself from the light. By the time I lowered it, he was gone.

Cassie sprinted to Mallory. I spun, dropping to my knees in front of Roman. I shoved my arms under his armpits, pulling him to his feet. "Are you alright?" I whispered. I knew he'd given me whatever power he could muster instead of using it to save himself.

"I'll be fine," he answered. "I just need a minute."

"What the hell was that?" Grady yelled from across the yard, walking past where Brynn still held Amina at knife point. He was smart enough to stop several feet from me. "You told him where the sceptre was."

"I had no choice," I growled, not in the mood for his attitude. "He was going to kill Mallory."

"So?" he questioned. "One life versus *millions*."

"Say we did nothing, and he killed Mallory. What do you think he would have done then? Do you think he would have stopped? Just given up and left? He would have just chosen someone else, worked this way through all of us until either we were all dead or one of us cracked and told him where it was."

"He's going to attack the island."

"Not right away," I countered. "He'll have to gather his forces, which means returning to Helwan. Then he'll have to get them onto the island through conventional means. He'll need his whole army, and not even a Chaos god is strong enough to teleport them all there at once. We have time to get there ahead of him and make our final stand."

"Kyndal's right, Grady," Brynn added, not taking her eyes from Amina. "We can warn the other Nomarchs, have them prepare the soldiers. They can reinforce the wards. It won't keep the hybrids or Set out, but it will prevent him from using any of his wraiths. Not to mention, we have Kyndal now, and we can use the sceptre to defeat him and put him back in the cage for good." Grady gave no response, instead grinding his teeth together as he contemplated the answer. Concerned by his silence, Brynn took her eyes off of Amina for one moment to look at her friend.

But that was all it took.

Amina lunged, knocking Brynn's arm away, forcing her to drop her dagger. Still holding one in her hand, Amina threw it with deadly accuracy and speed across the lawn. It whizzed past Grady, headed directly for my heart. There was no chance for me to duck, and even if I did, that would just leave Roman vulnerable. I spun, shielding a weakened Roman with my body. There was the unmistakable sound of metal tearing through flesh, and yet I felt nothing. I prepared for the inevitable pain, but it never came. I brought my hand up to my heart, expecting it to come away bloody, and yet it was clean.

I looked to Roman, panicked. "Are you okay?" I felt his chest, grabbed his arms, his torso, my hands shaking as they searched for some unseen wound. Had the dagger somehow hit him? He was covered in blood from the battle, but no fresh wounds as far as I could see. *If the dagger hadn't hit me, and hadn't hit him, who did it hit?*

I spun around, my eyes immediately dropping in front of me. Briar lay in the mud at my feet, the dagger embedded in her chest. She coughed, blood spewing from her mouth. "No!" I yelled, falling at her side. I reached for the dagger, ready to pull it out, but Briar's hand covered mine.

"Don't," she gasped.

"No, I have to," I told her, tears filling my eyes. "You have to heal yourself. I'll pull the dagger out and you can heal yourself. Everything will be fine." I knew I was rambling, but I didn't care.

"I always knew I would help you return to Awen," she said between coughs, curling in on herself. "Give me a proper funeral," she whispered, her voice so quiet, that without my enhanced hearing, I wouldn't have heard her. "Cleanse my soul so I may be at peace."

Then her eyes glazed over, and Briar took her last breath.

Chapter 24

Kyndal

The full moon shone above the canopy of the forest as I waited for it to be midnight.

The air was warm, my damp hair falling freely down the back of my black tank top. I'd finally showered this evening, my first warm one in recent memory, before putting back on my tactical gear.

After Set had disappeared, it'd taken the rest of the night and the next day to clear the dead and build the pyres. Together, Nero and I had pulled the fire from the burning trees. The last thing we needed was the Sheriff or rangers showing up at the compound after catching wind of a forest fire. Pulling that amount of fire into myself had reenergized my magic, healing any remaining wounds and bringing me back to full strength. The wood that hadn't been ruined was cut down, used to make five large pyres. Of the fifty soldiers Amina had brought with her, thirteen had been killed. Adding Briar to the list, left us at an even fourteen.

339

Three of the pyres were for them. It wasn't horrible considering what they'd been up against, and I knew it would have been worse if we hadn't been there to interfere. The other two pyres were reserved for the hybrids. They may be the enemy, but before that, they were our brethren. The least we could do was honor them in their deaths.

Amina had been arrested, her soldiers now falling under command of the Guard. Just as we suspected, many of them had thought I was as good as dead. After showing them otherwise, not to mention saving them from a brutal death, they were quick to rethink their allegiances.

The twelve torches had been placed in a circle around the pyres, the other elements prepared and waiting in their bowls on an old wooden bench behind me. I stood in front of them while I watched in silence as the others joined me in the clearing. Led by Roman, then Grady and Brynn, Amina's soldiers filed into the clearing, spreading out amongst the dormant torches. There was no sign of Mallory, Cassie, or Nero. The first two I knew were in Roman's house. Mallory wasn't fully recovered, and Cassie wouldn't leave her side until she was one hundred percent again. Nero was in the main house, guarding Amina, who was under twenty-four-hour surveillance until we could get her back to Awen and in one of the holding cells. Oddly, the Commander being in charge of the Governor's security didn't bring me the amount of trepidation I had expected it to. He'd saved Roman, fought on our side in the battle. I might not fully trust him, but I knew he hated Amina as much as the rest of us. He would never work with her.

Maybe I'd get lucky and he'd kill her.

The last people to come into the field were Isaac, Darius, and my aunt Allie. I had spoken with her earlier in the morning. She and Darius hadn't had the time to flee like we'd hoped. By the time they were ready to go, the hybrids were already here, and it was too dangerous to move. She and Darius had bunkered down in the house, only able to wait and hope that none of the hybrids found them. I'd sent Isaac to find them and bring them to the safety of the compound. At the moment, the compound was the only safe place for her, although I knew that wouldn't last. She'd gotten too deep into this world, and I wasn't going to be around to protect her forever. If I wanted to keep her safe, I was going to have to do something drastic.

When everyone had taken their place, I took a deep breath, stepping forward and calling to my power. My eyes turned a sharp red, the sounds and smells of the forest filling my senses. I raised my hands, the twelve surrounding torches bursting to life. The flames reflected off the deep hues of the shrouds wrapped around the dead, their golds, reds, blues, and greens dancing in the fire light. Roman, Grady, and Brynn stepped forward to stand alongside me. A united Guard, commanding the Kindred. "We come here tonight to honor the dead. To cleanse the souls of those who gave their lives so we could continue the fight."

Grady stepped forward, his eyes glowing green. Around him the dirt from the bowl swirled. "We cover their bodies with the earth, to remind ourselves from where we came, and where we shall all eventually return." The dirt spread across the clearing, lightly dusting the bodies.

"We cleanse their souls with water," Brynn added, her blue eyes shining as the water moved toward the pyres, "so they may find peace."

My eyes shone with tears, and my voice was scratchy as it rang through the clearing. "As fire consumes their bodies, we know they have not truly died, but live on the Other Side where we may one day be reunited."

Roman stepped forward, grabbing my hand. "As the air carries them to their final resting place, may we never forget their sacrifice."

He squeezed my hand, a silent signal. I called to the torches, all of them leaping to attention. The flames flew to the pyres, and we all stood in silence as the dead burned.

As the flames gave way to embers, the warriors slowly receded, until Roman and I were the only ones left. Grady and Brynn had been the last to leave, each placing a soft hand on my shoulder as they passed. I knew they were headed back to check on Amina. After all that had happened, Brynn wouldn't let her out of her sight for long.

I stared at the pyre closest to me, at where Briar's emerald colored shroud had been consumed by the flames. I'd cleaned her up myself, washed the blood from her skin, combed her hair. "I barely knew her," I said. "I barely knew her, and she sacrificed herself for me. Why would she do that?"

Roman moved behind me, wrapping his arms around me, enveloping me in his embrace. He kissed the top of my head. "Briar believed in you. The first time I met her, she said she knew you would be the one to deliver the Kindred from darkness. That through her, you would return to Awen."

The tears I'd tried so hard to hold back broke through, spilling down my face. For once, I didn't try to stop them, not when it was just Roman to see. "And you think this is what she meant?" My voice cracked. "That she would die so I could live? How am I worthy of that kind of devotion?"

Roman tightened his grip around me, wrapping me in his strength and power. "She saw the same thing in you that I see. That anyone around you feels. I'm not just talking about your power, either. It's your loyalty, your devotion, your heart. You are amazing. I've never met anyone else like you."

His words filled me with pride. Roman was an exceptionally tough critic—and for him to say such things—I did not take them lightly. I craned my neck, kissing him on his jaw. "Tonight was too close," I told him. "There was a Chaos god in our home. Miles away from my family, my friends, all those I care about. This can't happen again."

"It won't," he assured me. He didn't know how right he was.

"I know," I answered, the idea that had been permeating in the back of my head taking full form. "And I know how to make sure of it."

"You want to do what?" Allie demanded.

I leaned against the fireplace in Roman's house, even though no flames crackled in its hearth. The remaining Kindred, the nearly forty of them, milled about the main house, packing their things and preparing for us to leave. Only the inner circle was privy to our meeting, the silence sigils ensuring we wouldn't be overheard. "It's the best thing for everyone. Trust me," Brynn implored her.

"You can't lock yourself out of Marienville, I won't let you." Allie crossed her arms.

I popped my knuckles, finally facing my aunt. "It's not up to you," I said softly. "We've already discussed it and this *is* going to happen. Think about what has happened in the last twelve months. All the wraith attacks, the innocent people who were killed. Let's not forget you were kidnapped and nearly killed, too. My enemies know that they can threaten you, threaten the people here to get a reaction from me. Marienville has become a weakness, and the only way to keep you safe is if I'm no longer attached to anything here. This is the only way you will be safe."

She scoffed, throwing her hands in the air. "If you've made this decision already, why even bother telling me at all? Why not just do the damn spell or whatever and leave? You clearly don't need me."

I pursed my lips at her choice of words. "Actually, we do." I looked to Roman for support.

"Every big spell requires an anchor," he began. "Something to tether the magic to in order to keep it going. Usually we could use some sort of celestial event. An eclipse, or a full moon. The full moon has already passed, we can't wait for next month to do it, and there won't be an eclipse any time soon. So, in order to get the amount of power we need for this spell to work, we need a living being to sustain it. A life force."

Allie stared at him blankly, obviously not understanding. "They want to bind the spell to you," Darius translated. "It'd be like the wards in Awen, but instead of only keeping out wraiths, it would include all magic. As long as you are alive, no wraith, or hybrid, or Kindred would be able to set foot within Marienville."

The gravity of our decision settled in as Allie fell back onto the couch behind her. Grady moved over, as if uncomfortable being that close to her. "But—" she responded, weakly fighting back. "But that's all of you." She looked up to Darius, to me. "I'd never see you again. Either of you."

"You're the only human we can ask this of," Roman said soothingly. "You're the only one that understands."

Allie dropped her head into her hands, her shoulders rocking with soft sobs. Darius reached down rubbing his hand across her back. I had to look away, unable to bear the sight of it. I was ripping her happiness away from her, her future with Darius. The fact that he didn't object spoke volumes about his loyalty to the Kindred. To the Guard. "I'll do it," she said finally, lifting her head. "I'll be your damn anchor."

"You're wrong," Isaac's voice sounded from the back of the room. He'd been turned away from us, staring out into the forest through the glass wall.

"Isaac, you know this is for the best. . ." Roman tried convincing him, but Isaac interrupted.

"You're not wrong about the spell. You're wrong that Allie is the only option as the anchor. There's another choice."

"Who?" he asked.

"Me."

"Isaac, no," Allie cried, and I loved her for it. Even with the great emotional hardship it would create for her, the last thing Allie wanted was for someone else to take her place. Isaac raised his hand, cutting her off.

"I can't use my element, the tonic sees to that. If you bind the spell to me, I won't have to take my tonic anymore. The wards will keep the poison in my blood from manifesting. I'm no help in a fight against hybrids, and I'll never be able to step foot in Awen again. Let me do this. Let me help the Kindred one last time."

I walked across the small living room, wrapping my arms tightly around Isaac. "Thank you," I said, as much for his admission as his choice. He wrapped his long arms around me, pulling me in tightly. Isaac and I had been through a lot together, and I understood how difficult it was for him to admit he couldn't fight anymore.

"When do we do it?" Isaac asked as I pulled away. I glanced at Roman, who stood silently against the wall, his eyes glued to the floor.

"Tonight," Brynn answered. "We leave for Awen at first light. The spell has to be completed by then. I'll need at least an hour to prepare."

"I'll help you," Roman offered in a surprising gesture. Brynn nodded, grabbing The Book of Breathings from the coffee table before the two of them walked to the back door. I tried to catch Roman's eye on his way by, but he kept his eyes glued to the floor. I watched them through the yard, well past when they disappeared into the forest, until I could no longer feel him through the bond.

Isaac placed his hand on my shoulder, his touch gentle. "He's upset."

"I know," I answered. "He just needs some time to adjust."

"Time isn't something we have a whole lot of," Grady pointed out, ever the buzzkill.

I turned to my aunt, to Darius. "Even if you're not the anchor, you realize this isn't a perfect solution. You know that Darius. . ."

She raised her hand, cutting me off. Tears shone in her eyes, but I knew better than to mention them. "I know exactly what this means. But with all you've given up, how can I complain about what is being asked of me?" She turned to Darius. "When it's safe again, we'll find a way to be together." My heart ached at the pain in her voice, at what she was willing to sacrifice for a world she should have never been a part of.

"What exactly is the plan?" Isaac asked, pulling my attention.

"We'll divide our forces. The Guard will take Amina back to Awen and meet up with Astrid," Grady explained.

"I want Nero to go with us," I interrupted. The whole room went still, everyone staring at me. "What?" I asked them.

"Nero?" Grady asked. "Crazy, psychopath Nero?"

"He fought against Set, and he's still a Nomarch. Like it or not, that's going to matter. We need him in our corner."

Grady held up his hands. "Fine. Once in Awen, the first thing we need to do is get to the sceptre. We've been running tests on it for months but none of us have been able to handle its dark magic. Hopefully with Kyndal back, we'll finally have enough power to use the damn thing."

"I can do it," I said confidently. I'd handled the sceptre briefly in Cairo, knew what the magic felt like. "Set said he helped Maat write The Book of Breathings. Since the spells in the book drain our power, then the sceptre has to be the same way. You say the three of you combined magic to use it, and it still was too much?"

Grady nodded. "It drained Brynn, and Roman and I passed out once or twice." I raised my eyebrows, shocked to hear him admit it. "We never pushed it past that point. If it is like the spells in the book, when we run out of magic it will start to drain our life force. We didn't want to risk it."

"Adding me in has to be the final piece. If Marius's Guard was able to use the sceptre to kill Set, and that's a *big* if, they would have had to combine power to do it. And by that point Davina had already been turned into a hybrid. There would have been only three of them."

"Apparently numbers aren't as important when one of them is a Descendant," Grady threw in, his statement surprisingly lacking his usual snark.

"Speaking of Marius," Isaac added, "ever think about just asking him how he killed Set the first time?"

I shook my head. "My dreams don't work like that. I don't get to ask questions." I didn't bother explaining that I hadn't dreamt of Marius, Davina, Maat, or anyone for months. Not since Set took me prisoner. In fact, I hadn't dreamt at all until the night Roman found me.

"And the rest of us?" Darius asked. "Where will we go while the Guard is in Awen?" I didn't miss the look of pain that crossed my aunt's face at Darius including himself in the war.

"All of Amina's soldiers here are loyal to the Guard now. You will go with them to Cairo and find Sandra Cartwright. She's been collecting rebels and building a base there for months. Make sure she is brought up to speed. We'll send reinforcements as soon as we can, as many as we can spare. If we aren't successful stopping Set in Awen, Cairo will be his next stop, and you will be our last hope in keeping him from breaking down the wall to the Inbetween."

"Who will lead these warriors when the Guard is gone?" Darius asked. Good question. While they might be in our service now, I definitely didn't trust one of them to lead the group until they got to Sandra.

"I will," Mallory rasped from the stairs. She'd been upstairs, sleeping and recovering. While she was obviously better than she had been, she still looked like hell. The left side of her face was one giant bruise, and she leaned heavily on the stair railing. Most of her injuries were invisible to the eye, but that didn't make them any less real. Set had fed from me once and I understood the toll it took on a person. Behind her, Cassie stood as if she expected her girlfriend to faint at any moment.

I crossed the living room, nervously watching until Mallory's foot hit the safety of the floor. "You're hardly ready," I lightly admonished. "Darius can lead them to Cairo. Sandra will resume command then."

"Like hell," Mallory growled, grimacing slightly. "I outrank him. I have decades of experience on him. Even wounded I could kick his ass." I crossed my arms. "No offense," she added as an afterthought, as if she just now realized how her words could be offensive. I rolled my eyes. *Gemini.*

Darius raised his hands in the air, defensively. "No offense taken." Smart man to not argue with her.

"Fine," I conceded. "You will lead the soldiers into Cairo. But once you arrive, you will defer to Sandra." And with those simple words, part of me wondered if I'd just sentenced my friend to death.

Chapter 25

Roman

I stood on the tarmac of the small private airport just outside Marienville. The sun hadn't fully risen yet, the colors just beginning to paint the sky. Behind me, two planes were fueled and ready to go. The warriors were loading the plane headed to Cairo. We had cleaned out the compound the best we could the night before, stripping it of weapons, books, medical supplies, sustainable food, clothes, absolutely anything we thought could be useful to us. With the new spell in place, we wouldn't be going back, not in Isaac's lifetime. Cassie was escorting Mallory onto the plane, only pausing at the last moment to look back at me. She smiled softly, patting the pocket of her jeans, where I knew she'd tucked the note I'd written for my mother. My small attempt to let her know I was alright. Cassie would see to it that it was delivered.

I raised my hand, pressing it against the invisible wall in front of me. I could feel the magic humming through the barrier, and if I focused hard enough, I saw a faint sheen of multi-colored light that extended from the ground all the way above the tallest trees. It surrounded the town, protecting it like a dome.

"Weird, right?" Isaac asked. He was only two steps in front of me, and yet a world away. I could no more step inside the boundary than he could leave it. As the anchor, the boundary only held as long as he stayed in Marienville.

"Where will you go?" I asked him.

He shrugged, no doubt pretending to be more nonchalant than he felt. His home life was always a touchy subject. "I don't know yet. I haven't talked to my dad in months. He probably thinks I ran away or died or something. I might crash at Allie's if she'll let me."

"School?" I asked.

He sighed. "Maybe. I'll have to go back eventually, I guess. I'm behind on everything, but I have a couple months to figure that out."

"I bet there's a certain tiny blonde who will be happy to see you return. She could help you get caught up."

Isaac grinned at the mention of Lydia Warner, his onetime girlfriend. I hadn't asked about her in months, but last I knew things were left pretty unsettled. The bond tugged at me and I glanced over my shoulder to see Kyndal standing at the stairs to the plane, the only person left on the tarmac.

The first plane, the one headed to Cairo, was already barreling down the runway. She motioned for me to join her. "I guess it's time. Listen, I said some things the past few months," I started, trying to put into words the things I couldn't say the night before.

"Don't," Isaac interrupted. "I don't need you to explain. I know you were just looking out for me. I don't take it personally. And I don't need some grand goodybe. Just go kick some ass. If you get in a pinch and need some advice," he smiled, his signature Isaac humor seeping through, "you know where to find me."

I nodded, ignoring the swell of emotion. "Even without your magic, you're always going to be one of us. You'll always be Kindred, and you'll always be family. Don't forget that."

The flight to Awen was short. The island was currently inside the Bermuda Triangle, only three hours away from Marienville by airtime. If Kyndal was right, and Set had to return to Egypt before attacking the island, we had gained a large head start. The four of us had barely slept the night before, finalizing plans for returning to the island, coordinating with those who were headed straight to Cairo. Even when all of that was finished, we'd still stayed up until the sun began to chase away the stars, taking the opportunity to spend what we knew would be our last night together in Marienville, possibly anywhere. It was our last opportunity to speak freely because in Awen there were always people listening, people plotting against us.

We slept in shifts during the short flight, two of us sleeping for an hour and a half, then switching. We needed more sleep than that, but someone had to stay awake at all times to keep an eye on Amina and Nero. The Commander leaned lazily against the wall of the plane, sharpening a dagger in his lap. I kept as close of an eye on him as I did the Scorpio Nomarch. It was Kyndal's choice to bring him along, and although I agreed with her on a strategic level, his presence made me uneasy. I hadn't spoken to him since he saved me in Marienville, and while I was avoiding him for now, I knew I wouldn't be able to forever.

We entered the vortex around the island as we began our descent. The wards were strong, imbued with the strength of the four elements. It was impossible to cross through them without feeling their power. They pulled on our strength, testing us to see if we were worthy to cross onto the island. If you weren't strong enough to withstand them, the wards would reject you, or worse, kill you.

I closed my eyes, absorbing their magic, allowing it to flow through me, keeping as much for myself as possible in order to strengthen my power source. The last time I'd been in Awen, I'd attacked Amina's sentries and stolen their greatest artifact. That, plus returning with their Governor in shackles, Awen was going to be dangerous. Even though Astrid had been working for months with other Nomarchs to dethrone Amina, the Governor still held the majority of support within the Council. We were going to have to contend with them first if we stood a chance in defeating Set, a fact much easier said than done.

With the wards ripping through me, and my magic wide open, the bond flowed freely, an open highway from my magic to Kyndal's. Her emotions were easily accessible, something I couldn't help but look closer at. We were rarely given a moment to ourselves to speak privately, but at least I could check in on her, even surrounded by others. She was laser focused on the task at hand, no doubt strategizing how we were going to pull this off, but deep underneath all that I felt a sense of uncertainty.

Regret.

Sensing me digging around in her emotions, Kyndal's head snapped up, locking eyes with me. We hadn't spoken since leaving Marienville, not about the implications of the wards we put around the town. *What's wrong?* I mouthed at her. She shook her head in response, then looked away. I pushed down the bond, a sharp poke that forced her to look back at me. I raised my eyebrows, making it perfectly clear I didn't buy that nothing was wrong. *I'll be fine*, she mouthed back. *Talk later. After.* I nodded, reluctantly dropping it for now.

The island came into view not much later, the sparkling colors unmistakable. The red tile roofs reflected the sunlight, the clear blue water of the river winding between the houses, wrapping itself around the mammoth arena that sat at the center of the city. I remembered the first time I'd seen Awen, how I thought it was directly out of a mythology book. Something that belonged more to the past than the present. Maat's Hollow loomed on the far side of the island, its barren, rocky cliffs at odds with the lush vegetation that dominated the rest of the landscape.

As soon as our wheels were on the ground, we all stood, grabbing our weapons and settling them into their various sheaths and belts. The plane came to a halt, the door opening to the humid island air. Not thirty seconds later, a familiar face poked her head into the plane.

"Well, look who it is," Daniela joked, greeting us all. "If this isn't the biggest group of criminals I've ever seen." Her eyes bounced around the plane, taking stock of all of us on board, of the weapons strapped to our belts, our backs, hidden in our boots. We hadn't traveled light. They lingered on the two Nomarchs at the back of the plane until she finally turned to Kyndal. "Descendant. Long time no see."

Next to me, Kyndal's face lit up at the sight of her friend. It'd been too long since they'd seen each other. "Daniela," she responded. "How you been?"

She shrugged, her black curls bouncing around her face. I couldn't help but think she was oddly happy considering the circumstances. "Can't complain. No one has tried to kill me recently, so there's that. Although something tells me that's about to change."

"How many soldiers do you have at your disposal?" Grady asked, clearly in no mood for the banter.

"I have five stationed right outside, ready to accompany you to Chambers. The rest are spread out throughout the route, blending in. You won't see them unless it's absolutely necessary."

"Should we expect resistance?" Brynn asked. *Good question.*

"Anything's possible," Daniela admitted, "Although it's highly unlikely considering the state of things."

"What do you mean?" Kyndal asked.

"It's easier to show you," Daniela answered.

"Let's move out," I ordered everyone. Grady grabbed Amina's cuffs, yanking her to her feet. He had reinforced the cuffs with twine, spelled with his element to make them unbreakable. He all but pushed the Nomarch down the plane steps, only her quick reflexes keeping her on her feet.

Amina glared at Daniela as she passed, "I should've known it was you working against me. You've always been jealous of my power. Threatened by my strength. This is treason," she spat through her teeth. "I'll see you executed for this."

"A friend of mine works in the Hollow," Daniela responded, completely unafraid of being out in the open, her cover as the leader of the rebels confirmed. "He told me that before you were a Nomarch, you were responsible for imprisoning the Surori sisters." Kyndal's head snapped over, surprise bursting through the bond. Clearly that bit of information was news to her. "I met them not too long ago, and believe me when I say that time has not made them kinder. I'll make sure that when you're imprisoned, your cell is next to theirs. I'm sure they'll remember you."

Brynn, who had exited after Grady, snickered and pushed Amina forward. Kyndal and I held back, waiting for Nero to exit before us. No way were we putting him at our back.

We combined with Daniela's soldiers, starting the trek toward Council Chambers. The airstrip wasn't technically a part of the city. It sat just outside the heart of Awen, but we would have to cut right through the center in order to reach our destination. I looked behind me to the stone watchtowers that lined the coast. Soldiers were posted in each of them, but where they were supposed to be faced outward toward the sea, they all turned inward, their eyes following our small group as we left the airstrip. Kyndal's shoulder bumped mine. "What?" she asked.

I turned back to the dirt path we walked. "Eyes in the watchtowers," I responded. "Everyone will know we're here now." There may not be electricity in Awen, but there were ways of talking to each other, of spreading messages quickly.

"Good," Kyndal responded. "The time for secrets and deception is over. It's time everyone knows what's happening."

We rounded a corner, the path underfoot turning from dirt to stone. This was the beginning of the marketplace, one of the busiest parts of the whole island. We should have been able to hear the buzz of Kindred working in their shops, of foot traffic through the streets, and idle chatter of people as they crossed each other's paths. It was early in the day still, nowhere near the curfew. Instead, the streets were empty, the silence louder than if I had screamed at the top of my lungs.

"Where is everyone?" Kyndal asked.

"Astrid called for a special public session of the Council. Those that were brave enough to leave their houses are in the chamber with the Nomarchs," Daniela explained.

"Brave enough?" Grady questioned.

"After the executions in the arena, Amina gave her sentries full executive power. The first thing they did was shut down the marketplace. They extended the curfew to all hours of the day. Soldiers are expected to report to work and then directly back to their quarters. Anyone caught convening in the streets is beaten and thrown in the Hollow. After a while, people quit risking it and stopped coming out of their houses at all."

"That's disgusting," Brynn commented.

"We are at war," Amina snipped from the head of our small group. "Allow soldiers too much freedom during war and they lose their resolve. They think of love and laughter, and other petty things rather than killing the enemy. You must keep them separated, focused. My sentries pulled them apart to make them stronger. Sharper."

"You isolated them," Brynn bit at her. "An army is only as strong as each individual. Soldiers need a purpose, to fight for a cause, and there is no cause greater than saving those you love. When you pull them apart, they forget why they should fight in the first place."

"Why aren't the other Nomarchs doing anything about this? Why don't they do anything to stop it?" Kyndal asked.

"They did," Daniela countered. "They got you here."

"Where are the sentries now?" I asked Daniela.

"They'll be outside the main chamber, guarding the door."

"Good," Kyndal answered, an unnatural chill coming through the bond with her words. Kyndal's emotions always reminded me of various forms of heat, no doubt an influence of her element. Wild and moving quickly like fire, part of me was never quite sure what she would do next. Now her words didn't hold any heat, but a sharp, measured coldness, like when lava is cooled too quickly and turns to sharp crystal.

The shadow of Council Chambers came into view as we walked through the eerily quiet streets of the city. We ascended the large staircase, the etchings of the House symbols on the pillars the only thing there to greet us. It wasn't until we entered the building, our boots echoing off the stone walls, that we met another soul. Just as Daniela had promised; it was the sentries. They took one look at our small group, at Amina locked in shackles, and ran forward, creating a human wall between us and the entrance to the throne room. Their tall, silver spears gleamed in the sunlight at their sides. A quick count told me there were fifteen of them, three times the size of our group. At the center were the Fire Users from the corridor outside where the sceptre had been kept. Brynn and I had kept them all alive when we'd stolen the sceptre, although one of them, my least favorite of them all, now sported a large scar across his left eye and down his face.

Grady, still holding firm to Amina's cuffs, stared down the sentries. "Let us pass." I had to give him points for trying to keep it diplomatic and not immediately pulling his dagger on them.

"Release the Governor," the sentry demanded.

"That scar is cute," Brynn pointed out, noticing the same thing I had. "Was that my dagger or Roman's that did that?" The sentry stared at her, anger seething just under

363

the surface. Brynn wasn't fazed. Not even for a moment. "What do you think, Roman? Was that you or me?"

I shrugged. "Tough to say. We were so busy kicking their asses, and all sentries look alike to me."

"We have business with the Council," Daniela announced. "Let us through."

The sentry's eyes changed, a lighter flicking to life at the same moment. Although he didn't move, fire jumped from the lighter to his spear, the tip of it now engulfed in flames. He lowered the spear, pointing the end of it directly at my heart. Next to me, Brynn leapt forward, the sharp end of her sai pointed at Amina's throat. I hadn't even seen her pull her weapon. "Try it and your Governor dies at your feet."

I wasn't connected to Brynn the way I was Kyndal, but I knew she meant every word she said. Even so, the sentry did not move. I raised my eyebrows at the flaming spear. Usually, I'd be strategizing how to disarm him, how to get around his weapon, but I didn't have to. I could already feel the power building next to me.

Before the sentry could make a single step forward, the flames leapt off the spear, now held firmly in Kyndal's hand. "I wouldn't," my Rafiq threatened, her voice low. That same edge permeating every word. "No matter how strong you are, I promise you—I'm stronger." I smiled at the sentry, at the shock that was clearly registered on his face. In a split second, I called to my power, using the closeness of Kyndal to increase my strength. The wind ripped through the open corridor and I shoved it at the middle sentry, at those that stood on either side of him. The burst rocked them all backward, lifting them off their feet. They flew into the stone walls behind them, those in the middle knocking into the double doors that led to the throne room. They burst open, the sentries skidding several feet down the stone ramp that led to where the Nomarchs sat.

The voices inside the chamber, that before had been nothing but a low murmur, came to a screeching halt as everyone turned and looked at the Guard.

Chapter 26

Kyndal

The silence didn't last long.

Once the initial shock wore off, a hushed whisper rippled through the people, a mixture of confusion, outrage, and excitement, no one quite sure what to comment on first. *The Guard arrested Amina,* one whispered. *I'd heard they were all dead,* another said. *There are the Taurus and Scorpio. Where are the other two? Kyndal, do you see Kyndal? That's Nero, the Aries Nomarch. He betrayed us for Set. Why isn't he in chains? I see her, the Descendant. That's her!*

Their voices mixed together into an almost indistinguishable blur as we fully entered the throne room. I hadn't been in this room in what seemed like a lifetime. The last time I'd been here, the Guard had been sent by Astrid to Marienville. We'd thought at the time that she was sidelining us, kicking us out of the war, when in reality she was liberating us. She'd arranged for Sandra to meet us in Marienville with the box that held Set's soul so we could use it to track him down.

While the thrones were in the same place as they were then, much had changed. There now sat a large table in the center of the wheel. What looked like various maps, parchment, and books were scattered over the top of it. And while the throne room was capable of holding a significant portion of the Kindred warriors, only half the space was taken up. Every inch of empty space represented the fear and tyranny Amina had been imposing on my people, every inch giving me another reason to fight.

We descended through the people, stepping over the sentries that still writhed on the floor. The small crowd parted instinctually, allowing us to pass unhindered. At the bottom of the decline, the Nomarchs stood from their thrones, various looks of shock and excitement playing across their faces as they took in the group coming down to them.

Next to me, Roman was tense, his eyes scanning every person looking for threats. There were weapons all around us. A blacksmith with a hammer in his belt, another warrior with a dagger strapped to her leg, the person next to her carrying a short sword. Every person I saw was armed in some way, although that wasn't surprising. No one had ever been shy about their weapons in Awen. There was no one to hide from here. Roman didn't watch for weapons, though. I realized he watched their hands, to see if anyone was reaching for them. We didn't know who was our enemy anymore. Who supported Amina and would only follow her rule. I followed Roman's example, eyeing those we passed, but I quickly realized no one was reaching for their weapons.

They were too busy staring.

Grady and Brynn pushed a bound Amina into the center of the wheel. The Governor held her head high, that nose of hers permanently stuck in the air, even though her typically pristine exterior was rumpled and disheveled. She clung to the final shreds of her dignity until finally she came face to face with Astrid.

Grady kicked the back of Amina's legs, dropping her to her knees in front of the Cancer Nomarch. Roman and I stepped forward, standing on either side of Grady and Brynn. A united, completed Guard standing proud in front of the Council. From the corner of my eye, I saw Nero wander over to the empty Aries throne, his hand resting on the arm of the seat, although he didn't dare sit.

I waited for the Nomarchs to do something, to say anything, but they all stood in silence for what felt like an eternity. Who would be the first to make a move? Would it be Maks, the sharp-minded Leo Nomarch? No, he was too cunning to be the first to voice his thoughts. Zayna, the decadent Nomarch from House Taurus? Roman told me she was a strong supporter of Amina, something made obvious as she stared at the bound Governor five feet in front of her.

From the Gemini throne, a loud voice hollered, "What in the hell is he doing here?" Cyrus's booming voice echoed through the room. It took me a moment to realize he hadn't said *them*, but rather *he*. Cyrus wasn't talking about us, but Nero. Nero stared back at him, his dark eyes dancing with mischief, an evil smirk on his face as he basked in one of his oldest enemy's discomfort at his presence.

"Good to see you, Cyrus," Nero drolled.

"Get the hell out, traitor," he spit back, his eyes turning a bright yellow.

"Why?" Nero taunted, surprisingly keeping his power beneath the surface. "I was invited here by the Guard. Besides, I am a Nomarch still, am I not? My seat still sits empty. I belong here as much as anyone."

"The Guard cannot invite anyone. They are the tools of the Council, soldiers who follow orders."

"In case you haven't noticed," I interrupted, my voice cutting through the room although I had not moved to raise it. "We aren't taking orders from anyone anymore. Now have a seat."

Murmurs broke through the people at my words. It was unheard of to speak to a Nomarch in such a way. Cyrus cut his gaze to me, to Amina at our feet, as if seeing her for the first time. "You have brought disgrace to the Kindred people and the High Nomarch Council with your actions.

You stole the was-sceptre, attacked your own people, and now you have kidnapped your Governor. And in it all, all you have managed to do is sign your own execution orders." We'd all been taught from the beginning that they were better than us, more powerful. After all, they were the oldest in our Houses, and with age came strength. Cyrus was a strong warrior, but he was not stronger than me.

No one was.

I was the strongest Kindred on the planet, and although he might appear to outrank me, we both knew there was a difference between pretend power, an unearned title handed to you, and the real thing. Power earned through reputation and action. I called to my magic, my eyes cutting red. "I said, sit down!" I yelled, the torches on the walls blasting forward with fire to punctuate my point. Yelps of surprise rang from the audience. I let the torch closest to Cyrus fly the furthest, just over his head so he could feel the heat of my flames on his face. His eyes grew large with fear as he looked at the torch behind him that had already returned to normal, as if nothing had happened. He said nothing, but wisely sat back on his throne. The room went quiet again, even as more people were shuffling into the area surrounding us. Just as Roman thought, word of our arrival had spread, and the people were pouring out of their homes to see the returned Guard. "I am done listening to the idle prattle and empty threats of the Nomarch Council. Now *you* will listen to *us*."

"Tell us what you came here to say," Astrid encouraged, her icy blue eyes peeking out from behind her long silver hair that fell over the front of her white tunic. This moment was as much her crowning achievement as anyone's.

I took a deep breath, looking to my Guard. First to Brynn, a woman I'd grown to respect despite our rocky beginning, then to Grady, a man who had betrayed me, and yet I knew was in danger of becoming a good man. Finally, to Roman, my Rafiq. I loved him more than I could describe in words, not because we were fated to be together, but because I chose him. He challenged me, respected me, supported me, and I knew that with him by my side, I could take the next step waiting for me.

I could take control of our people and defeat Set.

"I know many of you have been told stories about the Guard, about me. That we're traitors, that we've disobeyed the Council, broken Kindred law. I'm here to tell you that the rumors are true."

A collective gasp broke through the people. I waited for them to die down before I continued. It was one thing for people to think you'd committed a crime, it was a completely different thing to admit it. "It's true that I've disobeyed the Council. When we were ordered to sacrifice the life of a loved one to protect The Book of Breathings, I disobeyed and allowed our enemy to get the book in order to save my aunt because I knew the law was wrong. When I was ordered to succumb to a Council ruling I deemed unfit and unfair, I challenged it and demanded to be tried by The Blinding of Truth by Falsehood because I knew the law was wrong. I risked my life and the lives of my friends to save the man I love, and when we entered the Guard and took our oaths swearing to deny our love, I broke Council law again." I looked to Roman, his blue eyes clear and full of love. "We both did, for we knew the law was wrong. We stole the sceptre from the clutches of a ruler that would see our greatest weapon locked away and out of the hands of the only people capable of using it to protect us from the greatest threat we have ever faced. And when the Guard was denied permission to leave Awen, the law was broken again as my Guardsmen risked their lives to rescue me from the clutches of the Chaos God Set. And now we stand before you, alive and ready to lead our people against Set because we were not the ones that were wrong for breaking the law. The law was wrong."

Roman took a step forward. "The law is wrong, because the ruling body, the Nomarch Council, has been corrupted. I have been Kindred since I was twelve years old. I grew up in this world, and know as well as anyone the inner workings of our politics. As most of you know by now, I was raised by Ezekiel Sands, who besides Astrid of House Cancer, was the longest sitting member of this Nomarch Council. He taught me to respect and fear our law, and yet the law is the very thing our Nomarchs have hidden behind as they continually make decisions to hurt the Kindred. In the past year, I have been betrayed by three Nomarchs. First, my adoptive father Ezekiel, whose true allegiances were known by none, then my actual father Nero." The murmurs were replaced by gasps as Roman revealed his true heritage. He cast his eyes sideways, to where the Commander leaned against the throne. "Although he has recently proven to be a friend. The final betrayal came from our Governor, Amina of House Scorpio."

Brynn stepped up. "I am House Scorpio. I was ordered by Amina to enter The Blinding of Truth by Falsehood on behalf of our House. I hoped to compete and bring honor to our House, but just before the games began, Amina told me my true purpose. She had visited Kyndal the night before and gravely wounded her. My mission was to capitalize on her weakness and kill her."

Shouts ricocheted through the room; the people outraged. Amina, the Nomarch that had always presented herself as full of honor, was doing her dirty work behind closed doors. Grady, although he kept a dagger in his hand, raised his arms to hush the crowd that had at this point grown to capacity. "Amina was not the one who defeated Set and gained the was-sceptre in Cairo. Although her soldiers initially attacked us, we eventually worked together to infiltrate the Egyptian Museum and enter The Hall of Two Truths. It was Kyndal that crossed the river into the Inbetween and returned with the sceptre, and it was her sacrifice that allowed us to escape with the weapon." Memories from that night flooded into my head, the pain of it all still fresh in my mind.

"Amina has been lying to you from the start," I added. "I am not on Set's side, nor did he kill me. I've been his prisoner for the last six months, and if it weren't for the Guard, I would still be in his clutches."

Roman continued. "Amina let you think she was trying to defeat Set by letting the Guard practice with the sceptre, the whole while knowing we weren't strong enough to use it. Knowing that we needed a full Guard. That we needed the Descendant of the Original Aries."

"And when my Guard finally did liberate me from Set and his hybrids," I said, "Amina responded by attacking my home town, threatening the safety of innocent humans in order to draw me in and kill me before you all knew I was free."

"Lies!" Amina shouted from her position on the floor. The first words she'd spoken since entering the throne room. "Everything they say is lies!" she repeated.

I ignored her desperate pleas, as did the others. Roman raised his hand to hush the crowd. "The Guard has the was-sceptre in our possession, here in Awen." Not one hundred percent true, but I didn't miss the slight nod from Astrid. She would hand the weapon over without a fight. "Set knows the sceptre is here and he will come after it. He is preparing his army as we speak and we must prepare as well. We will make our final stand in Awen. From this point forward, the High Nomarch Council no longer exists." More shouts. "No longer will power be given, but instead earned. The Guard presents this choice to the High Nomarch Council: relinquish your thrones and help us lead our warriors into battle, or refuse and face the Hollow. If we survive, those of you who chose to fight with your people may be considered for Nomarch again, when we hold free elections."

"You cannot demand we step down," Elias protested, the Aquarius Nomarch rising from his seat.

"They just did," Daniela bit back. "You will not make it out of this throne room without choosing. Decide. Now." All around us, warriors, people who I'd thought were drawn here by their curiosity, began to creep closer, their eyes glowing with power. As they weaved through the crowd, I noticed two things. One, all their weapons were drawn. Secondly, I recognized some of them. There was Travis, who I met at Daniela's house. Not far from him there were two others I remembered seeing inside the Hollow. These weren't just warriors. They were members of the resistance, loyal to Daniela.

And now loyal to the Guard.

Grady's hand was creeping toward his dagger, his eyes intent on the crowd. He'd sensed the change in power just as the rest of us had, but was yet to realize who they were. That they were on our side. I placed my hand atop his, shaking my head slightly at him.

Riley, the Capricorn Nomarch stood. She'd taken over for Ezekiel and had only been a Nomarch for just under a year. "I stand with our people. I relinquish my title as Nomarch."

As if it were the simplest thing in the world. Without another word, she stepped off her throne and stood in the crowd, among the people.

Aquarius was next on the wheel, all eyes on Elias. He stared back at everyone defiantly, although I could see the beginnings of fear. "This is mutiny." No one responded, we didn't have to. It only took one more look around the room before it became obvious how he would choose. Angry as he was about losing his title, he feared the Hollow more. "Fine," he spit. "I will fight."

Joran from House Pisces stood next, his eyes the clearest blue, although I was sure he wasn't pulling any power. He always made me uncomfortable, as if he saw things I couldn't. That no one could. "It has long been predicted the old gods would return to walk among us. Although it has been many years since I held a weapon, it will be my honor to fight in this great war and die if it is asked of me." Grady raised his eyebrows at the eloquence of his answer, no doubt a little unnerved by its extreme undertones, just as I was.

All eyes turned to the next seat, to the Aries throne and where Nero still stood nearby it. He shrugged. "I'm in." Short, simple. I shook my head. That man really pissed me off. Through the bond, it was obvious Roman felt the same.

The wheel continued, and one by one, the Nomarchs stood and made their decision. By the time we'd made it through all of them, we stood at seven to five. Riley, Elias, Joran,

Nero, Madigan, Maks, and Astrid all chose to fight. Zayna, Cyrus, Gabriel, and Haru refused. Amina wasn't given a choice. She was going to the Hollow no matter what to await a trial and proper sentencing. There was no choice in the world that would allow her to escape facing penance for what she'd done.

I looked around the throne room, at those who stood with us, at those who had refused and would soon be dragged to the Hollow. The strength of magic in the room was electric, the warriors looking to the four of us to tell them what to do next. To lead them into battle and protect them from Set. "Now what?" Grady whispered.

"Now we prepare for war."

We wasted no time getting to work.

Daniela and her soldiers escorted the five Nomarchs to the Hollow, acting on orders to keep them separated from each other, making sure their cells weren't even in shouting distance of one another. Once they were properly locked up, she would make sure those Amina had wrongfully imprisoned were released and returned to their quarters.

The throne room cleared out quickly, all of the warriors leaving with instructions to prepare for the upcoming attack. They were organized into groups, each one led by a former Nomarch. Joran led the first group, taking them to strengthen the wards and outer defenses. Set would have to attack the island the old-fashioned way, and we needed to be on the lookout for his ships. Riley and Madigan took another group, pulling the weapons and tactical gear from the various armories and distributing them among the people. They were also in charge of setting up stations, rotations, and routes for the warriors. Where they would be placed and for how long, what roads they would use if forced to retreat. It wasn't often we had the chance to prepare for a battle, and we were taking every advantage we could get. We were going to need them. The last group was led by a reluctant Elias, who went to the infirmary, preparing it for what would almost assuredly be countless injuries. Hard as it was to admit, there was no way we were making it out of the battle without injuries or losses.

"And us?" Astrid asked, referring to the remaining former Nomarchs. Herself, as well as Maks and Nero.

"You're with us," I answered simply. "I want you to take me to the sceptre."

"It's hidden in the old ruins your Guard has been training in on the edge of the city. Protected by our own type of wards. We'll escort you there."

I nodded brusquely, our small band of warriors exiting the throne room. I had never seen the ruins before, only knowing what they looked like through Roman's description. According to him, the ruins were the perfect place to practice with the weapon. Out in the open, and far away from any residences in case something went wrong. As we finished weaving through the city streets and they came into view, I saw exactly how right he'd been.

Filled with an ancient beauty, the ruins were made of the same limestone as the rest of the city, although there were more places where the stone had cracked and weathered than there were in perfect condition. The roof was almost completely gone, but whether it was torn away by the elements or simply by time and neglect, I wasn't sure. The vines around the columns on either end were brown and withering, but with a simple touch from Grady, they turned to green, and bright orange, pink, and purple flowers burst forward from them. Astrid cut right through the pillars without even a glance at the growing wildlife and entered the training arena. The sand was soft underfoot, the familiar training circles drawn in chalk. She continued through the other side, rounding the corner out of sight. The others stopped to wait, so I did as well. There were large braziers in the corner, although they appeared dark and covered in soot from disuse. I couldn't help but wonder why they hadn't been using them. "It didn't feel right without you here," Roman whispered in my ear. I shivered as his breath danced along my neck, a reaction he didn't miss. "I refused to light them until you returned."

I leaned up, smiling at him before placing my hand on the nearest brazier. So close to him, to the rest of the Guard, it took almost no power at all to light it. It roared to life, its counterpart doing the same on the opposite edge just moments later. Nero gravitated to one almost out of instinct, running his fingers through the flame to grab a piece for himself. He rolled it in his hands, before slowly pulling it apart and extinguishing it.

Astrid returned a moment later, holding the was-sceptre, wrapped in soft velvet. Even without seeing it, I could feel its power. I'd always thought it felt wild and reckless, but now I recognized the feeling for what it really was. It was Set. The sceptre had been created for him and held the same dark signature as his power.

Carefully Roman approached Astrid and unwrapped the velvet, revealing the weapon beneath. The metal inlay swirled with life. Once it had reminded me of mercury, but now I saw the same thunderstorms that raged in Set's eyes. Roman lifted the weapon, and through our bond, I could feel the strength of its power, radiating through him and down our magical connection. "We've never managed to use it for more than a few minutes," he explained. "The magic is the same as The Book of Breathings. It feeds on our life energy. Brynn found a spell to lengthen how long we can use it, but we were scared to push too far." I knew all this already, Grady having explained it to me.

"We won't need a spell," I answered simply. The magic inside the sceptre called out to me as I reached and took it from my Rafiq. Call it destiny or intuition, I knew I was the missing piece. That with the Guard complete, we'd be strong enough to wield it. I'd known it the moment I held it in The Hall of Two Truths. It was why Maat had allowed me to take it in the first place. "You ready?" I asked the others.

Brynn nodded, understanding perfectly. She whispered quietly, the words rolling off her tongue with practice and ease. It took only moments until we were connected to one another, our strength and magic flowing endlessly from one to the other. I lowered the weapon pointing it at one of the limestone walls. There were no more words to whisper, no spell to use this time. Just as I had when I'd brought Roman back to life, and when I'd entered the river under the museum, I acted on instinct, willing the magic from the Guard, the magic contained in my blood to take control. I funneled that magic down my arms and through my hands, releasing it into the sceptre. The metal warmed under my hands, the power growing until lightning shot from its end, blasting into the wall. The limestone crumbled and when the smoke cleared, there was a large hole ripped through the wall.

I looked up at Roman, "How do you feel?" I asked him.

Excitement lit up his eyes. "Fine, barely a pull at all."

I spun around, swinging the sceptre in my hand and aiming at the opposite wall. Again, the sceptre fired, blasting a hole in the wall. I waited for my power to deplete, for me to feel like the sceptre was draining everything from me, from the others, but I didn't feel anything. In fact, I felt the opposite. I was invigorated by the power in my hands. This time I looked to Grady. "Nothing," he responded to my unspoken question.

I dropped to a knee, slamming the bottom tip of the sceptre into the sand at the same time. This time the electricity burst through the sand, skipping over the top of it like a living net, crackling until it met resistance in the limestone walls.

I remained kneeling for just a moment before rising back to my feet and looking to the others. They stared back at me with looks of awe and fear, all of them except Roman. He looked at me with nothing but intense pride and satisfaction. As if he knew this was exactly what would happen when I finally got a hold of the sceptre. Maybe he did.

"Well," Grady said, always the one to break the silence. "You're officially the most terrifying of us all."

I laughed. "It's not just me. Any of us can use it now. As long as the four of us are connected." Even though I didn't ask for it, Roman brought me the velvet cover, wrapping the sceptre back up. Although it didn't eliminate the weapon's strength, it worked to quiet it for now. "The sceptre is too powerful to use in open battle against Set. If any Kindred get in the way of it, they'll be annihilated."

"No kidding," Brynn added.

"We'll have to lure him to a specific location," Roman tacked on. "One we can control. Once we have him subdued, we can perform the spell to pull his soul out of Ezekiel and into the box."

"The arena," Astrid added. "It's the obvious place to pull him in. Enough space to fight, but the walls will contain any sceptre blasts. It's as controlled as it gets. Everything we need."

"Set is smart," Nero said. "He won't come to the arena if he thinks it's a trap."

"He may be smart but he is also egotistical and narcissistic. We'll bait him into the arena by playing on those weaknesses," Astrid answered. "You said you told him I had the sceptre?"

"Yes," I said.

"Fine, then I'll be waiting in the arena with the sceptre. He must think I'm alone until the very last second. Once he's there, you can begin the ritual."

I nodded. "Fine."

Nero piped up again. "If you're alone, he'll smell a rat. You should take some soldiers with you to make it seem like you're at least attempting to hide from him. And me, you should take me. I'll see to it that you get the hybrid sacrifices you need."

"You, why?" Roman asked.

"To see that it's done. If you all fail, Set will have my ass, I'd rather that didn't happen."

I snorted. Could always count on Nero to be self-serving. For once, that selfishness worked in our favor. "What do we need for the spell?"

Brynn took a deep breath. "It's a dirty one, as you all know. Four sacrifices, one House for each element. Unless you guys know anyone lining up to be sacrificed, we'll need to capture hybrids and bring them in to complete the ritual."

Grady nodded. "We can keep them in the cells under the arena. You can sacrifice them there. Set won't even know what's happening." I tried not to think too much about how he knew about those cells.

"Once we complete the spell, I'll perform the last piece and lock him in the box. Then you all can deliver him to the Hollow and make sure he stays there this time, " I said.

"No." The word came out simply, forcefully and I not only heard it aloud, but felt it in my bones as it ripped down the bond.

"No?" Maks asked, speaking for the first time since entering the old ruin.

"No," Roman repeated, glaring at the former Nomarch before looking at me. "You will not lock him in the box. I'm not going to allow you to sacrifice yourself to put him in there."

I huffed a breath. "We've already discussed this," I began.

"I don't care," he threw back. "We're discussing it again."

I pinched the bridge of my nose. I hated arguing with Roman, even more so in public. "We have no other choice," I tried again.

"I agree with Roman," Grady said. "We can't just let you die." I rolled my eyes. Of course he would side with Roman on this issue, it was the only thing they'd ever agreed on.

"For the record," I threw at him, "you don't get to *let* me do anything. It is not your choice to make."

"Brynn?" Grady asked, searching for help.

She stepped forward, her eyes uncharacteristically soft. I already knew what she would say, how much it would hurt her to do it. "Kyndal's right. It's her choice." I smiled sadly, nodding at the woman in thanks.

"We're at the eleventh hour," Astrid added, no doubt attempting to be diplomatic. "It takes something powerful to lock Set's cage and Kyndal's blood is the only thing we know of that is strong enough to work." I appreciated her help. Astrid had always approved of using me to seal in Set. She would gladly sacrifice my life to save our people.

As would I.

"And what happens if you die in battle?" Roman demanded. "Or if I do? There are no guarantees as to what will happen out there. If one of us dies before we lock away Set, all of the Kindred are doomed. It's a bad plan."

My heart sunk as I listened to him fight this. As he grasped for straws in order to find any alternative that didn't include sacrificing me, for although he mentioned his own death, I knew he didn't fear dying. Only losing me.

I placed my hand on his arm, running my fingers down his skin until I laced them through his own. "Set needs me to make more hybrids. He won't kill me, he can't. I am, and therefore you are, the safest people out on the battlefield." Over his shoulder, I noticed Nero staring at us with great interest, his dark eyes focused on where our hands were joined. I could almost see the wheels turning in his head, and a part of me was desperately curious to know what he was thinking. What did he think of his son, of the man he had become?

Roman pulled his hand away, blind rage roiling down the bond as he stalked over to the other side of the sands. I let him go, gave him his space. I didn't try to talk him out of his rage. It was better if he was mad at me, it would make it easier for him to accept what would happen. Easier for him to move on if he hated me for my choice. I turned to the old Nomarchs, unable to look at my Rafiq. "If we don't manage to stop Set in Awen, there is a backup plan. Sandra Cartwright has been gathering soldiers in Cairo. Soldiers that deserted their compound after Amina took over. We sent Cassie, Mallory, and Darius, along with a small band of Amina's former warriors to meet up with them. They are setting up eyes on the museum, and they'll be there to confront Set in case he makes it through us. They'll do their best to hold him off until reinforcements arrive."

Nero scoffed. "If Set makes it to Cairo, there won't be any reinforcements to send because we'll all be dead."

Chapter 27

Roman

The sun was setting on my first night back in Awen.

I reached the bottom of the cliffs, the light glowing brightly on the western face of the mountain in front of me. I leaned back to see the top, the grass and vegetation on the flat top already cast in shadow. Within the next hour, the whole island would be covered in darkness.

I'd wandered through the city for hours, checking on the preparations. We couldn't risk anything going wrong. Couldn't leave anything to chance. The warriors were hard at work, the former Nomarchs surprisingly holding to their promise to join in this fight. While I was happy they were helping, a part of me couldn't help but wonder how long that cooperation would last after Set was defeated.

The arena was ready for the dispossession spell, Brynn had seen to that. She'd memorized the spell we needed, made sure we all had done the same. We didn't want to rely on using the book during the fight. It would be tucked safely inside the library, locked in with the other special collections items. Under the arena, each of the Cardinal directions were marked, and we knew exactly which cells to use when we sacrificed the hybrids. Their deaths would activate their elements just as they'd done the first time, inside the Hollow, creating a maelstrom of power that only those inside the circle would be protected from. The biggest trick was going to be getting Set into the arena and inside that circle.

The barren face of the Hollow loomed not too far away, the roar of the waterfall echoing off the rockface. I called to my power, using the wind to push me to the top of the cliffs, to where I knew she would be.

She sat with her feet dangling over the eastern edge of the cliffs, staring off into the ocean. Her figure was silhouetted in stars, the red pommel sitting darkly above her shoulder. She knew I was here and yet she didn't turn. Even as I came and sat next to her she stayed facing forward. Tension spread out between us, the bond tight, fraught and strained. For a while, neither of us said anything, just sat with each other staring out over the ocean. The water was quiet, the waves calm. Combined with a clear sky, I felt like I could see miles outward. "Thinking of jumping?" I eventually asked her, attempting to break the tension.

Thankfully, she chuckled. "I did once."

I turned in complete surprise. "What?" She'd never told me about it.

She smiled at me, the sight of it mending my heart and then breaking it all over again. How could I live without her? Without the sight of that smile? "Cassie and Isaac brought me here once, the first time I came to the island. I'd had my head down, totally focused on training, lost in grief over you. I wasn't doing a great job of blending in, to say the least. There was a whole group up here, laughing and playing. Just enjoying each other's company. I just remember thinking that if they were all able to find a moment of happiness, I could too. So, I jumped." She paused. "It was the most freedom I'd felt since becoming Kindred. The first real moment of joy I'd felt after you were possessed. It was when I decided to live life again." The wind pushed a piece of hair out of her ponytail. Out of instinct I reached up to tuck it behind her ear. She leaned into my touch briefly, but then pulled herself away as if she thought better of it. "Sorry."

"Sorry?" I repeated. "For what?" Kyndal never apologized.

"That's not fair of me. I know you're angry with me."

I reached out, cupping her cheek. I was incapable of sitting this near to her and not touching her skin. "I am angry, unbelievably so. I can't imagine living in this world without you. But that doesn't mean I don't still love you." The bond pulsed with heat and I knew my words were getting to her.

Regardless of what she was feeling, she held her resolve. "If you came up here to try and get me to change my mind, you're wasting your time. I've made my decision."

I huffed a breath. "I know."

Her mouth, which had been open, no doubt preparing to interrupt me, promptly closed. "What?" she asked a moment later.

"I said, I know. I understand you've made your choice. I just came up here to tell you I've made a choice, too."

She scrunched her eyebrows, fraught with confusion. "Okay." She let the word drop.

"I've decided that I'm not going to quit trying. I'm going to fight until the very last moment to save you, because while you might be only one person to everyone else, you are *everything* to me. I've lost so much in my life. So many people have left me behind, but not you. You've never given up on me, and I refuse to give up on you."

She leaned over, pressing her soft lips to mine for the briefest of moments. I tightened my grip on her, pulling her closer, intensifying the kiss. She didn't object, leaning into me, her lips surrendering under mine. We'd had so few private moments since I got her back, I couldn't help but soak it up. She reached up, digging her fingers into my hair. I still hadn't had a chance to get it cut, and it was unusually long at the moment. The way she gripped it, used it to glue my body to hers, made me never want to cut it again. I didn't know which of us moved first, but suddenly we were laying back in the soft grass, and her hands were at the hem of my shirt. She pushed it up, and I raised off the ground only long enough for it to go over my head. We both knew this was probably our last night together, and it seemed we were driven by the same impulse to spend it together, wrapped up in each other. I reached for the buttons of her tactical pants just as a small clap of thunder rumbled through my chest. We pulled apart almost simultaneously.

"Was that thunder?" she asked, her eyes were feverish, her lips swollen from my kisses.

I looked out to the ocean. Where just moments before the sky had been clear, the ocean calm, there were now thunder clouds building on the horizon. Kyndal rolled off me and I called to my power, just as Kyndal's sparked to life next to me. Now pulling from the elements, we could see further. Not only were there dark clouds forming, but lightning cut through them, lighting up the sky and revealing under them, "Ships," I whispered. Dozens of them. We'd been wrong, we didn't have until tomorrow to prepare for battle. We were out of time. I reached blindly for my shirt, yanking it over my head, our moment of passion forgotten. "We have to go," I said to Kyndal. "We have to go now."

I ran to the northern edge of the cliff, just in shouting distance of a watch tower. "Raise the alarm!" I shouted to the guard there. "Light it now!"

He didn't hesitate, grabbing the torch next to him and reaching up to light the brazier that sat atop the stone. An ancient alert system meant to notify the Kindred of an enemy's arrival, the flames flew to life, glowing brightly. I stared off in the distance to where I knew the next watch tower was placed. "Come on, come on," I whispered.

"There!" Kyndal shouted. Another flame, another brazier lit. Shouts rang out through the streets as one by one the braziers went up until the whole island was rimmed in fire. "We need to find Grady and Brynn."

I grabbed her hand and we raced for the western side of the cliffs. We didn't pause when we reached the edge—not for a moment—as we leapt into the air only falling briefly before I used my element to slow our descent. We landed easily, just as a dark cloud over us rumbled with thunder, lightning striking down mere feet in front of us. We leaned back, shielding our eyes from the brightness of the light, and when we lowered them, two hybrids stood, eyes glowing green and blue, their daggers drawn.

I drew my dagger just as Kyndal drew Batil. In her open hand, a fireball grew, the tongues of the flame licking over her wrist. The magnitude of her power coursed through me, filling me with strength. Lighting struck further behind the hybrids, deep in the city, and screams sounded from the people as they realized what we already had.

The enemy had arrived.

Kyndal launched her fireball, not meant to injure, but to maneuver the enemy where we needed them. We ran after as it raced directly for the heart of the Earth User hybrid. He dodged, rolling out of the way and separating himself from his comrade. We capitalized, running straight down the middle, splitting the two hybrids. I dropped low at the same time Kyndal swung high, our blades cutting through the flesh of the hybrids. I turned, driving the tip of my dagger through the heart of the felled hybrid, just as Kyndal blasted hers at point blank range. We didn't stop to make sure they were dead. There wasn't time.

We raced through the streets of Awen, barreling toward the southwestern side of the island. Brynn and Grady were supposed to be in the infirmary, doing one final check, confirming Elias had done his job setting it up. We rounded the corner to the infirmary's street, ignoring the screams coming from the center of the city. Twenty feet before the entrance, the doors burst open and Grady and Brynn ran through, their weapons drawn.

"How many?" Grady demanded.

"Twenty ships, maybe more," I answered. "If they're all full, that's at least four thousand warriors. They're already getting past the wards. Set is teleporting them in through the thunderstorm somehow." We'd taken stock of our warriors last night. Our numbers stood in the low three thousands. Not all of those were soldiers. Although every Kindred received basic training, many worked jobs on the island and hadn't seen battle in years. Decades.

"We need to get to the arena," Brynn yelled.

The streets were buzzing with activity, the warriors pouring out of their houses and various shops, throwing on gear and securing weapons as they ran to their assigned positions. The wind had kicked up, bringing with it even darker storm clouds. Thunder rumbled, fingers of lightning cutting through the clouds, and yet not a drop of rain fell. Soldiers stopped in the streets to stare above them, the ominous presence of the clouds having appeared seemingly out of nowhere.

Thunder rumbled again, lightning striking straight down into a nearby dirt road, but we didn't slow down to fight the hybrids I knew would come with them. Let the others take them. We had a job to do.

The arena wasn't far away as the crow flies, but through the curved streets, it was about a mile run from the infirmary. We sprinted at full speed, the lightning strikes coming faster with each step. They landed in the streets, broke through the roofs of houses, pounded into the training building and armories, anywhere our weapons were expected to be.

Thunder cracked again, this time so closely overhead, I felt it rumble through my bones. Lightning struck down in the alley of the building we ran past, four hybrids falling quite literally on top of a Kindred. She screamed as three of them held her down, the final hybrid holding his hand over her heart preparing to feed. I skidded to a stop, turning back to the alley. "Roman, we can't!" Brynn yelled.

"I can't leave her!" I shouted back, already moving toward the alley. I called to the roaring wind, and with a scream, it flew through the alley and threw the hybrids off the woman. Three of them went flying, but the fourth didn't move and when he turned to glare at me, I realized why. He was an Air User like me. It didn't matter though, because moments later, a fireball tore down the alley, blasting the hybrid in the chest. He hit the wall, dead.

By the time we made it to the arena, the lightning was coming so quickly, it was impossible to count the strikes. The walls had been repaired, almost all signs of Ezekiel's attack erased from the great arena. Beyond them we could already hear the clanging of metal. The hybrids had made their way into the arena. Brynn tore open the iron gate, revealing the sands beyond, but two steps in and a hybrid leapt from the stands, landing on her back. She fell to the ground, rolling through the attack and turning with sais in hand. She threw the one, embedding it in the leg of the hybrid. He grunted, then ripped the sai out, throwing it back at Brynn. She dodged, the weapon landing harmlessly in the sand. Suddenly, the hybrid began to sink, the ground at his feet turning into quicksand. Unable to move, Kyndal ran up behind him, shoving her sword through his heart.

She turned to Grady, giving him a wicked, approving smile. "Man, that move really is a bitch."

We ran toward the center of the arena, where Astrid, Maks, and a small group of warriors were fighting off a much larger group of hybrids. Astrid's silver tunic shone in the darkness as she spun through her enemies, twin blades in her hand, the hilts stark white as if made from bone. Not far from her, Maks fought fiercely, blood splattering across his face as he felled another hybrid. Beyond them, barely visible in the darkness, was the wooden box that I knew held the sceptre. I could feel its power radiating from here, calling to us to use it.

Fire ripped from a nearby brazier, headed straight for Astrid. Maks was occupied, unable to use his power to stop it. Grady's voice carried on the wind as he spoke the words to combine our powers. I stepped forward, pushing the wind out in front of us, swiping the fire wide and into the stone wall. Kyndal returned the favor, building a fireball of her own, throwing it at the hybrids. They scattered, the fireball scorching the earth where they had been standing just moments before. Brynn leapt forward, her eyes glowing a magnificent blue. She spun low, swiping at the legs of the closest hybrid, an Air User. She jumped backward missing the blow, right into the waiting hands of Astrid. She'd dropped her blades and now held the hybrid on either side of her face. Without so much as a flick of her finger, the hybrid's face contorted and twisted, then water began leaking from her mouth, ears, and nose. She fell back, grasping at her neck. Astrid didn't hesitate. She picked up her dropped blades, ramming one through the hybrid's heart before tearing it away, the blade soaked in blood.

We worked our way toward the middle of the arena, working with the other soldiers to clear the hybrids there, but for every hybrid we killed, two more arrived. Kyndal led the way, her fireballs catapulting through the enemy, dropping each one they touched. She was beautiful to watch, like an avenging angel cutting down demons. Those she missed, Grady, Brynn, or I picked up, focusing on a physical assault in order to keep our magic available to Kyndal.

A Fire User dropped right in front of me, cutting me off from the others, a living flame already in his hand. He flung his hand outward. I was too close to completely miss the blow, but I managed to turn, taking the brunt of the pain on my back. The fire singed through my shirt, and I hissed at the pain of it. When I turned back around, the hybrid's blade was already coming down fast. I lifted my own dagger, more sparks flying as the metal collided. Suddenly a sharp heat sliced across my abdomen, an echo of Kyndal. I shouted in pain, losing focus for a split second. The hybrid capitalized, snapping my head to the side with a nasty right hook. I staggered, then kicked out with a heavily booted foot, connecting with the hybrid's gut. I swung a sharp left across his jaw, payback for the hit he landed.

Then I landed another one. And another. My abdomen screamed with pain each time, and finally on the third hit, I put my element behind it, snapping his neck. He dropped the ground, his body still and yet I knew he wasn't dead. I twisted the dagger in my hand before finishing him off.

I lifted my free hand to my side, my fingers coming away red. If the echo was this bad, Kyndal had to be badly injured. I searched the battlefield for her but came up empty. There was no sign of her and the fireballs had stopped flying. The lightning flashes continued, too bright, making it difficult to see through the bodies. I could feel Kyndal, but in the chaos I wasn't able to narrow down her location.

I caught sight of Grady. His nose was bloodied and his gear torn across the shoulder. He jumped and spun, landing a full kick to the face of a Water User hybrid, sending her across the sand.

"Grady, where is Kyndal?!" I yelled to him.

He held his hands up high. "I don't know! There's too many to see!" he shouted back.

A surge of power barreled down the bond, emanating from the other side of the arena, under the old dais. It was Kyndal's magic, but mixed with the darker edge of the was-sceptre. She must have gone for the weapon, knowing we weren't able to stop the sheer number of hybrids coming into the arena. Lightning ripped across the sands, but this time it didn't come from the skies. It tore through a line of hybrids, ten of them dropping at once. The sceptre hit them in their shoulders, their abdomens, their hands, it didn't matter. One glance of the sceptre's power and they disintegrated instantly.

Kyndal appeared from under the dais, her sharp red eyes matching the ruby pommel of Batil tucked in the scabbard on her back. She limped slightly, even as the sceptre swirled with life in her hands. She lowered the weapon, and the closest hybrids, the ones who had been fighting Astrid and Maks, turned and ran from its power. Kyndal didn't allow them to escape. Silently, and with a cold stillness I'd come to associate with this new version of her, she fired the sceptre and laid waste to the hybrids as they sprinted for the exits. The dark magic of the sceptre filled the arena, the acrid smell of smoke and burnt flesh filling my nose. As the sceptre ripped through the arena, the lightning strikes from above stopped almost immediately, the number of enemies left to fight slowing until none remained.

I looked around in the darkness, my chest heaving. Kyndal, Grady, Brynn, Astrid, Maks—we'd all survived. I ran to Kyndal, placing my hand carefully on her wound, ignoring the spike of pain in my own abdomen. "You alright?" I asked quietly. I knew she hated to be babied.

"I'm fine," she answered brusquely. "Does Nero have the hybrids in position?"

"I don't know," I responded quickly. None of us had had the time to check and relying on Nero was not something I was comfortable with.

Thunder sounded again and the wind whipped around us as the cloud overhead swirled. Different than the rest of the storm, this cloud sang with magic and darkness, the kind that could only come from a god. I stared in awe as the cloud seemed to increase in size, the lightning pooling together until it struck in one giant lightning strike in the center of the arena. We closed our eyes to shield from the light, but I already knew who we would see when we opened them again.

"Set," Kyndal sneered.

He hadn't come alone. At least twenty hybrids flanked him, their eyes glowing with the promise of blood. The basic frame of Ezekiel was nearly unrecognizable at this point, his skin pulled so tightly across his bones that it appeared to be made of leather. His veins protruded outward, running a deep red that matched the color of his eyes. If I watched closely enough, I could see electricity skitter through his veins. Kyndal had told me he'd been feeding at extraordinary levels, and this was no doubt a manifestation of the magic that afforded him. Shadows curled around his neck, underneath his arms, and around his feet, their darkness swallowing the night. The god stood in the center of the arena, cracking his neck. "Hello, Kyndal. I've missed you." I stepped forward, putting myself between Kyndal and the god. He snickered, a sound that reminded me too much of my adoptive father. "No need to play the protector, Roman. We both know I would never hurt her."

From Set's right, one of Astrid's soldiers screamed, running full tilt at the god, her dagger raised high in the air. Not a single hybrid lifted a finger to stop her. "No!" Brynn shouted, but it was too late. Set turned, raising his hand. Although Set never touched her, the soldier stopped midair. With a single flick of his wrist, he snapped her neck, dropping her limp body to the ground.

"Dammit, Set. Stop this!" Kyndal screamed.

He turned back to her, his veins nearly glowing. "Gladly," he sneered. "Just give me what has rightfully belonged to me for thousands of years."

"The sceptre doesn't belong to you," Astrid answered, the tiny woman standing with her back straight, completely unafraid of the god in front of her. "It is the property of Hermes Trismegistus and Maat, and therefore, the Kindred."

Set surveyed her, his lips pursed with disapproval. "Astrid, correct?" he asked. "I've seen you in Ezekiel's memory. You belong to the old world, as I do. How disappointing that you appear as distasteful as he remembered." Set turned to all of us. "Let me provide you all with a short history lesson." Kyndal stepped slowly around me, positioning herself to fire the sceptre. "The was-sceptre never belonged to Maat or that pitiful excuse for a god you call Hermes Trismegistus. It was *mine*, and she stole it from me when she stole my kingdom. Do not worry though, I will return it to her when I rip down the veil between this plane and the Inbetween. I will bury it in her black, broken heart."

Kyndal fired the sceptre. Set, moving almost too fast to track, simply stepped to the left and out of the line of fire. The lightning bolt tore through one of his hybrids, disintegrating him immediately. Set didn't even pause to brush away the ash.

Behind him, the other hybrids roared with rage at the sight of their fallen comrade. Set gave a slight nod, and the hybrids broke toward us, coming in a wave of darkness.

Not far from me, Brynn was whispering under her breath even as she ran toward the enemy. The rest of us followed, and just before we collided, a shield snapped tightly around the Guard. Our daggers clashed, metal against metal, sparks flying around our heads. The Fire Users tried to grab a hold of the sparks, to use the fire to their advantage, but everywhere they tried, their magic fell useless against our shield.

Set stood at the back of it all, watching with the sort of disinterest that only came from someone who didn't care about the lives of others. We fought fiercely, striking down as many hybrids as we could. Kyndal still brandished the sceptre, and while it didn't pull on our power, the shield did, and I could feel it weaken as the hybrids continued to hammer us with the elemental attacks.

Just as I drove my dagger through the heart of a Water User hybrid, the braziers bolted to the giant fountains inside the arena, burst to life. I'd felt no push of power from Kyndal, and the hybrids weren't strong enough to light them mid-battle. The source of fire could only be coming from one place.

Yes, I thought. *Nero must be sacrificing the first hybrid.* The first element, Fire stood as the representative for the southern cardinal direction. Inside the diamond, Set turned, his storm-cloud eyes taking note of the new flames. He seemed to pay it no attention, maybe playing it off as something Kyndal had done, but then he looked closer. He searched the arena, as if he was just now really paying attention to his surroundings. His eyes found the chalk line drawn in the sand and followed the diamond whose four points pointed at the Cardinal directions. Brynn was the first to cross the chalk line, into where the elements couldn't touch her. She'd disposed of the hybrids in her way, even with one of her sais lost. She walked slowly, heavily favoring her left leg even as she staggered toward Set. Grady was only steps behind her, his russet hair wild and sweat-slicked. He eyed Set as he reaffirmed the grip on his weapon. I followed my Guardsmen across the line. "You think you can rip me from this body?!" he shouted at us. "You don't have the strength."

Heat stirred in the bond, Kyndal's power roaring to the surface. Invisible to everyone but me. "You're right. We don't," I agreed. "But she does." The sceptre ripped lightning across the arena. It slammed into Set's shoulder and he staggered backward, his hand clutching his shoulder. He pulled his hand away, his fingers stained with a dark red blood. When he whipped back to us, his eyes churned with the promise of violence, his skin smouldering under his hand.

Hope swelled in my chest at the sight of his wound. Kyndal stepped inside the boundary and I couldn't help but look to her. The same excitement coursed through her as did me.

The sceptre worked.

It can hurt him.

A roaring wind ripped through the arena, immediately extinguishing the flames. The Air User had been sacrificed.

Halfway there.

We just needed to hold on a few minutes longer.

Our excitement was short-lived as Set's shoulder stitched itself together, the wound disappearing as if it never existed. Sand ripped at us, a thousand tiny cuts, tearing our skin. Astrid and Maks, who were both still outside the diamond, were pushed back against the arena wall and held there, their feet dangling just off the ground. They writhed and fought against their invisible prisons, but they were nowhere near strong enough.

Set stalked forward, closing in on the Guard. Three more steps and he'd be on us. Kyndal aimed the sceptre again, this time at his chest. The lightning flew, but the god was prepared this time. He held out his hands, absorbing the magic. He staggered yet didn't fall, gathering the lightning in his hands. He raised his arms, molding the magic over his head, forming a giant orb of electricity that crackled with dark magic. I expected him to throw it at us, but he turned, launching it with god-like strength toward the Hollow.

The orb slammed into the side of the Hollow. On contact, the mountain shook and a bright, multicolored light appeared along the surface of the mountainside. It was familiar to me, the sight of magic. In this case, the anti-magic wards that kept the prisoners from using their magic. Those wards were the only thing that kept the prisoners from escaping their cells.

We barely noticed that the wind had quit, and the formerly dormant fountains were bubbling with water. Nero had sacrificed the third hybrid. The dark magic spread outward along the Hollow, slowly eating at the wards, swallowing their light until they completely disintegrated. It would only be moments until the creatures and criminals locked inside the mountain would realize they had access to their powers again. The prison would be full anarchy.

Set took another step forward.

Only two steps away.

Kyndal fired twice, but the Chaos god leapt in the air, over our heads. He landed behind us, both Brynn and Grady raising their daggers to attack. Set grabbed them both by their throats, launching them across the sands as easily as someone would a doll.

We were so close. There was only one more element to sacrifice. We had to keep him in the diamond for just a little longer.

I lunged toward the god, dagger first. He kicked at my wrist, and I lost grip on my weapon. Undeterred, I reached over pulling the dark sword, my father's sword, from Kyndal's back. I struck at Set and yet he grabbed my wrist again, ripping the sword from my hand. He threw me to the ground, and brought the sword down across my back, the blade ripping through skin and muscle.

I screamed in pain, Kyndal's roar immediately following. I dropped to my knees, the back of my shirt already soaked with blood. My eyes went blurry with pain as I leaned forward, digging my fingers into the sand. The heat of the wound screamed with every breath, as I tried to remain conscious. I focused on healing my wound, knowing it would heal Kyndal, but my magic was failing with every passing breath. It slipped further and further from grasp. Astrid and Maks lunged toward us, the former Cancer

Nomarch reaching for her bone blades. "No!" I shouted, managing to lift a hand to stop them. "The wards! You have to fix the wards!" If those wards stayed down, the island would be overrun with prisoners hell-bent on getting their revenge.

Kyndal, somehow still on her feet, held the sceptre like a spear, facing down the Chaos god with zero fear in her eyes. The Guard was still connected in magic, her emotions barreling down the bond, making it difficult to know where she ended and I began.

Determination.

Rage.

Bloodlust.

She built her power, preparing to fire the final shot, the one that would put him down until the last element could be sacrificed. The metal of the sceptre churned in her hands, but before she could release its magic, Set grabbed ahold of the weapon, his hand just above hers.

The moment his hand touched the sceptre, a burst of dark magic shot from the sceptre, knocking everyone backward.

I landed awkwardly on my back, growling when the sand dug into the filleted skin. My vision blurred again, the sights and smells of the arena pulling away from me. The last thing I remembered was a brief moment of feeling like I was floating.

Then everything went black.

Chapter 28

Kyndal

I groaned at the pain burning in my back.

I wasn't used to things feeling hot, not anymore, but that was the only way to describe this pain. A searing heat that cut through my skin from my left shoulder blade to right hip. I'd tried to heal it. I sent it as much power as I could spare, and while I managed to numb the pain a little, the wound wasn't mine to fix. It was an echo of the wound Set had given Roman. I wouldn't heal completely until he did.

I was laying on the ground. Not the hardpacked sand of the arena, but a cold, rocky surface. It was pitch black, but I already knew where I was. There was no wind, no rustling of the tropical trees that populated Awen. Instead, the air was stale and heavy with moisture I knew came from the river. Set had teleported us off of Awen, and there was only one place he would take us.

I pushed myself up slowly, screaming when I moved too quickly and my back protested. "Roman?!" I called out. "Grady?! Brynn?!" No response came, but I knew they had to be here. I could still feel our connection.

I checked my own magic supply. The well was there, my magic depleted from staying connected to the others. Roman was hurt, and if the others were too, their magic was forcing them to heal themselves and they were using pieces of my strength to do it.

"Set!" I yelled, my fingers searching blindly across the floor. "Where are you, you bastard?!"

He didn't answer, but from far away, there was a strange sound I couldn't identify. A continuous popping that reminded me of food sizzling in a pan on the stovetop. I shuffled on my hands and knees through the darkness until my fingers stumbled over something metal. I fumbled over it, my hand finally finding purchase on the hilt of a sword. I grabbed the weapon, using it to push myself to my feet.

I pushed my power out, attempting to light the torches I knew were bolted to the cave walls. I only managed to light the closest one. I grabbed it, yanking it from the wall to illuminate where I knew the staircase would be. Hieroglyphics shone in the orange firelight, confirming where we were.

The Hall of Two Truths.

My torch didn't help me see too far, just enough to realize the sword in my hand was in fact Batil. Set had held it last, used it to cut through Roman's back. I didn't see the Chaos god anywhere in the antechamber, or the was-sceptre, for that matter. As I limped closer to the tunnels, the strange sound grew louder and rainbow light flickered at the other end of the tunnel. I finally realized why the sound was familiar. It wasn't a sizzle, but rather a boiling of water. Set was breaking down the barrier between us and the Inbetween, boiling the water in the river in the process.

I had to stop him.

I didn't make it a step before a hand reached out of the darkness, wrapping itself around my ankle. I swallowed a scream, holding the torch low to see the source of the sharp grip. "Brynn?!" My chest was heaving from the effort it took to speak. She was slumped awkwardly against the cave wall, the left side of her head cut and bleeding.

"Don't go in there alone," she rasped. "He'll kill you."

"Shh," I reprimanded softly. "You need to save your strength." I didn't bother to explain all the reasons she was wrong. An argument just cost us precious time. I whipped the torch past her, searching for the others. Not far from her, Grady was sprawled out on his back and from the looks of it, he'd landed awkwardly on his ankle. It was obviously broken and facing the wrong direction. It would be painful to heal, but it wouldn't kill him. Just past him, Roman was laid out on his stomach, his black shirt wet with blood. I stumbled past Brynn, lighting a torch over her head on my way to Roman. He had to heal himself. If he didn't, neither of us were going to make it long enough to fight Set. I reached my Rafiq, placing my hand carefully on his shoulder. I was surprised to find another body beyond him. His large frame was folded in on itself, his gear covered in dust.

Nero.

I didn't know how he'd made it here. I understood the Guard. We were connected through power and magic. When Set teleported me, it took them with me. But Nero, I didn't understand.

The Commander coughed, dust flying out of his mouth. Carefully, I pushed Roman aside to free him and he groaned and sat up slowly, his dark gaze settling on me. "Where are we?"

"The Hall of Two Truths. Tell me you finished the ritual."

He shook his head, more dust falling from his hair. "The Earth User wasn't dead yet when he sent us here. We're still short one sacrifice." I gritted my teeth, seething. "What are we going to do?"

"Listen to me," I said, every ounce of my being hating that I was about to put this amount of faith in Nero. "The Guard can't leave. We're the only ones strong enough to fight Set.

You have to go find Cassie and Mallory. They are with Sandra and her rebels. We need their help."

"I have no idea where they are," he argued.

"Just listen!" I shouted, cutting him off. Pain exploded in my back and I fell forward, forced to focus on my breathing until the pain subsided. Next to me, Roman stirred slowly as if the pain had woken him. I wasn't worried about the noise drawing Set's attention. He was fully preoccupied with breaking through the barrier. "They were sent here with instructions to watch the museum. You shouldn't have to go far. Just make yourself visible, and *they* will find *you*."

Nero pulled himself to his feet. I didn't miss the short glance he gave his son. "Try not to die while I'm gone." I wasn't sure if the words were for me or Roman. He stumbled toward the stairs.

"Wait!" I hissed, my hand around the hilt of Batil. I raised my arm, the muscles shaking from pain and adrenaline. The blade pointed at him, an unspoken offer. His hand twitched toward the weapon, but at the last minute he hesitated. "Take it! Dammit, take it before I change my mind! It's yours anyway." I hated to give it back to him even now, but I couldn't send him off unarmed. He took it from me, the dark hilt fitting perfectly in his hand. He stared at it with adoration although it'd only been a short amount of time since I'd taken it from him. Without another word, he ran for the stairs.

Roman stirred again, this time trying to push himself off the ground. "Not yet," I warned him quietly. "You're still hurt pretty bad. You need to heal yourself before you move." Roman didn't respond, but I felt the pull on my magic as he started to slowly heal himself. I lifted the back of his shirt, pleased to see the angry wound was already starting to knit itself together. He wouldn't take enough power to heal it completely, just seal the wound. Nearby Brynn had roused Grady. He was propped up on his elbows, Brynn kneeling at his feet. The sizzling still came from the tunnel over her shoulder, the sound growing louder than before.

We were running out of time.

"Kyndal, come here, I need you," Brynn summoned me. I looked to Roman, and he gave me a small wave off, giving me permission to leave him.

I dropped next to Brynn. "What do you need?"

"His ankle is broken and dislocated. I'm going to have to pop it back in place, then set the bone before he can heal. I need you to hold him still, because this is going to hurt like hell."

I shuffled around to the other side of Grady, pushing him up to a sitting position. I ignored his grunts of pain as I sat down behind him, one leg on either side before pulling him into my lap. I folded his arms across his chest and braced mine over his. "Try not to enjoy this too much," he panted.

"Funny," I responded. "I was just going to say the same thing to you." It was a lame attempt to lighten the mood, but seconds later a crack echoed through the cave, and Grady bucked against my hold. I held tight as he fought against me and bit down on his scream. He squeezed his eyes shut, tears leaking from the corners. The crack was followed quickly by a loud pop. His eyes burst open, a beautiful earthy-green glowing in the small amount of firelight.

"There, it's done," Brynn announced. Grady almost instantly relaxed, but I held him a moment longer before releasing my grip. I backed away gently, making sure he was able to hold himself up. I was the closest to the tunnel now, the sound of the sceptre breaking through the barrier, pounding in my ears. The wild magic of Set was leaking out of the tunnel, a dark invitation.

Roman pushed himself to his feet. His face was still pinched with pain, but the echo had almost completely subsided, so I knew his pain was manageable. "We need a new plan," he said to us, all while he searched over me. My face, my body. Checking to see if I was alright. He pushed through the bond, too and I sent him what reassurance I could.

"I sent Nero to find Sandra and the others."

"What about the ritual?" Brynn asked.

I shook my head. "It's incomplete."

"We're screwed," Grady added.

"We're not screwed!" Roman threw back.

"Explain to me how we aren't," he argued. "We don't have the sceptre. We have no fourth sacrifice, and even if we did, we don't have the cage to put him in anymore. It's back in Awen! There's no other way to kill him."

"What do you want to do then, Grady? Quit?" Roman demanded. The two men continued to argue, but their voices became nothing but background noise as my brain churned, looking for another solution, another way out.

"Maat," I said quietly, simply. My voice wasn't loud, but the men still shut up to listen. "Maat can help us. She is strong enough to defeat Set."

"I thought she already turned you down," Brynn responded.

"Yeah, well that was before Set was going to rip down the barrier between our worlds. She doesn't have a choice anymore. She can get off her ass and help!" I barked, my temper flaring.

"What's your plan?" she asked.

"I need to get to the river. I can cross to the Inbetween and talk to Maat, but we'll need to move quickly before Set fractures it too much. You guys will just have to hold him off for as long as you can while I'm over there."

"Uh, Kyndal?" Grady asked as he pushed himself to his feet, heavily favoring his left ankle. "I think it's too late for that."

"Why?" I asked.

He pointed over my head. I turned and stared down the dark tunnel. I couldn't see anything, but the hair on the back of my neck stood up, every Kindred sense I possessed standing at attention.

"Wraiths."

Roman

Wraiths poured out from the depths of the tunnel.

They were unlike any wraith I'd ever seen before. Every Kindred knew wraiths didn't have a form of their own, that was why they possessed humans, in order to exist on this plane as a corporeal being. What ran down the tunnel, crawled along its walls, was dark as night, but instead of being an inky shadow like they should have been, these wraiths had legs, arms, a body and head of their own. Through whatever dark magic that lived inside him, Set had given them bodies. I wasn't sure how to kill them. I wasn't even sure they could be killed.

Out of habit, I reached for the dagger in my belt, only to find the sheath empty. I'd lost my weapons back in Awen. Kyndal reached down to her boot, pulling out her tiny ring dagger. She offered it to me, her eyes cast down. I understood why. Where she was going, a dagger would do her no good.

I accepted the dagger, allowing my fingers to linger on her hand. Her eyes snapped up, and her beautiful, fierce red reflected my own gold. I didn't know what I'd done to deserve a woman like her. Strong, smart, and fiercely independent, loving her had been the honor of my life. I knew this could be the last time I looked into her eyes, the last time I touched her skin. I pulled her to me, pressing my lips against hers, in a brief yet powerful kiss that said everything I'd never be able to. "I'm with you until the end."

"Until the end," she whispered.

Two by two, the Guard ran for the tunnel. Kyndal's hands lit up as she launched fireballs ahead of us. I pulled the air from the antechamber, and although it was heavy with moisture, I fed it to her flames, turning her fireballs into walls of fire. The wraiths screeched at the sight of the flames, crawling higher up the walls and onto the tunnel ceiling. Grady and Brynn had managed to hold on to their weapons, and their daggers shone in the firelight as they leapt, dragging their blades through the wraiths above us. The metal sliced through the living shadows, splitting them in half, turning them to ash.

They could be killed.

The other end of the tunnel wasn't far, but the opening was barely visible past the outpouring of wraiths. Small crackles of light burst past them as the sound of Set's dark magic ripping open the river grew closer and closer. We hadn't dropped the shield around us. Although wraiths had no elemental powers, we couldn't risk not being prepared for everything. We were surrounded by the elements in this cave, able to easily pull more power, and the spells that combined our magic and protected us thrummed with strength as Grady busted through the wall of wraiths. The ones he missed, Brynn, Kyndal, and I cleaned up. "There's too many!" Grady shouted. He was right. As long as the barrier was breaking open, more and more wraiths would enter this plane.

We'd been running, but Kyndal suddenly stopped, placing her hand on the rock wall of the tunnel. Fire sparked from her fingertips, and as if following an imaginary line of gasoline, the fire spread along the rock. Wraiths screeched and screamed as they burnt to death until every inch of the walls, the ceiling, were covered in flames. I could feel the heat of the flames as they crackled all around me, the tips of the flames nipping at my arms, and yet I did not burn. A protection of our shield. With the way clear, at least for the moment, we ran through the tunnel of fire and toward the river.

Set was on its banks, kneeling down at the water's edge. The tip of the sceptre was placed in the water and electricity popped through Set's veins, down the sceptre, and into the water. The river rolled wildly under the touch of the dark magic. Behind him, a wraith slithered out of the water's edge, the inky form taking shape in front of our eyes. Kyndal didn't hesitate. She reached for the fire at the tunnel's mouth, launching a piece of it at the wraith and disintegrating him on the spot.

The shadows wrapped around Set churned as the Chaos god turned his head. He did not raise from the water's edge or release the sceptre. Instead, his free arm raised, a pulse of magic bursted forth. It hit the four of us like a ton of bricks, pushing us backward toward the tunnel and Kyndal's flames. Our feet slid on the slick rock, but we pushed back against it. It slowed our movement, managing to keep us upright. The heat of the flames grew near again as they popped and crackled in my ear. They pushed against our shield, and although it did not yield, I could feel the magic pulling out of us too quickly. We wouldn't be able to hold the shield for much longer with it under duress. We needed to move forward. If Kyndal was going to make it to the Inbetween, we had to get Set away from the water's edge.

Brynn, as if she had read my mind, lifted her arms in front of her and then parted them. The water in front of Set, where he'd laid the sceptre, split in two, leaving the sceptre in dry air. The wraith that had been climbing out of the water fell back in, dropping under the surface. His spell temporarily broken.

A loud noise thundered through the tunnel, coming from the antechamber. The pounding of feet followed, the familiar presence of Kindred filling my veins. Nero was back, and from the sounds of it, he'd found the others. Set, whether he had realized the same thing, or was simply annoyed at Brynn's interference, finally stood from the side of the water, fully intent on us.

Brynn released her hold on the water, and it settled quickly back to normal. The room was small, the air limited, so I focused on the fire roaring in the tunnel. The others wouldn't be able to get to us through it. They didn't have the same protection we did. I called to the air, to the oxygen that fed the flames, extinguishing them a little at a time as the strength built in me. Kyndal's magic joined mine, forcing the flames to bend to my will. They were wild and powerful, but slowly they receded until all the flames had gone out. The power was overwhelming, more than I'd ever pulled before. I knew I couldn't contain it, only aim it. I faced the chaos god, releasing my hold on the magic, sending a microburst of wind at Set. It wouldn't hurt him, but it could buy us time. The magic hit him like a wall, knocking him back into the sharp rocks behind him. The sceptre rattled at his feet.

I didn't even get a chance to turn. To tell her to go, or to say goodbye. The moment the sceptre hit the ground, Set's hold on us vanished. Grady and Brynn broke toward the weapon, and Kyndal ran for the river. I stood, almost frozen in place, as I watched her dive into the water and disappear beneath the surface.

Chapter 29

Kyndal

I stood in the endless white sand of the Inbetween.

Last time I'd been in the Inbetween, the sun had been bright, the landscape warm. Although I could see the sun in the sky still, it gave no warmth. Just as before, there was nothing around me for miles. Only mound after mound of never-ending desert, and yet unlike before, it was all shrouded in gray.

"You've returned," her voice skipped over the sand.

I turned to see Maat standing behind me, but instead of the white chiffon dress she'd worn before, now it was a multitude of jewel tones, beautifully contrasted with her dark skin. *The colors of her wings,* I realized. It was the only color in this gray wasteland.

Last time, I'd fallen to my knees at the sight of her, but this time I stood with my back straight as I greeted the goddess, the keeper of the Inbetween. "We need your help. Set is breaking down the barrier between our worlds."

She looked around her. "I noticed."

I scoffed at her unconcerned tone. "You need to help us."

"I told you once, child of Aries, I cannot enter your plane. I cannot leave the Inbetween, Duat would fall to ruin."

"Duat is going to fall to ruin anyway! If you do nothing, the Inbetween won't even exist anymore! You're the only one strong enough to defeat him! To keep him down for good." *Why couldn't she see that?*

"That is partly true. But I will not leave the Inbetween," she repeated.

I turned, digging my nails into my hair. I bent my head back and let loose a scream. It flew over the sand, a never-ending echo. "How can you refuse to help us? I'm willing to give up everything! To sacrifice my *life* to defeat him, and you won't even lift a finger!" I didn't care that I was screaming at an ancient goddess. I was pissed.

Maat appeared in front of me, although I had never turned around. She grabbed my hands, her jeweled-eyes staring into my poor imitation. "I know what you are willing to sacrifice, that is your destiny and burden as a Descendant. But you were not listening, child. I did not say I would not help." Images flashed in my head, ones I knew she was putting there. They moved quickly, but each was burned into my memory as if I'd thought of them myself. My breath came quickly as I examined what she was showing me. "Do you understand now, child?" she asked kindly. "Descendant blood is the only thing that can contain a god. The lock to his cage."

I nodded. "Yes," I whispered. I understood. I understood for the first time exactly what I was capable of.

"Good," she responded. "Then see it is done."

The sunlight disappeared, replaced with the soft moonlight reflecting off the river. I was back in the Hall of Two Truths, somehow miraculously dry. No doubt a parting gift from Maat. The cavern was empty, but the sounds of battle raged in the antechamber. I was instantly reconnected with Roman, with the rest of the Guard. The images Maat placed in my head were still at the forefront of my mind as I ran through the tunnel to join the battle.

To see it done.

I noticed several things quickly. Nero had been successful, and our reinforcements had arrived. Set was battling not only the Guard, but now Mallory, Cassie, Nero, and dozens of rebel Kindred. From across the dark cave, I saw the brilliant blonde hair of Sandra Cartwright as Roman's mother fought in the thick of it.

From somewhere, hybrids had appeared to support their master, as well. I shouldn't have been surprised. We wouldn't have been the only ones with a back-up plan. Set must have left them behind before attacking Awen. Bodies littered the floor of the antechamber, Kindred and hybrid alike. When I'd entered the river, the others were going for the sceptre, but Set held it in his hands now, blasts of its dark magic bursting through the cave.

For the moment, no one had noticed me. I took the opportunity to do what was necessary. I ran around the edge of the battle, to where Nero was fighting a hybrid. He still wielded Batil, cutting it across the leg of the hybrid and dropping him to his knees. I came up behind the hybrid, snapping his neck. He fell to the ground, Nero finishing him off with the blade through the heart.

His chest heaved with exertion as he looked to me, the blade at his side dripping with blood. "Thanks."

"I need your help."

Roman

I felt her the moment she emerged from the river.

The bond had been heavy, and I was almost weighed down as her anchor to this plane, but when she came back, the weight was instantly lifted. I'd expected her to come blazing through the tunnel, returning with a vengeance, Maat at her side, but it didn't happen. Instead, I'd felt her approach the antechamber quickly, but she didn't rush to the middle of the fight like I'd expected.

The Guard was holding off Set, the three of us only surviving thanks to our shield. Sandra had arrived with the rebels without a moment to spare, helping us push Set out of the river cavern and away from Kyndal. Sandra tore through the tunnel, daggers flying, the sight making my heart swell. I had not realized how empty her absence had made me feel until I saw her again.

Another blast of the sceptre ripped through the cave, and I rolled to miss its blast, hiding behind one of the larger boulders. It hit a Kindred soldier who wasn't quick enough to get out of the way. She was gone moments later, as if she never existed. Past where the soldier had just stood, I caught sight of Kyndal running on the far edge of the battle. She stopped to help Nero kill a hybrid, then leaned forward to whisper in his ear. Another lightning bolt tore through the cave, the blast knocking off a piece of the boulder I was hiding behind. I was forced to duck lower to avoid being hit by debris, but when I looked again, Nero was handing his sword over to Kyndal without hesitation. There was a small pull on the bond, and the sword lit up, flames crawling over the tip to her hand. She reached over, pulling a piece of flame and gifting it to my father.

I stared at them, confused. What could the two of them possibly be scheming? Whatever it was, I knew it wasn't good. I knew I had to stop them.

Another bolt hit the wall over my head, the rock crumbling down on me. By now, a hybrid had taken notice of where I was hiding, forcing me to jump back into the action. The hybrid's dagger came down hard, but I raised my own to match. I'd taken the weapon off a dead hybrid, knowing the ring dagger wasn't going to cut it in a battle like this. I kicked out at the hybrid, pushing her back, straight into the grasp of Cassie and her blades. She was dead in moments.

I looked back to where I'd last seen Kyndal, but she wasn't there. She was tearing through the hybrids, her fire sword laying waste to the enemy. She felled one of the two hybrids Mallory had been battling, our friend finishing off the other. Behind me, Grady and Brynn did everything they could to fend off the hybrids as Set continued his onslaught of power. A shout rang out as Brynn didn't move fast enough to avoid one hybrid's blade, his dagger cutting through her side. Grady stepped forward to defend his Guardsman, and in two moves, the hybrid was dead and Grady was hauling Brynn to a safe place to heal herself.

Frantic, I ran toward Kyndal, my blade slicing through every hybrid that got in my way. I reached Cassie first, stopping only long enough to help her defeat her opponent. Together, the two of us headed for my Rafiq. We found her fighting back to back with Mallory, beautifully in tune with the woman that had taught her so much as they fought back the enemy. When Mallory dropped low, Kyndal spun Batil high. When Kyndal was forced to turn her back, Mallory's dagger was there to cover. Fire burst from the sword, igniting the handful of hybrids who had made the mistake of thinking they had the two of them defeated.

I reached Kyndal, clasping my hand across her forearm. "Where's Maat?"

She shook her head. "She's not coming!" she yelled over the roar of the battle.

I sent my dismay, my questions down the bond, not bothering to ask them aloud. "What are you planning with Nero?" I demanded.

The bond tightened, a sure sign she was about to lie. "Don't worry, I know what to do. Maat told me." Without warning, she grabbed my shirt and pulled me to her, kissing me hard on the mouth. It was so fast, I barely had time to register the touch before it was gone. She pulled back just inches, her breath mingling with mine. "It'll be okay, Roman. *I'll be okay.* I have a plan. Trust me." *Trust me.* The words rang through me as she put the strength of our bond, our love, behind her request.

Trust her.

I wanted to. Desperately. But Kyndal had made it very clear she didn't value her life as much as I did. I ran through the facts. Set's cage wasn't here. Maat wasn't coming to help. We had no way of imprisoning the chaos god. Without any of those, the best we could hope for was to weaken him enough that we could leave with the sceptre until we came up with another plan. Whatever secret Kyndal was keeping, there was no way it ended in her sacrificing herself. There would be no point in it.

From behind me, a hybrid screamed before they attacked, and Kyndal raised her sword to stop the blow that would have landed across my shoulder. I spun, blasting the hybrid away from us and into the wall. I turned back to Kyndal, determined to get more information from her, but she was already gone.

"What is she doing?" Mallory asked.

I gritted my teeth, shrugging. "She says she has a plan," I responded. "We do the only thing we can. We trust her."

Begrudgingly, I followed my Rafiq and leapt back in the fray with the others, dodging through the random shots of the sceptre as they tore down The Hall of Two Truths one bolt at a time.

Trust her, I repeated.

I'll be okay, she'd said.

The four of us reached the far side of the antechamber, where Set was waiting. There were only a handful of hybrids remaining, but Sandra would make sure the others finished them off and cleared the way for us. We joined Grady and Brynn, the six of us facing down the Chaos god. The magic of the Guard still thrummed through me, even though we were all beaten bloody and using more magic than we ever had. I spared a quick glance to Grady. His face was pale, his eyes strained. I knew the magic was pulling hard on him, and I was worried if we expended too much more, he'd collapse.

Set twirled the sceptre in his hand as he looked across the line of Kindred soldiers staring him down. His shadows wrapped around his arms and legs, leaked from where Kyndal had wounded his shoulder. His eyes churned, the sceptre pulsing in his hand. This was it. This moment would decide the fate of the Kindred.

The fate of the world.

Mallory attacked first, her metal staff coming down hard across the sceptre. Set had kidnapped Mallory, tortured her using his dark magic, she had as much right as anyone to want him dead. She didn't flinch at his defense, dropping low, stabbing at his leg at the same time Brynn jumped in, her sai swiping at Set's arm. Set blocked Brynn, but Mallory's blow landed, the sharpened end of her staff cutting through the meat of Set's leg. The god roared, magic flying from his center, pushing Mallory and Cassie back several feet and onto the other side of the remaining hybrids. Grady, Kyndal, and I pushed forward, joining Brynn, each of us brandishing our various weapons.

The four of us attacked the god, slicing, cutting, stabbing at any part of him we could. The sceptre pushed at our shield, and I could feel our magic waning, cracks in the shield leaving us vulnerable. Grady managed to swipe his blade across Set's arm, but he retaliated with a backhand that sent Grady flying to the other side of the cavern. With a scream, Brynn brought her weapon down on his leg, her blade cutting through his thigh, just above where Mallory's cut had landed. She yanked the blade out, blood covering her weapon. Set growled and grabbed her by the neck, throwing her backward toward Grady. The god's chest heaved, a dark-red blood leaking down his extremities. I knew none of the hits were fatal. We were managing to harm his vessel, but we were doing nothing to attack the god inside the body. If we killed his shell—the man that used to be Ezekiel—Set would still live.

Kyndal and I were the only ones left standing. Me with my dagger, Kyndal with her fire sword. Our magic was leaking out, our strength waning. Even so, our determination held strong and we leapt as one on the god. He raised his sceptre, our weapons coming down hard on the metal of it. The sceptre seemed to absorb the hit, stealing the strength of our power on contact. We stepped backward, perfectly in tune. Through the bond, I knew exactly what move she would make before she did it. Kyndal swept her fire sword high, but the god ducked under its flames, allowing me to bring my knee up high and directly into his face. I heard the satisfying sound of bone breaking under my knee, and when the god pulled back, his nose was bleeding. It wasn't much of a hit, but it was enough. It had distracted him *just enough.*

Kyndal let loose a shriek, a bloodthirsty battle cry, and moments later, she brought the black fire blade of Batil down across the wrist of Set. The flames cut through his wrist, severing the hand that held the sceptre. The god roared, the cavern shaking with the power and rage of it. The ground under my feet shook and I had to work to stay on my feet.

Kyndal's eyes were a livid red. The same cold heat that I'd felt before streamed down the bond as she stalked toward the god. She switched Batil to her left hand, grabbing the severed hand with the other. Slowly, she peeled the sceptre from the stiff fingers still wrapped around the weapon. When the sceptre was free, she dropped the hand onto the hard floor. I flinched as it landed with a wet thud. I expected her to turn the sceptre on Set, and yet, she turned away.

What is she doing? She has the advantage.

Now is the opportunity to strike. To end it all.

Instead, she threw the sceptre out into the antechamber and it clanged on the ground not far from my feet.

"What are you doing?" I shouted. She didn't respond. Didn't even acknowledge me.

Instead, she twisted the onyx blade in her hand, the blood-red pommel of Batil fused by fire, to her hand. In that moment I understood what she was going to do. Why she hadn't come back with Maat. Why she had seemed so sure of herself since returning from the Inbetween.

I'll be okay, she'd said.

No, she wouldn't be.

"Kyndal, no!" I shouted, preparing to stop her.

Out of nowhere, a body hit me at full speed, spearing me to the ground. I struggled against my attacker, but strong arms clamped down around me, forcing me to stay on the ground. "Don't," my father whispered.

I pushed against him, thrashed my body trying to break his hold, but he held strong. "Let me go," I demanded.

"I'm sorry, son. I can't."

With a single step forward, Kyndal grabbed the chaos god by the shoulder and drove the sword into his chest.

Kyndal

The sword slid through Set's chest, the blade stopping just before his heart.

The god screamed and dropped to his knees, looking up at me, even as thunderclouds rumbled in his eyes. "You stupid girl!" he sneered. "That blade cannot kill me."

I pushed the blade further, until I felt it cut through the muscle of the heart. I didn't quit pushing, not until the hilt of Batil rested against Set's skin. "I don't need it to kill *you*. Just *him*."

He laughed, even as blood bubbled through his mouth. "I stopped the ritual and you have no cage to keep me in." Stupid, arrogant god. Even in his defeat, he couldn't see it yet. He was already dead.

A pang of panic ripped down the bond from where I knew Roman laid incapacitated not five feet away. I ignored him. Nero had done what I'd asked of him. He'd been the only person I could ask for such a terrible favor. "I don't need a cage," I pointed out, reveling in this moment. Ezekiel had killed my parents. My brother. He was the reason all this evil had come into my life. "Only Descendant blood can lock in a god. When Ezekiel dies, you lose your host. You'll be driven into the nearest replacement—me." I twisted the blade again, pushing it upward, knowing it would be the final blow. "I will be your cage," I whispered in his ear. "Maat sends her regards." I pulled my blade free, allowing his body to drop to the cave floor.

Shadows leaked from the gaping hole left by my blade. Set's soul trying to escape his dying host. I dropped the blade, preparing myself for what came next. "Kyndal, don't do this!" Roman's voice ripped through the cavern. I risked a glance, pleased to see Nero still held him down even as my love thrashed and pushed against his jailer. Roman beat his arms against his father, kicked at him with all his strength. Nero took every hit and yet did not release him. The wind kicked up around me, his desperate attempt to reach me, and yet Nero did not let go.

The others stepped forward, Mallory and Grady determined to stop me if Roman couldn't. I raised my hand, a fireball at the ready. "Don't come closer," I commanded. They wisely listened. The Guard was still connected through magic, and I was pulling my fill. The others were nowhere near strong enough to challenge me. The shadows grew out of the body that had once been Ezekiel Sands, swirling around my foot, traveling up my leg. *This was it.* Set's magic was so cold it burned, but I held tight to the fireball, refusing to let my friends interfere. With one final breath, Set's soul climbed up my torso, and pushed its way down my throat. I didn't resist it, even though every fiber in my being knew it was wrong, knew I should thrash and fight. This is what Maat had shown me. It was the only way to defeat Set, even if it meant my ruin. So, I stood still, allowing Set to possess me, his dark magic corrupting my internal fire.

The power was instant. I felt him spread out through my limbs, working to take control of my legs, my arms. He moved through every part of me, until only a sliver of myself remained. My power was still there, as strong as ever, but instead of a burning heat, it was a fire made of ice and crystal. A dark flame that I somehow knew would be as black as Batil's blade if I chose to release it. I held on to the tiny piece of myself, that piece that sounded like the bubbling of Cherry Run and smelled of burnt leaves and a hint of engine oil. I fought against Set's control, knowing it was my only chance of pulling this off. I didn't have to last long. Just long enough.

Hands grabbed ahold of my shoulders, hands that were shaking me, and through the pain, through the wall that was growing thinner between me and Set, I felt a light breeze. I didn't know how he got loose of Nero's grip. At the moment, I wasn't capable of caring. Roman shook me, yelling my name. "The river," I managed to say. "Get me to the river."

He picked me up, cradling me against his chest as if I weighed nothing at all. He ran through the tunnel, holding tight as I writhed in his grip, screaming as the power of Set ripped through me, the icy fire burning away all that was good about me, all that was free and strong.

Moments later—years later—the cool water of the river lapped against my skin. Roman had laid me down at the water's edge. He knew he couldn't go any further. I would have to be the one to complete the final step. I groaned at the strength of the god inside me. He was pushing me back, retreating from the river. He knew if we went under, he wouldn't return. Neither of us would. I clung tight to that final piece of myself, to the fact that the fight would be over soon and I could finally rest.

Then I rolled into the blackness of the water.

When I opened my eyes again, I was laying on the white sand. It stuck to my wet arms, to my neck and face, the fine grain of it like sandpaper against a raw nerve. Set still roiled inside me, I could hear his screaming echoing in my ears. I curled in on myself, clamping my hands over my ears to try and stop his deafening roar. I coughed, some distant part of me recognizing the blood that stained the sand.

"You've done well, child." Her voice was distant, barely audible past Set's screaming. My vision was blurring, and from my place on the ground, I could only barely make out her sandaled feet.

"It hurts," I groaned, tears falling from my eyes. "He's killing me." I knew it was true. "Please make it stop. Just make it stop."

Maat dropped down, her beautiful face coming into view. She placed her hand on my head, brushing back my sweaty hair. Her other hand laid gently over my heart. Inside me, the chaos god lunged at her throat, demanded I end her life. I pulled back on the impulse, tightened the leash on my self-control. It was almost over. Just a moment longer. "I understand. You can stop fighting now. Your job is complete."

A sense of overwhelming calm filled me, and I uncurled my body, rolling to my back.

I was done.

I fulfilled my destiny.

I could rest now.

I surrendered to the pain inside of me, allowing everything to disappear, letting go of that last piece of myself.

I surrendered completely and then everything faded to darkness.

Chapter 30

Roman

I knelt on the edge of the river that divided our world from the Inbetween and wept.

She'd lied to me.

She'd told me everything would be okay, that *she* would be okay. And then she'd driven her sword into the heart of a chaos god.

I'd laid on the hard floor of the antechamber, trapped by my father, too weak, too injured to get out of his grasp until it was too late to save her. To stop her from sacrificing herself.

Again.

Boots thundered down the tunnel behind me, but I didn't turn. The hybrids were dead. The wraiths were gone. There was no more threat. "Where is she?" the voice demanded.

"She's gone, Grady," Brynn answered, her voice further behind his. She'd always been the only one strong enough to agree with Kyndal. To believe that sacrificing her life was worth it in order to serve the greater good. Even so, there was no missing the pain in her voice.

"What the hell do you mean, she's gone?!" Grady yelled back. He didn't understand. He hadn't seen her go under the water. He hadn't seen the dark depths of the river pull her under so deep she wasn't even visible anymore. Someone should tell him what happened. I should tell him. *How long ago had that been? Two minutes? Ten?* "She can't just be gone! What the hell happened back there?!"

I knew the last question was directed at me, but I couldn't bear to form the words. My Guardsmen stood on either side of me, yelling and raging at each other. Another set of boots ran my way, a familiar presence dropping to her knees next to me.

"Roman?" Cassie said softly. "Roman, your hands are burnt. Do they hurt? Tell me where it hurts and I can fix you."

I didn't respond. How do you tell someone that you can't be fixed? That the physical injuries didn't matter because there was a gaping hole in your heart that could never be filled.

As if from a distance, as if it were happening to someone else, Cassie's light, yet confident touch probed at the bruises on my face, the giant slash across my back. She grabbed my hands, tried to open them to reveal the thick bands of blood and ruined flesh, but I refused. Held them tight into fists. The others were still yelling at each other, and I thought I heard more people join us, but I wasn't sure.

I wasn't sure of anything anymore.

More tears fell, and yet through them I noticed another face drop into view. Her blonde hair was stained red in places and a gash cut across her left cheek bone. She knelt in front of me, her strong yet slender hands cupping my cheeks and wiping back the tears. Hands that I knew had been cut and tortured to near ruin, just like mine were now. She shouldn't bother with me. More tears simply fell in place of those she removed. "Roman." Her voice cut through the fog that had separated me from everyone else. Her voice.

My mother's voice.

"I can't feel her," I whispered. My voice was hoarse. I think I'd been screaming earlier. "She's gone. I can't feel her anymore."

I felt Grady's eyes move to me. I knew he was checking my power signature, searching for any signs of my connection to Kyndal. His silence said enough.

The bond was gone.

"I know, honey," my mother cooed. A voice she used when I was young and the memories of my sister's death would creep into my dreams. "I know it hurts, but you can't do anything for her now. We need you to open your hands so Cassie can look at your burns."

I still didn't unclench my fists. "They aren't burns."

"What are they, Rome?" Cassie asked this time.

"They aren't burns," I said again, but I let her unfurl my hands. She hadn't been burning when I'd held her. I'd carried her to the river, but her skin hadn't been burning. "She was cold. So terribly cold." I broke out of my trance, looking to my mother. My sister. "*I'm so cold.*"

I hadn't been talking to anyone in particular. I damn sure hadn't expected a response, but from behind me, near the mouth of the tunnel, a deep voice answered. "It's Set. His magic eats at the life force of the host. He absorbed her power, inverting it and turning it dark." The voice belonged to my father. To the man that held me down and forced me to watch Kyndal leave me. Again.

Without warning, I jumped to my feet, faster than anyone could stop me. "You bastard!" I screamed, lunging toward the man. He was slightly taller than me, held more weight and muscle than I did, but none of that mattered. I was faster, and I was pissed. "This is all your fault!" My fist ricocheted off his cheekbone, his head snapping to the side.

443

I grabbed him by the front of his shirt, pulling him to me. I hit him again. Again.

Blood poured from his nose and out the corner of his mouth, but he never once tried to defend himself. Never once tried to stop me. "You did this!" I screamed, my tears obscuring my vision again. "I could have stopped her! I would have stopped her!" Strong hands grabbed at my arms, pulling me backward and off my father who was lying limply against the cave wall. "No!" I bellowed, my element echoing my demand off the surrounding rock. "Leave me alone!" I thrashed against who I now recognized as Cassie and Mallory, breaking free and lunging toward Nero again. I swung again, this time his nose breaking under my fist. I pulled back, prepared to hit again, when a pulse of magic, a pulse of pure *power* hit me square in the heart.

I cried out from the shock of it. I fell to all fours, my ruined hands scraping along the rocky ground. Unlike the cold, brutal power of Set, or the fiery strength of Kyndal, this power was pure, untainted, undiluted. It spread from my heart, moving down my abdomen to the hollow space where the bond was supposed to live. Inside the power I could feel all four elements. The heat of a flame, the rush of the air, the smell of wet earth. "Roman, what's happening?" I heard Cassie shout.

"It's not me," I managed to respond between gasps for air. "It's not me."

The magic burrowed deeper, the pain worse than any I'd ever experienced. Worse than when I'd been branded, tortured, even killed. Even so, I somehow knew I wasn't in danger, that the pain wasn't mine, not really.

I screamed at the top of my lungs as the elements spread through every inch of my muscles, my nerves. The power was too much to contain. Too much for one person to handle alone. Eventually, my voice gave out and still my mouth remained open in a silent scream. The others clustered around me, their voices frantic, and yet none of them knew what was happening, how to help.

Just when I didn't think I could take anymore, the power burst out of me in a shot, a cord of pure magic. It flew across the cave, past my friends that still hovered over me. Some part of me that had been broken, lost, snapped back into place, and a small kernel of warmth took hold in my gut. Mercifully, the power softened. It became easier to take, easier to withstand as it found its home. I groaned again, this time not in pain, but exaltation.

The familiar feeling, the sixth sense I'd come to rely on, cherish, and identify as the Rafiq bond was back. And if the bond was back, that meant she was too.

I didn't have Grady's gift. I couldn't read power signatures. But as clear as if it were written in blood, I tracked the invasive power across the cave. As powerful and painful as it had been, it was equally beautiful. It was made of multi-colored light, the most stunning jeweled tones I'd ever seen. I looked to the others. Could they see it too? They were all staring at me. None of them followed the magic. I tracked the light as it moved away from me and toward the river. As it moved toward the body that I not only saw, but felt, lying on the river's edge. A body that hadn't been there moments ago.

If I didn't know better, I would have said she was sleeping. She laid on her side, hair falling out of her ponytail and obscuring parts of her face. Her chest rose and fell in even breaths. Her skin was perfect, not a single mark on her. I opened my fists, searching for the ruined flesh that had been there moments before. They were covered in dried blood, but no other signs of my wounds remained. Whatever magic healed her, had healed me too.

Grady was the first to catch on to what was happening, no doubt his power sensing things others couldn't see. "It's her!" he gasped.

As one, they all turned toward the river, each letting out their own versions of surprise and awe at the sight of my newly returned Rafiq. Left alone, I tried to push myself to my feet to join them. *I had to get to her. I had to touch her.* My wounds may have healed, but I was weak from blood loss and my power was completely depleted. My knees gave out underneath me, and I dropped back to the floor. I closed my eyes, focusing on my breathing, thinking around the pain that still lived inside me. Every part of my body was screaming at me to quit. She was back. She was alive.

I'd done my job. But that wasn't enough. *I have to see her. I have to touch her,* I said to myself again.

I reopened my eyes, determined to make it to her, but the floor shook and blurred underneath me. I dropped to all fours again, crawling toward the river. At the first step, my elbow buckled underneath me, and I fell to the ground. I rolled to my back and closed my eyes, no longer strong enough to fight the impending darkness.

Kyndal

I woke to the sound of water.

Not the soft lapping of the river, but the roaring of ocean waves as they crashed against rocky cliffs.

I had been dreaming. Not the same dreams I'd had before, where Marius, Davina, or Roman were actually there, but a dream that instead conjured a memory. I'd been dreaming of the summer I was ten. We'd gone on a trip to the Gulf of Mexico, and my brother was trying desperately to bury me in the sand. My parents sat not far away, my dad with his nose stuck in a mechanical book, my mom sitting in her lounger, admiring the ocean. We'd spent the whole day at the water, not leaving until the sun had disappeared beyond the horizon and it became too dark for us to see. When I woke, I could still see the vision of my father's smile in my eyes, the sound of my mother's laugh in my ears.

The room was dim, lit in the soft purples and blues from outside. It had to be very early in the morning, just before the sun made its appearance. I laid still, staring at the ceiling. It was ornate, the molding a thick wood, probably something stupidly expensive like mahogany. In its center hung an equally extravagant chandelier. So different from the cracked ceilings made from stone and rock that I'd become accustomed to. The opulence played at a different type of memory, one I knew wasn't exactly real. I'd never been in this room before, and yet the chandelier was familiar to me.

I was in Astrid's house in Awen.

I'd visited Roman here once, the first time we'd spoken in our dreams.

I pushed myself up slowly, every inch of my body screaming at me in protest. The last thing I remembered, I'd rolled into the river, my body riddled with wounds, my internal organs on fire with the power of Set's dark magic. Now, my skin was perfect, if not a touch pale. Although there was not a scratch or bruise to be seen, inside was a different matter. There was a bone-deep pain, one that permeated every inch of my body. One I knew would take a very long time to fully repair. I searched for my magic, pleased when I was able to find the well where it resided, although I didn't dare touch it. Not yet.

Grimacing through the pain, I managed to sit all the way up and smiled when I was fully able to take in the room. Unsurprisingly, the floor was littered with sleeping bodies. Grady was posted in an armchair, Brynn sitting and leaning against the wall not far from him. Cassie and Mallory were spread out on the floor, their hands intertwined. Apparently none of them had ever heard of a bed, or at the very least, a pillow. Unlike me, they were all still peppered with bruises and cuts. Either it hadn't been too long since the fight, or they'd all refused to heal themselves. They were stubborn enough to do something like that, just as they were stubborn enough to refuse to see to their own needs in order to make sure I didn't wake up alone. The others faded away as I looked next to me. He sat awkwardly in a chair, leaned over the bed, his head laid out on the comforter, "Roman."

He woke at the sound of my voice, his head lifting slightly, his eyes opening slowly as if he could barely pull himself from sleep. His chin was covered in facial hair, much more than I'd ever seen on him before. More time had passed than I'd realized. It had been too long since he'd shaved. Since any of us had taken care of ourselves. "Kyndal?" he said quietly.

I reached out, running my fingers across the scratchy hair on his jaw. "Hi," I answered simply. I didn't know what else to say. Would he hate me for what I'd done? I'd confided in his father behind his back, worked to keep him out of the way. I lied to him and did the one thing I'd promised not to do. I wouldn't blame him if he never spoke to me again.

"Never," he answered, as if I'd asked the question out loud. "I could never hate you. Part of me is so pissed at you for what you did, but it was also the bravest thing I've ever seen."

"Is it really over?" I asked. *Part of me didn't believe it.*

He nodded. "Set's gone, for good this time. Grady checked your power signature the second you returned from the river. There are no signs of him or his magic anymore. You did it. I don't know how, but you did it."

The details were fuzzy, my brain still foggy from pain and trauma. I cleared my throat, my vocal chords scratchy. "I think Maat pulled his soul out of me. I don't remember much of what happened while I was possessed. Just that it—" I stumbled. "Just that it hurt. And his power was cold, so cold I felt like it was burning me. I never understood. . ." I began, but my throat clogged with tears. "I'm so sorry, I never really understood." Roman had only spoke about his possession once, when we first went to Siberia. The way he'd described it then, I thought I understood the pain he'd gone through. Almost unconsciously, Roman looked down at his open hands. I followed his gaze but saw nothing out of the ordinary. Whatever he was looking at was a ghost of a wound. "It was stupid and arrogant of me to think I knew what you'd been through." I shook my head, more mad at myself than anything. "No one understands. . ."

"Unless you go through it," he finished for me. I nodded, ignoring the hot tears streaming down my face. Slowly,

Roman reached over, grabbing my wrist and turning my hand over, his thumb brushing lightly over my brand.

I waited for him to start, to tell me everything that happened, and yet he never did. He simply sat in silence, his hand under mine. I wondered if he didn't want to tell me. If the news was too bad to hear. We may have won the war and defeated Set, but I knew we did not get out unscathed.

How many had we lost?

"Your wounds are healed," I said after a while. "Just like mine. I'm assuming that's not a coincidence."

He shook his head. "No. I think it was Maat's thank you gift to us both." His thumb continued to work back and forth over my palm. A soothing, even rhythm. "I've never been so scared as I was when you drove that sword into his heart."

My heart twisted at the emotions behind his words. "Me neither," I admitted. "When I went into the river the second time, I didn't expect. . ."

"You didn't expect to come back," he finished for me. I didn't deny it. We both knew he was right.

"I'm sorry," I said again, the words not as difficult to say as they used to be. I moved my hand from his cheek and ran it through his hair. He needed a haircut. "Once Maat showed me what to do, I knew I didn't have a choice. It was always going to be me in the end."

Roman gave a little half shrug, a move that looked dismissive, although I knew it was anything but. "I understand." He huffed a laugh. "Sort of."

I looked around at the others, their changed and cleaned clothes at odds with their marred and wounded skin. "Just tell me."

Roman paused, the same way he always did when he didn't want to deliver bad news. "I'm not sure you're ready. It's bad."

I took a deep, steadying breath. "Tell me the worst."

Chapter 31

Roman

I ambled down the steps of Astrid's house, cracking my neck.

It was still the middle of the night, the house, including all our uninvited guests were still fast asleep.

But *she* was awake.

I rounded the corner to the kitchen and stopped in my tracks. Sitting at the table with a half-drank bottle of bourbon in front of him, was Maks. I was struck by memories of Astrid in that very spot, her long pale blue nightgown covered by her silver hair. Maks looked terrible, his eyes swollen and red from tears. Although I wasn't exactly in a position to judge. My own appearance was substandard at best.

"Sorry," I said immediately, attempting to move out of the kitchen. "I didn't think anyone else was up."

"It's fine, Sands. Have a seat." He lifted the bottle high in the air. "I'll share with you, although you'd have to get your own glass."

I didn't point out that he wasn't using a glass, just moved to the cabinet to get a tumbler. I poured myself a generous amount, although I set it in front of me instead of drinking from it. "Kyndal's awake."

"I heard," Maks responded, taking a large pull from the bottle. "How did she take the news?"

I wasn't sure why he was asking. If he'd heard her wake up, he must have heard the rest of our conversation. I answered anyway, "About as expected. She was upset she missed the funerals."

"She's been out for eight days," Maks responded sarcastically. "Not exactly like we could wait."

"All the same. She would have liked to have been there to pay her respects to the soldiers. And to Madigan, Astrid, and Daniela." At the last name, I did reach for the glass in front of me, taking a generous drink. Maks lifted the bottle, too, although I knew it was the former Nomarch's death that drove him to it, not that of the once-rebel leader.

"That couldn't have been easy," Maks said, his only attempt to make me feel better. Frankly, I was surprised he'd even tried. He was lost in his own grief. I remembered how he'd stood vigil by Astrid's pyre, his tears flowing openly and without shame. His heart was broken by her death. It was so obvious, I don't know how I hadn't seen it before. He was in love with her. I shook my head. So much had gone wrong during the battle, it had been difficult to know where to start. "Did you tell her the other part?" he asked.

I nodded slowly before taking another drink, a larger one that emptied the tumbler. I'd barely set it down before Maks refilled its contents. "Yes. Took everything I had to convince her she couldn't get out of bed in that exact moment and start hunting. I had to wake up Grady and Brynn before I could even leave the room. I wouldn't put it past her to try and escape."

Maks scoffed. "If she did leave, I might be tempted to join her. Over one thousand Kindred are killed and somehow that bitch Amina slithers away. She deserves to be hunted down and killed. Slowly." I didn't disagree. According to the official reports, the wards had only been down at the Hollow for under ten minutes, but some of the prisoners, the ones that hadn't been in there long and still had their strength, were able to rebel and escape. Amina and a handful of her most loyal sentries were among them. Maks and Astrid had done everything they could to hold the Hollow, but they were overwhelmed by sheer numbers. Astrid had fallen protecting Maks, ran through with a dagger by Amina herself. There'd been no sign of them since. Best we could tell, they'd stolen one of Set's ships and used it to disappear.

Although part of me knew she wouldn't stay hidden for long.

"Mallory sent word to all the compounds around the world. If she surfaces, we'll find her."

"Have you spoken to your mother?" Maks asked suddenly. The usual bitterness when Sandra was mentioned was missing. How much things had changed in the last year.

I paused a minute, surprised by his change in subject. "We spoke before we left Egypt. I think you can understand why she wouldn't want to join me in Awen." Even though the Nomarch Council didn't exist anymore, there was just too much bad blood for her to trust coming here anytime soon.

"There will be many changes, I think," Maks said, as if he'd read my mind. "Maybe someday she will return."

"Someday," I agreed.

Kyndal

It was two more days before Roman let me leave my room. I went as far as down the hall to the bathroom in order to clean myself up. It was another additional day until I finally went outside. I wanted to argue with him, to tell him he was being overprotective, but I couldn't bring myself to do it.

Truth was, I was exhausted, and I was hurting. Turns out that when you let a Chaos god possess your body, it takes some extra time to heal yourself.

When I did eventually step outside, I wasn't fully back to normal, but I finally convinced him I couldn't stay in that bed any longer.

Besides, I had been summoned to the old throne room. I'd spent my last several days of bed rest to pepper every visitor with questions.

Who was in charge now?

Was someone taking proper care of the injured?

How were we recovering after the destruction done to the island?

From what they told me, the Guard and the surviving Nomarchs—at least those that had chosen to fight on our side—were working together to pick up the pieces. Mallory had taken over leadership in what used to be Daniela's rebel group. Cassie was back to running the infirmary, Brynn, Grady, and Maks keeping court in the old Council Chambers. Roman had taken on the responsibility of getting the soldiers back to proper training hours. At least when he wasn't hovering at my bedside.

They'd been working tirelessly, keeping things going, waiting for me to be ready. They'd all refused to make decisions about the future of the Kindred without me present, even when the old Nomarchs pressured them to. I'd earned the right for my voice to be heard.

I walked out of Astrid's house and into the sunlight, Roman at my side. We were in the thick of summer and the day was hot. In just a few short days, the House would change, and Awen would move, and yet I knew the island would keep its sunny, balmy weather.

Brynn and Grady were standing out front, their backs to us. When the door clicked shut behind me, they both turned my way, welcoming smiles on their faces. I walked forward, wrapping my arms around Brynn first. "I know you hate hugs, but you're just going to have to deal with it."

She laughed, and I swore I heard tears in her voice. "I'll deal with it this one time—but no more!"

I started laughing, too, even as I wiped the tears off my cheeks, ones I hadn't even realized had formed. The bond tugged gently behind me, drawing my attention. It wasn't anywhere as strong as it had been, but I knew it would return with time. I moved to Grady. He wrapped his arms around me. I expected him to let go quickly, to feel awkward hugging me, but he didn't. He held tight, and I found myself squeezing him back just as hard. There were no words exchanged between us, there was no need for them. Not after everything we'd been through.

I returned to Roman's side, looping my fingers through his. The four of us walked slowly through the streets of Awen, toward what used to be Council Chambers. He looked down on me with that crooked smile of his I loved so much. "What?" I asked.

He shrugged. "Nothing. I just think that's the first time I've heard you laugh in a long time. I didn't realize how much I missed that sound."

I pushed up on my tiptoes, kissing him lightly on the lips. He held on a moment longer, neither one of us missing out on the importance of being able to do that in public. Even a month ago, that would have been enough to get us thrown in the Hollow.

"Get a room!" Grady yelled back at us playfully.

We pulled away, both of us smiling stupidly at each other as we followed after our fellow Guardsmen. The city was damaged again, signs of the hybrid attack in every piece of broken stone and burnt road. My heart ached for the damage, for the hundreds of lives I knew had been lost, but a part of me knew we would rebuild, that we would come back stronger than ever. We finally made it to the steps of the large building, the four of us collectively pausing. This time there were no sentries, no guards to stop us.

We may have won the great war, but there was much left to do. At the next full moon, the Kindred would hold their first free election, choosing their House leaders for the first time in their history.

Roman's hand brushed my arm, sending shivers up my spine. "Stop worrying," he whispered.

I snorted. "How? There's so much to do."

"It's okay if you're not ready. You don't have to fix everything in one day. You can take the day for yourself. We can start tomorrow at sunrise."

I raised my eyebrows, smiling playfully at the love of my life. My Rafiq. I stepped onto the bottom step, pulling him along with me. "Sunrise? I see no reason to wait. Besides," I tugged him to me, kissing him once more, "I hate mornings."

The End

ACKNOWLGEMENTS

At the end of this series, it is nearly impossible to thank every person who has helped me along the way. From the people that came to my speaking engagements or allowed me to speak in their classrooms, to those who put up with my incessant questions about small details. In particular, thank you to Thea Rademacher at Flint Hills Publishing. We have been on quite a journey together over the last several years, and thank you for seeing it through. As always, thank you to my friends and family for your unwavering support. To my parents, thank you for forcing me to have a bedtime when I was younger, and yet allowing me to lay in bed and read until I fell asleep. To my husband, thank you for supporting me on all those nights when I put my headphones on and worked until I couldn't keep my eyes open any longer. To my daughter Avery; even at your young age, you inspire me to work hard, to do more. You make me believe I can do anything. And finally to you, the reader. Thank you for reading this series, for loving these characters. I hope they have resonated inside you, as much as they have me.

About the Author

Whitney Estenson was born and raised in Topeka, Kansas. The daughter of two teachers, she spent her summers swimming at the pool. Through the years she played several sports, including softball, basketball, volleyball, and running track. While traveling to the next tournament, an hour or several states away, Whitney always brought a book. It was on these long trips that she developed a love of supernatural and fantasy stories.

After high school, Whitney attended Washburn University, graduating with a Bachelor of Arts in English Education in 2009. That summer, she married her husband Josh in a seven-minute ceremony on a Jamaican beach. When she returned, she began her teaching career and has been teaching middle school ever since. In 2012, she received a Master of Science in Educational Technology from Pittsburg State University. In 2013, Whitney and Josh welcomed their daughter Avery.

Follow Whitney on Facebook: The Ascendant Series by
Whitney Estenson,
Instagram: the_ascendant_series,
and her website: theascendantseries.com